In the Company of
Shadows

The Night's Road: Book Three

Empire

Of

Dirt

Andy Monk

Part One

Hunger

Chapter One

Upon the Road, Principality of Anhalt-Dessau, The Holy Roman Empire - 1630

"We are going to die."

"You *may* die. I will not."

As reassurances went, it wasn't the best.

He fixed eyes front, teeth gritted. Not that there was anything to see. The storm reduced their world to a circle a few paces across; beyond that, a gauzy, shifting curtain of snow faded from white to grey to black nothingness.

We need to find shelter.

He stopped himself saying it again. Morlaine heard it well enough the first time he'd said it. The second and third too. Better to save his breath.

Still, what did it matter? They were already dead, and freezing solid was not the worst of the potential endings awaiting them. He shouldn't complain, really.

His gelding, which he'd named Plodder, hung its head as it ploughed through snow already reaching its fetlocks and deepening rapidly. Steam rose from the horse; he supposed it was warming him a little. Till Plodder keeled over from the cold, anyway.

To their left, somewhere, the Elbe flowed. It could have

been a few dozen paces away or a league. There was no way of telling. As was her want, Morlaine shunned the roads as well as the daylight, making their progress from Madriel all the slower.

Behind them, Solace and Lucien followed, shadows in the snow.

Time was difficult to keep a hold of, but it must have been over an hour since the ex-mercenary captain uttered a word. Another blessing!

His whole body was numb from the intense cold, which meant, for once, his ruined arm felt no worse than the rest of him. There wasn't a breath of wind; the snow fell about them thick but even in slow fat flakes. If there'd been wind to cut through them, they'd likely have all died hours ago.

Apart from Morlaine, of course, she showed not the slightest trace of discomfort.

When he totted everything up, there really were lots of reasons to be cheerful. Perhaps he should start whistling a jaunty tune to serenade their good fortune!

"There is shelter ahead," Morlaine's words were startling in the utter silence of the night.

The demon loomed over him on the back of her monstrous mount, Styx. Snow had settled in the creases of her hooded cloak, like veins of marble cutting through black basalt.

Her senses were keener than anyone else's, the horses included, but even her eyes could surely see nothing through a veil of snow so thick God might have finally given up on the world and erased it.

"How can you tell?" he took no hope from her words. Hope always made everything worse.

2

"I can smell the blood..."

"Not a fire or a hearty broth, too, I suppose?"

After a pause, "No... just blood."

"I won't expect a comfortable night then."

"As long as there is shelter for the horses, it will suffice."

"Delivering our frozen corpses to Magdeburg without the horses will be much harder."

"Yes," the demon agreed.

"One might think you care more for the horses than the rest of us."

"They are better company."

Morlaine, he well knew, did not make jokes. Which at least made her a more bearable companion than Lucien.

He settled back into his saddle and stared into the emptiness.

They had been roughly following the Elbe for the last week as it flowed through Saxony and now the Principalities of Anhalt before reaching the Archbishopric of Magdeburg. They had skirted a wide arc to avoid Wittenberg, the largest city between Madriel and Magdeburg. Progress had been painfully slow, but other than snow, cold and discomfort, they avoided trouble, so perhaps Morlaine's methods were not entirely without merit.

The war had ravaged the Principalities of Anhalt; little good waited ahead, though, right now, he'd happily trade the blackened cinders of his soul for fire and hot broth.

The Devil, he imagined, was currently doing excellent business in Anhalt.

Plodder plodded on. Too tired for even their proximity to Styx, who had spent most of the last week trying to bite or kick any of the other horses foolish enough to pollute the brute's air, to unnerve it. The cold and snow subdued even that creature's foul temper.

Another blessing to add to the list!

He considered whistling again but nothing suitably chirpy came to mind.

"There..." Morlaine said a few freezing minutes later.

"Where?" he leant forward, saddle leather creaking under him. Nothing but snow fuzzing the darkness lay before them.

When he looked back to the demon, one gloved hand rested on her sword's hilt.

"Trouble?"

"Trouble is like the sea. It is without end."

He found the familiar worn grip of Old Man Ulrich's sabre.

This is the sort of thing that happens when you start counting blessings...

Slowly, out of the snow, something dark emerged.

Buildings.

"God be praised!" Lucien cried behind them.

The possibility the Good Lord would ever lift a finger to help the likes of Lucien Kazmierczak, suggested the Almighty might not have been paying proper attention.

Still, finding anything out here other than a cold death did seem to border on the miraculous.

"What is this place?"

The demon reined Styx in, "A farm of some kind, I would imagine."

He could still make little out, but if it was a farm, it must be a gentry's estate; the buildings were too large for a peasant's.

As Solace and Lucien brought their mounts to a halt abreast of them, Morlaine slipped smoothly from the saddle. She stood motionless, one hand on Styx's bridle, the other upon her sword's pommel. Head cocked, she seemed to be sniffing the freezing air.

He glanced at Solace, but the folds of her hood obscured her face. Shoulders slumped; her head hung forward.

"My lady?"

"All is well," Solace replied, without turning, her voice almost consumed by the silence.

He thought nothing was well, including his mistress, but kept his own counsel. He dismounted Plodder with a grunt and little grace, his boots immediately sank into the crisp snow.

"Anything?" he asked Morlaine.

"Death," she said in her usual happy-go-lightly manner.

"Death is everywhere," Lucien, a featureless shadow against the snow, slipped from his horse, "but let's introduce ourselves regardless. I am sure the owners will be delighted to offer every hospitality to such worthy Christian travellers as us."

"Check the main building; I will stable the horses," Morlaine said.

Lucien pulled a lantern from his saddlebag before the demon led the horses away, leaving the three of them huddled together.

"Which do you think is the main building?" he peered into the gloom.

"We shall explore and discover!" Lucien boomed in the

5

kind of voice often accompanied by a hearty slap on the back. Thankfully, in this case, it wasn't. The urge to punch the bastard in the face might have been overwhelming otherwise.

Lucien moved to the nearest wall and beckoned them to follow. Once close enough, he could see it was stone, solid and well-built.

The mercenary hunkered down, Solace and he spread their cloaks to shelter Lucien as he laid a thick scrap of leather out on the snow. It took some time and a considerable amount of inventive cursing to get the tinder to take and then light the lantern from it, but he was grateful for the warming glow when it finally came.

"We need to get inside," Lucien straightened up, hurriedly pulling his gloves back on.

"Amen," he muttered.

He handed the lantern to Solace without comment. Lucien didn't draw any of his many weapons but kept a hand on the hilt of his sword.

They edged along the wall, passing small, dark windows. He pressed his nose against one but learned nothing except no candles or fires burned within.

An unlit house in the depths of a winter's night was not unusual, but he felt uneasy all the same.

The unease swelled as they passed the next window. He pulled up abruptly and called the others back. Solace raised the lantern when he pointed. A handprint, fingers splayed wide, dirtied the glass.

A bloody handprint.

Lucien sucked in air through his teeth. Solace already

looked ghostly, but the sight of it paled her further.

She is thinking of The Wolf's Tower.

So was he.

His father's blade hissed from its scabbard. Lucien's did the same.

Silently they moved on, boots pushing through undisturbed snow. Nobody had come this way for a while. The snow had started falling at dusk; he tried to take some heart from that, at least.

Along the house, the lantern light revealed a door, which did nothing to reduce his unease.

Who left their front door open in the depths of a winter's night?

"I will go first..." Lucien pushed the door with his blade before glancing over his shoulder at him, "...you will bring up the rear."

"Why should I go last?"

"Because there is much less chance of you hitting me with your big, sharp sword that way," Lucien grinned. He really did possess a most infuriating grin.

"Do as he says," Solace changed the lantern to her left hand and drew the fencing dagger she carried from her belt.

They should probably wait for Morlaine, but he bit down on suggesting it. The thought he needed the demon for anything rankled even more than Lucien's infernal grin.

Lucien and Lady Solace entered the unlit house and he followed.

*

The silence seemed even deeper.

The still wintry night muffled the world's natural sounds, but it felt more profound inside. A house *should* make noise, mimicking those within its care. But the door didn't squeak upon its hinges, the boards made no creak under their boots. Nothing.

The lantern illuminated a hallway. Sturdy, solid. It was a sizeable house. A country estate rather than a mere farmhouse. The home of landed folk, she imagined.

A drift of snow covered the threshold; nothing else appeared out of place.

The bloody handprint smearing the window suggested that would not last.

The hall was wide enough for her to walk at Lucien's side, but she kept a pace behind his shoulder, on the left, to avoid the swing of his sword arm.

The lantern light bobbed around them, illuminating unadorned plasterwork.

"Anybody home?" Lucien shouted.

"Is that wise?" Renard shuffled from one foot to the other.

"I've always been famed for my good manners..." Lucien moved forward when the house remained silent.

She followed, trying to keep focused, trying not to think about creeping through The Wolf's Tower, following a lantern's glow, terrified of what it might reveal.

I am not that girl...

No. That girl was nearly a year dead. She had yet to find out who she was now, but it was not that petty, frivolous, cosseted creature.

The first room they entered contained a jumble of

overturned furniture. No bodies or blood, but the room carried the unmistakable reek of urine. Broken bottles glistened as she swept the lantern back and forth.

"Reminds me of some of the more memorable parties I've attended," Lucien said, stepping aside once certain the room was deserted.

"Brigands?" Renard asked, keeping one eye on the corridor from the doorway.

"Or an exceedingly poor choice of house guest," Lucien scooped up a bottle. Sniffing it, he pulled a face, "Better used for cleaning than drinking..."

The clatter when he dropped it again was louder than it should be in the stillness. She wished he would stop making unnecessary noise. Not just because it would alert people to their presence, but that every sound here seemed a profane intrusion. Like a crude joke at church.

"Whoever did this is days gone... hopefully," Renard said, still hanging back in the doorway.

Lucien picked his way through the room to the fireplace.

"I don't think so," the mercenary said, after pulling off a glove and crouching by the hearth to run fingers through the ashes, "this is still warm."

"How long?" she asked.

"This fire was alight before sunset," Lucian wiped the ashes onto the front of his britches, "so someone was here before sunset."

Her eyes moved to the window, "And they left in the snow?"

"It didn't start snowing till dusk," Renard reminded her.

Lucien's boots crunched glass underfoot as he returned to

9

her side, "We can't leave, so let us hope they have."

"And if they haven't?"

He shrugged and squeezed past Renard back into the corridor, drawing a pistol to accompany the sword in his right hand.

She exchanged a look with Renard. His shrug was somewhat less assured than Lucien's.

The next room was as wrecked as the first, with the addition of several dark pools on the floor.

"Blood?" she asked.

Lucien poked the nearest stain with his foot, "Not yet completely dry either.

Again, memories of The Wolf's Tower bubbled to the surface, darkened rooms and pools of blood on a winter's night. She resisted pulling the cloak more tightly about her. It wasn't the chill making her shiver.

The kitchen was the largest room. It, too, had been ransacked; everything that could be broken lay in pieces. A body curled in one corner, a woman, grey-haired and simply dressed.

"Is she dead?" she asked Lucien after he crouched beside the figure.

He nodded without checking for a pulse.

"No need to come closer," he said, standing and putting himself between the body and her when she approached.

"I am not a child, Captain. I have seen death."

Lucien sucked his cheeks in and stood aside.

The woman's head was no more than a bloody pulp. She'd been bludgeoned to death, and, by the state of the corpse, her attacker had carried on with the bludgeoning long after she died.

The lantern light danced in time to her trembling hand.

Lucien's eyes stayed on her; she refused to turn away from the dead woman. A servant, most likely, by the cut of her blood-stained, brains-splattered dress. Older, slightly built. It was impossible to tell more, given how little of her head remained.

"My lady..." Renard called.

"Yes," she looked over her shoulder.

"You should see this."

Renard stood on the other side of the kitchen, too far for her to make out anything much, though she could see no corpse.

She turned and made her way through the broken furniture, smashed remnants of bottles and jars and sundry other debris. Lucien followed.

Ulrich indicated the floor with his sword.

An unlit candle sat in the middle of a chalk pentagram scratched onto the flagstones.

"Witches," Renard cast an eye about the shadows.

"This..." Lucien jerked his head at the dead woman, "...is the work of brigands, not witches."

"Or they were witches and..." she let the words trail off.

"Witches are generally burnt, not beaten to a pulp."

"Perhaps... we need to check the rest of the house."

Lucien nodded, Renard looked miserable, but as he usually looked unhappy, she didn't read much into his hangdog expression.

The mercenary sheathed his sword and plucked the candle from the pentagram.

"What are you doing?" Renard asked.

"Casting more light…"

"But-"

"'tis just a candle, nothing more," Lucien sniffed it, "definitely no virgin's blood in this. I'd be able to tell."

Renard shot Lucien a venomous look.

Lucien lit the candle from the lantern's wick, and they explored the rest of the house. Each ground floor room had been turned upside down, but they found no further bodies nor blood.

"Perhaps the woman in the kitchen lived alone," Renard said at the foot of the stairs.

"With her black cat and broomstick, perhaps?" Lucien suggested.

"Best we check upstairs," she said before they could start squabbling. Sometimes she felt more like she'd become the mother of two quarrelsome little boys than leading a quest to rescue her brother and avenge her father.

They picked their way through the upstairs rooms one by one. There were five in total, each one ransacked.

The bodies were in the last.

Lucien stood in the doorway, blocking it with his broad shoulders.

"You do not need to come in here," he said quietly, candle in one hand, pistol in the other.

"Yes, I do," she said.

Lucien shuffled aside.

Renard sucked in a breath behind her as she swung the lantern, taking in the scene. It was the largest upstairs room; a fine bed occupied most of it.

The bodies of two women lay on the bed, lashed together and facing each other. Both naked, both with their throats hacked open.

A third body was tied to a chair at the end of the bed. A man, naked too. He bore terrible wounds, his eyes had been put out, and he'd been castrated, presumably before his throat had been cut. Only when her eyes refused to linger on the man did she notice the pentagram drawn beneath the chair, some of the chalk scuffed away by bloody footprints.

For the first time in days, she felt hot. She moved to the window, putting aside the lantern to force it open. Freezing air made the urge to vomit recede.

"What... happened here?" she asked, eyes fixed only on the pale reflection upon the black glass.

"Mother and daughter," Lucien's boots creaked over the boards, "both raped numerous times. The man, husband and father, forced to watch. Whether they killed his wife and daughter before they took his eyes... I cannot say."

"But why?"

"They wanted money, valuables or information, so they tortured him to get it. Or a punishment, a warning to others... or perhaps just for the fun of it."

"And the pentagram.?"

"I... do not know."

"Sacrifices to Satan?" Renard asked.

"Who knows..." Lucien sighed, "...but best we do not linger here."

The snow still fell thick; they could be trapped for days.

"We should bury them," she said.

13

"The ground is frozen, my lady."

"We can't just leave them," she thought of her people, slaughtered in The Wolf's Tower. She'd seen those killed in the Red Company's assault, though not Father or the women and children.

She forced herself to turn and stare at the three cold corpses in the bedroom.

Would it have looked very different to this?

"Is this the work of men... or..."

"Demons?" Renard finished the question.

"The monsters you seek are few," Lucien replied, "men capable of monstrosities, however, are many. So, I'd wager this the work of men."

"Is this the way the world is now?" she whispered.

"My lady," Lucien said, "this is how the world has always been...".

Chapter Two

A Farm, Principality of Anhalt-Dessau, The Holy Roman Empire - 1630

They found Morlaine in a barn with the horses.

"How many bodies?" the demon asked, sitting, back against bales of straw, eyes narrowing at the intrusion of their light.

"You knew?" Solace demanded.

"I smelt death."

"You could have warned us!" he blurted.

"No one in there could have done you any harm. A warning wasn't necessary."

When he made to protest, she closed her eyes and pulled her hood back up.

He shot the others a glance; Solace looked too pale and exhausted to speak while Lucien moved to their provisions. Morlaine had been busy; the horses were unsaddled, rubbed down, watered and fed by the looks of things. Their gear stowed in three neat piles beside their sleeping rolls and blankets.

"Anyone hungry?" Lucien asked, rummaging through his saddlebag.

Solace slumped onto her blanket and shook her head.

He joined his mistress.

Morlaine sat opposite them, silent and unmoving, almost nothing but another shadow in her long cloak.

15

"I'll keep watch till dawn," Lucien pulled some dried beef from his pack.

"Best you sleep," Morlaine said, "I'm better suited to the dark."

Lucien shrugged, chewed and sloshed icy slush around his canteen as he ambled over to join them.

"You know, if we sleep in the house, we could have a fire and-"

"No," Morlaine and Solace said together, though he suspected for different reasons.

"Luckily, Lucien Kazmierczak is well used to the cold..." he said through his chewing before adding "...and corpses."

After the horrors he'd witnessed in The Wolf's Tower, he thought his hide might have hardened, but the images of those poor people in the farmhouse lingered behind his eyes. Perhaps one day, that might change, allowing him to look upon such things and remain unmoved.

He didn't like the man he was now very much but suspected he would like that one even less.

Lucien hunkered down next to him, tearing off chunks of dried meat with his blackened teeth and recounting what they found to Morlaine. No emotion troubled the man's voice; he could have been talking about the weather.

"What do you think?" Lucien asked when the demon stayed silent.

"I think I was right not to go inside."

"Should have told us; I could have passed on seeing... *that*," he said.

"If you choose to walk the Night's Road, you will see worse. Prepare yourself."

He was going to spit that it wasn't his choice, but he kept his peace. There was always a choice. He didn't have to follow Solace. He'd shattered his word and soiled his honour when he'd helped Saul and the Red Company breech The Wolf's Tower, so, really, what was keeping him here? The fact he'd spent Solace's silver to save an orphaned child in Madriel? Debt and honour? Nothing more?

His eyes dropped to his mistress; she'd turned her back to the lantern light, curled on one side under her blankets. He didn't know if she slept, but he reached over and pulled the upper blanket over her shoulders.

When he looked up again, Morlaine was staring at him, or, at least, he thought she was. There was little face to see deep within the shadows of her hood.

"What do you think happened? The work of demons?" he asked, irked by her attention without knowing why.

"Vampires? I doubt it."

"'tis not the sort of thing Saul would do?"

"Indeed, but the chances of us stumbling randomly upon his handiwork are unlikely. Whatever happened, it's not our business. The war strips away flesh to expose that which hides underneath. Best we leave it behind us as quickly as possible."

Lucien belched and picked at his teeth before hunkering under his blankets, "Turn the lantern down, lad, eh?"

"You don't seem troubled by what we found in there?" he made no move towards the lantern.

"Troubled? Lucien Kazmierczak is cursed with a gentle soul. Anyone will tell you that. But what does being

17

troubled give you, apart from a poor night's sleep? Would you sleep better believing demons did that? If so, believe it. You wouldn't be the only one. Satan doesn't make men do things like that. Trust me. Lucien Kazmierczak knows a thing or three when it comes to what men are capable of."

With that, Lucien pulled the blankets over his head. After a minute or two, soft snores broke the silence.

"Sleep," Morlaine said.

He had no more interest in sleeping than eating but bundled the blankets on himself and settled down. The alternative would be talking, which was even less appealing.

He didn't expect sleep to come. The eyeless, pain-wracked face of the man tied to the chair and the despoiled bodies of the women on the bed danced too vividly before him for that.

So, when his head next jerked up, it was a surprise to find dawn's light softening the barn's shadows.

Solace still slept; Morlaine sat as if she had not moved a muscle. Lucien was filling his face again.

"Breakfast!" Lucien beamed, "Best meal of the day."

"Barbarian..." he said, but softly.

The air bit into him as he tossed the blanket aside and climbed to his feet with the grace of a new-born foal.

His bad arm ached; the fingers of his left hand so stiff he could barely bend them. It hurt worse in the cold, as if his broken body needed to remind him how he'd come by the bloody injury lest he ever forgot.

At least a few paces worked the stiffness out of his legs.

He peered through a crack in the barn door. The icy

breeze watered his eye and blurred his vision.

Outside, snow still fell, though only a smattering of lazy flakes now floated out of the leaden sky.

"How long do we have to stay here?" he asked, returning to the others.

"We'll not get far till it thaws," Lucien didn't look up, "still, it'll keep everyone else away. Best we're not here when the bodies are discovered. It might provoke a few awkward questions."

"We should bury them," he tried to stamp some blood into his toes.

"There's more snow, and the ground will be even harder than last night," Lucien snapped back his cup, grimacing.

"What are you drinking?"

"Schnapps," the mercenary grinned, "the water's frozen solid. Who said winter's all bad, eh?"

He rolled his eyes as he paced, "So, we just wait?"

"I have some dice…" Lucien offered.

"We leave as soon as it thaws," Morlaine pulled down her hood, "we can't risk the horses in this weather."

"Agreed," Lucien knocked back more schnapps.

He settled down, back against the wall, blanket wrapped around him. There was nothing else to do but wait and shiver.

*

"Do you think it's getting warmer?"

She blew in her hands as they stood shoulder to shoulder in the doorway.

"If it gets any colder…" Renard grumbled.

19

The door was a small one in the side of the barn, with so much snow piled against the main doors they wouldn't budge. A lot more must have fallen while they slept.

The door looked over fields rolling down to the Elbe, a gunmetal ribbon cutting through a world turned white all the way to the misty horizon.

A collection of buildings huddled by the river. A village. A few curls of smoke floated upwards. With any luck, none of the locals would fancy the walk through the thick snow to the farm.

The grey daylight revealed a once prosperous estate. Several sturdy outbuildings circled the even sturdier farmhouse, though paint had peeled here and there, cracks cobwebbed some of the windows, lichen and moss blurred the stonework. Like the rest of the world, it appeared to have fallen on harder times.

Who had lived here? Why had they died? Who killed them? What happened in the hours before their deaths?

She didn't know. Though she couldn't help but wonder if anyone had stood within the rubble of The Wolf's Tower since they left and asked similar questions.

"We could be here for days," Renard's eyes rose to the sky. Although no snow was falling, it still sported a sombre, threatening hue.

"I remember one winter, snow laid thick on the ground for months," she said, sticking out her boot to paw a hole.

"You should be careful. If you spend too much time around Morlaine, you may end up as cheerful as her, my lady."

She chuckled at that and immediately felt guilty.

Renard eyed her like he might a dog that had started acting peculiarly.

She'd been so furious with him since Madriel she could understand his wariness. A distance had grown between them while they travelled, and she'd shunned his company to keep her temper in check. It was time to let her grievance go. The silver was gone to save a child she didn't know, but as much as she hated admitting she needed anyone, she understood she needed Ulrich Renard.

"I've told you before, you don't need to call me, *my lady.*"

"There isn't?"

"No. We are friends."

"We are?"

"You saved my life, Ulrich. Twice. That counts for something."

"You saved mine... just the once, though."

"But my life is at least twice as valuable as yours."

He thought about that, then nodded, "I would say so."

That made her smile, and she turned her eyes to the distant Elbe.

The river flowed all the way to Magdeburg. And *Graf* Bulcher.

Her smile faded.

"We should pray for a quick thaw," she said.

"Do you think the Lord still listens to our prayers?"

"Of course. We do his bidding."

Renard looked sceptical but settled for running a hand through the bristles of his beard rather than telling her she was spouting nonsense.

She wasn't doing God's bidding. She was doing Lord

Flyblown's. And her own, personal, demon's. Vengeance.

Nothing else mattered.

"We should go inside; 'tis warmer," she said.

"'tis less cold," Renard stood aside but made no move to follow her.

"I will keep watch," he said when she stared at him.

"No one will come in this snow."

He shrugged, "The air is better out here."

"I am sorry," she said, not expecting the words till they escaped her mouth on a steamy breath.

"My lady?"

"For my anger. It was petty and unbecoming. There are still things more valuable than silver. Perhaps I lost sight of that for a while. I am glad you have not."

Renard looked uncomfortable and shuffled his feet.

"You are the only person I trust in the world, Ulrich."

"Even though I betrayed you?"

"The irony is not lost on me," she turned her bottom lip between her teeth, a habit she'd had since childhood, "'tis not so important what you do at the beginning as what you do in the end. You stood with me, stayed by my side when all hope was dead. I will never forget that."

He nodded.

The words felt clumsy and awkward. Did she mean them, or did she just need him too much to risk losing him? She wasn't at all sure.

When she made to leave him, Renard said, "With your indulgence, I will always call you *my lady*."

"Why?"

"Because..." a smile she might have thought of as shy

ghosted his lips, "...you are. And always will be."

A fat water drop splashed on Renard's cheek.

His eyes broke with hers to look up at the barn's roof.

"The snow is starting to melt," he wiped a hand across his face.

"See? God does listen to us."

"Then perhaps he will destroy the Red Company without us?"

"Perhaps..."

Her gaze drifted to the farmhouse.

"...though I fear there may be too many monsters in the world for even the All Mighty to deal with alone. Therefore, he needs our help..."

Chapter Three

"If we take the road from Dessau, and the thaw doesn't turn it into a quagmire, we can be in Magdeburg in three days," Lucien's eyes swept across them before settling on Morlaine, "two if we travel by day. One if we push the horses."

"We travel by night and cross country," Morlaine said.

Only the drip, drip, drip of melting snow interrupted the silence following the demon's words.

He was eager to be away from this cold, awful place but otherwise wanted to take as long as possible to reach Magdeburg. God might indeed require their help hunting monsters, but that did not mean he had to provide his assistance any way but grudgingly.

Lucien turned to Solace when she said nothing to contradict Morlaine. The mercenary pushed himself to his feet with a grunt.

"We leave at dusk then," Morlaine said, smoke-blackened glass hiding her eyes again.

They had spent another long chilly night in the barn but had awoken to find blue skies and snow slipping from the roofs. Sunlight snicked inside, cutting through the shadows in dazzling spears the demon carefully avoided.

Lucien stared at the bales of hay stacked in the corner of the barn they camped in.

"Whoever attacked this place, they weren't soldiers," the mercenary said.

"No?" Solace asked.

"A foraging party would not have left winter feed for horses."

"They took everything else," he said, "Perhaps they wanted to move fast. Wagons of hay slow you down."

"Perhaps," Lucien conceded.

They had searched the farmhouse thoroughly. There was no food, and everything else of value was missing, down to the pots and pans in the kitchen.

As they started to collect up their gear, Morlaine jumped to her feet, head tilting.

"People are coming..."

They all stopped and looked at the demon. His stomach sank. He could hear nothing but dripping water and the occasional gust of wind. He distrusted much about the demon but not her unnaturally keen senses.

He hurried to the side door facing the distant village and opened it a crack.

His stomach fell further.

"Shit..."

"What is it?"

He turned to find Solace and Lucien had followed him to the door.

"Riders."

"How many?" Lucien asked.

"A dozen or so."

"Oh," the mercenary relaxed, "I thought it was something to worry about!"

Solace ignored the fool, "Can we get away?"

"They'd see us. And by the time we leave, they'll be here."

"A fight it is then!" Lucien beamed, drawing his pistols.

"We don't even know who they are!" Solace protested.

"Does it matter?" Lucien cocked the first weapon.

"Of course it matters!"

"There are four corpses in yonder farmhouse. They will want someone to hang for that."

"But it was nothing to do with us."

Lucien raised an eyebrow, "Are you confident in your powers of persuasion, my lady?"

"We don't fight unless we have to!"

"What if it's the men who attacked the farm?" he asked.

"Unlikely they would return to the scene of their vile crime, but..." the Captain shrugged, "...we only need to kill three each. Lucien Kazmierczak has often faced worse odds and walked away with a happy smile upon his rugged but handsome face."

"Oh, please do stop talking such shit!" he all but screamed at the idiot.

Lucien's only reaction was a wink.

He wanted to punch him.

"Bickering will not help us," frost dusted Morlaine's voice as she collected up her few belongings and began stuffing them into a saddlebag.

"What do you suggest we do?"

"You may do as you wish," she said, straightening up, "but I cannot go outside. The sunlight is too bright."

"So-"

"We go and greet them," Solace said, her face strangely

slack for a moment.

"Greet them?" he blinked.

"Yes."

"But-"

Solace brushed past him on the way to the door, "We can't outrun them, we can't fight them, and we can't hide in here."

"Why not?"

She paused to look over her shoulder, "Because doing any of those things will make it appear we had something to do with what happened in that farmhouse."

"What if *they* had something to do with what happened in that farmhouse?!" he cried.

"They didn't," she said.

"How can you..." he let the words fade.

Solace smiled and turned back towards the door.

Was that her *sight*, or just wishful thinking?

He supposed he would soon find out.

When he looked at the others, Lucien pulled a face, "Lucien Kazmierczak has done much in his time; following the orders of a slip of a girl is a new one. Still, 'tis always worth trying different things. And, if she's wrong, then we will kill them."

"Are you not going to say anything?" he turned to Morlaine as Lucien sauntered after Solace.

"It is as good a plan as any."

"Are you going to stay here and make some tea for them, then?"

"We don't have a fire to boil water."

He peered at her, but, as ever, Morlaine's face remained

straight and expressionless.

The demon slung the saddlebag over her shoulder and headed off in the opposite direction.

"Where are you going?"

"I will hide. I can't leave the barn. Don't worry about me; I've done a lot of hiding over the years."

"What about Styx and the rest of your gear."

"Think of something to explain it away."

"Like what?"

"I recommend lying. It can be quite effective," with that she tossed the saddlebag atop the bales of hay and scrambled up after it.

He turned away and hurried after Solace and Lucien. Best he didn't know exactly where Morlaine intended to hide.

It would be much harder for the approaching riders to torture her whereabouts out of him that way...

*

The hooves of the riders' horses clattered on the cobbled courtyard patchily emerging through the melting snow.

Renard had miscounted; there were not a dozen horsemen but thirteen. An inauspicious number.

For a moment, back in the barn, she'd been struck with the absolute certainty talking to the newcomers was the only option that would not result in their deaths.

The *sight*. She'd assumed. The uncanny ability to sometimes just *know*. A gift she had sworn never to again ignore after it warned of what would befall The Wolf's Tower. However, as the rider's reined in their mounts, doubt eroded that assumption down to mere hope.

The men were grim-faced and heavily armed, though, given these dark days, few people who ventured beyond their settlement's walls were likely to be anything else.

"How accurate is this *sight* of yours?" Lucien muttered from behind her shoulder.

"Keep your hands away from your weapons, Captain," she replied, her voice much calmer than her heart or stomach.

Despite their wary eyes and lack of smiles, none of the newcomers drew their weapons.

"Who are you?" One of the men demanded; he appeared the youngest of the group, little older than her, with suspicious, restless eyes beneath a burnished helm. A fur-lined cloak hung from his shoulders.

"We sheltered from the snowstorm in the barn," she kept her chin up and gaze fixed. Father once told her authority came from always sounding like you knew what you were doing even when you didn't have a clue.

"Unlike old Enoch to be charitable, I hope he didn't charge you too much to sleep in his draughty old barn," another rider laughed, vaulting from his saddle. He was young and well-dressed, too, though he wore a wide-brimmed hat rather than a helm.

"Now comes the awkward bit..." Lucien said under his steaming breath.

Enoch. The old man on the chair, blinded and castrated.

"We were unable to ask permission," she said, "everyone inside is dead."

The young man in the hat stopped in his tracks. Several of the horsemen behind him exchanged glances as hands drifted towards weapons.

"What have you done?!" the first man to speak edged his horse forward. The helm made it difficult to be certain, but she thought the two men similar enough to be related.

"Nothing," she kept her eyes fixed on the dismounted man, hoping he was in charge. She preferred the confused expression on his face to the anger lancing across the other man's. The rest of the riders were men-at-arms; they were waiting to do what they were told.

"What-"

"Quiet, Joachim!" the young man in the hat held up his hand. Joachim shot him a surly look but stilled his tongue.

The man took a couple of steps forward. He was fair-faced and carried himself well, straight-backed and purposeful. Good boots, thick cloak, a fine-looking sword hung from his belt. A nobleman of some kind. She wondered if she knew the family.

Eyes narrowing, he scanned the barn and the other scattered outbuildings.

"How many of there are you here, *fraulien?*"

"Just the three of us," she ventured a small smile, "this is not a trap if that is what you suspect, sir?"

He nodded, "Traps are often set with tempting bait..."

"I am no man's bait," her smile evaporated.

Without looking back at the riders, he barked, "Paasche, take some men and find Enoch."

"Yes, my lord," a burly man clambered off his horse and beckoned three others to follow him.

"What lies inside," she warned when the young nobleman's eyes returned to her, "is not pretty."

"Few things are these days."

30

"Even by the standards of our times, they did not die easily."

He gave her a look that suggested he thought she knew little of blood and death. She was just a girl, after all. A split lip probably looked like a bloodbath to such a delicate little thing.

She shrugged off the irritation. Better he think petty, patronising thoughts; it'll make him less inclined to suspect the slaughter was anything to do with them.

Joachim jumped from his horse, "Who are you?" he demanded, pulling the helm from his head.

"You must excuse my brother; he's always been the headstrong one."

Up close, she could see the similarities, and the differences. Joachim had a gaunter face and thinner lips but shared the same shock of blonde hair, sharp cheekbones and long nose. It was in the eyes, however, that the differences and similarities were most striking. Both were blue-grey, but while Joachim's were restless and narrow, his brother's sparkled as if continually suppressing something he wanted to laugh at.

"My name is Celine Lutz... my lord."

"Wh-"

"You must forgive my manners, *fraulien*. The times we live in," he swept up her hand to kiss it, "I am Lebrecht, heir to the *Markgräf* of Gothen. This is my little brother, Joachim."

"Lebrecht..." Joachim growled as his brother released her hand.

A young Prince of the Empire. A dashing one too. Had Father ever tried to make a match of them? The thought her younger self might have been well pleased with the suggestion bubbled somewhere within, but she ignored it. That foolish girl was as dead as the rest of Tassau.

Despite the many insufferable hours Tutor Magnus forced her to pour over his wretched old maps, she'd didn't recall the *Markgräfschaft* of Gothen, but that was no mystery. She did not know the names of all the stars in heaven either, and the myriad statelets of the Empire numbered almost as many.

"And what brings such a beauty to-"

"And who are *they?*" Joachim cut Lebrecht off mid-flatter as he glared at Renard and Lucien.

"My retainers," she said, meeting Joachim's hostile eyes.

"You appear harmless enough, but they-"

"I lost my estate in Lustria to this infernal war. The only family I have left is in Naples; they are escorting me there. Nobody travels this land without armed men anymore," her eyes moved to the soldiers behind the two brothers, "do they?"

"Indeed, they do not," Lebrecht said, "but Anhalt does not lie on any route between Lustria and Naples that I am aware of."

"It does not. We are heading to Magdeburg, my Father, God rest his soul, had investments there; I need them to secure my future and reach Naples."

"I am Lucien Kazmierczak," Lucien beamed, stepping forward, "renowned soldier and adventurer. You may have heard of me, my lord?"

"I can't say that I have."

"Well," Lucien's grin didn't falter, "you are very young.

Nevertheless, despite only being in this good lady's employ for a short time, I can wholeheartedly vouch for her honesty, integrity and virtuous nature. 'tis as she said 'tis. And Lucien Kazmierczak's word is famed from Calais to Cairo!"

"I'm sure it is," Lebrecht's attention moved to Renard, "And you, boy, are you famous too?"

If Renard had any thoughts about being demoted from husband to retainer, he didn't show it. However, if he was trying not to look shifty, uncomfortable and suspicious, he was failing miserably.

"My name is Ulrich, lord."

Lebrecht's eyes snapped back to her, "And you have no one else?"

"If you are wondering whether I have men hidden about the farm intent on doing you ambush, my lord, then no. There is no one else. I would hardly put myself here if I did," she conjured her sweetest smile and made sure the blade on her belt remained concealed, "I am not much of a fighter."

"Two men are insufficient to ensure a lady's safety during these dark days..." Lebrecht was all charm and smiles, but he wasn't a fool and only a fool travelled abroad without suspicion at their side.

"I did have a third, Morgen, but he died on the road. Brigands. Once I have my money in Magdeburg, I will hire more."

"Prudent," Lebrecht said, "though reaching Magdeburg may be difficult, an Imperial force is blockading the city."

"Then best we do not tarry, my lord. We would already be

there if not for the early snow."

Before Lebrecht could answer, the burly soldier, Paasche, burst from the farmhouse, "My Lord, you must see this!"

"I am sorry if he was a friend..." she said.

"Enoch the Miser was no man's friend," Joachim exchanged a glance with his brother.

"Excuse me, *fraulien*," Lebrecht turned on his heels, but not before telling Joachim to keep them where they were and get their men to search the rest of the farm.

"Aye," Joachim said. Once his brother was out of earshot, he said, "Lebrecht has always been a fool for a pretty face. Rest assured, *Fraulien* Lutz, I am not..."

Chapter Four

One of the men with Lebrecht was not a soldier.

"'tis clearly witchery! The question must be put, my lord!"

Lebrecht cast a weary eye in Pastor Josef's direction. There were many in the Empire who blamed witches for all the world's ills and would gladly burn anyone they didn't like the look of just to be on the safe side. The Pastor appeared to be one of them.

He thought of the blood-smeared pentagram on the floor under Enoch the Miser's mutilated corpse and kept his face even. The man might be a zealot, but he had more to work with here than he was probably used to.

They had gathered in one of the rooms that was not an abattoir while Lebrecht's men searched the farm. He hoped Morlaine was as good at hiding as she claimed.

They had found an unbroken chair for Solace; Lucien and he stood against the wall behind her. The Gothen men hadn't taken their weapons, which was something.

Besides Lebrecht, his brother and the Pastor, Paasche and another soldier guarded the door. Both men kept their hands close to their swords.

"These terrible crimes had nothing to do with us, Pastor," Solace said, not for the first time.

"And yet here you are!" Josef stabbed a finger towards her triumphantly as if he'd just finished a long, heated debate with a blistering, undeniable act of reasoning.

Solace smiled and turned to Lebrecht.

"My Lord, you have seen the bodies, the rooms where these poor souls died. If we had been responsible, we would have been covered in blood. We are not. You have searched our gear; there are no blood-stained clothes."

"Blood is a bugger to get out; ruined many a shirt of mine," Lucien piped up.

Lebrecht ignored Lucien. The young nobleman didn't appear to know what to make of the mercenary. To be fair, he wasn't the only one.

"No," Lebrecht agreed, "We've found nothing."

"Enoch and his family have been dead for days; they've had plenty of time to wash or burn their bloody garments!" Josef spluttered. This time his finger shot towards the ceiling. He seemed to enjoy pointing.

"And why would we do that, Pastor?" Solace asked, voice reasonable, air light.

"To hide your diabolical and satanic crimes!"

"I meant," Solace's patient smile stretched a little wider, "why would we have gone to the trouble? Why not just leave?"

"You said it yourself; you were trapped by the snow!"

Solace turned her eyes to the window; bright sunlight dazzled in a clear blue sky.

"The snow stopped yesterday; we could have left at first light. We didn't..."

Because we are accompanied by a demon who cannot walk under the sun...

A thought very much best kept to himself.

Josef seemed to consider the point, then jabbed his finger in their direction again, "The question *must* be put!"

Lebrecht pinched the bridge of his nose, "We are going around in circles."

"My lord..." Solace turned her charm on the nobleman, "...you are clearly a wise and intelligent man; I am sure you can see we had nothing to do with this."

No quiver weakened her voice, no shake troubled her hand. She was confident and assured. Whether guilty or not, most young women would have shown some nerves if accused of witchery, especially if discovered surrounded by mutilated corpses and blood-smeared pentagrams. But not Solace. She had stood before Saul and his demons, and that crucible had hardened her, forged her, changed her into something else.

Of course, he, too, had stood before Saul, facing the monster alone while Solace scrambled down the side of The Wolf's Tower. He had survived. Yet the same crucible had produced a very different metal. He was afraid. He was scared, not just of Pastor Josef's accusations and the pyre's shadow but of everything.

Why would that be?

He supposed the metal that emerged from the fire depended on the quality of the ore that went into it.

He dropped his eyes to the scuffed toes of his boots.

"It seems unlikely-"

"My lord!"

Lebrecht waved down Josef's protest, "But this is a matter I must defer to my father."

"Father has enough on his plate," Joachim muttered,

arms crossed by the window.

"What do you suggest, brother? We build a pyre in Enoch's yard and burn these people?"

Joachim's expression suggested he didn't much care one way or the other.

"You and your men will accompany us to Edelstein. I apologise for the inconvenience, but I hope you understand."

Solace's smile faded, "That is most inconvenient; I must get to Magdeburg. As I explained, I have urgent business."

"With Satan himself, no doubt," Josef glared.

"With a banker," she snapped, "so, perhaps, not totally dissimilar."

The Pastor couldn't have looked more shocked if Solace had decided it an opportune moment to show the assembled company her breasts.

"Pastor Josef," Lebrecht said before Josef's outrage could provoke more pointing, "perhaps 'tis time to attend to the dead. We will take the bodies back to Ettestein for burial once the *Markgräf* has inspected them. Please ensure they are ready to be moved with haste and dignity."

He didn't look happy, in fact, he had the air of a man rarely inconvenienced by the emotion, but the Pastor mumbled a begrudging, "As you please, my lord," before departing with a swirl of his cloak.

"You must excuse him," Lebrecht said once Josef's footsteps faded away, "he is-"

"A piece of shit," Joachim interrupted, finding something outside to stare at.

Lebrecht shot his brother a disapproving glance but didn't

correct him.

"tis strange," Solace said, "all the churchmen I have met have either been the kindest or cruellest of men. I have never understood why."

Joachim snorted while Lebrecht smiled, but neither commented on the observation.

"We will depart for Ettestein as soon as the bodies are ready. I give you my word, I will do my best to minimise the delay to your journey."

Lucien stepped away from the wall, hitching thumbs into his weapon belt, "The lady has said quite clearly she wishes to go to Magdeburg..."

The smile on his face did not entirely mask the threat in his words or eyes.

Paasche mirrored Lucien's move. He was a big man, and not all his size was attributable to fat. Like the mercenary, he sported a long, extravagant moustache. But he wasn't smiling beneath his. The two soldiers eyed each other like two stags about to lock horns. Or, in their case, whiskers.

"My lady," Lebrecht said, "We must find out what happened to Enoch and his household. You understand this, surely?"

"Of course. Which is why we lingered here," she lied smoothly, "but we have told you all we know. Taking us to Ettestein will garner you no further intelligence. Even if you put the hot irons on me."

Lebrecht looked uncomfortable with both the words and how Solace stared boldly at him as she said them. In truth, he felt uncomfortable about it too. He didn't know how much sway Josef held, but people generally listened when men, particularly men of the cloth, started making accusations of witchcraft.

"I'm afraid I must insist..." Lebrecht said.

The soldier next to Paasche moved to the older man's shoulder while Joachim turned away from the window, unfolded his arms and let his hands drop to his weapons.

He supposed he should do likewise and join in with the mutual glowering and posturing. Instead, he stayed where he was. The more oil you sprayed around, the more likely some idiot would find a spark.

Solace did not flinch or cower and looked no more troubled than if discussing the place settings for a challenging feast. So, he followed her lead and prayed she knew what she was doing...

*

What on God's Earth am I doing?!

All sorts of things bubbled beneath, but she kept them from her face.

Lucien was not a subtle man. But that didn't make him wrong. If Lebrecht took them to Ettestein and decided they were responsible for the murder of Enoch's household, they would either hang or burn. But if they tried to fight their way out... no, if they were going to fight, they should have done it immediately, but the *sight* had told her not to.

At least, she hoped it had.

Now, all certainty had fled, and nothing whispered on the breeze.

The next choice was hers alone.

Out of the corner of her eye, she could see Lucien's hand

inching towards one of his pistols. She was sure everybody else could see it too.

She had no real idea if Lucien could live up to his many boasts, but Renard had but one good arm and drawing the fencing dagger in her belt was as likely to produce laughter from the four men facing them.

And another nine waited outside.

"Very well," she said, "we will come to Ettestein. But as your guests and as witnesses, not as accused. And my men will keep their weapons."

The tension eased from Lebrecht's face, "Agreed."

"And as you know I had nothing to do with this, we will not be denounced. On your honour, my lord."

"I do not believe you are responsible for this outrage, and I will speak accordingly. But my father is the law here, not me."

He spoke sincerely, as far as she could tell. And it appeared they had little choice.

"Your word is a fine currency, my lord," she smiled, dusted herself down and rose to her feet.

Lucien, a little begrudgingly it seemed, stepped back.

"We shall pack our belongings. And look forward to your hospitality."

Renard kept his peace until outside. The snow continued to thaw, but a bitter wind had kicked up, tugging cloaks and chilling skin.

"You trust them, my lady?" he asked as soon as no one could overhear him.

"No more than they trust us."

"If we get to Ettestein, we will be entirely at their mercy," for once, no grin accompanied Lucien's words.

"We have little choice. What do you know of Ettestein, Captain?"

Lucien's face crumpled, "Not much. A middling holding. A castle built in the days before gunpowder and cannon made such fortresses obsolete. The *Markgräf*... I do not know. Let us pray he is not a man with a fondness for the pyre."

"How far is it from here?"

Another shrug, "They do not have the look of men who have ventured far. My guess would be we will be there before sunset or shortly after."

"We could try and escape..." Renard offered.

"That would suggest we have something to hide..."

Renard lifted his head towards the barn, "We have."

"Morlaine?"

"She is hiding. Hopefully, she is as good at it as she claims."

"We are in enough trouble even without her," Lucien added.

"We have done nothing wrong," she insisted.

"Aye," Lucien agreed, "and we would not be the first people to march to the pyre clinging to that comfort..."

They packed their provisions and readied the horses in silence under the watchful eye of Paasche and a couple of his men. The barn was silent. If Morlaine was nearby the demon did nothing to give her presence away.

"How long will it take us to reach Ettestein?" she asked in a loud voice, though she supposed the demon's sharp ears would have heard a whisper just as well.

"Four hours without snow, brigands or imperials,"

Paasche said.

"The Imperial army?" Renard asked.

"Under Count Tilly, 'tis rumoured to be heading for Magdeburg to turn the blockade into a siege. We were looking for signs of it, though I doubt they will be here before the roads clear in spring. When they come, their foraging parties will strip this land of what little remains. We all hope the rumours are not true."

"And what does this army mean for Gothen?"

Paasche sucked at his remaining teeth, "Trouble."

"Your lord is a protestant?"

The burly soldier nodded.

"Does he oppose the Emperor?"

"Politicking is no business of mine. I just follow my lord's orders," Paasche said with a sniff, "best you pack quickly; the sooner we are away, the sooner we will be behind Ettestein's walls."

Walls were no guarantee of safety, but she doubted she'd get any more out of the soldier. And being too curious might raise suspicions further.

She resisted the urge to look over her shoulder when they walked their mounts out of the barn. Paasche had the air of a man who noticed things.

"My what a beauty!" Lebrecht exclaimed when they met up with the others in the courtyard. It took her a moment to realise he meant Styx.

The stallion pricked up his ears and threw his head, aware he was the centre of attention.

"Who's is he?" Lebrecht asked, moving to pat Styx's head. The horse snorted and pawed at the cobbles.

"Mine," she said without hesitation.

"Yours?" Joachim's eyebrows shot up.

"Why the surprise, my lord?"

"'tis a warrior's horse. Women should ride ponies or in carriages."

"Or better still, never leave the bedroom."

Lebrecht's laugh broke the initial shocked silence. Joachim only scowled.

While Pastor Josef, standing over four shrouded bundles laid out in the slush at his feet, just glared at her with distaste...

Chapter Five

Ettestein, Principality of Anhalt-Dessau, The Holy Roman Empire - 1630

Ettestein Castle perched on a low bluff overlooking the Elbe, dour and foreboding under skies that had returned to lead.

The road snaked towards the castle gates. They had seen no one since leaving Enoch's farm, though he'd spotted several fat plumes of smoke twisting upwards during the day.

Will there be anything left by the time this damn war ends?

He let the thought drift away. As they'd all be long dead before then, it didn't really matter.

To his right, Lucien slouched in the saddle, whistling through his teeth.

Solace rode at the head of the little column next to Lebrecht. She was easy to make out; Styx loomed over every other horse. He'd feared she might struggle to control that monster, but the stallion had been on his best behaviour.

But she was not acting like a lady should.

He twisted around to peer over his shoulder. Josef rode at the rear with the corpses. Two hung over Solace's mare, which they told Lebrecht belonged to their fallen comrade, Morgen. The Pastor was a grim-countenanced young man of pale skin and dark eyes. He wouldn't have cared for Josef even if he hadn't accused them of witchcraft. The man's gaze, he was sure, had not wandered from their backs the whole time.

Lost behind banks of thick cloud, the sun must be close to setting if it hadn't already.

Would Morlaine come after them now?

He assumed so. She seemed quite fond of her horse, if not the rest of them.

"What do you make of this place?" he asked Lucien, nodding at the grey walls of Ettestein.

"There *might* be women there..." Lucien said, with a twist of the mouth.

"That's your chief concern?"

"There will almost certainly be beer."

"There'll be no beer or women if they burn us at the stake..."

"Do you ever look on the brighter-lit side of anything, my friend?"

He focused his attention on the castle. Annoyed at himself for thinking he might get a sensible answer out of the fool. Maybe once the faggots around their feet were alight, he might cease with the bloody jokes.

The castle was larger than The Wolf's Tower, older too, he fancied.

They squelched past several simple dwellings, not quite

hovels, not quite cottages, sitting in the lee of the castle. All were dark, none looked well maintained, and no one was about in the twilight. Even this close to a castle, they might well be abandoned. The war was stripping the countryside to its bones; few felt safe without high walls to protect them. He suspected even fewer would once news of what happened at Enoch's farm spread.

His eyes fell to the tangles of Plodder's mane. High walls hadn't helped the people of The Wolf's Tower much.

The next time he lifted his gaze, the outer gates of Ettestein, sitting between two stout towers, neared.

As he watched, they swung open. Lebrecht and his men were expected and recognised, he supposed.

No voices greeted them; the men-at-arms who'd opened the gates offered no greeting as they trooped through the archway. No laughter, no insults, no banter.

The gate led through the outer wall; the main bulk of Ettestein sat above them on its stony bluff. Grey walls, turrets and conically roofed towers sprouted from the imposing keep.

More buildings sat inside the inner wall. Better kept than those outside, weak light glowed against the dusk from some; a scattering of peasants kept to their business, thin, pale-faced, eyes lowered. Again, all in silence.

"What a gay, joyous delight this place appears..." Lucien cracked.

He said nothing. But as they made their way up the track leading to the castle proper, they passed a circle of blackened ground; a few patches of snow remained, but the ash and cinders beneath were clear enough to see.

When he glanced at Lucien, he found the mercenary's eyes were already on the scorched ground.

A burning.

Lucien's gaze moved to his. His mouth tightened under his long moustaches, lips whitening. For once, no quip, joke or other idiocy escaped him.

They fled Madriel to escape the madness of a witch hunt.

But their flight had done nothing but deliver them into the midst of another one.

*

The *Markgräf* of Gothen examined her with narrow eyes. They had not left her for a moment since his sons brought her before him.

"*Are* you a witch?"

He paused, awaiting an answer, a greasy slab of chicken poised upon his lips. Apparently, the *Markgräf* always ate at six, regardless of food shortages and accusations of witchcraft and murder.

"No, my lord," she said, without flinching, though she could do little to stop her stomach rumbling at the aroma of roasted meat hanging in the Grand Hall. It had been a long time since she'd smelt anything so tempting.

The *Markgräf* sighed, deep enough for a steam of frosted breath to engulf the chicken. Then he gobbled it down.

A generous fire burned in the massive hearth, without dispelling the chill pervading the cavernous space. He sat alone at the imposing table, save for an elfin-faced girl to his right and the roasted remains of several animals before him.

The *Markgräf* wasn't a fat man, but the ravages of the war hadn't prevented food from reaching *his* table. Many of the castle's other inhabitants, she'd noticed as they had been marched through the fortress, were gaunt and thin enough to suggest few ate as well as their lord.

"I do not believe *Fraulien* Lutz and her men had anything to do with the murder of Enoch the Miser and his household," Lebrecht said. He stood at her shoulder, Lucien and Renard behind her. Joachim was also behind her, along with half a dozen armed men.

"No?" the *Markgräf* picked at the chicken carcass before discarding it and slumping back into his high-backed chair as if it were too bothersome a chore to pursue.

"No, Father."

"Pastor Josef thinks otherwise."

The Pastor disappeared as soon as he'd jumped from his horse in the cobbled courtyard in front of the castle's stables. Evidently, he'd been keen to whisper in the *Markgräf's* ear before anyone else could.

The priest wasn't in the room, but she doubted he was far. Other ears likely needed poison dripped into them too.

"'tis an obvious conclusion to reach," she said, 'tis the Pastor's calling to protect the souls of his flock from evil; I understand this. But we are no more than I say we are. Refugees fleeing the war. I have lost everything. My family, my home, my household. All I have left are these two men, four horses, the contents of our saddlebags, some assets of my father's in Magdeburg and my faith in Jesus Christ. I am at your mercy, my lord. But I am not a witch; we played no part in this foul crime. Other than discovering it."

The *Markgräf* spent a long time staring at her before speaking again. He had one of those faces that gave little indication of what was happening behind it.

"You speak well," he said, "but the Devil is well known for his silver tongue. Enoch the Miser died badly; I understand. A great inconvenience to him. And to me. If witchcraft was involved, and from what I am told, that fact is undeniable, 'tis beholden upon me to investigate the matter thoroughly. However well you speak, I need better evidence than that to be assuaged of your innocence."

"Your son gave his word we would be brought here as guests, not suspects; I-"

"My son's word is one thing. He is an honourable man. But 'tis not the word of the *Markgräf* of Gothen. Not yet, anyway. I will get to the bottom of this. One way or another."

"Father-"

"Be quiet, boy," the *Markgräf* shuffled his backside and took up his goblet.

"Father," the girl at his side spoke for the first time, "this woman cannot possibly be a witch."

"Is that so, Sophia?"

"Indeed. Witches are hideous crones; everyone knows that. The Devil despises beauty. She is far too pretty to be a witch!"

The *Markgräf* smiled, "Oh, how little you know of the world..."

Sophia, who, as his daughter, carried the title *Markgräfin,* raised her chin but said nothing more. She reminded her of the silly little girl she'd once been, who saw everything in simple colours and frittered away her days dreaming of handsome princes.

"However…" the Markgräf said, "…you do have a point. The Devil always marks his disciples. This is well known. If this woman is a witch, she will carry a sign of the pact she signed to sell her immortal soul. Therefore…" no hint of laughter softened his voice when he fixed his eyes upon her again, "…you will be examined accordingly. If your body is free of satanic marks, I will take that as evidence of your innocence, but if some unnatural blemish befouls your skin… well, then that will scream your guilt to these rafters."

She felt Renard and Lucien shuffle behind her, the creak of leather, the clang of metal. She lifted her hand a fraction to still them without looking around.

"As you decree, my lord," she said, keeping her voice even whilst trying to ignore the faint throbbing coming from Flyblown's mark upon the inside of her thigh…

Chapter Six

He tried to remember if Solace had any marks on her body.

Given he had been somewhat preoccupied with not dying the only time he had seen her naked, he doubted he'd given her body the attention it would otherwise have deserved.

In fact, he had no memory of seeing her naked at all. The feel of her skin against his as she had wrapped herself around his freezing body beneath the musty blankets in her father's hunting lodge, however...

He drained his beer and tried to push the memory away.

It was not becoming. She had saved his life; that was all that mattered.

He stared at the suds clinging to the bottom of the tankard.

His mistress being stripped and examined for a witch's mark wasn't seemly either. And if they found any, all of them would be for the pyre.

"Your drink is dry," Lucien said, turning back from the latest passing maid he'd failed to impress with his dubious charm.

"The world is full of disappointments."

"A disappointment easily rectified!" Lucien scooped up their tankards and bounced off in search of more.

They had been hunkering together in the corner of the

castle's enormous kitchen, where the men-at-arms and household staff ate and drank on long benches far enough away from the fires and ovens for the damp chill to seep into your bones if you lingered too long. Or didn't drink quickly enough.

Largely, everyone had studiously ignored them. The only thing likely to keep people away from you more than the possibility of the plague was an accusation of witchcraft.

As Lebrecht had insisted it was a matter of honour, he had promised Solace they were guests and not accused, they currently enjoyed the freedom of the whole castle rather than just its dungeon.

Of course, how long that arrangement lasted depended on what they found on Solace's naked body tomorrow. Such work required daylight, the *Markgräf* had decided. In the meantime, Solace had been given a room in the family wing while Lucien and he bunked down in the servant's quarters.

A tankard clanking onto the table brought his head up.

"That was quick?"

"Lucien Kazmierczak is famed for his ability to forage beer!"

"Finding a way out of this mess would be more useful."

"They'll discover nothing on her."

He peered at Lucien, "How would you know…?"

The mercenary's bushy eyebrows waggled up and down as he gulped beer.

"Horse shit!"

"Women cannot resist Lucien Kazmierczak's love. Trust me, 'tis well known."

Given the looks Lucien had been getting from the women in the kitchen, which covered the full spectrum of female disdain from distaste to outright disgust, that seemed even more questionable than Lucien's usual boasts.

He shook his head, "We should get out of here while we can."

Lucien shrugged, "It would not be easy. We are being watched. And running would be an admission of guilt. Better to wait."

"And hope Solace doesn't have a mark on her body."

"She looks remarkably unsullied to me," Lucien shot him a salacious grin he didn't care for.

"They'll find something," he sipped his own beer, "if someone is denounced, they always find *something*. A birthmark, a boil, a wart, a... a-"

"A freckle that bares an uncanny resemblance to a demonic turnip?"

"This isn't funny!"

"No, it isn't. But little in this world is, and we must laugh at something, even if it is only our own deaths. Otherwise, life would become very dull and depressing. And what would be the point of that?"

Lucien slouched and looked pleased with himself. For some reason.

He tried to wash the sourness from his mouth, but the ale was weak and poor.

"We are being watched?"

"Of course," Lucien nodded; if he had any reservations about the beer, he wasn't showing them, throwing more down.

"'tis fortunate Morlaine is not here, then we would already be doomed."

"Now I can attest with certainty that she has no mark on her body!"

"I wonder if we'll see her again."

"She is close."

"Really? She couldn't have left the farm till dusk; how would she know where we are?"

Lucien leaned in and dropped his voice beyond its normal boom, "She's drunk my blood, Solace has drunk hers. As I understand it, that means our souls sing to her. She can find us."

He wasn't sure if he found that reassuring or depressing.

Lucien returned to his beer, "Don't talk of our mutual friend; walls have ears."

"We're being listened to as well?" he looked around; no one sat within a dozen paces of them. Witchery and the plague.

"Best not to do anything strange or different. We are just two men-at-arms awaiting our mistress' orders. Nothing more."

Grudgingly he had to accept, on this matter at least, Lucien had a point.

"So, what should we do that won't draw attention to ourselves?"

"Just behave like all right-thinking fellows do when enjoying another lord's hospitality," Lucien tipped his tankard towards him in salute, "Get shit-faced drunk and find some passable maids to pester for a fuck..."

*

"You do not dress like a woman?"

"The road is not a place for pretty dresses. I need to ride, to run, to fight if necessary. 'tis not what I would choose, but as the war has stolen most of my choices from me, what is one more?"

"You could borrow one of mine?"

"Thank you, my lady, but I would not wish to inconvenience you. Especially if I am for the pyre."

Sophia blinked at that, linen-cheeks flushing.

"Forgive me. My humour tends to be bleaker than it once was."

The *Markgräfin's* eyes drifted across the room. Although comfortable she doubted it one of the castle's better ones. Still, for a stranger suspected of witchcraft, it offered more than she could have hoped for. A large bed, a fire that struggled with the draughts, a small window and a few functional pieces of furniture. It also had a man-at-arms outside the door, which she assumed was not the norm in Ettestein's guest wing.

"Lebrecht is trying to persuade Father to dispense with the indignity of having you examined," Sophia said.

"I am grateful."

"He likes you."

"He does?"

"I can tell."

"You are close to your brother?"

"Oh no, he hates me."

She couldn't help but laugh.

"I believe I am a source of great irritation to him."

"You are his little sister. I believe such things are expected."

It was Sophia's turn to laugh.

"Do you have a big brother?"

Her own smile faded, "I did, but..."

"Oh..."

They sat by the fire on the room's two functional chairs, close enough to almost burn her legs but not close enough to keep the chill from her nose.

Another long pause, before Sophia announced brightly, "I like your hair!"

Her hand rose to flick through her shorn locks. She still sometimes expected to find the same long tresses Sophia sported, teased into elaborate and artful plaits. A nobleman's daughter always had to be prepared for the unexpected arrival of a suitable prince.

"Another concession to practicality. And upon the road, 'tis better to be mistaken for a boy."

"I would like to have my hair cut short, but Father would throw me into the pig stye if I ever did such a thing."

"Your hair is beautiful. You should treasure it. Mine was much like yours not so long ago."

Sophia blushed and looked pleased. She was pale and fey but pretty. No doubt a relief for her father, ugly daughters could be an expensive burden.

"What manner of man is your father?"

"He is kind. When he can be. But the world weighs heavily upon him, I think. The war can make monsters of us all..."

From the mouths of babes...

Before she could ask more, the door opened. Lebrecht let himself in. A scowl immediately creased his face at the sight of his sister.

"Sophia, you should not be here!" he closed the door quickly behind him.

"I have yet to be turned into a toad," she said, folding her hands into her lap.

"It can be difficult to tell. You've always looked like a frog, and they are so much like toads."

"Pig!" Sophia spat.

Lebrecht stood between them, facing the fire.

"How did you get in here? The men were given strict instructions..."

"'tis my natural charm. A smile, a flutter of the eyelashes. No man can resist my requests."

Her brother snorted, "My sister is most deceptive and manipulative. She will make some *lucky* man an excellent wife one day."

If Torben had not been so afflicted, would this have been how we would have been? Hiding our love for each other behind banter, insults and japes?

A cold sadness no fire could ever thaw settled upon her heart.

"And why are *you* here, brother dearest? You should not be in a lady's chamber at night. Or any other time for that matter."

"No business of yours," he jerked a thumb towards the door, "now hop off back to your lily pad before I tell Father of your latest misadventure."

Sophia made a noise in the back of her throat as she rose

to her feet, brushing away the creases in her skirt, "Well, at least I will find someone to marry *me.*"

Lebrecht shot his sister a sour glance.

"I shall see you tomorrow, Celine. We will become good friends once this nonsense is resolved."

With that, she gave her brother a frosty smile before departing with a suitable slam of the door behind her.

"I apologise for my sister; she can be... difficult."

She nodded, "I was not so very different once."

"You speak as if you have the weight of many years upon your shoulders?"

"The war ages us all."

"Indeed."

"But your sister is correct; you should not be here. If someone takes umbrage at a birthmark or mole, it would not look good for you."

"No one will find a witch's mark on you."

"You speak with a rare confidence for a man who has never seen my body."

That brought a blush to Lebrecht's cheeks. It was rather fetching, she had to confess. She wondered again if Father ever tried to make a match with the *Markgräf* of Gothen.

"In these days, it does not pay to stand against the church's wishes, even for a nobleman. My father must be seen to be thorough. I apologise for the indignity, but I believe you will suffer no more than that."

"But what if I am a witch?"

A pained smile twitched his lips, but no comment.

"When we rode in, we passed a patch of scorched earth. A burning?"

"Nobody important."

"Everybody is important to someone, but I am not important to anyone here."

"You have my word, my lady."

She hoped that had some value but only bowed her head in acknowledgement.

"But if I did not murder Enoch, who did?"

Lebrecht wrung his hands, "I do not know."

"Why were you visiting his farm?"

"A business matter."

She raised an eyebrow.

"He borrowed money from my father. The repayment was overdue."

"And now he is dead?"

"Repayment is more difficult."

"The land is ravaged, my lord, awash with men capable of the most heinous acts. I have seen these things with my own eyes. I would contend the culprits were such men. The pentagrams and the like merely an amusement, a distraction, a deception. They are long gone."

"Let us hope."

"Indeed."

"And my men?"

"I believe they are currently attempting to drink the castle dry."

"You are having them watched."

"Of course. For their own safety. They will come to no harm."

Lebrecht loitered, looked uncomfortable, then coughed, "I should leave you to your rest."

When he moved to the door, she asked, "Who will be inspecting me tomorrow. Pastor Josef?"

"No, we have a woman. She knows what to look for."

"I see..."

"I am sure she will find nothing. And you will then be able to enjoy the hospitality of Ettestein properly."

"I wish only to be free to go to Magdeburg."

"Of course. But 'tis Christmas the day after tomorrow. You should join our feast. It is the least we can do."

"You are too kind, my lord."

Lebrecht shuffled his feet and looked like he had something else to say. If he did, he changed his mind and bid her goodnight.

She sat a while, staring into the flames.

Eventually, she said, in the lowest of voices, "My Lord Flyblown, I believe this might be an opportune moment for a word..."

The only answer was the crackle of burning wood in the fire.

Chapter Seven

Lucien had found someone willing to talk to him.

Which meant he didn't have to.

Something worth celebrating at last!

He was slightly drunk. Perhaps more than slightly.

It'd been a long while since he'd drunk so much. He remembered downing a lot of *bottler* with Morlaine after Madleen attacked him, but it hadn't gotten him particularly drunk. That night he could have emptied the cellars of every tavern in Madriel and stayed sober.

The memory of Madleen brought the momentary lifting of his spirits to a crashing end.

He finished the remnants of his latest beer with a sour scowl.

The occasional sound of clanking or scrubbing floated out of the kitchen proper. Work was finishing for the night. In a few hours, the servants would rise to start preparations for the next day, but the kitchen was winding down for now. A handful of determined drinkers clung to the benches in the dining hall; most had come and gone. All avoided them, despite Lucien's insistence on trying to strike up a conversation with anyone foolish enough to venture within half a dozen paces of him.

He remembered what castle life was like. A small, enclosed community; everybody knew everyone else's business as well as they did the smell of their own shit.

News of what happened at Enoch's farm was common knowledge, as was Pastor Josef's accusation.

The cold shoulders suited him just fine. He had no desire to talk to anyone, save Solace. Assuming she really had finally forgiven him for spending her silver getting Seraphina into Madriel's overcrowded orphanage.

But Solace wasn't here. She got to stay with the better sorts. For now, at least. Of course, if she had an unfortunate birthmark, they'd all burn together.

He pushed the tankard away and rose to his feet.

He had to grip the edge of the table for a second or two to stop his arse plonking straight back down again. The ale must have been stronger than he'd thought. Or he was even more watered down than he feared.

"Bed," he managed to mutter when he got his legs to take him past Lucien.

"The night is still young!" the mercenary beamed. However much beer he downed, he doubted the fool would ever become less irritating.

He grunted and left him in the company of the two bearded men who, for reasons best known to themselves, hadn't given Lucien the evil eye and conjured an excuse to be somewhere else.

Some time later, he found himself in a dimly lit corridor, boots scraping on cold, worn stone.

Was their room down here?

Perhaps he should have paid more attention. And drunk less ale. Probably both.

His shoulder slumped against a wall.

Would staggering around the castle drunk and lost make him appear more or less like a witch?

Footsteps echoed in the gloom. As he wasn't moving, he decided they were unlikely to be his.

Three figures emerged behind him. Perhaps they would know where his room was?

Two of the men he didn't recognise; broad, cloaked, armed. The third made his heart sink.

"Pastor Josef..." he said.

A dark, sombre suit lacking any embellishment, black hair, long but thinning, pale face, high cheekbones above sunken cheeks, restless eyes. A man who could equally be much older or younger than he appeared. Either way, he seemed well suited for shadowy corners.

Josef nodded as he came to a halt; no smile accompanied it, *"Herr...?"*

You would have thought you'd at least go to the trouble of learning the name of someone you wanted to burn on the pyre.

"Renard," he straightened himself. He saw no point in lying. He wasn't pretending to be Solace's husband here, "Ulrich Renard."

"Is there any reason you are skulking around the castle in the middle of the night?"

"I'm lost. Your ale is stronger than I expected."

The sin of drunkenness was far safer to confess to.

"Our brewer is famed for his ale. Perhaps someone should have warned you."

"I don't suppose you know where my room is?"

"Please, walk with me..."

64

The notion the pastor was as likely to be taking him to the dungeon as his room flitted across his mind. Neither of Josef's companions looked like priests.

He fell in step, the other two men behind them.

"What happened at the farm, *Herr* Renard?"

So much for small talk.

"'tis as my lady said."

"I have a nose for lies. 'tis twitching now."

Josef boasted a long and straight nose. He could well believe the Pastor was quite adept at sticking it in places other people would prefer he didn't.

"We sought shelter from the snow, came across the farm and found the dead inside. As you saw them when you arrived. We considered burying them, but the ground was frozen," he said carefully. He felt much less drunk suddenly.

"I am a servant of God, a minister of the church. 'tis my duty to root out the Devil's minions wherever they are. I take that duty very seriously."

He concentrated on planting one foot in front of the other.

"I need to discover what happened at Enoch's farm..."

"We've told you all we know."

"Perhaps... but if you *are* hiding anything, now is the time to tell me."

"Why now?"

"If you confess and denounce your fellows, it will save both your soul and your life..." when he said nothing, Josef added, "...I am a man of my word, *Herr* Renard. I am quite prepared to swear upon the Holy Bible..."

This, of course, was how the madness worked. Frighten

someone enough that they confessed and denounced others hoping they would go to the pyre in their place. Everyone knew what happened to those accused of witchcraft; they always put the questions with hot irons, hammers, chisels and pliers. You suffered to the point that either your courage or sanity failed; many would take such an offer, for the threats Josef and his ilk made were not idle.

But he had stood before Saul the Bloodless, who knew far more about torture and terror than someone like Pastor Josef ever would, and had stayed at his mistress' side. Why would he do anything differently now?

Do you run, or do you stand?

In the end, so many things came down to that.

He stopped and turned. Josef halted to meet his eye. Anticipation played across the priest's face, like a maid before her first kiss.

"We found the farmer and his family dead. They were already dead when we arrived. Whoever committed the crime left long before we got there. I know nothing else. My mistress knows nothing else. I have nothing more to say to you."

Josef's mouth twitched. He looked not so much like a maid denied the kiss she'd been expecting but one who'd received a slap in the face instead.

"Then you are damned..." he said, voice even despite the anger in his eyes.

He thought the priest's men would seize him then. If they did, he would not go quietly. His good hand found the hilt of his father's sword.

Josef's lip curled into a sneer as he shook his head before

brushing past him. The two other men, blank-faced, followed suit and all three of them headed off into the shadows ahead.

He let his hand fall to his side, though he curled it into a fist and then flexed the fingers as he watched them till both they and the echo of their footsteps disappeared.

He would never betray Solace again. He might hate her, or at least what she was becoming, but he loved her too. As much as he feared what Josef might do, he knew what honour he still possessed bound him too tightly to his mistress for that.

But he doubted Josef would make his offer to him alone. Solace would betray him no more than he would her. They had suffered and shared too much.

Lucien, however...

Would the louche mercenary's bravado extend to facing the hot irons and the flames to stand with them if it came to it.

Or would he give that maid the dark kiss she so craved?

*

She'd hoped her dreams might take her to the grey plains where the damned and the monsters roamed so she could speak to Flyblown. Removing the mark he'd put of her inner thigh, five elongated red welts, would greatly help her avoiding the pyre and fulfilling the deal they had struck.

As it was, sleep barely troubled her and what little she found took her nowhere, bar from one side of the bed to the other and back again.

She sat up long before dawn's grey light caressed the

narrow window.

Had she made a terrible mistake?

Should she have fled, hid or fought when Lebrecht and his men arrived at Enoch's farm? The *sight* warned her not to, and she'd sworn to always listen to it after what befell The Wolf's Tower.

But what would the *Markgräf's* woman make of Flyblown's mark? After all, it *did* signify a pact with a demon...

It was impossible to conceal; Flyblown had not appeared to remove it, fleeing the castle would be akin to climbing Ettestein's highest tower and announcing her guilt with a trumpet.

What do I do?!

In the end, she clambered from the bed, blankets wrapped around her to throw logs on the fire's glowing embers. The wood first smoked, then caught the flame, casting an orange glow about the unlit bedroom.

The only sound to disturb the night other than the crackle of burning wood was the occasional creak or clank from the other side of the door, presumably as the guard changed or paced to relieve the boredom of the long, cold night.

Neither sleep, inspiration nor Lord Flyblown visited her before a maid arrived shortly after dawn with porridge and elderflower tea. The woman said nothing and left the tray unbidden upon the room's small table, immediately rushing out again, no doubt fearing some evil might befall her if she lingered too long.

After splashing near-freezing water on her face and dressing, she made herself eat. She had little appetite, and the porridge, thin and tasteless without sugar or honey to sweeten it, did nothing to give her one, but she forced every spoonful down regardless. Who knew when her next meal might be.

An hour later, two men-at-arms arrived.

"Come with us, please, *fraulien*," the older of the two said. Neither smiled.

She'd never seen them before. It was probably too early for Lebrecht to come and personally escort a guest/prisoner to her stripping and examination.

"Where are we going?"

"Come with us, please, *fraulien*," the older man said again. Still no smile.

Having little choice, she nodded, showed them what a smile looked like and headed for the door.

Outside, the corridor was empty. One of these two must have been her most recent guard.

"This way," the younger man placed a hand on her elbow and steered her left. He had an ill-advised beard, no more than downy wisps, that made her think of an unkempt hound for some reason.

"I don't require manhandling," she snapped, staring at him. Both his gaze and hand fell away. He didn't know she was a *Freiherr's* daughter, but she resented his disrespect all the same. It was such a petty trespass compared to so many of the others she'd suffered over the last twelve months, but it irked her all the same.

"Where are we going?" she asked, wishing she had put more clothes on. Winter chill seeped deep into the castle; she didn't want anyone to mistake a shiver for fear.

"The *Markgräf's* orders," the older man replied. She

wanted to bark at him that she'd asked *where,* not *why* but held her tongue.

Ettestein seemed far more of a labyrinth than The Wolf's Tower; they had quickly taken enough turns and descended narrow, twisting staircases for her to hopelessly lose her bearings.

But they kept going downwards.

With no windows, only the feeble greasy light of flickering rushlights set in niches lit their way.

The *Markgräf* wanted her examined in the morning when the daylight would expose any witch's marks. But if that was the case, why were they leading her down to part of the castle where no sunlight fell?

A grin split his beard when she swivelled to look over her shoulder at the older soldier. The younger man gripped her arm.

"No slacking now, eh, witch?"

"Where are-"

The older soldier silenced her with a cuff to the back of the head, forceful enough to send her staggering forward.

"No need to make a fuss, bitch; we're here now. And right comfy you'll be too!"

The younger soldier sniggered at his companion's words; a high-pitched nervous laugh spluttered in her ear as he grabbed her arms.

A door opened; darkness awaited on the other side.

"What is the meaning of this?"

That earnt her neither a cuff nor a reply. Instead, the younger soldier shoved her inside. She resisted, but he was too strong and she'd left her dagger in the bedroom with the

70

rest of her gear.

A final shove sent her staggering into the room. Neither man followed. The door slammed behind her, then the rattle of key and lock.

The room was larger than she expected and not as dark as she first thought.

A single candle burned upon a table. Beyond the candle, a figure waited, motionless and expressionless; his face, lit by the wan flickering light below him, remained half hidden in shadow.

Pastor Josef indicated the chair opposite him.

"Please sit; we have so much to discuss..."

Chapter Eight

He woke to pain and torture.

The pain might be from his throbbing head and the torture from whatever infernal racket Lucien was making, but, for a few bilious breaths, he doubted Josef could inflict worse.

"What... are you *doing?*" he growled, deciding he really didn't need to open his eyes.

"'tis a madrigal. Lucien Kazmierczak is famed from La Rochelle to Livorno for his angelic singing voice. There is no finer way to awake from your slumbers. Unless you have a comely maid to hand, of course. Sadly, you are not a maid, comely or otherwise, so..." Lucien burst into song again.

"You sound like you're boiling a cat in oil."

Lucien paused mid-wail, "I am singing in Italian. The language of passion and love!"

"Very well, you sound like you're boiling an Italian cat in oil. Please stop. They're already looking for an excuse to throw us on the pyre."

When Lucien immediately recommenced belting out his madrigal, Ulrich slowly peeled open his eyes. The mercenary faced the window, arms thrown out to either side.

"Why don't you have any clothes on?"

"I sing much better when I can feel the air on my

bollocks."

"Is that a traditional singing technique?"

"Nope. 'tis of my own devising," Lucien, breath steaming with the cold, turned around, grinning proudly.

"Ye gods! You're... *aroused!*"

"Of course. I'm singing about love, beauty, passion. Why wouldn't I be?"

Ulrich rolled over to face the wall, "Get dressed man! Someone might walk in!"

"Why would that matter? Even without the stimulation of music, 'tis the most natural thing in the world for a man to awake engorged. Don't you?"

"No!"

"How odd... you should get that looked at. The fact I was unable to find a maid to assist with my lust last night is also a factor. A very rare occurrence. Hopefully, once this witchcraft business is sorted, the locals will be more obliging."

He continued to stare at the wall until the rustle of clothing indicated Lucien was tucking everything best kept out of sight away.

When it seemed safe, he kicked off the blankets and dragged himself to his feet with only a minimal groan. Lucien leaned against the wall, grooming his moustaches.

"Do you sing when dressed?"

"Not so much."

"In that case, never take your bloody clothes off around me again!"

Lucien laughed, a booming, phlegmy rattle only a fraction less agonising to his head than the mercenary's singing.

While he pulled on the few garments he'd bothered to take off before falling into bed, Lucien peered out of the window. It appeared to be sunny.

"Josef asked me to denounce you and Solace last night," he said.

"Yes, he tried the same with me."

"He did?"

"Uh-huh."

He carefully sat on the edge of the bed to contemplate pulling his boots on. The big toe of his left foot peeked back out of his sock at him.

"What did you say?"

Lucien looked over his shoulder, "I told him his life would become immeasurably happier and more fulfilling if he started trying to fuck women instead of burning them at the stake."

"How... did he take that?"

"He went away to give my advice due consideration..." Lucien shrugged, "...I fear the infallibility of my argument may have induced a crisis of faith..."

"Let us hope..." he concentrated on his boots, unsure whether to believe Lucien or not.

By the time he'd found his way back to their room, the mercenary had been snoring soundly. Oddly, the sound hadn't been much different to his singing.

"What did you tell him?" Lucien put his back to the wall and crossed arms across his chest.

"That I had nothing to add to what we'd already told them. He didn't seem best pleased."

"Do you think he'll make a similar offer to Lady Solace?"

74

"He'll get the same answer if he does," feet squeezed into boots, he stood up again. At least this time, the manoeuvre required no accompanying groan, "and call her Celine here."

Lucien nodded as he headed for the door.

"Where are you going?"

"Breakfast! Sausage and ale. Given the state of the world, the sausage here is mainly gristle and rind and the beer tastes like horse piss filtered through Beelzebub's shit-stained undergarments, but… 'tis still the best way to start the day!"

His stomach gave a slow, queasy roll that made him want to fall back into bed, boots and all.

Before his knees could give way, the door flew open and the *Markgräf's* younger son burst in, armed men at his shoulder.

"Where is she?!" Joachim demanded, eyes blazing.

"And a good morning to you too, sir!" Lucien beamed, tucking thumbs into his weapon belt.

"Who?" he asked, knowing full well who Joachim was talking about. His weapons remained on a chair in the corner. The prospect of sausage and ale hadn't been enough to start him strapping on his own arms.

"Your mistress."

"In her room, as far as we know."

"She isn't. She's gone!"

Lucien pointed at the window, "'tis a lovely morning; perhaps she's taking some air…"

"The guard at her door said she never left her room," Joachim squared up to Lucien, the mercenary was taller and broader, but that didn't stop the *Markgräf's* son from putting his toes against Lucien's. Behind him, three soldiers fanned out as best they could in the small room.

"We don't know where she is," Lucien said, not giving an inch, though his smile faded.

"Well then," Joachim sneered, "are you saying she vanished into thin air?"

"Of course not."

"No, that would be ridiculous," Joachim said, cocking his head, "unless she is a witch..."

At Joachim's shoulder, the men-at-arms drew their weapons...

*

The table was old and scarred.

Aside from the single candle in a black iron stick, there was a pile of blank parchment, a quill and inkpot and, for reasons she decided it best not to think about, a hammer.

"Sit," Josef said again.

"Why am I here?" A chill seeped into her bones, her breath steamed, the air tasted of wet stone and unwashed clothes.

"I have questions. You have answers," his eyes flicked to the hammer, then back to her before he added, "but there is no need for unpleasantness."

"The *Markgräf* said a woman would examine me for a witch's mark, but the light here is poor for such work. And I see no other woman."

"The *Markgräf* is not the authority here when it comes to witchcraft. I am."

"Is that so... Pastor...?"

"The church takes precedence in these matters. I am the Church's senior representative in Ettestein, therefore…" he opened his palm, "…please sit."

The chair wobbled and squeaked under her weight as she did as he asked.

The single candle illuminated little beyond the table. From the way their voices echoed, the room was large enough for the deep shadows surrounding them to conceal others, but she thought they were alone.

Did Josef's duties stretch to torture? She didn't think so, but no one had ever been accused of witchcraft in Tassau, so she had no direct experience of how these things worked.

Once settled, she met Josef's eye.

"I am not a witch."

"Would you tell me if you were?"

"I do not know. As I am not a witch, I have no inkling of how one might behave."

Josef pursed his lips as if considering her words. Then he produced a long iron nail from his pocket. He placed it next to the hammer.

"Our Lord, Jesus Christ, suffered upon the cross for our sins. Nails like these hammered into his flesh…"

Assuming he had a point, she said nothing and waited for it.

"Can you imagine such suffering, *Fraulein?* Cold metal, hammered into your flesh, binding you to a wooden cross where you would hang in the burning sun for hour after agonising hour…"

She kept her tongue.

"I often wonder..." Josef spun the nail around with his finger until the tip pointed towards her.

"I prefer to think of our Lord's mercy, charity and kindness."

"Indeed. But without the sacrifice, who would remember those things?"

She sighed, "If you wish to discuss theology, Pastor Josef, I'm sure Ettestein boasts more comfortable surroundings."

Josef made a few more circles with the nail.

"You know nothing of Ettestein."

"No. Nor, in truth, do I wish to. I have business in Magdeburg. From which you are detaining me."

Josef's eyes rose from the nail.

"Business? With whom do you have this business?"

"A man named Yannick. A moneylender. Among other things. He undertook business on my father's behalf. He holds money due to me as my father's sole heir," the lie came without hesitation. It was one she'd been practising.

"I know of no man called Yannick."

"How well do you know the moneylenders of Magdeburg?"

Josef sniffed and straightened. Then picked up the quill, dipped it in the inkpot and scratched out a few words onto the first sheet of parchment.

"Yannick? He sounds like a Jew."

"I couldn't say. I've never met him."

"You have papers pertaining to your inheritance?"

"No."

"Regarding your father's business with this Yannick?"

"No."

Quill poised above paper; Josef raised an eyebrow.

"The war took my home. My father and brother with it. Everything save what I could carry burned."

"If this Yannick is a Jew, I wish you good luck getting money from him without paperwork to support your claim. You know how *those* people are."

"I can be most persuasive…"

Josef found this amusing.

"Does the perilous state of my finances have any bearing on whether or not I have sold my soul to the Devil?"

"Well, if you are prepared to sell your soul to a Jew…"

"Until recently, matters of finance were my father's concern. I am merely dealing with his choices."

"The sins of the father."

"My father committed no sins."

"Then he must have been a saint," Josef's words had a sharp edge, but she didn't query them. She had other concerns.

"Do you intend to torture me?"

Josef adjusted himself. His chair squeaked too.

"If you do, I suggest you get on with it. Questioning me about my father will tell you nothing about whether I had anything to do with Enoch's death."

"I have no desire for torture. I find the idea loathsome, but we must confront evil with whatever tools one has at one's disposal." His eyes returned to the hammer and nail beside the parchment.

"I am not evil. I just wish to be free of this wretched war."

"As do we all," Josef scribbled a few more words, "I asked both your men to denounce you. I told them if they did, it would save their own souls. And their skins."

"They both refused."

He raised his eyes, "You say that with confidence?"

"They are good men. Neither would lie to save themselves."

"'tis a wicked world, my lady. Are you so sure?"

"Yes."

"And if I made the same offer to you..." Josef pushed the nail around in another circle until it pointed at her again, "...would you denounce them?"

"They have done nothing to denounce. So, no."

Josef picked up the nail and held it towards her, "If I placed this against your skin, would you denounce them?"

"No."

"If I took this hammer and used it to drive iron deep into your flesh, would you denounce them?"

"No."

"If I did the same to them, would they denounce you?"

"Everyone has a limit to the pain they can endure. I do not know theirs'. But I know mine."

"Do they love you?" he asked, dropping the nail.

Her laughter surprised even herself, "I have no idea. But I doubt it."

"But you are beautiful. Men will sacrifice much for beauty."

"I had not taken you for a flatterer, Pastor Josef."

"I am not."

"And yet..."

"Beauty is a kind of magic. A spell, even. It can ensnare."

"As mad as this world has become, 'tis not enough to send someone to the pyre, surely?"

"On its own. No. But the Devil uses many weapons. He is

cunning."

She folded her hands in her lap, "What do you want? To see me burn? To see my men burn?"

"I seek only the truth. Enoch the Miser died a horrible death. His wife and daughter despoiled, used, before their throats were cut like slaughtered pigs. His maid bludgeoned to a pulp. I want justice. Nothing more."

"Then we want the same thing. I had nothing to do with their deaths. The kind of men who killed them are much the same as those that destroyed my home, killed my family and everyone I ever cared for," her voice tightened as she tried to keep it even.

"And what kind of men is that, *Fraulien?*"

"Monsters. They are monsters."

Josef nodded, easing himself back into his chair, "Many monsters walk in the world of men. Perhaps more than most of us truly appreciate."

"And you think I am a monster?"

"No, actually, I don't."

"You... don't?"

Josef shook his head.

"You accept I had nothing to do with Enoch's death?"

"I do."

"Then... why... I don't understand?"

"I know you didn't kill Enoch the Miser because I know who did."

"Who?"

Josef's only reply was to smile.

And spin the nail once more.

Chapter Nine

"She hasn't left this castle!"

The *Markgräf* didn't look happy. In fact, he looked bloody furious. Joachim mirrored his father, Lebrecht wore an expression more akin to bemusement. Lucien was scowling, too, though he suspected the mercenary captain was more annoyed about being kept from his sausage and ale than anything else.

"How can you be so sure?" Joachim asked when the *Markgräf* did nothing but glower at him.

"Because she wouldn't have gone without us. Or our horses."

"How do you know the horses are still here?" Joachim seemed to be taking on the talking responsibilities this morning.

"Are they gone?" he asked.

Joachim's eyes flicked to his father and back, "No. All of her gear appears present too."

"Then she hasn't left the castle!" he insisted, only just keeping from emphasising the point with some profanity.

"Of course, if she's a witch…"

"She isn't a witch!" he spat, "and she hasn't magicked herself away, or flown off on a broomstick!"

Two men-at-arms stood on either side of the door. The vehemence of his words was enough to make them both step forward, hands on their sword hilts.

The *Markgräf* looked at the men and then back to him. When he forced himself down into the chair before the nobleman's desk, the *Markgräf* glanced at his men again and shook his head. They stepped back in unison, but their hands remained near their swords.

"I'm sure there is a simple explanation," Lucien said, lounging on his chair as if settled before a tavern's fire for the night.

"Such as?" the *Markgräf* asked. Although he spoke softly, the nobleman possessed the kind of voice you paid attention to.

"Perhaps she went for a walk?"

"The guard would have noticed," Joachim sneered.

"I have commanded soldiers for many years. I have never underestimated the capacity of fighting men to lie through their teeth whenever they don't follow orders," Lucien swivelled to grin at the men by the door, "no offence, boys."

"So, you're saying the guard is lying," the *Markgräf* asked.

"The simplest explanation is almost always correct," Lucien opened his palms toward the *Markgräf*, "Occam's Razor…"

"You are a student of philosophy?" The idea anyone, least of all a nobleman, might be impressed by any of the absurdities spouting from Lucien's mouth was one the look on the *Markgräf's* face severely tested.

"Oh, no, my lord. I am but a simple soldier. But I have wandered far and wide enough on my travels to have seen many things. Lying soldiers are one of the more common ones."

"Who was on *Fraulien* Lutz's door this morning?" the *Markgräf* asked his sons.

"Tibor," Lebrecht replied.

"How would you rate him?"

"He is young..." Lebrecht said, "...and easily bored."

The *Markgräf* pinched the bridge of his nose and sighed. He looked tired; bags, like faint bruises, swelled beneath his eyes.

"Talk to him again. Robustly," when Lebrecht only nodded, he barked, "Now!"

"Yes, Father," Lebrecht gathered himself and hurried from the room. Joachim's eyes followed his brother to the door, something close to a smirk decorating his face.

"You are searching for our lady?" he asked.

"Of course," the *Markgräf* said, "and we will-"

A red-faced soldier bursting into the room cut off the sentence, "My lord, excuse me-"

"What?"

"There are soldiers at the gates."

The *Markgräf's* eyes widened, Joachim's head snapped around.

"Whose?"

"The Emperor's."

"Invited for Christmas?" Lucien asked.

As he shot to his feet, the Markgräf appeared much less impressed with that comment.

His son and the two men-at-arms trailed after the nobleman. Lucien climbed to his feet and made to follow them.

"Where are you going?"

"Best we see what is going on."

"But what about… *Celine?*"

"Do you think she has deserted us?"

"Of course not!"

"Then she is here somewhere."

"She could be in trouble."

"Women usually are."

He hurried after Lucien.

"We should look for her."

"Where do you suggest we start?"

Lucien lengthened his stride to keep up with the *Markgräf*.

"But we-"

"Imperial soldiers are at the gates. We need to know what is happening; it will be a lot harder to find our lady if the castle is under attack. Information is the most valuable weapon in any soldier's arsenal…" Lucien glanced sideways, "…first rule of soldiering, that."

He tried to think of something cutting to say in reply, but nothing materialised.

The cold slapped his face when they left the castle. The sky might have been a deep blue, but the air was bitter enough to suck the breath from your throat.

Outside, people scurried in all directions. Men to the outer walls, women, children and elderly into the castle.

Boots slapping on the damp stone steps, they reached the battlements overlooking the road snaking up to Ettestein. And the men and horses now filling it.

"Not enough to take the castle," Lucien announced as they caught up with the *Markgräf* and Joachim.

"What are you doing here?" Joachim glared at them.

"Thought you might need all the swords you can get," Lucien shot back.

"They're not here to take the castle," the *Markgräf* said, cloak ripping about him in the wind.

"No?"

"They're here to ensure I send no men to aid Magdeburg."

"You were planning to?"

Joachim glanced at his father, who ignored him.

"The city has requested help. I've yet to decide. I am sympathetic, but I am waiting on word from my liege, the Prince of Anhalt-Dessau. Who is something of a ditherer."

"Then this gives us the excuse to make the right decision," Joachim stared at the men below.

The *Markgräf* followed his son's gaze but didn't answer him.

"Magdeburg is ruled by fools," Joachim spat.

"How so?" Lucien asked.

"They think Gustavus Adolphus will come to their aid to defend the faith. He won't."

"You know the Swedish king well?" Lucien rested his hands upon the worn old stones of the battlements.

"I know he's much more interested in seizing land than defending protestants from Imperial persecution. He has joined the war to conquer the Empire's northern territories. If he holds the ports, he controls the Baltic trade and the gold that goes with it. Magdeburg is too far from his interests to waste men there. Though the Emperor sending troops to put down rebels will reduce the number available to fight him, so I assume his emissaries are encouraging the good burghers of Magdeburg to sacrifice themselves to aid his ambitions."

"My son," the *Markgräf* said, with a thin smile, "is something of a cynic."

Lucien was right. He reckoned around two hundred men sat under the imperial banners. Far too few to take the fortress by force. But probably enough to keep the *Markgräf's* men from going to Magdeburg. If they tried to cut their way through, they could do it, but they would lose a lot of men in the process. And it would also be considered a direct attack on the Emperor.

Whatever the *Markgräf's* preferences, his men would not be going to Magdeburg any time soon.

And neither would they.

*

"Are you going to tell me who murdered Enoch and his family?"

Josef continued to stare at her. He stared for so long that she became sorely tempted to grab his hammer and start beating the table with it, if not the sombre priest himself.

"I believe so," he finally admitted.

When he immediately returned to staring, she raised an eyebrow.

"I need to know that I can trust you."

"You can trust *me?* You've accused me of being a witch, threatened me with the pyre and abducted me. You have a peculiar way of building trust, Pastor."

"Abducted is a little strong."

"I am free to go then?"

He cocked his head, "There is no one here to stop you

leaving."

"And yet the door is locked."

Josef fished a key from his pocket and tossed it onto the table.

It was the Pastor's turn to raise an eyebrow, "You remain seated?"

"I am bedevilled with a curious nature."

"Bedevilled…"

She offered a pinched smile.

"Why do you need to trust me?"

"Because there is no one here that I can."

"Is the *Markgräf* not an honest man?"

"The *Markgräf* is a monster."

"I have met monsters, he-"

"The most dangerous monsters wear masks," Josef glared at her before his eyes returned to the nail.

"Did the *Markgräf* kill Enoch and his family?"

Josef rolled the nail back and forth below his finger. The look of concentration on his face reminded her of a small boy. "The *Markgräf* owes Enoch a great deal of money," he stopped rolling the nail, eyes rising to meet hers, "he *owed* a great deal of money."

"The *Markgräf* owed money to a farmer? We were told Enoch was the one with the debt?"

"They lied to you. Enoch was a rich man with fingers in many pies. Like your friend Yannick, he was a moneylender too."

"So a number of men owed him money?"

"Yes," Josef conceded, "but none as much as the *Markgräf* of Gothen. And he has history."

"We all have history."

"He killed his wife."

"Why are you telling me this?"

"Because I don't want him to kill you too."

"To the casual observer, Pastor Josef, it would appear you have been the one keen to kill me."

He sat back. Then snatched up the quill and started scrawling on the parchment with the frenetic haste of a man who had thought of something extremely important he needed to record before it squirmed away from him.

"No," he said, when he finally stopped scratching, "what appears to be the case is not always the case. Masks. Roles. Expectations. You see?"

The only thing she was starting to see was the possibility that the Pastor was not entirely sane.

But she nodded anyway.

When finding yourself in a locked room with a man whose sanity you were starting to question, agreeing seemed prudent. Even more so when he'd brought a hammer.

"Excellent!" Josef beamed, clapping his hands hard enough to make her blink. It was, she thought, the first time she'd seen him smile properly.

It didn't suit the dour set of his face.

"May I ask what happens now?"

The smile faded.

"You are going to help me ensure the *Markgräf* pays the price for his many crimes, sins and abominations."

Several questions leapt to mind. She ignored them all.

She was sorry for the suffering of Enoch and his household, but it was no business of hers. She had too many of her own wrongs to put right. All that concerned her was reaching Magdeburg and finding *Graf* Bulcher, from whom she would slice the whereabouts of Saul and his Red Company, one bloody, dripping word at a time.

At this moment, the thing keeping her from that task was sitting in a locked room with Pastor Josef. Get out of this room and she'd face the next obstacle, escaping Ettestein before she was burnt alive.

One problem at a time.

"How can I help?" she smiled, knowing a smile suited her face much better than it did Josef's.

"By denouncing the *Markgräf.*"

Her smile faltered.

"Denouncing?"

"Indeed."

"To whom."

"To the world. To the church..." Josef stretched out a hand and, eyes still fixed on her, let his fingers dance down the hammer, "...to me."

"I know nothing about the *Markgräf.* I saw nothing at Enoch's farm to-"

"You don't need to know *anything*," Josef snapped, "you just need to denounce him. Use your imagination. Say you saw him cavorting with demons dancing around Enoch's corpse or fucking Enoch's wife and daughter with a rolling pin. It doesn't matter."

"But that would not be true."

Josef's fingers caressed the hammer's shaft, "Trust me, whatever you can think of, that man has done worse..."

"You are asking for a lot of trust."

"Trust is the glue that holds our world together; without it..." he waved his free hand at the door, "...you've seen what's out there, haven't you?"

"Yes... I have."

"Then you should give me your trust. It will work out better for you that way."

"And, if I feel I cannot trust you, Pastor? If I refuse to denounce the *Markgräf*?"

Josef sat back, "Well... *someone* has to burn for what happened to Enoch the Miser..."

"The *Markgräf* is a powerful man. You are a pastor..." it was her turn to shrug.

"I have the authority and power to send you and your friends to the pyre. The *Markgräf* has enemies. I can assure you, once the wheels start rolling, he *will* be destroyed..."

Josef picked up the nail, pushed the tip against the wood and began hammering it into the table.

"Whatever you decide, I require an answer by the time this nail is buried in the wood," his eyes found hers, hammer poised in mid-air, "who is set for the pyre, *Fraulien*, you or the *Markgräf*?"

The hammer fell again...

Chapter Ten

"Occam's Razor?"

"William of Occam, an English monk. Long dead. Also known as the principle of parsimony. When examining competing propositions, the one with the least assumptions is most likely correct."

"And that applies to our lady how?"

Lucien put his shoulder against the battlement and lowered his voice to ask.

"What are the possible explanations for her disappearance?"

He bit his lower lip, checking off the possibilities by raising a finger of his good hand in turn, "She has deserted us and escaped the castle. She's gone off on her own somewhere for... reasons unknown. She's being held against her will..." he stared at his little finger for a second or two before shrugging "...she really is a witch and has magicked herself away."

Lucien raised a hand to mirror his, "She has shown herself loyal to you, saved your life and in return owes her own life to you; she would need a motive to explain such behaviour, and if we do that, then we still need to make assumptions as to how she could have escaped Ettestein unnoticed. If she simply took herself off, we need to assume she has found somewhere none of the men searching for her would think of looking and, as for being a witch, well, that's bollocks."

"Which leaves us with..."

"Occam's Razor leaves us with the most plausible explanation. She is being held against her will."

"But by whom?"

"The *Markgräf* has no reason for such a song and dance; if he wanted her held, tortured and denounced, he need only snap his fingers."

That made sense. Which was unusual for Lucien, but then Christmas was supposed to be a time for miracles.

"His sons?"

"Lebrecht seems quite keen on our lady, so-"

"He does?"

"You haven't noticed how he looks at her?"

He shuffled his boots on stonework worn smooth by centuries of passing feet.

"Not really..."

"His intentions might not be honourable, but..."

Ulrich cleared his throat and looked sharply towards the imperial soldiers making camp out of musket range.

"The other one then?"

"Joachim. Harder to read. Possible, but he acts the part well if he actually does know her whereabouts."

He returned his attention to the mercenary captain.

"Who else?"

"Have you seen Pastor Josef this morning?"

He hadn't enjoyed the pleasure of the dour-faced young priest's company since their encounter the previous night.

"No."

"He has asked both of us to denounce the other and our lady. Perhaps it is her turn?"

"She would not denounce us."

"Perhaps not. But she is a woman. In the eyes of bullies and cowards, a more malleable target than redoubtable men of principle and arms such as our good selves."

He would use far earthier terms to describe Lucien Kazmierczak, but he took the point.

Beyond the walls, a group of five riders approached the castle gates beneath an Imperial pennant.

"Perhaps they are hoping for an invitation to the *Markgräf's* Christmas feast? Not many feasts around here at the moment, I'd wager..." Lucien observed, noting the horsemen.

They had edged away from the *Markgräf* and his son, who were deep in discussion with several of their officers. At least the arrival of the imperials gave them something more urgent to think about than witchcraft.

"So, we must find Father Josef?"

Lucien nodded, "If we root out that weasel, I suspect our lady will be nearby."

No one raised the alarm when they slipped away, which he took to mean they were free to search for Solace themselves.

Ettestein was a broody dark slab atop its craggy outcrop, full of nooks, crannies and hidey-holes. Quite where they should start, he couldn't imagine, but the sight of Lebrecht hurrying across the mud from the castle proper dragged his mind from that question.

"You have company," Lucien cheerfully hitched a thumb over his shoulder at the gates.

"I heard," the young nobleman shot them a questioning look but didn't break his stride.

"Did you learn anything from the guard, Tibor, my lord?" he asked as Lebrecht strode past.

"Yes..." Lebrecht snapped, "...I learned we should employ men better capable of controlling their guts."

"My lord," Lucien said, "have you seen Pastor Josef this morning?"

Lebrecht stopped and turned, the mud' squelching beneath his boots, "No..."

"Neither have we. I suspect our lady's whereabouts might be linked to the Pastor's. He asked us both to denounce her last night..."

"Josef can be... overly zealous... but..." Lebrecht's words faded, he shook his head, "...we can't spare men to look for her now. You two search for her and bring her to me. If you encounter difficulties, you have my authority to do what you think necessary."

"And if Josef is putting the question to our lady...?" Lucien asked.

Intervening in a witchcraft investigation was a bold move, and one not often considered by people keen to avoid having their feet roasted.

Lebrecht met each of their gazes in turn, "Stop him. My father is in charge here, not Josef."

They both watched him as he hurried on towards the outer wall.

"You ever punched a priest?" Lucien asked.

"No."

"They tend to squeal, scream and bleed much the same as other men."

"Good to know."

"Of course, punching other men usually doesn't get you burnt at the stake."

"I'll take the risk."

Lucien smiled and gave him a knowing look before patting his back as if they were friends, "C'mon, let's find her…"

Most of the *Markgräf's* men-at-arms were on the outer wall, leaving the castle to the servants, who were generally much easier to intimidate. They seemed no more inclined to talk to them than the previous night, but no one admitted to seeing Pastor Josef that morning.

It didn't seem likely he would be in his rooms, but, lacking a better place to start, they headed there after getting the location from an old man with a fold of scarred skin where his left eye once resided.

"What do you think will happen with the Imperials?" he panted as they hurried up one of the castle's innumerable spiral staircases.

"Given the history of the last twelve years," Lucien replied, seemingly not out of breath at all, "they'll probably commence hacking lumps out of each other sooner rather than later."

"'tis Christmas…"

"Then perhaps their piety will keep them from slaughter until the day after tomorrow."

Josef's rooms were near the castle's chapel. There was also a small church amongst the wooden buildings clustered between the castle and outer walls, but he roomed close to the family. Presumably so he was nearby whenever they felt the need to be told they were going to burn in hell.

When no response came to Lucien's fist hammering Josef's door, he put his shoulder to it.

"Do you think Lebrecht's authority stretches to breaking down doors?" he checked each way to ensure no one was coming down the corridor.

Lucien tilted his head as if thinking about it before shrugging, "Fuck him…"

It took another couple of charges, and a few carefully chosen curses, to break the lock. Neither the sound of splintering wood nor the swearing attracted any attention. They hurried in.

There was a desk, a couple of chairs, a multitude of books and a cold fire. No Josef. No Solace.

Lucien wrinkled his nose and rested a hand on the pommel of one of his pistols. There were two other doors, one to the left, one to the right. Lucien headed to the left while pointing to the other.

The right-hand door opened onto a space only slightly too big to be a cupboard. Clothes hung on pegs, a couple of sturdy trunks took up most of the floor, shelves held more books and piles of loosely bound papers. Jesus men did love their words.

Only a murky light penetrated the narrow window's dirty glass, but it was enough to reveal that Josef wasn't here.

"Anything?"

"He didn't sleep in his bed last night," Lucien called from

the other room.

"Perhaps he made it this morning before going out?"

"Possible, I suppose..." Lucien grunted, "...priests *are* a fucking strange bunch."

He was about to shut the door of the little storage room when something caught his eye.

He crouched down, "Lucien..."

"What is it?" the Captain appeared in the doorway.

He held up the fingers he'd dabbed the stain with, "Blood..."

"What do you think is in those trunks?" Lucien came to his shoulder as he straightened up.

What if she is in there...

He loved her and he hated her. What she was doing terrified him, and her death would release him from the madness of her vengeance. But the possibility of losing her, sudden and real, didn't make him think of freedom and salvation.

It just filled him with aching loneliness.

When he did nothing but stare at the chests, Lucien brushed past and hauled the first trunk's lid open.

It contained nought but books, papers and old musty air.

He let out a breath he didn't know he was holding.

Lucien let the lid drop.

"More books?" the mercenary captain asked, moving to the second trunk.

"Books don't bleed," he nodded to the floor; a second, smaller, dark smear soiled the floor.

No inane quip followed. Lucien opened the second trunk. They stood there looking into the chest for a second before

Lucien ran a hand through his hair and spat on the floor.

"Shit…"

"So… what would Occam's Razor have to say about that?"

From the trunk, Pastor Josef's dark eyes stared up at them from his slack, bloodless face.

*

Pastor Josef's dark eyes stared at her across the table from his slack, bloodless face.

There wasn't much of the nail left protruding from the table, but the gaps between each blow grew longer as Josef looked quizzically at her, hammer poised in mid-air, awaiting an answer, no expression on his face, but something she could not name twisted in his eyes.

The hammer fell.

A little more nail disappeared into the splintered wood.

The Pastor's attention snapped back to her.

"One more," he said, "perhaps two…"

"Save your strength."

"You have decided? I should exchange hammer for quill to record the *Markgräf's* heinous and demonic crimes, yes?"

"The *Markgräf* may have committed any number of heinous crimes, demonic or otherwise, but I have born witness to none of them. And I will not falsely denounce a man."

Something rippled along Josef's lips, and he slammed the hammer against the nail without looking, driving the black iron into the wood and shaking the table so violently she half expected it to cleave clean in two.

"Your honour does you credit…" Josef hissed.

In truth, her words had little to do with honour. She may have spent her life cocooned within The Wolf Tower's thick walls, but she still knew enough about how the world worked to know denouncing the most powerful man in the room was more likely to result in your execution than his.

Josef pushed back his chair and rose to his feet.

Of course, her current problem was that the most powerful man in this room was the one lightly tapping a hammer against his leg as he walked towards her.

"I have more nails in my pocket," he stopped behind her.

"Do you believe you can frighten me into denouncing the *Markgräf?*"

"No. I'm merely trying to persuade you what is in your best interest…"

She tried not to flinch as Josef pressed the cold metal of the hammer's head against her temple.

"Why do you hate the *Markgräf* so?"

"Hate?" Josef moved the hammer down the side of her face and then along her cheekbone, "I don't hate him. I am just trying to make the world a better place. That's what we men of god do, isn't it?"

Josef giggled.

It wasn't the kind of sound you wanted to hear from a man holding a hammer to your skull.

"I could write the denouncement? All you'd need to do is sign it. I take it you can write?"

"I'm signing nothing."

"Are you absolutely certain…?" he traced the line of her jaw with the hammer.

"Positive!"

She brushed the hammer aside, sprung to her feet and glowered at the pastor. If he wasn't a head taller than her, she would have jammed her nose hard against his.

"I don't care who you are or what you want. You have no authority over me and I'm not giving false evidence against anyone. If you do me any harm, I swear my men *will* kill you..."

"Such... bravado..."

"Trust me, Pastor... I've stood before more frightening creatures than you..." her eyes moved to his hand and back, "...I've been threatened with far worse than a hammer too..."

"Have you now?" Josef flashed a toothy grin. Then his free hand shot out and squeezed her right breast.

"A nice bit o' tit you got there, so you have..."

She jumped to her feet, startled as much by Josef's voice as his grasping hand. The accent had wavered with those words, like a mimic tripping over his tongue.

"Who are you?" she backed away, leaving the small island of light cast by the solitary candle.

"Oh, just a humble servant of God, shepherding the faithful through these difficult times..."

He sounded like Josef again, but the leering mocking grin didn't fit his face half so well.

Her eyes darted back to the table where Josef had tossed the key.

His gaze followed hers. He laughed, a rough, barking noise this time, "You don't think that really *is* the key for the door, do you?"

She said nothing. Poised on the margin between the last of

the candlelight and the encircling shadow, conflicting urges to flee the madman and avoiding the absolute darkness pulling her in both directions.

His laugh spluttered into a chuckle, "No... you're going nowhere. We need to get to know each other a lot better yet, don't you think?"

Josef's hand stretched out of the gloom as if to caress her face. She ducked under it and headed back to the table, snatching the key before spinning to find Josef hard behind her. Straight-backed and unmoving, as if he hadn't scampered after her at all. As if he had been standing just there all along.

"You doubt my word?"

She made a fist around the key.

"I doubt everybody's word."

"Best you do. Honour is not what it was. As well you know..."

She ran for the door, expecting Josef to try and stop her, but no feet but her own slapped the stonework as she dashed across the room. It was little more than a suggestion in the shadows, and she had to find the keyhole by touch before sliding the key in.

It refused to move when she twisted.

"Perhaps you believe me now?"

She turned to find Josef's pale face upon her shoulder. Again, standing like he'd been here all along. She hadn't heard him running after her, he was not breathing heavily, and his skin remained as pallid as ever in the darkness.

But he must have chased after her...

Reaching past her, Josef placed his hand on top of hers

102

that still held the key. His touch chilled her from the skin to the soul.

Flyblown's mark smarted on her thigh.

"Now we've established you're not going anywhere, we'll have time to get to know each other better, to learn about trust and how doing what you're told makes life much easier…"

She tried to squirm away from him, but fingers clamped around her wrist, iron-tight and then he was pulling her back to the table. She stumbled and fell to her knees, but Josef just yanked her forward till she sprawled on the cold, old stone. Then he dragged her behind him, paying no more attention to her cries than he did the weight of her body.

Josef threw her across the table, scattering paper, ink and light. The back of her head smashed against the tabletop, stunning her. Before she could regain her senses and push herself upright, Josef had pinned her wrist, hammer in the other hand.

She screamed as he swung it, but it crashed next to her wrist, a black metal blur in the shaking candlelight.

"Best you keep still, so it is," Josef said, not sounding like Josef again.

He was nailing the sleeves of her jacket to the table, pinning her to it.

She clawed at his face while trying to tug her other hand free.

Stars exploded in the darkness.

"For feck's sake, I told you to keep still so I did you dozy bitch!" someone shouted.

She lay dazed, blood trickling down her face.

Had he broken her nose?

It seemed the least of her worries. The silly girl who'd lived in her stone tower would have been horrified by the prospect of a broken nose, but, really, did it matter anymore? You didn't have to be pretty when all you wanted from the world was vengeance.

Cold fingers gripped her cheeks hard enough to make her mouth pop open.

"Now you stay nice and still, why don't you'? Makes not a spit o' difference to me if I put one o' these nails through you arm rather than you coat. Understand me?"

The hand moved her swimming head up and down when she said nothing.

"There's a good girl..."

Soon after, the hammer started driving more nails into the table, making the world vibrate around her.

Then the blackness washed in and the hammering echo faded into the distance...

Chapter Eleven

"Do we tell anyone about this?"

"Josef wanted us thrown on the pyre. Now he's dead, and our lady has disappeared. What do you think?"

"Occam's Razor?"

"The most likely explanation is Solace killed him and then escaped."

"Proves Occam and his bloody razor is a load of shit then, doesn't it?"

They both stared at Josef's corpse folded into the trunk. The corpse stared back.

He reached down and closed the pastor's eyes. He'd always hated looking into the eyes of the dead.

"We need to tell Lebrecht," he decided, straightening up.

Lucien didn't appear convinced.

"Someone is going to find the body soon or later, if anyone sees us here…" he jerked his head at the corpse, "…plus he's been dead for hours. One of the maids saw our lady this morning when she took her breakfast. She couldn't have killed the pastor, but if they don't find the body till tonight…"

"Should have fought our way out of Enoch's farm when we had the bloody chance."

He looked at the mercenary, "She knows what she's doing."

"She's a *child*, lad. She knows fuck about fuck."

"Then why are you following her?"

Lucien said nothing and lowered the trunk's lid on the corpse.

"Morlaine…" he said.

Lucien looked awkward, which was a novelty.

"You're not following Solace; you just want to be-"

"Enough," Lucien snapped.

"Damning your heart as well as your soul, then?"

Something flared in Lucien's eye. Ever since meeting the man, he'd thought him nothing but a louche, boorish fool, but for just a few heartbeats, he glimpsed something dangerous lurking beneath the mercenary's bravado.

"You know fuck about fuck as well…"

This wasn't the time or the place. And whatever his relationship with Morlaine, it wasn't really any of his business. Aside from the fact consorting with a demon would see them all burn.

"C'mon," he brushed past Lucien, heading for the door, "we need to report this."

He expected Lucien to protest, but the mercenary fell silently in step, closing the door to Josef's rooms after them. The damage wasn't obvious with the door shut. The corridor remained deserted, and they passed no one on the stairs.

How long till someone found Josef's corpse?

He discarded the temptation. If they knew where Solace was and could get out of Ettestein unnoticed, he'd be prepared to leave Josef where he was and avoid the additional suspicion and awkward questions. As it was,

106

Solace was missing and a small Imperial army sat on the other side of the gates, likely with orders to ensure no one left the castle.

Lucien was uncharacteristically quiet.

An air of brooding thoughtfulness hung about the Captain. It didn't trouble him any. So long as Lucien kept his mouth shut, he could have the air of a pigsty about him for all he cared.

"Where is *Markgräf* Lebrecht?" he barked at a soldier as they returned to the frosty sunlight. The sons of a *Markgräf* carried the same title as their father, which he supposed could get confusing.

The man-at-arms was as friendly as anyone else in Ettestein, which is to say he looked at him like he was something his wife would make him scrape off his boots before letting him into the house.

"With the *Markgräf,* talking to the papists. What's it to you?"

He exchanged a glance with Lucien, who offered only an unhelpful shrug in reply.

"We need to see him."

"So does the Emperor; wait your fucking turn," the soldier shook his head and hurried off.

"He could do with a few lessons in manners," Lucien watched the man disappear around the corner.

"What do we do now?"

"Tell anyone else, and we'll be disarmed and locked up till the *Markgräf* finishes his chin wag with the Imperials. Which could be five minutes or Christmas Day, depending on what they want. And if Solace is in trouble..."

I wish he'd stop talking sense, 'tis even more irritating than the bullshit...

"So... we search this place one room at a time till someone tells us to fuck off or they find Josef's body?"

"He might not be missed for a while..."

He stared at Lucien, "He's the castle's pastor. 'tis Christmas! He will be bloody well missed when he doesn't turn up to give his sermon!"

"The Empire rolling up to their gates might buy us a little extra time...?"

"Very well, we search for Solace until Lebrecht finishes with the Imperials, then we tell him about Josef."

Lucien peered at him, "You say that like you're in charge, lad."

"Let's not waste time arguing about who has the bigger cock, eh?"

Lucien's grin stretched, "That'd be a short argument..."

He headed back towards the castle, "Where do we start?"

"Tibor," Lucien said with a confident nod.

"Tibor?"

"The soldier guarding our lady's room-"

Lucien stopped and swept off his hat as a maid descended the steps from the castle's entrance.

She seemed to think about spitting at them but simply stuck her nose in the air and ignored them as she breezed past.

"Do you think finding their pastor stuffed in a trunk will make them any more amenable to us?" Lucien asked, plonking the hat back on as he followed the sway of the girl's hips.

"Depends how good his sermons were…"

Lucien chuckled at that.

As if I haven't got enough to worry about, now his bad jokes are rubbing off on me…

He paused on the steps, "Is Tibor not likely to be on the walls with the rest of the men?"

"We will ask around," Lucien said, hurrying inside while slapping his hands together against the cold.

As it turned out, Tibor wasn't on the walls. He'd upset Lebrecht enough to spend his day cleaning out the castle's shit pits instead. Unlike most of Ettestein's inhabitants, he appeared happy to talk to them, though, when the alternative was shovelling shit, that wasn't much of a compliment.

Ettestein didn't have a moat and the Elbe wasn't close enough to shit directly into, so the castle's privy chambers dropped their wares into a number of pits surrounding the castle. The lucky Tibor's job for the day was loading it onto a cart to dump outside the castle. Assuming the Imperials didn't object.

Tibor, a scrawny young man, rested on a shovel only marginally thinner than him and yanked down the kerchief he'd tied around his mouth and nose.

"Every man has the right to go for a shit once in a bloody while…" he grumbled.

Lucien wrinkled his nose at the steaming pit behind Tibor, "Seems everybody else here does."

Tibor snorted and pulled a sour face.

"Tell us what happened with our mistress this morning?" he jumped in.

"Not much to say. Sat by her door for half the night. Nothing happened. Rosalind turned up with some porridge for the win.... err, the lady. She came back an hour later to collect her bowl and... the lady was gone," Tibor nodded and leaned forward a fraction, "vanished even, you might say."

"She didn't vanish," Lucien growled, "she left the room whilst you were contributing to that shit pile."

"Or someone took her," he suggested.

Tibor shrugged, "Can't say. Didn't see nothing. And now I've gotta shovel shit all bloody day."

Several plops in the pit behind added more work for him.

Lucien's eyes rose to the privies jutting out from the castle on stone corbels high above. More shit fell from one of the holes.

"Impressive shitting..." the mercenary noted, head lowering to track the flying turds until they splattered into the rest.

"If you enjoy watching shit so much..." Tibor thrust his shovel in Lucien's direction, "...please, be my guest."

Lucien gave him only a toothy grin in return.

This wasn't getting them far.

"And you saw no one else other than this maid, Rosalind?" he pressed, trying to get back to greater concerns than excrement.

"No one," Tibor said, dropping the shovel to his side once more.

"Perhaps we should find Rosalind and-"

"Nah," Lucien stepped forward and grabbed Tibor by the collars of his battered coat.

110

"Hey!"

With little apparent effort, Lucien carried the squealing man to the very edge of the shit pit.

"Now, tell us the fucking truth, or you're going to take a bath in there!"

Tibor tried to break free of Lucien's grasp, but the mercenary simply extended his arms. Tibor's boots momentarily scuffed the wall of filthy stone marking the pit's boundary, then he was over the stinking pile contained within.

"I don't know anything!"

"How about a *headfirst* bath?"

"I don't know fucking anything!"

"How about I hold your lying mouth under that filth until you do! Now tell me!"

Lucien shook the man hard enough for him to rattle.

"Alright! Alright!"

Lucien swung him around and dropped him onto the muddy ground, before standing over him, "Well?"

"Fleischman paid me to piss off for five minutes."

"Who's Fleischman?"

"One of *Markgräf* Joachim's men."

"The order was from Joachim?"

"No. He just said… they needed to take the witch somewhere. I don't know where, or why. Didn't want to know."

"How much does it cost for you to disobey your orders then?" Lucien leaned over the cowering man.

"Not about money. Fleischman's a cunt. If I'd refused, I'd probably have ended up…" he looked back at the shit pit,

"...somewhere worse than there."

Lucien prodded him with his foot, "Trust me, whatever he says, I'm a far bigger cunt than this Fleischman prick can ever dream of. In fact, Lucien Kazmierczak is famed from Gothenburg to Genoa for being a cunt of *enormous* proportions."

"I can vouch for that," Ulrich said, looking around to ensure no one was in sight.

"So... what else can you tell me to stop me from throwing you in there and seeing how much shit I can get you to swallow, eh, lad?"

*

She didn't know how long it took for her senses to fully return, but the hammering had ceased by the time they did; only faint grey light dusted the arched stone ceiling. And she couldn't move.

"You keep nice and still now, why don't you," a voice said. Pastor Josef. Except it didn't really sound like him at all. The accent and intonation were all wrong.

She craned her neck but couldn't see the speaker.

The candle was no longer on the table, hence the gloominess.

She tugged at her arms, stretched at forty-five-degree angles from her body, but neither moved. She couldn't sit up either. Her long travelling coat was nailed to the table.

Oh, yes, all that hammering.

But at least Tutor Magnus would have been proud she remembered what forty-five-degree angles were...

"I said keep still, didn't I now?"

A hand grabbed a fistful of her hair and banged the back of her head against the table. When she cried out, a cold finger pressed her lips, "Ssssh..."

She stayed still and silent. The finger went away.

Her head throbbed and so did her nose.

"What are you going to do to me?"

The only reply was boots on stone. Then a hand squeezed her knee.

A figure stood at the other end of the table, blocking what little light there was.

"I'm not sure I approve of your clothes. Dressing like a man..." the hand wandered up her leg, fingers digging into her thigh, "...there's a reason women wear dresses. You know what that reason is?"

He chuckled when she said nothing, then moved his hand to her crotch.

"'tis so 'tis easy for a man to get at her cunt, so it is."

Josef hadn't bothered nailing her britches to the table.

So she kicked him.

The angle wasn't good enough to connect with his groin, but she thought she got close.

Still, Josef only laughed rather than yelped.

Disappointing.

At least he took his hand away from her thigh.

Flyblown's mark was smarting fiercely. Was it trying to tell her something? Besides don't ever let a madman nail you to a table, of course.

The figure moved behind her. Metal scraped against metal; something cold and hard pricked her forehead. A nail.

"Now, what if I told you that if you don't denounce the

Markgräf, I'll hammer this nail into your head?" Josef asked, without the peculiar accent this time.

"I'd say you'll have some explaining to do when they find my body."

"Do you think I wouldn't do such a thing, girl? Whack this here long iron nail with me big heavy old hammer till it splits your skull? And keep hammering till 'tis buried in your brain?"

"What has the *Markgräf* done to you?"

"Done? Absolutely nothing?" he pressed the nail harder against her forehead, "Now answer the question!"

"I won't denounce him."

"Why?"

"Because it isn't true."

Josef laughed; the pressure on her forehead eased.

"True? Why does it matter if something is true? You'd rather me hammer a nail into your empty little head than tell a lie, eh, girl?" Josef's accent wavered again.

"If I denounce the *Markgräf,* I'll be dead anyway. So, why should I? What's in it for me?"

Josef took the nail away.

"What's in it for you? Now, that's much more like it. That, I understand!"

"Why are you speaking in a different accent?" she asked to mask her relief.

"Because the accents are the hardest feckin' bit, so they are!"

"Why-"

"What about an eye? What if I stuck this nail in your eye, would you denounce the *Markgräf* then?"

She ground her teeth together, the nail hovering above her left eye.

"No."

"But if you did, I wouldn't turn your eye into goo and smear it all over your pretty face like gooseberry preserve on a slice o' very fine white bread. That's something for you, isn't it?"

"Do you think anyone would believe my denouncement if it has clearly been tortured out of me?"

Josef sniffed, "No one complains about all the witches tortured into confessing nonsense and then roasted alive. So, yes, I would."

"He isn't some peasant. He's the *Markgräf*. He is the law here."

"No, he isn't..." he touched her again, but this time to stroke the hair she'd kept hacked short since The Wolf's Tower fell, "...I am..."

He moved again, taking the nail with him, to begin circling the table. Head lowered as if in thought.

"What is this about?" she tried to work her right arm free but couldn't get it to budge a fraction.

"You have spirit, girl, I'll give you that. Of course, I knew that anyway but 'tis always nice to have an impression confirmed."

"You speak as if you know me."

"Oh, I know you alright! Maybe not as much as I'd like..." his hand ran down her leg. She jerked it away from his touch. Provoking another chuckle.

"I'd never seen you before yesterday. I've never heard of Gothen, let alone been here!"

"Most people would say whatever was asked o' them when faced with the prospect o' pain and death. They might take longer to betray family, children, lovers, but, in the end, even them. They might say otherwise, but when you hurt someone enough, all the fine promises they've ever made turn to dust. Pain is a price even love eventually cannot pay. 'tis just a matter o' degree. As most things are. And trust me, I know. I've seen a lot o' pain, so I have."

Josef walked as he talked, head lowered, seemingly not looking at her but at something in his hands. A nail, probably.

She strained to pull away from the table. It creaked under her shifting weight, but nothing gave.

"But you... I think you'd rather take a nail through your thick skull or have your comely eyes smeared over your face rather than do what I asked. Maybe you'd denounce the *Markgräf* in time, but not your friends..." he stopped at the end of the table and braced his hands upon it, "...not young Ulrich. You'd never denounce him, would you now?"

She gave up straining against the nails and raised her head to stare at the man standing before the candlelight, heart beating faster as Flyblown's mark started to burn.

"Which is a strange thing, considering he betrayed you and everyone else in The Wolf's Tower to save his own skin, don't you think, Lady Solace...?"

Chapter Twelve

Having a pistol shoved in his face clearly startled Fleischman.

To be fair, it was not the sort of thing you expect to happen while you're fucking.

"Excuse us, ma'am," Lucien said to the young woman obligingly bent over a barrel for Fleischman's benefit, "We need to have a word with the gentleman here; we won't be keeping him from his business for too long..."

The girl didn't scream or make a fuss. In fact, she looked a lot less put out than Fleischman as she peered over her shoulder at them. Of course, she wasn't the one with a pistol in her face. On this occasion, anyway.

"Now..." Lucien clamped his free hand on Fleischman's shoulder, "...why don't you just ease yourself out of there while we ask you a few questions. No need to keep the young lady from her chores for that... there we go... good... oh, *really?* Hardly worth the bother for *that*, was it, *Fraulien?*"

Lucien walked Fleischman backwards, the soldier's gait restricted to a shuffle by the britches around his ankles.

The maid jumped up and tugged her skirts back into place, cheeks aflame.

Ulrich smiled reassuringly at her.

As was often the case with his reassuring smiles, the

recipient didn't seem in the least bit reassured.

"We're not going to hurt anyone," he said, dispensing with the smile and opening his hands.

She still lingered, looking wary. Perhaps the way Lucien's pistol pressed into her lover's head undermined his reassurances.

"Sorry for giving you a fright," he said, "why don't you run along."

Lucien shot him a disapproving look, but he wasn't going to tie the girl up or worse.

"Just keep quiet about this, eh?"

She nodded and edged towards the door after glancing at Fleischman, cock shrivelling in the frigid air.

"And if you think about going to fetch help for *Herr* Tiny Dick," Lucien warned, "we'll be sure to let everybody in this castle know what you've been doing when you should have been scrubbing the floors. Understand?"

She froze. Wide-eyed. Glanced at Fleischman again and then nodded at both Lucien and him.

"And if you fancy a drink later," Lucien grinned, "I'll show you what a real man has in his britches..."

She hurried for the door, but he stopped her with an outstretched hand. And the coins in his palm.

"By way of an apology," he said, "for any embarrassment caused."

Most of the castle thought they were in league with the Devil, and they'd just caught her bent over a table with her arse on display. But in hard times money was money. So, she scooped it up after only the slightest hesitation and a near-silent thank you before hurrying off without meeting his eye.

"How much do you pay her?" Lucien tapped Fleischman's temple with his pistol.

Fleischman's jaw was so tight he looked in danger of shattering his remaining teeth.

"And don't tell me she bent over for the fun of it, not for... *that*. She must have been getting *something* in return..."

"Lucien..."

"Yes?"

The mercenary was starting to enjoy himself too much.

"Maybe we should get down to business?"

He crossed to the door, checked the corridor and shut it properly. They were in a storeroom in one of the lesser-used wings of the castle. Tibor told them Fleischman had an arrangement with several maids and was as likely to be here, collecting on one, as anywhere else.

His information turned out to be correct. What the threat of having your head pushed into a pond of shit could do to a man's tongue was amazing.

"Where is our lady? he demanded, crossing the room before Lucien could start mocking the size of Fleischman's cock again.

"You're gonna pay for this. I-"

He punched Fleischman in the face.

The soldier staggered back into Lucien, who at least managed not to shoot him while he kept his feet.

"Cut the lies. You have an Imperial army at the gates, and you're here fucking a maid. But that's nothing compared to the shit you'll be in when the *Markgräf* finds out you disobeyed his orders and took our mistress from her room this morning. So start talking."

"I-"

He punched him again.

"Did that sound like another lie coming out of his mouth?" he asked Lucien.

"Definitely. I've heard a lot of them in my days."

Blood trickled from Fleischman's lip when he straightened up; eyes burning, he said nothing.

He knew the type. A hard man, the kind that thought everyone below him was put on God's Earth for his amusement, who strutted along with their shoulders back, chest out and chin jutting forward. Tall, broad, neat beard flecked with grey, time starting to carve lines around sharp blue eyes, a mouth well-suited to a sneer or a cutting aside.

Oh, and not to forget, a very small cock.

"Where is our lady?"

Fleischman spat blood on the floor.

He reached for one of the blades hanging from his belt.

The soldier's eyes followed the hand.

"Where is our lady?"

Fleischman shook his head.

He'd never tortured a man before. He suspected Lucien was better at this sort of thing, but Solace was his mistress. He loved her and he hated her. She had already taken him down a dark road leading to a place he did not want to go. A road that would pass many places he had no desire to visit.

And this was one of them.

He slid a knife free.

It was a short blade. He'd slept little in the gloomy

daylight hours they had spent with Morlaine since leaving Madriel. There was little to do after eating and before sleep eventually came. Working his whetstone was one of them.

He held the knife up so Fleischman could get a good look at the razor sharp blade.

Lucien watched him with interest.

He doesn't think I've got the nerve for this kind of work...

He stepped forward, grabbed Fleischman's balls and pressed the knife's edge against them.

Fleischman was looking at him with interest, too, now.

"Where is my lady?" he held the man's eyes as well as his balls, "and if she's dead, so are you..."

He tightened his grip, the cock still sticky from the maid. He could smell her on him; he could just about remember what a woman smelt like.

For a moment, Madleen's reflection danced in the soldier's widening eyes. Pretty, frightened, desperate, lonely Madleen, who he hadn't been able to save.

Fleishman's Adam's apple rose and fell.

Then he blinked.

"Pastor Josef wanted her..." he said, his voice weak and high. Did he always sound like that, or did it have something to do with the sharp cold metal pressing against his balls?

He tightened his grip further, enough for Fleischman to wince and whimper.

"When?"

"*Please...*"

A tear welled in Fleischman's eye. He was making a man cry. How did that make him feel? Was this an honourable thing to do? Even for the woman you both loved and hated? What would Old Man Ulrich say from the other side of his tankard, bleary eyes fixing on him, a drunk's wisdom poised upon beer-frothed lips?

"When?"

"This morning! Before dawn! He said God needed us for holy work!"

The man didn't look like he was lying. He looked like a man who would tell them just about anything to get him to take that oh-so-sharp blade away from his sticky little cock.

He glanced at Lucien, whose brow had furrowed.

Josef had been stone cold in that trunk. He couldn't say the hour of his death with conviction, but he was damn sure it was long before the sun had risen above the frost.

He eased the pressure and pulled the knife back a little.

"And you always do whatever God needs of you?"

"Josef paid us!"

That definitely had the ring of truth about it.

Lucien pressed the wheellock pistol harder against Fleischman's temple, reminding him that having his balls sliced off wasn't his only concern, "Where did you take her?"

"The upper catacombs. The eastern ones. I left her with Josef. He didn't want us to stay. We locked the door and that was the last we saw of her. As far as I know, she's still there."

"We?"

"Ulger. My... friend."

"And where is Ulger now?"

"On the walls."

"Which is where you should be?" Lucien asked.

Fleischman nodded.

"But you decided your cock needed warming, eh?"

"Yes!"

He stepped back.

Fleischman sucked in a breath.

He raised his blade and pointed it, "You're going to take us there now. If my lady isn't there, I'm going to cut your balls off. If she has been harmed, I'll take your eyes as well. If she's dead... I'll do to you whatever was done to her. Understand me?"

Fleischman nodded. Sweat glistened on his skin as he trembled. Though the room was a mite cold to have your britches around your ankles and your cock hanging out.

"Let's get going then, lad," Lucien shoved Fleischman forward, "and if any clever ideas pop into that dark empty space between your ears before we reach this room, remember, I've killed a lot more men than you've fucked maids with that tiny little cock of yours..."

*

She knew the answer but asked the question anyway.

"Who are you?"

"Aren't you going to protest you've never heard o' anyone called Solace?" she thought he was smiling, but with what little light there was behind him, she couldn't be certain. Not that it mattered. A smile meant nothing when it sat upon a monster's face.

"Aren't you afraid the Red Company might get to hear that you're still alive?" that worthless smile stretched further.

123

She strained harder to pull herself free, but nothing gave. Perhaps unsurprisingly, given the unnatural strength used to hammer the nails into the table.

"Say your name…" she hissed.

"But why? You've worked out who I am, surely? Torben did say you're very bright… and he's rarely wrong about anything…"

The mention of her brother froze and burned, but she ignored it like she'd ignored everything in the world for the past year. Everything save vengeance.

"I want to hear you say it before I kill you."

He laughed at that. As she thought he might.

Fuck him. His head would be on a spike with the rest of them one day.

"I'm not sure if we were ever formally introduced. I am Wendel."

Wendel. The demon that took Captain Kadelberg's face to help the Red Company trick their way into The Wolf's Tower. One of those responsible for killing her father and stealing her brother, destroying her home and slaughtering everyone she knew and cared about.

Hatred, molten and visceral, surged through her.

"Ah, you remember me then, so you do."

She sucked in cold, stale air, trying to calm herself. Hatred and anger only got you so far.

She stopped straining against the nails. She wasn't going to break free of them.

Whatever the demon wanted, she'd already be dead if he was here to kill her.

"You've taken Josef's face this time?"

124

Wendel nodded, "And his life. Not necessary for the trick, but it makes things simpler. I need to study a subject first, you see. Like an artist before his muse, so I am."

"When?"

"Last night. When he got back to his room... well, I let him say his prayers first. I'm a civilised fellow, after all."

So the Josef they had seen yesterday had been the real one. She supposed he had to be; even with another's face, the demon would not have been able to ride in the daylight with Lebrecht, Joachim and the others.

"Why are you here?"

The demon tapped the end of her boot, "You're the one nailed to a table; what makes you think you get to ask the questions, girl?"

"Because I know nothing of any use to you, and as you haven't killed me yet..."

"Oh, I wouldn't read too much into the fact I haven't killed you. Killing isn't always a quick business with us. You could ask your Dadda about that, so you could."

The rage came again. So hard she wanted to scream at the shadow-cloaked ceiling. She didn't. That would mean he was winning, and she would never let any of these bastards win again.

"So," she repeated, "are you here to kill me?"

"Actually, no," Wendel shrugged, "'tis nothing personal. Under other circumstances, I'm sure you'd make great sport and excellent meat. But this time, I was asked to ensure you're unharmed. Till I leave you, at least, after that, you're on your own."

"Who asked?"

"More questions! You have an endless supply, so you do!"

"Who?"

The humour, if that wasn't too strong a word for it, faded from his voice, "Your big brother…"

"Tor-"

"Enough! Mouth shut, ears open. Or do I need to nail your tongue to the table too?"

He raised a hand, another nail pinched between thumb and forefinger.

She wanted to talk, to scream, to shout, to spit. She wanted to claw his face from his skull. Instead, she did nothing.

Wendel curled Josef's lips into a smile.

"Torben sent me. To warn you to stop whatever daftness you're about. Go to Naples, he said to tell you. He still has affection for you, more than affection even. That's rare; such things do not always survive the change. After I changed, I raped and killed *my* little sister…" Wendel's gaze drifted off into the dark, "…but not everybody is the same. Heed his words, Solace. Find another path. Follow the Red Company, and you'll find only death."

"Death for you," she said before she could stop herself.

"Really? What do you think you can do? Saul let you live once; he will not grant the same mercy twice."

"Does… he know you're here?"

Wendel shook his head, "This is a personal favour for Torben. Saul would…" the words trailed away into a snort.

"How…" the words tore her throat, but she forced them out, "…is my brother?"

"Not the man you knew. But… he still loves you. And that,

believe me, is a rare thing, so it is. He wants you to stop, Solace. Live out your life, forget him, forget what happened in The Wolf's Tower. He has protected you so far. But if you continue…"

"How can I forget what you did…?"

Wendel lowered his head, "Live for yourself, Solace, not the dead."

"You stole my brother."

"He gave himself. And he saved you. And he continues to save you. If Saul knew o' this…" he shook his head, "…you'd be dead, I'd be dead, Torben… maybe Torben is too useful to him to kill. Maybe not. Regardless. This is the last warning, your last chance. Take Ulrich and your new friend and turn around. Save your life. Save their lives. Save the lives o' anyone else foolish enough to fall into your net o' madness. While you still can…"

Your new friend…

Lucien.

She fixed her eyes on nothing.

He doesn't know about Morlaine…

"How did you know we would be here?" she forced the thought away; as far as she knew, Wendel's talents did not run to reading minds, but wanted to give nothing away she didn't have to.

"Torben told me you'd be here. The day, the time…" Wendel sniffed, "…even the feckin' weather. 'tis uncanny. There are few things in this world capable of sending a shiver down my spine, so there is, but Torben…"

"Why did you kill Enoch the Miser and his family?"

Wendel wiggled a finger at her, "Now, in fairness, I can see

127

why you might jump to such a conclusion, so I can, given 'tis the kind o' entertainment we sometimes pass a night or two with. But that had nothing to do with me. Still, was convenient, gave Pastor Josef an excuse to whisk you away for this little chat."

She stared at him. As best she could.

"Believe me or not. I have no reason to lie..."

He started circling the table again.

"So... are you going to follow your brother's excellent advice?"

She said nothing.

"He did say you were stubborn. I offered to slit your throat and drink you dry – I find that an effective way to dissuade people from doing things you don't want them to do..." Wendel threw out his hands as he paced, "...but Torben weren't amenable to that fine suggestion. So, I'm left with only my powers o' persuasion, so I am. Not that I really care. If you continues this mad pursuit o' yours, well... you saw how things ended for this Enoch and his family, so you did..."

A cold smile split Josef's face.

"...that'll look like afternoon cake compared to what we'll do to you and your boys. Even if you don't care what happens to yourself, what about young Ulrich, eh? Saul wasn't best pleased with him. Saul the Bloodless ain't the kind o' fellow who takes kindly to rejection..." Wendel heaved his shoulders "...we all have our faults..."

He stuck his elbows on the table and leaned over her, face filling the world.

"Don't you care about anyone, Solace?"

"You killed everyone I cared about."

"I suppose we did. I can understand you hating us. But 'tis just our nature. We are no more evil than the cat or the fox."

She spat in his face.

He neither flinched nor wiped the spit away. He just looked faintly amused.

"You know that's as much as you'll ever be able to do to us, don't you? So, enjoy your moment. Does it make you feel better? No? You can spit at me some more if it helps..."

He laughed when she only glowered at him.

"Torben said, don't go to Magdeburg. There's nothing there but death. More death than you can ever imagine. Blood will run in rivers, the corpses will be piled higher than the Grey Hills. The World's Pain will consume the city and everyone in it. Go to Naples and forget him. He said to tell you that was what the owl would do..."

The bag of wooden animals and figures Torben had used to express the thoughts his mute tongue wouldn't allow. *The Owl* was intelligent. *The Owl* was clever. *The Owl* thought things through. *The Owl* always did the smart thing.

A tear bubbled beneath her eye.

Torben!!!

"Tell my brother..." she said, reining in each word to stop it becoming a scream, "...that I will not allow this. He is not a monster. He is not like you. Whatever he is now, he is still better than that. I love him, and I will never cease loving him. And I will spend every breath I have looking for him, looking for the Red Company. And when I find you, I *will* destroy you..."

She held Wendel's gaze and let hatred's furnace dry her tears.

"...I will do whatever I need to. I will avenge my father. I will avenge every last person you killed in The Wolf's Tower and Tassau. Man, woman and child. I will not go away, I will hunt you all down, and *nothing* will stop me. I will burn the whole fucking Empire till nought remains bar ashes and dirt if that is what it takes to see you all dead and my brother saved."

Wendel pursed his lips and slowly straightened up.

"Seems I've suffered a wasted journey then, so it does. Best I leave you to grub around in the ashes of your empire of dirt, Solace."

The demon turned away.

"One last question."

He stopped but didn't look back.

"Why did you try to make me denounce the *Markgräf?*"

"Just a bit o' fun to see if you would..." Wendel said, "...'tis always best to know your enemy, so it is. You wouldn't. Which makes me think you mean what you say. And that is what Torben is afraid of. I don't have his gift, but sometimes the future is not much of a mystery."

Wendel looked over his shoulder and smiled a grim little smile.

"Torben has no desire to be saved. He is at peace for the first time in his life. This is your last warning. If you ever do find us, my lady, your big brother will kill you quick as the rest o' us would..."

Chapter Thirteen

They let Fleischman pull his britches up and tuck his cock away.

They didn't want to draw more attention to themselves than necessary.

He went first, following Fleischman's directions. Lucien walked at the man-at-arms' side, a long-bladed dagger concealed beneath the folds of his coat.

"Only take's a second to slit your throat," Lucien cheerfully told him before they left the storeroom.

Every echoing footstep set his heart racing, but they encountered few people as they descended through the castle. Only servants and all at a distance. Most of Ettestein's garrison had taken the Imperial's arrival as a reason to muster on the walls, not to slip away for a sneaky fuck when no one was looking.

Old Man Ulrich would have had a thing or two to say about soldiers like Fleischman.

Perhaps feeling the need to make polite conversation Fleischman said, "The Pastor will see you all burn for this..."

"For what?" Lucien prodded him with the dagger through his cloak, "Interrupting your fornicating? Ulrich, remind me, doesn't the Bible take a dim view of such lewd behaviour?"

"Nothing good comes of it," he muttered, scanning the next corridor.

Sneaking around a castle reminded him of things he'd spent the last year vainly trying to forget. If they ever got out of here, he wouldn't moan about the cold and damp of the open road again. Almost certainly.

"All witches burn in the end," Fleischman's balls seemed to be getting bigger now he didn't have a knife against them.

"Lucky for us we're not witches then," Lucien shoved the soldier down the deserted corridor, "much further, Tiny Cock?"

Fleischman glared at Lucien, earning him another shove.

"I don't have a tiny cock!"

"If you don't get us to our lady soon, you'll have more to worry about than your laughably diminutive member."

"Lucien..." he warned. Goading the soldier wouldn't help with anything, apart from possibly passing the time.

Fleischman was red-faced and wide-eyed. If anybody got close enough, they would instantly realise he wasn't going for a friendly stroll with a couple of chums.

They walked on, nailed boots rapping worn stone. A sound that made his skin itch. It reminded him of shadows filled with monsters.

Monsters that still haunted the shadows inside him.

He shook the stupid thought away. The only monsters here were the human kind, and he needed to concentrate. Fear was an indulgence he could ill afford.

"Take these stairs down," Fleischman told them, nodding

at a door at the end of the corridor.

Voices called out from somewhere, not close and not alarmed, but he slowed all the same. Light speared through high narrow windows, but the shadows hadn't retreated far. Once the voices faded, he pulled open the door to reveal a staircase spiralling into darkness.

He looked back at Fleischman, who nodded again.

An unlit tar torch sat in a black iron cradle at the top of the stairs. He lit it from a rushlight burning in a niche in the corridor.

"How far down?" he asked, thrusting the torch into the stairwell.

"All the way…"

He exchanged a glance with Lucien, who swapped dagger for a pistol and pressed the wheellock's muzzle in the soldier's back.

"You don't look capable of being clever, Tiny Cock, so anything you try will result in a lead ball. Understand?"

"Understand, I'm going to piss on you after you're executed," Fleischman spat back.

"Aww, and just when I thought we were starting to build a little friendship…"

"Quiet!"

Lucien grinned and he headed down the stairs before the fool could wink at him.

More shadows. More echoing footsteps. More unwanted memories.

His palm slickened around the torch's shaft, eyes narrowing against its spluttering glare.

No monsters are waiting to pounce here…

He swallowed and concentrated on putting one foot in front of the other as they went down the thin, narrow and damp steps.

No one is here to make you cast aside your honour in return for your life...

Lucien and Fleishman moved behind him. Leather creaked, metal clanked. Breathing hard, his arms occasionally brushed the roughly hewn walls.

There is no one here to betray. Apart from Lady Solace, and you are here only to save her...

The staircase narrowed even more as they descended, squeezing the frigid air tightly around them. With each step, he expected the staircase's curve to reveal a figure in the torch's restless light. A corpse pale face, too large eyes, long, terrible, inhuman. Fangs bared.

Waiting, waiting, waiting.

Always waiting for him to come back to them.

Part of him wanted to turn and bolt back up; part wanted to run down. Whichever would get him out of this place first. It was only a staircase, but it felt like a tomb.

Instead, he forced himself to keep the same pace. One foot and one step at a time.

Eventually, the staircase revealed not a waiting demon but a solid wooden door. The stairs went no further, so he opened it without waiting for Fleischman's confirmation. And to fool himself he wasn't afraid.

The door revealed more darkness. They must be below the castle now, in the world where sunlight never reached. The air that rolled out was damp, heavy, old. Seldom breathed.

His guts tightened.

There were few reasons to bring someone down here.

So nobody heard the screams was one of them.

Fleischman's face was a blank as Lucien pushed the soldier through the door. No guilt, no worry. His jaw remained tight, but he didn't carry the weight of fear on his shoulders.

"If my lady has come to any harm down here because of you…"

Fleischman met his gaze, "All things are as God wills them."

"I'm the one with the gun in your back," Lucien patted Fleischman's shoulder, "so you'd best be concerned about *my* will for the time being."

"I am not afraid to die."

Lucien snorted, "The times I've heard that hoary old chestnut! Trust me, I've seen enough men die to know everyone pisses themselves at the end."

"Where did you take her?" he demanded.

Fleischman pointed down the corridor. It was narrow, the ceiling roughly hewn from rock. Moisture dripped to form black puddles on the stone slabbed floor.

They walked on in silence.

Several doors appeared out of the gloom. Fleischman shook his head as they approached each one. The corridor angled slightly downwards, towards the very bowels of the Earth for all he knew. Ettestein was old. And with age came secrets.

"Here," Fleischman said as they came to another door. Small, worn, and adorned with black iron studs.

He didn't share Solace's *sight*, but he didn't like this place.

Lucien stayed at Fleischman's shoulder. He said nothing, but his face had hardened, his nose wrinkled. No quips, no jokes. He felt something too.

He stood aside.

"Open the door," he told Fleischman.

"Why don't you? the soldier said, eyes flicking to his withered arm and back.

"Do as you're fucking told."

"It'll be locked. That door is always locked..."

"You said you locked the door. So, you must have a key," he said.

"Ulger has the key."

Before he could say anything else, a scream rolled out from behind the door. A cry of terror and pain.

It was a woman's scream.

And it tore him to the soul.

*

The demon wasn't going to kill her.

But she intended to kill him.

"Why do you do the things you do?" she asked before the shadows could consume him.

"*Why?*"

"When you were a man, would the things you do... the things you did at The Wolf's Tower, not have horrified you?"

"I was never a good man."

"But still...?"

He returned to the table.

"Yes," he admitted, staring down at her. Josef's eyes were mirrors, giving no clue to the demon's thoughts behind them.

"Then why?"

"The hunger."

"The hunger?"

"For blood. It drives us all insane in the end.

All vampires are mad...

Morlaine's voice breathed from the darkness.

"Are all demons the same?"

She knew they weren't, but she would not speak of Morlaine. Torben had told Wendel nothing of the vampire that hunted them. She didn't know why, but she thought it important. The *sight* said as much. So, she would say nothing about the dark-haired demon that walked the Night's Road with her.

"We are all mad, so we are."

"But do they all slaughter the innocent?"

Something that might have been discomfort flickered behind the face the demon wore.

"No..."

"Then why do you?"

"Because weak men become weak monsters."

"We all have a choice."

"So we do. Yours is to go to Naples and live a life or pursue us and die. Most likely badly."

"If the hunger for blood makes you a monster, then the hunger for vengeance makes me one too."

"But I cannot live without blood, you can live without vengeance, well enough, Lady Solace."

"No..." she whispered, "...I cannot."

"Then you'll die," he stroked her hair with fingers that

sucked the heat from her scalp.

"We all die."

"If it comes down to me, I'll make it quick. 'tis all I can offer."

His hand dropped, and he made to move away.

"Tell me of the man you once were?"

"Why is that of any interest? I am a monster now. 'tis all that matters."

Because Renard and Lucien are looking for me. Because you cannot leave this place till the sun sets. If they find me before then, we will kill you...

Flyblown's mark pulsed upon her thigh.

And then there will be one less of you to hunt.

"I wish to know the journey my brother has taken."

"Torben is not like other men."

"Tell me... please."

"I was... no one. Just a man. Unremarkable, so I was. My father was a farmer. I never got the taste for scratching the dirt, but I did develop a fondness for drink and whores. I had a quick temper. I got into fights. I lost a lot o' them," he smiled, "now I don't."

"And how did that man become what you are now?"

"I met a dark man upon a dark road," he shrugged, "I have no regrets."

"None?"

"None."

"Don't the screams haunt you?"

Wendel only laughed.

"They haunt me."

"Ah, but then you're just a wee slip of a girl, so you are."

"I've killed two of your kind," she held his eye, "and I will kill you, too."

Wendel patted her cheek, "No, me lovely. You won't be doing that."

"I killed your friend, Callinicus. Why should I not kill you?"

"Because I am not my friend, Callinicus..." this time, he slapped her cheek rather than patted it.

"I blew him to tiny pieces of meat. My only regret is I didn't get to see him die," she forced a smile, "I'm going to enjoy killing you. And this time, I will see it..."

She thought he was going to hit her again.

Instead, he laughed.

"Chalk and cheese you might be, but I can see your brother in you all the same, so I can."

His words lanced her. Torben was a card that trumped any she held.

"I killed a vampire in Madriel too. I stuck a knitting needle through her eye and into her brain. It was easy... the next one I kill will be easier still."

"I told Torben this was a waste o' time. 'tis not just vampires that are mad you see. Grief is like love. It can make a right royal fool o' you too."

Wendel scooped up the hammer from the table. From the look on his face, she feared he might take it to her head despite his promises to Torben. Instead, he put both hands around the thick wooden shaft and snapped it with no more effort than breaking a summer-dry twig.

The metal head clattered to the floor.

"Some things don't die easily..." he said.

"You'll find I'm one of them."

"Goodbye, Lady Solace. I hope we don't meet again," the demon dropped the broken halves of the hammer and once more turned to the shadows.

"I want to know about my brother!" she shouted after him.

This time he didn't pause.

"No, you don't. Just rest awhile. The candle will burn out soon. The dark helps me think..." his footsteps started to fade, "...don't worry, someone will find you eventually. Fingers crossed it won't be the pyre for you."

She tried to wrench herself free once more. This time something gave a little and tearing fabric replaced the clip-clop of Wendel's boots. But they didn't give enough.

The demon was leaving. One of the monsters who'd murdered her father, abducted her brother and destroyed her life. A slice of the vengeance she had dreamed of every day since she'd climbed out of the broken library window in The Wolf's Tower nearly a year earlier. Walking away, returning to the shadows and nightmares. Escaping her fury.

She craned her neck and stared into the darkness Wendel had scurried into. Her back lifted a fraction from the table.

But no more.

All she had left to hurl at the creature who'd stolen Pastor Josef's face as well as her life was a scream.

Chapter Fourteen

"Open the fucking door!" he yelled at Fleischman when it wouldn't budge.

The soldier did nothing.

He was torn between throwing his shoulder at the door or his fist at Fleischman.

Lucien stepped forward and planted his boot into the door.

"Release the witch and you doom yourselves," Fleischman said.

"Keep your trap locked," Lucien shot back, grimacing as he kicked the door again, "or you'll doom your worthless arse."

The door rattled and shook but didn't break. It was a lot sturdier than the door to Josef's rooms.

"Fuck you," Fleischman snarled.

He didn't see the soldier's fist before it connected with his chin.

He staggered back against the wall, the torch spinning from his hand.

By the time he could focus again, Lucien was grappling with the soldier, the pair bouncing from one side of the corridor to the other.

He fumbled for his sword, though there was little room to

swing the long blade in the narrow corridor.

Lucien cracked his forehead into the soldier's face. Fleischman screamed and sagged, blood spraying from his shattered nose. Lucien hurled the man to the ground.

The click of the lock broke the following silence. All their eyes turned to the door.

It swung open but revealed nothing beyond.

"'tis the witch's men!" Fleischman cried, though the blood streaming from his broken nose muffled the warning somewhat. Lucien's boot in his ribs discouraged anything further.

"Young Ulrich..." a voice floated out of the doorway, chilling his blood.

He scooped up the fallen torch and thrust it towards the door as best he could with his withered arm, the sound of shuffling feet on stone was the only response.

Lucien drew a pistol, kicked the door fully open and rushed inside.

The mercenary came flying straight back out to crash against the wall.

He wrapped the fingers of his bad hand around the torch and made to raise his sword. A figure emerged through the doorway. For a moment, he thought it a ghost.

"Pastor Josef..." Fleischman panted, pulling himself to his knees.

He took a step backwards, still gripping his father's sabre. He just lacked the strength to lift it.

"Josef's dead..." he managed to say when the cold stone pressed against his back.

"Ah, but here I am, alive and well, my son."

142

He hadn't known the pastor for long, but he doubted a smile half so sly and chilling had ever crossed his face.

The pastor was dead. Cold, dead and folded into a trunk. Face so pale he could have been drained of blood...

He wanted to run, scream, drop to his knees, take his father's sword, and slice the monster's head from its shoulders. To whisper, *Master...*

All he managed was to let the torch slip from the fingers of his ruined arm.

He'd seen this before. He'd ridden next to a monster wearing a dead man's face as he'd betrayed his oath, his lord and his honour. The only thing of worth a man truly owns.

Perhaps other monsters in the world could perform the trick. But he knew of only one.

"Wendel..."

"Ah, you remember me, so you do!" the monster placed hands over his heart, as his voice changed, "if you weren't such a wee misbegotten little shite, I might even be touched."

The hands fell to the demon's side once more.

"But probably not."

"Pastor," Fleischman said, finding his feet, "The witch's men made me bring them-"

"You're bleeding. How convenient..."

The monster still wore Josef's face, but the voice was his own, Irish roots tainting the German he spoke.

"Pastor...?"

"Come to me, my son, 'tis time for your last rites..."

"Stay away from him," he warned as Fleischman moved

unsteadily forward, "this is not Pastor Josef."

He should strike this creature down, but knowing their strength and speed so well, he left his sword where it was.

Better to try and reason with it.

And that was not cowardice at all. Not really...

"Why are you here?" he blurted.

Wendel hooked a thumb over his shoulder, his eyes not leaving the blood dripping down Fleischman's face, "She'll tell you later."

"My lady-"

"*My lady...*" Wendel mimicked, "...*master...* those kinda words come easy, don't they, boy? But what do they really mean, eh?"

Lucien groaned on the floor, starting to shake some sense back into his thick head.

The demon pulled his eyes from the bloody soldier, "A great steaming barrel o' nothing at fecking all, so they don't. If it weren't for the fact Saul would smell your blood on me, I'd kill you here. I promised not to hurt her this time, but Torben didn't say nothing about her yapping dog. So, I'll just give you the same advice I gave your lady, go to Naples, forget about the Red Company and make the most of your handful of empty years."

Wendel shot him a smile.

Then his face changed.

He'd seen it before. He'd hoped he'd never see it again. But it still caught his breath and made him push himself away, even though he already had his back to the wall.

Fleischman, who had never witnessed a man's face change into that of a bloodless demon, screamed. He was

144

still screaming when Wendel ripped his throat out.

The demon moved so fast. In the blink of an eye, Wendel was upon Fleischman, fangs in his neck. Arms flailed, wet screams echoed along the narrow stone corridor. Just as they had in The Wolf's Tower.

He should do something. His father's sword. Strike. Reclaim some honour. Show he was not a coward. Instead, he kept his back to the wall, unwilling to step across the torch at his feet, as if its greasy light offered some protection from the evil before him.

Fleischman's screams washed over him, freezing water, numbing him, making his whole body as useless as his withered arm. And within the dying man's cries the ghosts of the dead roared, all those lives taken because of his weakness and cowardice, because he valued his own life higher than theirs. Higher than his honour. If-

A roar and a flash startled him, making him shy away.

It took a second or two for the gears in his brain to catch and realise Lucien had discharged his pistol. And that Wendel twisted Fleischman into the path of the shot.

Fleischman slipped from the demon's grasp. A hole in his back to go with the ones in his neck. He was still twitching when he hit the ground, but he didn't expect the soldier to live for long.

Wendel puckered blood-stained lips, "Ooops…"

Lucien made to pull a second pistol free from his belt, but Wendel was already disappearing into the shadows, leaving only three words trailing behind him.

"Naples, Ulrich, Naples!"

Lucien regained his feet and fired after the fleeing demon.

The gunpowder flash revealed nothing.

The monster was gone.

*

Lucien finally managed to prise enough of the nails out of the table to allow her to wrench herself free.

"We have to leave now," the mercenary said again.

"No," she repeated, sitting on the table's edge and plucking the remaining iron from her coat.

Renard stood as pale and mournful as any ghost behind the tar torch he held, "Did... he hurt you, my lady?"

She shook her head.

"What did-"

"He had a message for me, nothing else."

"Message, my lady?"

"Later, we have no time. We must find him!" Her voice rose to a screech as she jumped to her feet, expecting her words to have settled matters.

"Josef is dead; there's a soldier with a lead ball in his back. We will be blamed. If they don't burn us, they will hang us," Lucien said.

"Wendel is here. In this castle. He can't leave before sunset. He's trapped!"

"So are we, my lady," Renard's voice was barely a whisper.

She headed for the door, stopping only when she noticed the flickering light of Renard's torch wasn't moving with her.

"I told you, there's no time to waste!" she shouted at them.

The two men exchanged a glance.

"What?" she demanded.

"How can we kill something like… *that?*" Lucien asked when Renard did nothing but stare at his boots.

"Everything dies. *I've* killed them, so I'm sure you can find a way."

"My lady-"

"One of them is here!" she walked back to them, the spit accompanying her words catching in the torchlight, "One of the Red Company is within these walls. Fuck Magdeburg! Fuck *Graf* Bulcher! Fuck all of them! We're not leaving here till I have that bastard's head!"

She glared at them in turn, hands on hips, chin jutting forward, "What? Are we scared?"

Lucien bridled at that; Renard kept looking at his feet. Some army she was gathering about herself.

She held out a hand, "Give me your sword; if you're not prepared to use it, I'll hunt the demon on my own!"

"Then you'll die," Lucien made no move to pass her a weapon.

"Renard," she thrust the hand at the other man, "give me your sword."

He refused to lend her his eye or weapon.

"Damn you both then!"

She twisted away and stomped towards the door.

Cowards!

One of the monsters who'd slaughtered her father and taken her brother was nearby. He'd come to give her a message, but she had her own message, and he was damn well going to hear it. She-

A hand clamped on her shoulder and pulled her back. She whirled around, expecting to see Josef's stolen face leering out of the shadows. Instead, Lucien loomed over her. He caught her wrist before her hand reached his face.

"Get your hands off me!"

Lucien gripped her arms, pinning them to her side.

"Calm down, my lady."

"Don't tell me what to do. I know what to do; I must kill that monster!"

"You'll avenge no one if you're dead!"

Renard moved to Lucien's side, "We are not enough to kill Wendel. Trust me, I have seen them up close. Without Morlaine-"

"I have seen them too! Don't you remember?"

"Yes, my lady, I remember..." Renard's eyes fell away. The torchlight danced around them. Renard was shaking. So was she.

She stopped struggling in Lucien's grip, chest and shoulders heaving as she panted. Beyond the two men, she tried not to see mocking figures prowling the thickening shadows.

She raised her eyes to hold Lucien's, challenging him. Eventually, he released her and took a step back.

"We must leave before the bodies are found."

"There is an imperial army at the gates..." Renard reminded Lucien.

She frowned, "Why?"

"To persuade Gothen to stay out of the Emperor's business in Magdeburg, we presume," Renard explained.

"Then we can't leave, can we?"

"While they are distracted, we-"

"No!" she snapped Lucien off, "We don't run. Not anymore.

Whenever we find one of those responsible for what happened at The Wolf's Tower, we don't run," her eyes slid to Renard, "We stand."

She thought that a good speech. Firm, passionate, steely. But with control. Not the petulant rant of a spoilt child she suspected and feared she still was and always would be.

Lucien and Renard, however, seemed much less impressed.

"And how do we stand?" Lucien asked, voice softer, "This demon, Wendel, may be here somewhere, but this castle's catacombs are large, dark and unknown to us. And we are but three. Everyone from Antwerp to Anatolia knows Lucien Kazmierczak is no coward, but he is no fool either."

She dropped her eyes. He was right, and she hated him for it. If they went charging blindly around these catacombs, they would likely find nothing but cobwebs before sunset, and Wendel would slip away. Walls and Imperial soldiers would present much less of a barrier to the demon than they did to them.

"And while we stumble in the dark," Renard added, "someone will discover Josef and Fleischman's bodies..."

She nodded, "Then there is only one thing we can do..."

"Yes, my lady," Lucien smiled, Renard looked relieved.

"We shall go to the *Markgräf* and tell him everything..."

With that, she spun away, not waiting to hear if their footsteps echoed after her.

Chapter Fifteen

He loved her and he hated her.

Right now, he feared her as well.

The *Markgräf* wasn't an easy man to read. Bright eyes set in an impassive face, few expressions troubled his features, his voice rarely changed in pitch. A man of little emotion or just one who kept his feelings hidden from the world?

If Solace scared the nobleman, too, he didn't show it.

"A demon?" the *Markgräf* asked, evenly enough, raising his wine glass but not sipping it.

"Yes."

"Who killed Pastor Josef and one of my men?"

"Yes, my lord."

"And now hides in my castle?"

Solace sprung to her feet so quickly the two men-at-arms standing behind the *Markgräf* took a step forward.

"I've already explained this. We are wasting time!"

The *Markgräf* might show little emotion, but he wasn't used to such a lack of deference, especially from a slip of a girl.

"You have explained little. And 'tis my time I am worried about wasting," he said, waving back his men.

"We could just hang them, Father. We do have other problems..." Joachim offered. Eyes drifting to the window and the Imperial force out of sight beyond it.

He wanted to step forward, calm Solace, placate the *Markgräf* before he sent them to the gallows or the pyre. Instead, he stayed behind his lady and next to Lucien.

Partly because that was his place but mainly because all he could hear was Wendel whispering in his ear.

Naples, Ulrich, Naples...

He fixed his attention on Solace rather than that taunting voice or the shake he could not still in the fingers of his good hand no matter how tight a fist he made of it.

She was shaking too, though not, he suspected, from fear.

"This monster cannot walk in daylight, 'tis trapped here until the sun sets," she jabbed a finger at the window, "we only have a few hours!"

"And this demon wears Pastor Josef's face?"

"Yes, for now, at least. But it can mimic anyone."

"Quite the adversary..." the *Markgräf* finally took a sip of his wine, swilling it around his mouth as if wanting to be sure it was to his liking before swallowing it.

"So, this demon could be... *anyone* here..." Joachim didn't share his father's penchant for keeping his feelings hidden. Scepticism and scorn dripped equally from every word.

"Yes."

"Even you?" Joachim stared at Solace. His lady stared right back.

"If I can stand the sun's touch, then I am not a demon."

Solace crossed the room and pressed her face against the glass of the narrow window.

With her back turned, Joachim and Lebrecht exchanged a glance.

"And this proves...?" Joachim threw his hands wide as Solace returned to the *Markgräf*.

"It proves I am not a demon," she held the young nobleman's eyes before adding with a thin smile, "why don't you try?"

"Father! We don't have time for this nonsense. Put them into a cell; we can decide what to do with them once the Imperials leave."

"That could be months," Lebrecht hunched forward next to his father.

Joachim shrugged.

Solace moved to the edge of the *Markgräf's* desk, again the soldiers behind him shuffled.

"You do not believe me then?"

"I believe Enoch the Miser is dead, as is Pastor Josef and one of my men. I believe you and your men are connected to all the bodies. There is one thing I know for certain, however..." he swished the wine around the glass, "...I am not a man who believes in coincidences."

"I-"

"Why?"

"Why, my lord?"

"Why is this demon here? Why is he killing my people? Why did he take you?" the *Markgräf* lifted the wine glass to his lips without taking his eyes from Solace, "And, perhaps most pertinently, why aren't *you* dead, *Fraulein* Lutz?"

The following silence was long and deep. He resisted glancing at Lucien as strongly as he did bolting for the door. He had given his oath, his word, his honour. He was bound to follow wherever Lady Solace led, even though he

152

knew full well she was leading them to the grave.

He wanted to drag her away from here, kicking and screaming if need be. To slap her face and scream at her that one of them was here and even if she could persuade the *Markgräf* and his sons to help, it would amount to nothing. They would all die.

At the master's hands.

Instead, he did nothing but watch as much as even his eyes wanted to flee.

Solace straightened her back and folded her arms to stare down at the *Markgräf* and his eldest son. Joachim, standing behind them, one shoulder against the book-lined wall of his father's study, she ignored.

"My name is not Celine Lutz. 'tis Solace von Tassau, *Freiin* von Tassau..." she said, "...I am hunting the demons that murdered my father, *Freiherr* von Tassau, slaughtered my people and destroyed my home. The creature within your walls killed Pastor Josef to take his place. He intended to kill me. And would have if my men hadn't found me. He killed your soldier escaping. He has taken many lives, men, women, children. He is evil incarnate. He drinks human blood. He has the strength of ten men. He is as fast as he is deadly. He can change his appearance. He is hiding in your home. My lord, I beg you for your help, as a man of honour and piety, to rid the world of this monster, to protect your people and avenge mine."

Disbelief didn't trouble the *Markgräf*'s face. Neither did concern, outrage or any other reaction. His eyes, however, did narrow as he stared at Solace. After a drawn-out pause, he put the wine glass down, "Perhaps if you told us this tale yesterday, two men might still be alive."

"There are men and monsters who I would prefer to think me dead. I apologise for the deceit, my lord. It was a mistake.

"Yes," he said, sliding the glass away, "it was."

Solace took another step forward and stood over the *Markgräf's* desk, "Please forgive my boldness, my lord, but time is short. 'tis best we do not waste it, one way or the other. Do you intend to help us or hang us?"

"You are indeed very bold, *Freiin* Solace..." the *Markgräf* said, his face still a mask, "...just like your mother..."

*

She squinted against the low winter sun.

The air was sharp enough upon the tower to steal her breath.

Hard to see, hard to breathe.

Had the *Markgräf* brought her up here just to escape prying ears or to discomfort her too? Perhaps both.

"We have little time, my lord," she said again, turning from the sun. How long remained until nightfall? Fearing the answer would discomfort her far more than the dazzling sun or biting cold, she ignored it.

"You look just like your mother," he said.

In a certain light, he looked a little like her father. The same neat beard flecked with grey, the same sharp features, the same build and stature. In his fur-lined cloak, sun glinting on its silver clasp, she could almost fool herself...

Many things in the world can discomfort you beyond

sunlight and temperature.

"I never knew her," was all she trusted herself to say.

"When I heard of her death…" his eyes, which were not at all like Father's, slipped away "…'tis a terrible world."

From their vantage point atop one of Ettestein's highest towers, they could clearly see the Imperial force pitching tents out of musket range. Curls of campfire smoke already sullied the sky.

"My lord, I would gladly talk of my mother, but the daylight does not last long at this time of year…"

"And your demon will flee with the night?"

"I don't know. He did not tell me his plans. But the night is his domain."

"There are things you are not telling me, I believe."

"Yes, my lord."

"For my benefit?"

"For both of us."

"I heard of Tassau's fall. I assumed it due to the war. You tell me otherwise. Why did these demons destroy your home?"

For me.

Guilt speared her again. Brighter and sharper than the light and air atop Ettestein Castle.

She didn't know this man. The days when she gave her trust without thought ended with her home. Her own life mattered nought beyond the fact vengeance would die with her, but there was Renard. Lucien and Morlaine too. Vengeance mattered more than all of them, but she would not squander their lives cheaply. Telling the *Markgräf* of Gothen anything was a risk. One she'd already taken. How

155

much further could she gamble her vengeance and their lives?

She thought of Wendel, somewhere in the stones below her, waiting to cloak himself in darkness and scurry off along the Night's Road to slaughter the Lord alone knew how many more innocents.

More lives lost because of her.

"A monster sent them, but not a demon. The mortal, flesh and blood kind. He sent them for his own twisted purposes. I intend to kill him as I intend to kill them all. But first, I will kill the demon under your roof."

The *Markgräf* turned away, resting gloved hands upon the pitted stonework; he narrowed his eyes against the glare.

"If you were anyone but your mother's daughter..."

"My mother... meant something to you?"

A rare smile broke his face, a fleetingly sad one, she thought. It made him look older.

"Something..." he echoed.

She glanced at the sun, already falling toward the distant tree line beyond the grey ribbon of the Elbe.

Time.

Slipping away.

"May I ask...?"

"I... wanted her to be my wife. So did her father, as did mine. All agreed it a fine match."

"But she..." her eyes widened at his words, "...loved my father?"

Frosty patches of snow remained in the places the sun had not touched. Something else crossed his face, it lingered for only a heartbeat, but it was enough to suggest the ice below her boots might be thin in more ways than one.

"No. She was yet to meet your father, but she declined my proposal. Her father - your grandfather - was not happy, but he was not the kind of man prepared to force his daughter's hand. Sadly, for me."

"So, she did not love you?"

"Love..." another sigh, another twitch, "...for the nobility, marriage usually has little to do with love. We marry for power, influence, money, alliance, prestige. We are all nought but pawns in the games our fathers play."

"Usually?"

The *Markgräf* gave her a long hard look. A year ago, it would have unsettled her. Now she met his eye and held it in a way some might consider unbecoming for a young woman before a man of high station.

"I loved your mother deeply," he said finally, "and I will believe she loved me too, until the day I die."

"Then why?"

He looked around, despite them being alone atop the tower. He had ordered his men to wait inside once he'd led her up here.

"You."

"Me?"

"She told me I was not the man destined to father her children, that her children were important, would be important and that nothing, not even love, should prevent their birth."

"She died giving birth to me," she said. A breeze picked up, strong enough to ruffle her short hair.

"I know," his voice dropped, "she knew too."

"She had the *sight*."

The *Markgräf* nodded, "I didn't believe her then, though part of me wanted to denounce her when she refused me... I am not a good man... not always."

"But you didn't?"

"No. My love outweighed my anger and heartbreak. And I didn't believe it till the day I heard she'd died giving birth to you. As she told me she would."

She pulled her own cloak around her against the wind.

"Who are you, Lady Solace?"

"I am... no one. I died a year ago."

He shook his head, "I don't believe that. The love of my life walked away from me because of you, even though she knew giving you life would end hers. And here you are. Standing in the very spot your mother told me she would not marry me. That must mean something. As I said downstairs, I do not believe in coincidence. God must have returned you to me for a reason..."

God and his reasons were unknown to her. But she understood why she was here well enough.

"I'm here to kill one of the demons who slaughtered my people. That is God's sole purpose for me."

"Perhaps..." the *Markgräf* tilted his head, "When I first saw you, I thought of your mother. Just a likeness, it seemed. One of life's curious little peculiarities, but no more than that. Still, it was enough to refuse Josef's demands to take you to the dungeons and put the question to you over Enoch the Miser's death. Now that I know who you are..."

"Who I am is not relevant, my lord. The fact a demon is

158

hiding in your home is," When he continued to stare at her, she asked directly, "Are you willing to help me hunt it down and kill it?"

"I could never deny my Eleonore..." a hand started to reach for her; a smile twisted his lips, and he let it fall back to his side.

"I am not my mother..."

"Perhaps not, but I will send men into the catacombs all the same. I-"

"No. You must empty the castle first. Wendel can change his appearance; he may no longer wear Pastor Josef's face. There is only one way to be certain anyone is not the demon..." she turned her face to the sun "...once everyone is outside, we will know whoever is left inside is our prey."

"I should make my entire household shiver in the cold? On Christmas Eve?"

"Only till sunset. Tell them 'tis for the benefit of their eternal souls..."

He sighed and clasped his hands before him, "Very well, my lady."

A smile broke her face, as radiant as the winter sun but far colder.

It was time to hunt..

Part Two

Thirst

Chapter One

Ettestein, Principality of Anhalt-Dessau, The Holy Roman Empire - 1630

"This is never going to work!"

Lucien slapped him on the back, irritating grin stretching from one irritating ear to the other, equally irritating, ear.

Which made the idiot the only person loitering in Ettestein Castle's shadow with a smile on his face.

People huddled together and shivered. Feet stamped, hands clapped and rubbed, breath steamed in plumes. Everybody looked as miserable as he usually felt. He supposed it made a change not to be the unhappiest man in sight.

A few hastily constructed fires burned between the castle and the outer walls. Women and children were being shepherded into the castle's outbuildings, but the men remained in the cold as there wasn't enough room for everyone.

The men-at-arms chosen to search the castle crowded together, a sergeant tying a red cloth around the right arm of each soldier. Lebrecht stood before the knot of men, ordering them to kill anyone they found not marked with a red cloth on sight.

"What spell did you cast on my father to get him to agree to this nonsense?" Joachim demanded of Solace as the four of them waited to one side.

"There is a great evil in your house. The *Markgräf* is dealing with it as any pious lord should."

Joachim looked like he wanted to spit but managed to swallow it and settled for a sour glare.

It was a good question, though. He had no idea how Solace persuaded the *Markgräf* to empty his castle on Christmas Eve with a hostile force setting up camp outside his walls. Should he be grateful? They'd likely be spending Christmas languishing in the dungeon awaiting torture and execution if she hadn't.

It seemed churlish not to be grateful. Yet...

He stared up at the great bulk of Ettestein rising above them.

One of his old masters was inside.

Horror and fear had coursed through him at the sight of Wendel, familiar and visceral. A dark flood sweeping him back to The Wolf's Tower. To his dishonour, to his shame, to his cowardice.

He didn't want to go back in there. He didn't want to stare into that creature's eye and fight to keep his knees from buckling once more.

Naples, Ulrich, Naples...

But he had no choice.

His attention drifted to the men-at-arms. Some grim-faced, others relaxed; most, however, simply looked bemused.

They had no idea what awaited them.

He opened and closed the fingers of his good hand. He shoved it in his pocket when that didn't stop it from shaking. Fortunately, people would likely put it down to the cold rather than fear.

When Lebrecht finished addressing the men, he joined them, a waspish-looking Sergeant named Bruner followed him.

"Can we get this done before my bits go numb?" Joachim snapped at his brother.

"Everybody is accounted for?" Lebrecht asked Bruner.

"Nobody seems to be missing," the man-at-arms replied.

"Seems?"

"We have a roster for the soldiers and permanent staff. Everyone taking the *Markgräf's* coin, but..." he shrugged, "...others come and go."

Solace turned her head to the sky; the sun was on the other side of the castle. He thought they had maybe ninety minutes till sunset. From the look on her face, Lady Solace thought much the same.

Not long enough. Not long enough at all.

"Let's begin," Solace stepped forward, only to find Lebrecht in front of her.

"No, my lady, this is not work for you."

"'tis not?" she tilted her head, "And how many demons have you killed, my lord?"

A mutter ran through the men. No one had seen fit to tell them why the castle had to be searched.

Lebrecht lowered his voice, "You are not to go inside until

it is safe. Those are my father's orders."

Solace's chin jutted upwards. She was going to argue, to spit and scream. Vengeance, at least part of it, hid within Ettestein's silent walls. Part of him wanted her to. The longer they tarried, the less time they would have to search for Wendel. The sooner night fell, the sooner the demon would be gone.

But he was honour-bound to protect her and keep her safe.

And there was nothing safe about what lurked inside that castle.

He moved to her side, "My lady," he said quietly, "best you do as they say. We are running out of time."

Her head snapped in his direction, frosted breath snorting from flaring nostrils. For a moment, just a moment, he didn't recognise her at all, as if something else living under her skin threatened to erupt from her flesh.

He had to force his feet not to step away from his mistress.

"I know what is in there," she managed to say, calmly enough, to Lebrecht, "you do not."

"My men are good. Battle-hardened. They can deal with one witch," he said.

"This is not a witch!"

Again, the eyes of nearby soldiers washed over her.

"I know what is in there, my lady," he heard himself say, "as well as you. Whatever happens today, you have other business in Magdeburg…"

The implication lingered in the frigid air with his breath.

Don't die here.

Wendel had only spared her to pass on Torben's message. If they cornered the monster, he didn't doubt the demon would gleefully slaughter them all.

Solace glowered at him along with the rest of the world, but when Lebrecht ordered two men to escort her to one of the outbuildings, she acquiesced without further complaint.

"Shall we get this charade over with, then?" Joachim said, although he did wait until Solace was out of earshot.

"My lord, this is not some bleak joke. I have seen what these creatures can do. If we find it..." he let his eyes slide over the waiting soldiers, "...some of your men will not make Christmas prayers."

Perhaps something haunted the cast of his eye or the timbre of his voice, but Joachim's smile, which was as much sneer as anything, melted away.

"Tell your men, only a mortal blow stops one of these things. Head or heart. Nothing else will kill it. Please... believe me. This is no witch. No caster of spells, mixer of potions, no practitioner of dark arts. This is not someone who can be put down in chains, tortured into confession and burnt at the stake. This..." he stepped disrespectfully close to the young nobleman, "...is a real monster..."

"I have the steel of my sword and the steel of my faith; I am sure such weapons will suffice against any... *monster.*"

He didn't like Joachim. In truth, there were not many he did. Even before the horrors of The Wolf's Tower, he'd been a distant, isolated man with few friends. But still, something about the *Markgräf's* son rankled and gnawed.

When you were about to face a foe, any fool was best avoided. An arrogant, cocksure, spoilt fool who gave orders, however...

Joachim snorted and whirled away, "C'mon lads, let's get this done. We're feasting tomorrow!"

A ragged cheer, probably as much to do with getting out of the cold as anything else, ran through the men as they started trooping after Joachim.

He looked at Lebrecht, "Your brother is going to get men killed."

"As much as 'tis not always apparent," Lebrecht said, "he does know what he is doing."

"With what's over there," he nodded at the outer wall beyond which smoke from the imperial camp's fires rose, "perhaps he does. But when it comes to what's waiting within *those* walls," he jabbed a finger up Ettestein's stones, "trust me, my lord, he hasn't got the faintest bloody idea..."

Lucien at his side, he began trudging after the soldiers, heart hammering and boots filled with lead.

*

The *Markgräf* was waiting for her.

"I trust you will be comfortable here until matters are resolved."

"I should be hunting that thing," she snapped back.

The *Markgräf* nodded at the two soldiers who'd brought her to the cottage. He didn't reply till they had left.

"'tis not work for a woman, my lady."

"I am not a typical woman."

A fire crackled in the hearth; she crossed the room to warm her hands over it. The cottage was one of the scores of humble buildings clustered between the castle and the outer walls. No doubt whoever lived here had been turned out for her benefit.

"I am aware of that," he said, joining her by the hearth, "you are Elenore's daughter, after all."

Though she kept her eyes on the flames, she felt the weight of his regard readily enough.

"Your wife, my lord...?"

"Died three years ago. Taken by a fever. And my name is Hendrick."

Wendel told her the *Markgräf* killed his wife, but she gave no more credence to that lie than any of his others.

"You loved her?"

"She was a good woman, but... she was not Elenore. No one else could be. So I have always thought..."

The fire's warmth spread through her, though the flush in her cheeks had little to do with the burning logs.

She stepped away and unbuckled the clasp on her cloak. The *Markgräf* hurried to take it from her shoulders.

"Thank you, my lord," she said, taking a seat close as he folded the cloak and placed it on a table.

He went to the fire, eyes remaining on her.

"What was my mother like?"

"Remarkable," he said. A smile softened the usually impassive face, "Even after all these years, not a day that passes..."

"I would have liked to have known her."

"She was beautiful, a gentle soul with a sharp mind. But... by God, there was steel in that woman!" he laughed.

It was the first time she'd heard him laugh, as if encircling

168

clouds parted to reveal something hidden from the world. The laugh soon faded, however, and the clouds quickly returned.

"Do you have the *sight*, Solace?"

"If I said yes, would you have me burnt?"

"No, of course not."

"I saw the remnants of a pyre when we arrived here."

"A maid confessed to cursing a pregnant woman who then lost her child," the *Markgräf* shrugged, "An unfortunate necessity. Such things cannot be tolerated."

"Confessed to Pastor Josef?"

He nodded.

"After he put the question to her?"

"Pastor Josef was a zealous man. He took his responsibilities seriously. As do I."

"And if I had not looked like my mother...?"

His eyes drifted away, "These are desperate times. We must have order; all else falls without it. Once the suspicion of witchery arises..." he sighed "...what must be done, must be done..."

"With respect, my lord, that does not answer my question?"

"No, it does not. But we shall see what my men discover in the castle; if we find this demon, then your claims will be proven."

"And if you find nothing?"

"Then the murderer will still be at large..."

"I see."

"'tis best you stay here until we finish searching the castle. For your own safety."

169

"Of course, my lord."

"We will talk later, I have matters to attend to."

"The Imperials at the gate? You think they will attack on Christmas Eve?"

"I would say no under most circumstances. They wanted only to pass on the Emperor's word and discourage any support for the rebels in Magdeburg. I would think it only a show of strength, but the man who commands them concerns me."

"Who leads them, my lord?"

"An ambitious man called Gottlieb, *Freiherr* Geiss."

"Many men trample the Empire beneath their ambitions these days."

He snorted, "True enough, but Gottlieb is my nephew. His side of the family has had designs on Gothen for many years. A spurious claim, but a claim nonetheless. The fact he leads the Imperial troops at the gates... disturbs me."

"Families..."

"Indeed."

The *Markgräf* moved to the door but stopped halfway across the small room, "If you do have your mother's *sight*, any knowledge of Gottlieb's intentions..."

"I do not have the *sight*," she said, keeping his eye.

"That is probably for the best..."

The words hung; his gaze lingered.

Then he was gone. Voices briefly arose. The two soldiers remained on the other side of the door. For her safety.

Of course.

She paced for a while, then wiped away condensation from the glass to stare out of the grubby window at the towering bulk of the castle. Eventually, she returned to the fire, troubled and uneasy.

Her mind kept returning to thoughts of Renard and Lucien scouring the castle for Wendel. It was larger than The Wolf's Tower, and she knew how many hiding places her home once boasted. Of course, Wendel wouldn't know the best ones, but he only had to hide for a few hours. The shadows outside the cottage stretched by the minute.

The castle didn't have many exits, but how long could they keep him bottled up once the sun set? And even-

"My lady of the Broken Tower..."

The voice yanked her attention back with a start.

A figure stood in the corner of the room furthest from the window; the gloom thickening into a shroud around it.

"My Lord Flyblown..." she eased herself back, "...you're a little late."

"*I am?* I find my timing is always impeccable."

"I called for you last night."

"Ah, I see, a misunderstanding! You think me some familiar perhaps? A supplicant being at your beck and call?" White teeth flashed in the too dark shadows, "Please, allow me to correct you. I am not that."

"Your mark upon my thigh, it might be mistaken as a witch's mark."

"Best you let no one see it then."

She climbed to her feet, the task harder than it should be. How long had it been since she'd slept properly?

"Sage advice, my lord, but I hoped it could be removed? I have no wish to burn upon the pyre."

"'tis part of our bargain. The signature on our contract. It

171

binds us. In more ways than one. I cannot remove it without nullifying our arrangement."

"I see..." she approached the figure despite the inordinate effort it took. Around her the room appeared to fall to night, though when she glanced at the window, soft winter daylight still pressed against the dirty glass, "...so your best advice is to keep my legs together. Perhaps our arrangement is worth less than the skin it sullies if that is all the assistance you can offer."

Flyblown wagged a long pale finger at her, "Funny you should put it like that..."

"I see nothing humorous," she came to a halt before him. The cold prickled her skin; she didn't know whether because she'd moved away from the fire or closer to Flyblown.

"Well-"

"We have one of them cornered. If we-"

"A pawn."

"I'm sorry?"

"You have a pawn cornered. A minor piece. And cornered is something of an exaggeration too."

"I want them all dead."

"Saul is the only one that matters. Without him, the Red Company unravels, and the natural order is restored."

"I don't care about the natural order. I care about vengeance!"

She spun away and retreated to the window.

Flyblown remained in the corner where the fading daylight no longer reached.

"And I want you to have it. We have a mutual alignment of

interests. Remember?"

"Why are you here if you're not prepared to help me?"

"I am here to help you."

She pulled her eyes from the beads of condensation running down the glass, "How so?"

"With sage advice..."

"I'm listening."

"The *Markgräf* has an army."

"If you can offer no better, take your damn mark from my leg."

Flyblown chuckled.

She raised an eyebrow, "Well?"

"Hendrick, *Markgräf* of Gothen, loved your mother."

"Your intelligence is slow, my lord; I already know that."

"And he still does."

"If you have a point to make...?"

Flyblown dabbed a finger at the air before him, "Do I need to draw a line between each point for you?"

"Evidently..."

He sighed deeply. The shadows swirling around him shimmered.

"Hendrick, *Markgräf* of Gothen wants you..."

It was her turn to laugh, "Don't be ridiculous!"

Flyblown's hand span in a circle, "Wheels and wheels and wheels around more wheels. The world turns, and everything that happens within the orbits of those wheels does so because a force exists to make it happen."

"I'm sorry, you are talking in riddles."

"Do you think you are here by accident, My Lady of the Broken Tower? That you stumbled into the castle of the

173

man who loved your mother, the woman you look so much like, at random? What are the chances of such a coincidence, do you think?"

"If you are saying 'tis God's will...?"

"God?" Flyblown snorted, "No! You are here at the behest of other powers."

"I-"

"You do not need to understand. You need an army to defeat an army. Hendrick, *Markgräf* of Gothen, has an army. You should be prepared to do whatever is necessary for him to give it to you..."

Her mouth slowly fell open.

But nothing at all came out.

Chapter Two

"The bastard could be anywhere."

For once, no grin creased Lucien's lips.

"And we'll find him," Joachim said, neither breaking stride nor looking over his shoulder, "If he exists."

The brothers split their men into a dozen groups to scour the fortress; both he and Lucien suggested they should lead their own groups on the basis they were the only ones with the faintest idea what they faced. Joachim refused.

"I want you where I can see you."

When Lucien stuck his tongue out behind the nobleman's back, he'd been unable to stifle a grin. Several of the men-at-arms smirked too. Whatever their nationality, belief, religion or principles, most soldiers shared a common dislike for the man telling them what to do.

The groups splintered to search Ettestein's many rooms, corridors, halls, storerooms, towers and catacombs. Lebrecht posted others to guard the single exit. It wasn't enough, but the *Markgräf* had refused to spare more. He needed the rest on the outer walls in case the Imperials decided to try something unbecoming for Christmas.

They had to make do with what they had.

He glanced out of every narrow window they passed.

And the time they had to do it in.

Four other men made up their group. All heavily armed,

they looked competent. No grizzled old timers or green youths. None said a lot. All looked alert enough.

But if they found Wendel, he expected most of them would die.

They searched room by room, nailed boots echoing in the silence.

Joachim was as good as his word; he spent as much time eyeing him as he did looking for Wendel.

"Do you watch your men so closely when you're hunting boar, my lord?" he asked as they ducked out of another empty room.

"Of course not. I trust my men."

"Take care, my lord; what we hunt today is far more dangerous than any boar."

Joachim snorted and headed down the corridor to the next room.

"How do you think the *Markgräf* will feel if we get his idiot son killed?" Lucien asked out of the corner of his mouth as he passed him.

He didn't answer, instead trailing at the back of the group, dragging his feet as they searched more deserted rooms.

Along with the other groups, they started in the high towers and worked down towards the dungeons and catacombs, locking doors behind them after clearing a corridor. He could have told them a locked door wouldn't keep Wendel where he didn't want to be.

They weren't locking Wendel out of the rest of the castle; they were locking themselves in with him.

He'd tried to warn them, but the *Markgräf* had put his youngest son in charge, and Joachim wasn't inclined to believe anything he said beyond the fact night would fall in less than an hour.

The longer they searched without success, the more the men around him relaxed, the more boredom set in, and the closer to the catacombs they got.

Ettestein was large, a thousand places to hide existed within its walls, but Wendel would be below ground, where no windows allowed the sharp winter sun to spear through; he was sure of it.

"What happened to your arm?" One of the soldiers, a tall hawk-faced Pomeranian by the name of Sack, asked.

While he was too busy glowering to answer, Lucien helpfully jumped in with his own explanation, "Too much wanking."

Sack sprayed spittle as he brayed like a drunken donkey.

He shot them both sour looks before moving on to the next room. They were working their way around the kitchens, a collection of pantries, larders, storage spaces and servant's rooms little bigger than cells.

The light was fading; they would need torches soon.

He opened a door on a room barely warranting a search; he could have leapt from door to wall in one bound. Although dark and windowless, enough light made it through the open door to show only a straw mattress on a rickety frame. The air smelt ripe with sweat and garlic.

They searched the kitchens. Food laid about the tabletops in various stages of preparation, left where it was when the *Markgräf* ordered the castle cleared despite the coming feast. Much of the Empire might be starving, but you would not have known it from Ettestein's kitchen.

Taubert, a stocky, flame-haired soldier with skin almost as pale as a demon's, sucked happily on a finger he'd dipped into a bowl of something as soon as Joachim turned his back. Noticing Ulrich's attention, he winked before going back in for more.

He moved on without acknowledging him. Restless, uncomfortable, irritable. The rich, fragrant aromas mixed with its unnatural silence to remind him of The Wolf Tower's kitchen. He continually expected to look up and see Henry Cleever, cross-legged on a table, examining Herman the cook's intestines with furious intent.

The shiver coursed through him hard enough to rattle his father's sheathed sword against his leg.

"Do you think he's gone?" Lucien asked, coming alongside him.

"We won't be so lucky; he's downstairs in the catacombs. I'm sure of it."

"Let's hope so."

"Better he has disappeared into thin air."

"You think?" Lucien pulled a face. Flour dusted the table they stood over; he drew a line through it with his finger.

He leaned towards the mercenary, "If Wendel is here, he will slaughter these idiots…"

Lucien shrugged, "And if he isn't, they will need to burn someone for witchcraft. Most likely us."

"Solace persuaded the *Markgräf* once…"

"The castle is talking of nothing but witchery now. Demons who can change their face! If we don't find Wendel and stop this, half the fools here will denounce the other half. Give it a few weeks and the Emperor will be able to

178

walk into an empty castle!"

Behind them, pots and pans clattered as Zukal, a bald Bohemian, stuck his shiny head in a cupboard.

"They reckon the cunt can change his face, not fucking shrink himself!" Doss, the final soldier in their group, yelled. Laugher echoed around the cavernous room.

Lucien patted his arm, "C'mon, the sooner we get into the catacombs, the better..."

That was very much a matter of opinion.

But he followed him all the same.

*

"What... exactly are you suggesting?"

"He's a man, you're a woman, 'tis a story as old as time itself. The man has something the woman wants..." Flyblown threw his arms wide, "...so the woman opens her legs to get it."

"I had not pictured you as quite so much of a romantic, my lord."

Flyblown conceded the point with a pull of his long face before letting his arms drop, "In truth, 'tis one of my few weaknesses. Although love tends to fool us all in the end.

"He is old enough to be my father!"

"A not altogether uncommon arrangement when it comes to rich men, I believe you'll find."

She pinched the bridge of her nose, "Are you seriously suggesting-"

"Oh, yes. I am," Flyblown smiled, seemingly drawing the skin tightly enough around his face to reveal the skull beneath, "I rarely make social visits. This... *appearing* is rather taxing for me. I am not as all-powerful as you might assume."

"But-"

"You want your vengeance, don't you?"

"Yes."

"I can't remember if you've ever said you'd do *anything* to achieve it. But people thirsting for revenge commonly do. Often with gritted teeth and a hissed intonation to emphasise the point. Sometimes *booming* with rage. Sometimes *icily*. But always some such. So, My Lady of the Broken Tower, are you prepared to do *whatever* it takes to put Saul's head on a spike?"

"Yes," she said again, though more quietly this time.

"Less you have not realised, you are going to war. You are pursuing a foe that is as vicious and ruthless as it is inhuman. People will die because of it. People under your command will die. Others too. Those in the wrong place at the wrong time. This happens when you unleash slaughter, however noble or just you may believe your righteous cause to be..."

Flyblown stepped forward. The shadows came with him.

"My Lady of the Broken Tower, you must realise you bring few weapons to this battle. You need more. And you should use *all* those you do possess."

Flyblown stopped before he reached the grey light falling through the window and cocked an eyebrow at her.

"You refer to my sex?"

"I do."

"My Lord Flyblown, I... have never even... kissed a man... I have no idea how to do this..." she threw out her palms

180

"…I'm but an ingénue."

"That is not necessarily a disadvantage. Virtue and innocence are highly prized. You should be prepared to trade yours for the things you need."

"An army?"

"A bigger one than you currently possess, at least."

"And you believe the *Markgräf* will give me his in return for…" she let the sentence wither unfinished upon her lips.

"He can be persuaded to give you more than you have now."

"With an Imperial army at his door?"

Flyblown wafted a hand behind him, "Oh, a trifle. Certainly compared to finding the love of his life he lost decades ago."

"The fact I do not-"

"No. That has no bearing whatsoever. Vengeance, my lady, always comes with a high price."

"One not paid in silver," she muttered, echoing Morlaine's warning from Madriel.

"Indeed."

"And how should I go about this… *seduction*, do you suggest?"

Flyblown raised his hands, "Oh, that is really not my field of expertise. But my advice is to treat the matter purely as a business arrangement. That's generally how the aristocracy treats these things. Decide what you want and need, then ask for at least twice as much. Negotiate from there."

"And in return?"

"Listen to what Hendrick, *Markgräf* of Gothen wants,

then... let him have a lot less than half..."

Flyblown's smile bordered on the feral.

"I believe I know how to negotiate. 'tis... in other matters, I am less certain."

"Other matters?"

"Seduction..." her cheeks seemed to have caught aflame, much to her annoyance.

"Oh, women have been figuring that out for millennia, my lady. I believe it will come naturally enough. I'm sure it will not prove as difficult as you fear. You're rather beautiful."

She rose and moved to the other side of the window; a river of grey light separated her from Flyblown's shadowy figure.

"Flattery, my lord?"

"Oh, do not fret. I have no interest in such trivialities as mortal flesh. I am a higher being these days..."

Dark, sharp eyes lingered on her from the far side of the waning light.

"What do I need to defeat the Red Company?"

"In battle? Thousands."

"Will I face them on a battlefield?"

"The future has a multitude of faces. All are hidden from me."

"The *Markgräf* will not give me thousands, no matter how skilled I turn out to be in the business of seduction."

"No. He won't. He does not have thousands to give."

"Then what should I be bargaining my virtue for, my lord? How much am I worth?"

"Whatever makes you stronger. It may not be on a battlefield, with neat rows of musket, horse and cannon,

but you will, one day, face the Red Company again..."
Flyblown turned his head, "...and it will not be one of them
alone."

"And my brother?"

He showed his teeth again, brightening the gloom, "That is
a problem for another day. Perhaps we should see how this
one ends first."

She followed his gaze to the window. The skies above
Ettestein Castle were darkening.

Night was coming.

Chapter Three

There were only two entrances to the castle's lower levels.

With no sign of Wendel above ground, he either remained in the catacombs, or he'd managed to evade their search and hide somewhere. Probably laughing merrily at their stupidity.

Broad stone steps led down into the catacombs. The light didn't stretch far.

Joachim was organising the groups of soldiers as they arrived at the entrance, a large square opening in the stone floor behind the kitchens. This was where supplies went down into the cool chambers below. People used a smaller entrance on the other side of the castle. Prisoners, guards, torturers, priests, he supposed. It had been the one Fleischman took them down that morning.

The doors would be closed and bolted behind them, and guards left to ensure no one who hadn't gone in came out.

"Has the sun set?" he asked Lucien while they waited, men milling around them.

The mercenary nodded towards the black oblong below them, "Hardly matters down there."

The men passed torches around. Armour clanked, leather creaked, boots scuffed on stone. A few men looked apprehensive. Most simply looked bored. No one looked scared, save possibly himself.

I shall fear no evil...

Monsters in the snow. Monsters in the dark. Monsters in the blood.

He had seen them. He knew. They didn't.

That's why nobody looked scared.

Should he say something? A rousing speech? A stony-faced explanation? A febrile warning?

Would it do any good?

He brushed past Lucien and went to Joachim; he was giving instructions to the men going into the catacombs, keeping them in the same groups of four or five.

"You don't have enough men," he hissed into the nobleman's ear.

"How many more should my father be pulling off the walls, do you think?"

"Send them in larger groups. Four men alone will not be able to kill this creature."

Joachim wrinkled his nose, "You haven't seen my men in action. When they're sober anyway."

A few of the nearer men laughed.

"And you haven't seen a vampire in action. I have. You are not sending them to drag some old woman off to the pyre... you are sending them to be slaughtered."

The laughter died.

Joachim turned to face him fully.

"Scared of the dark, eh?"

"No," he jerked his head at the waiting steps, "I'm scared of what's in *that* dark."

"You stay here then. There's plenty to do in the kitchens before we let the other women back in."

"My lord…"

Joachim whirled towards a portly soldier with a face seemingly rearranged several times over his life, "Sergeant Iskra, you open those doors to no one who doesn't knock three times. You let no one else down there and don't these two out of your sight. Send word to my father the castle above the catacombs is clear."

"Yes, my lord."

He tried to protest, but Joachim raised a finger in warning, "Another word and I'll throw you in a fucking cell and not open the door till next year!"

"But-"

Lucien's hand locked around his arm, "We understand, my lord, but please, be careful. Lucien Kazmierczak has seen many terrible things in his life, but never worse than what we think is down there."

Some of the anger drained from Joachim's eyes. Then he turned away, "C'mon lads, let's get this done."

"Well, that was helpful," Lucien said as the men lit their torches and began tramping down into the catacombs.

He shrugged the mercenary off, angry at himself for provoking Joachim.

But even more angry at the relief coursing through him.

What would Old Man Ulrich have said about his only son turning out to be a coward?

Whatever it was, it'd have been slurred by ale and wine.

A man only has his hon-

I fucking know, you fucking drunken old fool!

He retreated to a pile of sacks in the corner and turned his back.

Behind him, the clatter of nailed boots faded into silence.

How many of them would be coming back?

'tis not my fault if they all die. I tried to warn them!

He jumped and whirled around as something crashed. The heavy wooden doors had been slammed shut. Now a solid oblong of oak covered the catacomb's entrance.

Iskra stood over two younger men as they hunkered down to slide a thick wooden beam through the two doors.

Sealing twenty men in the lightless catacombs of Ettestein castle with a murderous, blood-drinking demon.

He'd endured a lot of bad feelings in his life, even more so in the last year. Another one gnawed him now.

Lucien ambled over and joined him. The mercenary pulled a face, "Maybe it'll work out for the best…"

"You think they'll be able to kill Wendel?"

"No," Lucien shook his head hard enough for his long moustaches to whip his face, "I meant it might save us from dying in the catacombs."

It seemed he wasn't the only one suffering a bad feeling.

"Did you mean to upset the young lord enough to save us?" Lucien asked.

"I only wish I were so devious…"

"Well, it gives us time to decide what to do next?"

"Next?"

"We'll either have to explain why the demon we claim killed the snivelling priest and that stringy piece of shit with the tiny cock can't be found, or…" he conjured a pained smile, "…how we let the *Markgräf's* youngest son become part of a demon's Christmas Eve banquet."

He blew out his cheeks.

Iskra was barking orders to the remaining soldiers left to guard the catacomb's doors; when done, he ambled over to them, thumbs tucked into his weapon's belt.

"The young *Markgräf* asked me to keep an eye on the pair of you for him. I get the impression he doesn't like you much. I haven't formed an opinion yet. You going to cause me any trouble?"

"No," he said before Lucien could say anything unhelpful.

"Good, then we'll get along fine and dandy then. Life's difficult enough, so I try never to make anything worse than it needs to be."

"Amen to that," Lucien said.

"Tell me," Iskra nodded at the sealed catacombs, "*is* anything down there, really?"

"There was this morning. We saw it kill your man. It wore Pastor Josef's face, but Pastor Josef was stuffed in a trunk with his throat slit at the time..."

Iskra pushed his lips together, "Never liked either of them, but still..." he had restless eyes, and now they flicked between the two of them, "...plenty are saying if there are any demons here, it's you two and your mistress."

"You have an interesting line in small talk, friend," Lucien grinned one of his less sincere grins.

"I'm from Neustadtl; we all speak plain there. Too busy fighting the fucking Turks for anything else..."

"Fair enough. But the *Markgräf,* the grown-up one, believes us enough to empty his castle on Christmas Eve. I reckon he knows more than feckless, gossiping wag-tongues, don't you?" Lucien said.

"You'd like to think so, but your mistress is... more than

fair."

"What we said happened," he growled, "trust me, you'll be more inclined to believe us when your friends come out of that hole in bloody little pieces."

Something made Iskra shuffle his boots back a step across the old stone floor.

"Then why aren't you down there?"

"Ask the *Markgräf,* the snotty-nosed one," Lucien said, "I don't think he likes us."

"Markgräf Joachim isn't much taken with anyone- ah, well done, lads!" Iskra turned away as men returned with chairs and what looked suspiciously like a crate of beer.

"Well," Iskra shrugged, "no reason not to be comfortable while we wait for the young lord to get himself torn a new arsehole, is there now?"

Lucien chuckled, "You know, I think we might get along, Sergeant Iskra."

*

How much am I worth...?

She'd asked herself that question several times since Flyblown made his suggestion. As the *Markgräf's* servants busied themselves conjuring a suitable table for a lord reduced to dining in a peasant's cottage, she asked it again.

The reflection in the window's dark glass held no answer.

Once, not so very long ago, when she'd spent her days combing her hair and nights dreaming of princes, she'd thought herself worth a handsome price indeed. Now, however, she measured the world through other commodities and different currencies.

All she wanted was vengeance, and that was not something paid for in silver.

"My lady...?"

She did not know the girl's name.

She'd arrived with two footmen and a table that took some conjuring to get through the door. While she laid the table, the men brought chairs. Fine ones. Made from mahogany, with padded seats.

Two of them.

She thought the number significant.

"Yes...?" she looked back from the window.

The girl had laid the table with cutlery, crockery, linens, candles, dried flowers. Wine and glasses too.

"Is everything to your liking... ma'am?"

Hesitation and uncertainty flickered over the maid's face, but no hostility.

"It looks beautiful. But why has it been set?"

Confusion replaced hesitation and uncertainty.

"Because the *Markgräf* requested it..." a faint smile played across thin, chapped lips, "...for your comfort."

"While everybody else shivers in the cold with their empty bellies?"

The maid's expression moved from confused to panic-stricken.

"What is your name?"

"Dorothea, ma'am."

"What is happening in the castle, Dorothea?"

The girl looked over her shoulder, even though they were alone in the room. Prudence was wise when practising the art of gossiping in a crowded castle.

190

"'tis said there are demons, ma'am. With horns, cloven feet, all stinky from the pit, come to feed us to the Catholics for Christmas."

"And where have these demons come from?"

Dorothea narrowed her eyes as if suspicious of some fiendish trap.

"Hell, ma'am."

"I meant, how is it they have come to be in Ettestein?"

Discomfort became the latest look to glide across the girl's face. She owned a fine array of expressions, but it wasn't immediately apparent if much else was happening below them.

When Dorothea said nothing and found something important to stare at on the end of her shoes, she added, "Please, speak frankly."

"'tis said you brought them, ma'am. But I never believed that! Any soul can see you're no witch."

"No, I am not a witch."

She was going to add she hadn't brought demons to Ettestein, but that wouldn't be true. If she hadn't come this way, Wendel would not be here. Pastor Josef and that soldier – she couldn't recall his name – wouldn't be dead either.

But she had.

And they had paid her price. Another price that couldn't be counted in silver.

"No, ma'am," Dorothea shook her head.

She slipped her hand into a pocket and found a coin. She handed it to the maid.

However, silver worked very well for many other things.

"For your trouble, Dorothea."

Another expression. Wide eyes and open-mouthed.

"I-"

"Yes, you can. 'tis Christmas. Even in these days, that still means something."

Dorothea's hand curled around the coin to spirit it away.

It was more than the girl earnt in a week, an unnecessary largesse, but she might need all the friends she could find.

And silver made you friends a lot quicker than blood and vengeance did.

"Thank you, ma'am... if there's anything else you need?"

"That will be all, thank you."

Dorothea smiled, her expression now warm and friendly.

She waited until the girl left her alone, then walked to the table and poured some wine.

Did wine help in matters of seduction? And negotiation?

The former probably more than the latter, but she drank deeply anyway. Whatever the benefits, it did not still the shake of her hand.

She returned to the window and wiped condensation from the glass again. Outside, a few feeble lights were all that marked Ettestein Castle from the night sky.

What was happening in there?

Were more men paying the price of her vengeance?

Renard and Lucien?

Both her *sight* and Flyblown's mark kept their council upon the matter.

Her guilt, however, was far more verbose.

This is my war, my battle...

Why had Torben sent the demon? Was he really beyond

192

salvation? Was she?

Her eyes moved from the window to the finely set table.

What was she about to do?

She drank more wine, then crossed the room to the fire. The logs had mostly turned to embers. She threw on more. And then more still.

Fire reminded her of Father. And why she was here. And why she would do whatever vengeance required. Whatever price, whatever currency. Silver, virtue, blood.

Vengeance was a capricious, hungry god. It required sacrifice, not faint hearts.

The night drew on.

The occasional voice reached her, but none sounded alarmed, so she stayed by the fire.

When the door eventually opened, she did not turn towards it.

"My lady..."

Hendrick, *Markgräf* of Gothen.

Other feet followed his into the cottage. Now she looked.

Servants busied themselves spreading cold meats, bread, cheese, pickled vegetables and dried fruits upon the table.

"Humble fayre," he said, "the kitchen fires are cold."

She wondered how many people across the empire with empty larders and rumbling stomachs this Christmas would consider the food laid out for her as *humble fayre*.

She did not join him at the table till the servants left.

"What news, my lord?"

"Nothing has been found; men still search the catacombs. My people are returning to the castle. My nephew and his troops are enjoying their first night in camp. I trust it will prove an uncomfortable one. The night is cold."

The *Markgräf* settled himself at the table.

She joined him.

"How is the wine," he asked, noting her glass on the table.

"Very fair, my lord."

"I hope dinner proves likewise. Again, my apologies for not being able to provide more fitting refreshments."

"In truth, I have little appetite."

The *Markgräf* refilled her glass.

"No matter."

She accepted the drink with a nod.

He poured one for himself, then sat back and stared at her.

"Given current events, one might think you would have no opportunity for entertaining?"

More voices floated by outside. Laughter. Still no alarm broke the night.

"Everything is in hand. 'tis a matter of priorities."

"And I am a greater priority than demons and enemies at your gates?"

"My nephew shivers in the cold. My men are searching for your demon. There is little more I can do."

She sipped the wine. And hoped it could indeed make these things easier.

"You should not have allowed people to return to the castle."

"My nephew has chosen to freeze. I will not ask the same of my people. If your demon is here, we will run it to ground."

You have no idea what you're dealing with...

"Tell me, *Freiin*, what are your intentions when matters here are resolved?" He reached for some bread, eyes lingering on her.

"I will pursue the monsters that destroyed my home. Until the ends of the Earth, if necessary."

"That is not a seemly ambition for a beautiful young woman."

He began smearing butter onto the bread.

"Seemly, my Lord?"

"The world out there," he waved his knife at the window, "is no place for a woman. Even without your demons. Barbarism and savagery consume the Empire; all that is good teeters on a precipice. Order, law, our freedoms, our wealth, our very future is under threat. The land is dying, the people starving, the Empire crumbling. Plague is rife. You would be better served staying within these walls where it is safe. Where I can protect you."

He tore off a chunk of bread and gobbled it in one.

"I've lived behind high walls all my life, my lord. They did not protect me. No matter how high you build them, any wall can be breached, any stronghold can fall."

"Nothing in this world is guaranteed, save the Lord's love."

"Of course…"

She tried to hold his eye above the dancing candle flames that separated them.

Am I really going to give myself to this man?

A better fate than *Graf* Bulcher's bed, to be sure. In truth, he was not an ugly man. Just old. He had to be several years over forty, at least. And the faint resemblance to Father stirred things best left unstirred. He was not the

195

kind of prince she had dreamed of, but he-

Oh, stop it! You are not that girl anymore!

She wasn't going to give herself to a man for flowers, love or comforts. Not to further familial ambitions, not for power or money. He had an army, and she wanted part of it.

And she would do whatever it took.

Forcing herself to hold his gaze, she played with her hair. The long blonde tresses were gone, hacked off and thrown into the fire to burn with everything else lost in The Wolf's Tower.

Still, had she not spent hour after hour in front of a mirror practising her most beguiling looks for the day her handsome prince rode through the Darkway? That prince never arrived, only the fat toad Bulcher. But perhaps those girlish daydreams had not been a complete waste of time.

"I must leave, my lord," she said, twisting a short knot of hair around her finger.

She had no pretty dresses to flatter, no powders and perfumes to enhance the Lord's blessings. She did have her mother's jewellery, but that silver and gold would pay for steel and leather, not to drape over herself. Despite her plain attire, the *Markgräf's* eye remained.

"To Magdeburg?"

"Yes."

"The city is under Imperial blockade; 'tis likely to be under full siege as soon as winter lifts. The Emperor's Edict of Restitution decreed the Archbishopric of Magdeburg, among others, must return to the Catholic faith; the city councillors refused, believing the Swedish king will come to their aid. The war is heading to Magdeburg, my lady, 'tis not a place a woman of quality should currently venture."

"I venture where I wish, my lord."

The *Markgräf* sighed and took a long sip of wine.

"So much like your mother…"

She sipped her own again, but just a little.

"The roads are not safe," he insisted, "I would not see you come to harm."

"Would your concern stretch to offering me your protection?"

He placed the wine aside.

"I have already offered you the protection of Ettestein's walls…"

"I want soldiers, my lord. Men-at-arms to aid my struggle, to avenge the wrong done to me and my family."

His eyebrows edged up in a rare display of expressiveness, "Soldiers… are highly prized at the moment."

"I know. My funds cannot equip and maintain the men I require to destroy my enemies."

"And how many men would that task take?" he looked faintly amused.

"I face an army. Therefore, I require an army to destroy them."

Still amused, he asked, "And how many of my men do you require for your army, my lady?"

She smiled. Sweet and captivating, she hoped. Her eyes held his.

How much am I worth?

"All of them…" she said, turning hair about her finger once more, "…I want all of them, my lord…"

Chapter Four

Lucien roared and clapped his hands.

Curses and sour looks broke out amongst the soldiers clustered around the table.

"I did warn you, boys, Lady Luck loves no other like she loves Lucien Kazmierczak!"

Lucien scooped up a pile of coins, an expression of such insufferable smugness on his face even he wanted to hit him.

He turned his back and stared at the barred doors in the floor.

His fellow guards decided to pass the time drinking and letting Lucien cheat them at dice. He didn't know the mercenary was cheating, but he seemed to be winning an inordinate amount. And, frankly, he wouldn't trust him not to cheat a babe out of its breakfast.

He had no desire to lose money (even if he had any) or get drunk. Old Man Ulrich idled away countless long nights of guard duty that way, and he had seen the man decay in front of his boyhood eyes. He would not walk down that path too.

As if to test his resolve, Usk, a young, burly soldier with the look of someone whose parents were related by more than just marriage, ambled over and held out a beer bottle.

"You don't want to steal our money too?"

"No," he said, eyes leaving the doors for only a moment.

Did he think Wendel would burst through it if he stopped looking for more than a blink?

Usk shook the bottle under his nose.

"No," he repeated.

Usk shrugged monolithic shoulders and started drinking it himself.

"I hear you wank too much?" the soldier asked after downing half the bottle.

He broke off from staring at the door to glower at the man.

A good-natured smirk did little to improve Usk's unfortunate visage.

"I shattered my arm escaping from monsters like the one down there. It withered in the socket during the year I spent living amongst the rubble and ghosts they left behind. Every other soldier died. Every servant. Every peasant. Every man, woman and child. Save my mistress and me," he leant towards Usk, "if I were you, I'd spend my time sharpening my weapons and wits rather than getting drunk and playing dice. This is no joke."

He twisted away from the young soldier without waiting for a reply and stormed out of the room. His hand had started shaking again.

The cold walls of Ettestein pressed in on him from all sides. Flickering shadows hid monsters and memories. Nightmares echoed. His legs wanted to run to open air, away from the lingering smells of musty stone and burnt tallow.

It was so easy to imagine himself back in The Wolf's Tower. That awful night when everything and everyone had died around him. Because he was a coward, because he'd sold his honour in return for his life and the promises of a demon with a liar's eyes.

Promises of blood, pleasure, strength, wealth. Promises of damnation.

He staggered, hand shooting out to find the wall, to convince himself he wasn't falling through the night, falling towards the ice clutching only a severed rope.

Falling toward endless pain.

Opening his eyes, he found a boy staring up at him, holding a bucket with both hands.

He fought down a scream.

He knew it was just one of the kitchen boys. The staff had been allowed back into the castle and would work through the night on the *Markgräf's* feast.

Still, part of him saw only a ghost. One of the children slain by the Red Company. The ones he heard in the stillness of each and every night. The ones who demanded to know why he'd left them to slaughter. Why was he such a coward? Why had he abandoned his oath?

"Are you sick?" the boy asked.

He swallowed. Then shook his head.

When the boy continued staring at him, he forced out a single word through trembling lips.

"No."

"You look sick," the boy backed away a step, "you don't have the plague, do you?"

"'tis nothing you can catch. Have you had plague here?"

"Not here. But in Halberstadt. So travellers said."

The boy's voice anchored him, allowing sense and sanity

to return. He was not in The Wolf's Tower; these stones held different fates, different memories.

"Best you get along. You have chores, yes?"

The boy nodded.

"Cook is pulling his hair out. Says if there is no feast ready for the *Markgräf* tomorrow, he will roast us instead. I think he is joking..." the boy let out a high-pitched laugh.

"I am sure he is," he said, though no laughter escaped him.

The boy smiled, then turned and hurried off down the corridor.

Noise came from the kitchen; voices cried, pots clanked, feet stomped. Normal sounds. The corridor was empty; a couple of torches restrained the darkness.

He put his back against the wall, and practised clenching and opening his right hand until the tremors subsided. Having one hand that didn't work was enough of a handicap...

Lucien appeared.

His hand might have stopped shaking, but his heart sank at the sight of the mercenary.

"Have all the demons of the pit come bursting out of the catacombs and you need me at your side to keep the satanic horde from swarming over Christendom?"

"Er... no..."

"Then why can't you leave me in peace?"

Lucien frowned, "I need a piss."

"Oh."

"Why don't you go and throw some dice? Maybe you could win back some of that silver you gave away in Madriel.

Might even cheer you up a little. I dare say stranger things have happened."

"There's a demon here. People are dead. More are likely to die soon if they haven't already. What's to be cheerful about?"

Lucien gave him a hard look, "Demons, of one kind or another, are *everywhere*. And people die all the time, a lot of them horribly. Life's short, my friend; best try and enjoy it a little before your turn comes around."

He pinched out a watery smile and tried not to hear the screams of women and children echoing through this castle as they had done in The Wolf's Tower the previous winter.

"Anyway," Lucien continued down the corridor, "my bladder is near sloshing over the top..."

"You're not cheating, are you?"

The mercenary stopped and turned, "Cheating! Why would you think a man as honest as Lucien Kazmierczak would stoop to cheating?"

"I imagine you're famed for it, no doubt from the armpit of Europe to the arsehole of Asia..."

Lucien slapped both hands over his chest, "You wound me!"

"*Are* you cheating?"

"Of course not."

"You'd better not be. We don't need to give them another reason to kill us."

"'tis only possible to cheat at dice if you have a loaded set, and the ones we are playing with are not mine. So, how can I be cheating?" Lucien threw his hands wide and gave him a long, intense stare... then winked before spinning away and sauntering off with a whistle on his lips.

"Oh, for fuck's sake…"

*

Hendrick, *Markgräf* of Gothen, didn't laugh outright.

Which was something.

Instead, he reached for his wine glass and drained it.

Once it was back on the table, he asked, "And what makes you think I might give you my men-at-arms?"

She sipped her own drink. Confident, worldly women, she imagined, drank wine while they used their wiles and a man's desires to get whatever they wanted. They just ensured they didn't get roaringly drunk in the process. She suspected that might be the tricky bit.

"You have not remarried, my lord?"

Something flickered over his usually impassive face, but it wasn't there long enough for her to identify. It still wasn't laughter, though.

"No. I have not."

"You are a wealthy, powerful man. Wealthy, powerful men usually have wives, do they not?"

"Wealth and power are relative, my lady."

"Indeed, but still…"

He sighed, "I have considered it. I loved Carolina. Not in the way I loved your mother. It was the kind of love that grew from a small seed. But grow it did. I miss her. I miss having a wife… I am not so old…" now he did smile, a small and rueful one.

"I can be your wife."

The *Markgräf* blinked.

"I'm sorry?"

"I will marry you. All I ask is you treat me with kindness, and I will fulfil every duty expected of a loving wife for the rest of your life. If you give me your men-at-arms."

"This... is not how such things work, my lady."

"Perhaps not. But the world has been turned upside down. There is an evil at large beyond that unleashed by the war. It has fallen to me to stop it, but I cannot do it alone. I am but a woman, after all..."

"I-"

"Please, excuse me, my lord. I don't wish to be rude, but time is short. I ask but that you listen and consider what I have to say. If it is not to your liking, rejection will not offend me. But my proposition is serious."

"I believe that, but what you ask..."

"My mother was the love of your life. I can see that simply by the way you look at me. When someone loses the love of their life, first to another man and then to the All Mighty, 'tis impossible to regain it. I am not my mother, your Elenore, but I look like her; I am the same age as her when you knew her. I am more like her than any woman alive. I am offering myself to you. I will love you, honour you and obey you. I will be yours. I will give you more children. I can give you the rarest of things. A second chance for your heart's true desire."

The *Markgräf* said nothing, but he poured himself more wine. His eyes didn't leave her. They seldom did, she'd noticed.

"But that is not all I can offer. My family is dead. I have inherited everything that belonged to my father. I am the

Freiin von Tassau now. And the last of my line. My home is in ruins, my possessions stolen, my people put to the sword. But the lands of Tassau are mine. More modest holdings than they were, my forefathers sold much of our land to pay off debts and bad investments. But some remain. Fertile farmland, woods full of lumber. There are holdings in Silesia too. They once held silver, but that is all gone. Still, the land remains. It has value. As your wife, all I own will become yours.

Surely, an offer worth consideration?"

He licked wine from his lips, speared pork from a plate and ate it slowly.

Silence hung between them.

Had she been too bold? Perhaps more seduction and less negotiation would have been a better approach?

"And you would remain at my side while my men chase these demons?"

"No."

"No?"

"I must face my enemies. I must see them die. I can know no peace till that happens."

"So... I give you my men in return for the promise you will one day come back and be my wife? That, my lady, is asking a great deal. You could die on your quest. So could all my men."

"You could ride with me as my husband. Or send one of your sons to accompany me, or any loyal lieutenant of your choosing to ensure my compliance. But, whatever happens, one way or another, I would come back to Ettestein, to your side..." she reached for the wine again "...to your bed."

"I cannot leave Ettestein defenceless."

"Then leave a son to rule in your name. What I face is difficult. But 'tis God's work. He brought me here for a reason. And that reason, I believe, is you. Is us. Together we can destroy the Red Company. A company of demons, my lord, what more could a man do to assure his assent to heaven...?"

"This is madness..."

She pushed herself to her feet. Ignoring watery legs and uncertain heart she crossed to his side.

Crouching by the *Markgräf,* she placed a hand atop his.

"The whole world is madness, my lord."

"You do not... you cannot... feel anything for me."

"My father was working to find a marriage for me. A match advantageous to Tassau and our family. Circumstances have changed; my father is dead. I am all that remains of my family. An advantageous match is the best I can hope for. My father would approve. He always intended my husband to be a Prince of the Empire."

He reached out, and cupped a hand around her face.

Is he going to kiss me?

Her stomach lurched. She had dreamed of a prince's kiss since she'd been a little girl. She was eighteen years old, and the only kiss she'd known had been Father's occasional peck on her cheek.

How would it feel? What if she did it badly? What if it was horrible? He was so old!

She smiled at him while she strangled the thoughts and feelings within.

She'd faced demons. She'd even killed some of them. She'd

fought on after all hope fled. She'd survived. And now she hunted evil. Now she walked the Night's Road. One day she would kill *Graf* Bulcher. One day she would kill the demons of the Red Company. One day she would kill Saul the Bloodless. One day she would find Torben and free him.

What was kissing a Prince of the Empire in comparison?

If she couldn't do that...

The *Markgräf's* thumb caressed the hair above her ear. Grey-blue eyes washed back and forth across her face. What went on behind them? Imagining? Desiring? Remembering? Looking for similarities or differences?

"Elenore..." he whispered.

Something twisted his face, something akin to pain.

"I can be whatever you wish me to be, my lord... whoever you want me to be."

"Are you even real? Is this some fiction, some fancy, some... spell?"

"I am who I say I am. You know this."

He caressed her cheek. Callouses from years of sword practice hardened the pads of his palm. His touch, however, was not entirely unpleasing. Her skin tingled beneath his. How would it feel on the rest of her?

A tremor ran through her.

Desire or disgust. She wasn't sure which. Perhaps both.

He stood slowly, hands finding hers, so she stood with him.

Tall enough for her to have to raise her chin to keep his eye, he was taut and spare of frame under his finery. Still a handsome man. Still a Prince of the Empire.

Yes, she could do this.

For Father. For Torben.

For vengeance.

She smiled up at him.

But mostly for a hundred men-at-arms.

Chapter Five

He paced to the kitchens and back several times.

Someone scowled or shouted at him whenever he wandered into that cavern of roaring fires and steaming pots. Told him to get his filthy boots out, to piss off and stop getting under their feet. They were busy with everything behind schedule.

He wanted to tell them a demon stalked the castle and an enemy camped at the gates, but he didn't think the cook, a man of both formidable belly and whiskers, gave a hoot about such trivialities. It was Christmas tomorrow, and he had to work through the night to prepare for it.

Every time he returned to the men guarding the doors to the catacombs, the soldiers appeared surlier and sourer than the previous time. Lucien's pile of coins grew ever larger.

How much did he need to win before they slit his throat?

He tried not to think of Wendel skulking in the shadows or the ghosts of The Wolf's Tower. He tried not to think of Madleen and Seraphina. He tried not to think of his own cowardice and dishonour. He tried not to think how his bad arm kept alternating between flares of pain and dead numbness.

There were a great many things, he noticed, he tried not to think about.

So, he thought of Solace instead.

As far as he knew, she was still outside the castle. He assumed she was safe. If Wendel wanted to kill her, he already would have done. No, he was here to deliver Torben's message and nothing more.

Would she heed her brother's advice? It seemed clear Torben did not want to be saved from the Red Company. He'd seen what the demons did and had made his choice regardless. Whoever, and whatever, he was now, he was not the man who'd walked into the darkness with Henry Cleever the night The Wolf's Tower fell.

But Solace could not, or would not, see that. She would continue her pursuit until they all died. The only possible conclusion to this madness. He didn't have either of their gifts to know the future, but that was clear enough to any fool.

And yet he would still follow her.

"I'm sure my father will appreciate your diligence."

Lebrecht's voice dragged him from his thoughts.

"My lord!" Iskra shot to his feet so violently his stool clattered to the ground behind him. Everybody else followed suit, save Lucien, who reached for more beer.

"Anything?" Lebrecht asked, walking to stand over the doors.

Iskra scurried to his side, "No, my lord. We've heard nothing since your brother went into the catacombs."

Lebrecht sighed and ran a hand through his tousled hair. He was a handsome young man, fair-faced, strong-limbed, tall, confident. There was a lot not to like, and he found it increasingly easy to dislike almost everyone.

"Should we go down?" the sergeant asked.

"Not yet. There are untold hiding places. It will take time to search. No one has come up, so our quarry must still be down there," Lebrecht's eyes flicked to him, "if there is one."

"He is somewhere..."

Lebrecht snorted, crossing to the table where Lucien still sat.

"You play dice?" the mercenary asked the young lord, wiping beer suds from his moustaches.

"Only fools gamble."

Lucien swept his eye around the room before replying, "I tend to agree, my lord..."

A couple of near-murderous glares came Lucien's way.

Three sharp knocks rattled the doors.

When he drew his father's sword, every pair of eyes snapped from the doors to him. Save Lucien, who busied himself counting coins.

"Take no chances," he advised.

Lebrecht nodded and they gathered, weapons drawn, as Iskra oversaw two of his men pulling free the bar to the catacomb doors.

Below came the sound of scuffling feet and low voices. He didn't relax the grip on his weapon till the doors opened, and Joachim's scowling face emerged up the stairs, followed by his men.

"I've enjoyed better Christmas Eves," he spat.

"Did you-"

"Not a damn thing. Save rats. I didn't realise we had so many bloody rats..."

Lebrecht scratched his head, "Best go get some food, the-"

"No!" he stepped forward, "Is everyone accounted for?"

"Yes, of course" Joachim said.

"Iskra?" Sergeants tended to know faces a lot better than noblemen.

The Sergeant swept his eyes across the group, lips moving wordlessly, until he turned to Lebrecht, "Everybody's here, my lord."

"I didn't lose anybody," Joachim moved alongside his brother, "the rats aren't *that* big..."

"Every man should say his name and place of birth," he said, not loosening the grip on his sword.

Joachim rolled his eyes.

"My lord, the demon can change his face. I've seen it. But he can't take a man's memories..."

"Do it," Lebrecht ordered.

Some of the soldiers exchanged uncertain glances with the men standing next to them as they spoke in turn. Iskra nodded along with each name until only Joachim remained.

"Joachim of Gothen," he said, "and I was born here."

"Ask him something only your brother would know?"

"What was your nanny's name?"

"Matilda," the young nobleman replied instantly, "the one with the ridiculously big tits."

Laughter rippled around the room.

Finally, he slipped his sword home, eyes moving to the stone steps disappearing down into darkness.

"Then he's still there."

"Can your demon turn himself into a rat? They're the only thing down there."

"Seal the catacombs," Lebrecht told Iskra, "and I want the doors guarded through the night."

212

Iskra did as ordered, despite Joachim's weary shake of the head.

"Is that it?" he demanded.

"What else can we do?" Lebrecht shot back, "We've searched the whole castle... Perhaps he slipped away..."

"Or he was never here in the first place..." Joachim waved the men off to the kitchens to find food.

"He's still here!" he fought the urge to grab the man and start shaking him.

Joachim turned away, muttering under his breath. Which didn't do much for his temper. A hand curled around his arm. Lucien had finished counting his winnings.

He wanted to shake the man off, but he was right. Picking a fight with Joachim wasn't one he could ever win. And they already faced one fight they could never win.

"I take it our cousin has done nothing while I've been chasing geese?" Joachim asked his brother.

Lebrecht shook his head, then slapped Joachim's back, "Come, Father wants to talk to us about something."

"Does he want us to start building some pyres?" he glanced at them.

Lebrecht leaned into his brother, said something sharp in his ear, and then shoved him towards the door.

"And what should we do?" he asked.

"Go and see your mistress; she wants you," Lebrecht said.

"And try not to kill anyone else," Joachim added, earning himself another shove from his brother.

"I have the impression that fellow doesn't care for us much," Lucien said.

"I wonder what the *Markgräf* wants to see them about?" he

wondered aloud as the brothers left.

"The Christmas feast, probably. Nobles always put their stomachs first."

He wasn't sure; he was getting another of his bad feelings.

*

"I'm sorry, my lady? You're doing... *what?!*"

"Marrying the *Markgräf.*"

She thought she'd said it clearly enough, but Renard blinked again as if he still hadn't heard her correctly.

Lucien, who, on seeing food spread over the table, had immediately slumped uninvited into a chair, continued shovelling whatever came to hand into his mouth. To be fair, neither she nor the *Markgräf* had eaten much.

"But... why?"

"He has an army."

Renard blinked once more. He still looked dumbfounded. So, she explained further.

"I need an army."

He still looked blank.

"How many men?" Lucien sloshed wine into the *Markgräf's* glass.

"We have yet to agree the details. He hasn't agreed to marry me yet. He wants to think about it. But he will say yes."

Lucien frowned, "And how will this work? He will let you head off into the blue yonder chasing the Red Company with his army?"

"As I said, we'll deal with the practicalities later. We'll have a few days before the wedding."

Lucien sucked something from his teeth, wine poised on his lips, "Romantic…"

"Why would he want to marry you?" Renard asked.

She raised an eyebrow.

"More importantly, why would he give you his army?" Lucien added.

"In answer to the first question. Why wouldn't he? I am young, healthy, heir to the lands and title of Tassau. Some men might even go so far as to say I am fetching…" Turning to Lucien, she continued, "…and to answer the second question. He'll give me whatever I ask for because my mother was the love of his life, and I, apparently, bear an uncanny resemblance to her…"

Renard crossed to the table. Lucien was already pouring wine for him by the time he got there.

"Fuck…" Lucien said, whilst Renard threw the wine down his neck.

She returned to her chair, shaking her head, "I really must discuss the concept of deference with you two at some point."

Lucien raised his glass, "Congratulations and good health to the new *Markgräfin* of Gothen!"

"As I said, he hasn't agreed yet."

"He has eyes in his head. I'd *definitely* give you my army."

"You left your army in Madriel," Renard said.

"They weren't technically mine…"

She held out her hand. When Lucien just stared at her, she waggled her fingers.

"Ah…" he leant over the table, plucked Renard's glass from his hand and passed it to her.

Renard scowled.

"As the junior member of our company, you can drink out of the bottle."

"I am not-"

"Enough! We need to talk about Wendel."

Renard scowled some more but took the bottle to the fire.

"I'd rather talk about the wedding," Lucien pinched meat from the remains of a chicken leg, "Lucien Kazmierczak is famed from Antioch to Algiers for his weddings."

"I'm not going to ask."

"Six," Lucien tipped his glass in her direction and winked.

"I'm still not going to ask..." she turned her eyes to Renard, "There was no sign of the demon?"

Renard shook his head.

"Perhaps he did get away. If he wrapped himself in enough clothes, he could stand the daylight. Morlaine can, after all."

"Perhaps," Lucien said, "And perhaps better he did."

"I want him dead. I want them *all* dead."

Lucien stared at her. Renard stared at the fire. Neither said anything.

She wiped the back of her hand over her mouth; she'd said those words with enough vehemence to spray spittle.

"I should speak to the *Markgräf;* his men must continue searching the castle. And the walls, Wendel will have to climb the walls with the gates shut, and-"

"A word of advice," Lucien held up a greasy finger.

"Yes?"

"A prospective bride would be wise to keep her nagging to a minimum until *after* the wedding ceremony..."

She almost threw her glass at him. Instead, she glowered, lips pressed tight together.

Then, much to her surprise, she burst out laughing.

Renard stepped away from the fire, face creased with concern before realising she wasn't having some manner of fit or demonic possession. Had he ever seen her laugh properly?

The laughter subsided; she couldn't remember the last time she'd laughed so heartily. It had felt rather good. She drank a little wine. Both men eyed her carefully.

She shook her head.

"I am quite well."

"Laughter suits you," Lucien tipped his glass in salute.

"I've had precious little to laugh at recently."

"Well, you have a wedding to look forward to now!" Another salute.

That removed the last trace of a smile from her lips, "Yes, I do…"

"My lady," Renard stepped away from the fire; Lucien retrieved the bottle from his hand to top up his glass, "perhaps you should not act so hastily, marriage-"

"I need more men."

"But-"

She shook her head, "If the *Markgräf* is agreeable, we will wed. And I will have an army to hunt down the Red Company."

Renard didn't look happy. Lucien was starting to look drunk.

She leaned into them and lowered her voice, "We are here for a reason. What are the chances that we stumbled across a man who loved my mother, is widowed, wealthy, and has the men we need to destroy the Red Company? This cannot be a coincidence. 'tis God's will."

"'tis a shame God was looking the other way when the Red Company arrived at The Wolf's Tower," Renard snatched the bottle back from Lucien only to find it empty.

"God would not have brought us here if it were not for our benefit! God is not so perverse!"

"In my opinion," Lucien offered, "God is *exceedingly* perverse. A whimsical, contrary fellow who takes great delight in arranging our lives so that we continually walk into doors, slip in horse shit and fall flat on our faces, always at precisely the moment that most inconveniences our sensibilities, ambitions, hopes and dreams." The mercenary looked around the room, "For example, we seem to have now run out of wine just as I was beginning to get a taste for it..."

Renard found a stool and perched on it.

"Have you considered it might not have been God who brought us here, my lady?"

"Who else could?"

"Your brother."

"How..." the words dried in her mouth.

"We are only here because of what we stumbled upon at Enoch's farm. If that were done for our benefit so you would meet the *Markgräf...*"

"What are you saying?"

"Your brother sees the future, my lady. Ours, his, Saul's too, presumably. Perhaps a better way to stop you pursuing him is for you to be married."

218

"But marrying the *Markgräf* will help me find Torben."

"Will it?" Lucien asked, "A man might make any promise to get a woman into his bed. Whether he will honour those promises afterwards... and, this may surprise you given my noble reputation for integrity, I am speaking with some experience here..."

"I appreciate your counsel. But neither of you gentlemen are my father."

"You'd be far less pretty if that were the case," Lucien conceded.

"Trust me, I know what I am doing."

She knew no such thing, the words as much for her benefit as theirs, but a leader should always sound like they knew what they were doing even when they didn't. Had Father told her that? Or Lutz? Tutor Magnus? She couldn't remember.

Lucien gave her a look that suggested she was too young to know much about anything but remained wise enough to keep the thought to himself.

"And what about... our mutual friend?" Renard asked.

"What about her?"

"We can hardly go blundering about, travelling only at night with an army at our backs."

"And Morlaine is more useful than a hundred men-at-arms," Lucien added quickly.

"There are untold bridges sitting between us and Saul the Bloodless. We'll cross each one as we come to it..."

219

Chapter Six

He could not shake the thought of a man touching Solace from his head. The idea knotted his stomach and kept tightening.

He did not understand why.

She was his mistress, a noblewoman. The aristocracy always wed for material gain before anything else. Those born to privilege, wealth and power dedicated themselves to maintaining and improving their station above all other things.

If the Red Company had not destroyed their old lives, she would likely have been married off by *Freiherr* von Tassau to someone very much like the *Markgräf* of Gothen. A rich older man looking for a young wife, either for himself or his son. So, this was completely natural.

But the Red Company *had* come.

Their lives were not as they once were. He didn't look upon Solace von Tassau as a noblewoman anymore; she was not a *Freiin* or *Baronin* in his eyes. Not an aloof young woman of privilege unlikely to even notice his existence. Now she was... what? His captain? His companion? His friend?

That seemed too bold a claim.

But something more than his employer.

He loved her. He hated her. He feared what she was becoming and where she led them. But he had given her his oath. And what fragmentary honour he still possessed. She had saved his life. She had stripped naked and wrapped her body around him to keep him alive. They had shared a bed in Madriel. Apart from the impropriety of sharing a bed in the first place, nothing improper had occurred.

So, what was she? What were they? Why did the possibility of her marrying this lord, this stranger, this rich older man, disturb him? Thoughts and feelings swirled like sycamore seeds in a storm.

What if he was unkind, cruel? What if he had... strange desires? Everybody knew how peculiar the aristocracy could be. That was what centuries of marrying your cousins got for you. What if he hurt her?

Why did he care?

Did he care?

Yes, he cared. She was the one person on God's Earth he did care for. She'd saved his life. Forgiven his betrayal, his weakness. They had stood shoulder to shoulder against demons and expected to die together. That meant something, didn't it?

It was only natural he should be concerned. That didn't mean *anything...* of course not, nothing at all.

He paced.

He liked to pace when he had thinking to do.

Pacing or drinking.

But pacing was better.

He'd seen what drinking did to you. Like fucking your cousins, it was best avoided.

Torches flickered and hissed in the corridor, but they only

created small islands in the dark. Up in the fancy apartments, candles and oil lamps burned with abandon, but on the castle's lower floors only smoky tar torches or feeble rushlights held back the night.

Tamburro, the *Markgräf's* steward, a Genoese who waved his arms too much and smiled too little, had appeared at the cottage with a couple of servants to move Lady Solace to, "more fitting accommodations." Which turned out to be a suite of fine oak-panelled rooms high in the castle. A distinct improvement to the room the *Markgräf* originally put her in.

Was that significant?

Probably.

He couldn't help wondering how close the *Markgräf's* rooms were but decided it too impolite to ask.

The suite came with adjoining rooms for servants, which he and Lucien had squeezed into. The mercenary had immediately kicked off his boots and fallen asleep on one of the cots.

Unable to even rest, he'd told his mistress he would look for Wendel.

"You should not go alone," she'd said, eyes drifting towards the door to the servant's rooms, through which Lucien's snores reverberated.

"I don't trust the *Markgräf's* men have been thorough enough... but he's likely gone. He's delivered your brother's message; there's no point him lingering here. Especially as he must know we've been looking for him."

"Be careful, Ulrich..."

"Yes, my lady."

In truth, he had no intention of searching for Wendel. He just didn't want to listen to his unwanted thoughts competing with Lucien's snoring for his attention. The *Markgräf* had posted two men outside their door; whether to protect or detain, he wasn't certain, but they said nothing when he left the rooms, though he felt their eyes on his back readily enough.

Lucien's snoring proved easier to run away from than the whispers haunting his mind.

Life bustled and pulsed throughout the kitchens, but shadows and silence filled the rest of the castle. Occasional voices and footsteps echoed, but he saw no one. During the long dark nights of winter, most people took to their beds as early as possible. Light was expensive and sparse, bed the easiest place to keep warm.

Perhaps talking Solace out of her plan was a better use of his time? However, he'd grown to know her well enough to understand that once she'd set her mind, little he could say or do would alter it.

He'd seen what the demons of the Red Company could do. He doubted a hundred men-at-arms could stand against them. All her madness would achieve was sending more souls to their doom.

But if not a hundred, how many? A thousand? More? Perhaps Solace should aim higher and try for the Emperor himself?

He snorted out a plume of frosted breath at that.

More footsteps. He paused by a flickering torch, but no figure appeared, and they quickly faded.

He shivered, though not entirely from the cold.

Better he went outside, where the air didn't taste of tallow and tar, and the moon might wash the world with a little light.

And the memories might not be so sharp.

The sounds and stinks of Ettestein reminded him so much of The Wolf's Tower. When he had wandered alone after Callinicus' death, not knowing who he was or where his allegiance lay. Whether he really had sold his soul to a devil with a liar's eyes or whether redemption and escape were possible.

Those memories had haunted him every night since, along with the ghostly cries of the children he'd left to die.

Naples, Ulrich, Naples…

That's what he should be telling Solace, but she would listen to that advice no more than she would the counsel of the birds or the wind.

He walked on. Past closed doors. Through pools of pale light and wastelands of shadow.

He reached a spiral staircase, meaning to go down and take the freezing air. Footsteps rattled from above. His heart quickened. Remembering.

Pretty thing, come to me…

The urge to turn and run almost overwhelmed him. Tremors shook his arms, and it was all he could do to not sink to his knees.

The footsteps grew louder. The clank of metal, the rasp of leather, the clip of nailed boots on the stone steps.

Just a soldier.

Probably.

But not Alms.

He was not here. He had not come for him or his soul.

Wendel was not here anymore either. The demon had fled with the coming of the night. His business done. It was no one, it was no one...

It was Sergeant Iskra.

He nodded, the soldier nodded back, a faint expression, part amusement, part disdain dusting his craggy face in the gloom. Perhaps he'd heard a rumour that Lady Solace might soon be the mistress of Ettestein. Few secrets lasted long within the confines of a castle.

"Christmas tidings, Sergeant," he managed to say.

Iskra replied with a weary grunt and hurried on down the stairs. He'd intended to go that way but went upwards instead, not wanting to risk the Sergeant becoming talkative at the bottom.

He assumed they had found no sign of Wendel, the Sergeant would have said.

The next floor was dark and deserted. No lights burned beyond the stairwell's doorway; a narrow window allowed a sliver of moonlight to dust the corridor. He walked to it, footsteps echoing. Hundreds resided inside Ettestein's thick stone walls, but such was the depth of the stillness up here he could have been the last man on Earth.

Perhaps Wendel had slaughtered everybody. Lucien snored loudly enough to mask all manner of horrors.

He shook his head. Too many bleak imaginings were not good for a man's soul.

Cold glass pressed against his nose as he peered through the window. A thin moon hung above the Elbe; below, torches danced on the castle's outer walls. Figures patrolled the battlements. Nothing else moved.

For a while, he watched the night, wiping away the condensation of his breath from the glass to make out the stars mottling the sky alongside the crescent moon, serene and peaceful. You could lose yourself staring into the heavens if you considered them for long enough.

Eventually, he sighed and pulled himself away. The view would be better outside. Maybe he'd find a spot up on the walls from which he would see no marks of man at all.

Iskra must be well clear of the stairwell by now.

This was as high as these stairs reached. He had no desire to stumble around in the dark, so he would retrace his steps and make his way out of the castle. Perhaps the freezing night air would chase away his thoughts. His ghosts and demons were harder to dispatch, but emptying his head might at least allow him to find a little sleep later. Lucien's snoring permitting.

Something glistened on the floor between the silver light spilling through the window and the torch at the top of the stairwell.

His breath caught.

Crouching, he ran his fingers across the floor. They came away stickily familiar.

Blood.

A bloody footprint.

Once more, he wandered The Wolf's Tower. The tracks of killers soiling the floors.

He let out a soft, strangled moan. It sounded like he shared the darkness with a frightened animal, keening its fear.

226

As much as he wanted to curl into a ball, he forced himself to his feet, hurried to the stairwell and snatched the torch from its cradle. Returning to the corridor, he kept the burning flame low. Other prints soiled the stone, blurry and indistinct but clearly footprints.

Someone had walked through a pool of blood.

He stopped, holding the torch out before him. What would he find if he followed the tracks back to their source? Licking his lips, he knew the answer to that well enough. A corpse.

Probably one with a neck wound.

Wendel hadn't left Ettestein after all.

Indecision rooted him to the spot. The flame in his hand writhed, his heart thudded. Which way should he go? Onwards to find the body or follow the tracks and chase Wendel. Before he escaped. Before he hurt anyone else.

Master...

He shook the thought away. He had no master.

Only a mistress.

Should he go to Solace? His first duty was to protect her. But if Wendel wanted to hurt her, he would have that morning. He could have opened her veins and drained her dry long before Lucien and he found her. But he hadn't then. So why would he now?

Why not just slip silently away?

Hunger?

He'd fed from Josef last night. Morlaine didn't need to drink blood every day. Why should Wendel? Why leave a corpse to be discovered? Why risk raising the alarm before he slipped into the night...?

He spun on his heels.

The marks on the stone steps were fainter. Each more indistinct than the last. He hurtled past them, breath rattling, throwing out clouds of steam ahead of him.

He should get help. Lucien, at least, but he was afraid there was no time, and anyone else wasn't likely to do anything but take him to one of the *Markgräf's*. And by the time they believed him...

It'd be too late.

The slaughter would already have started...

*

It was the night before Christmas.

Nothing stirred within the castle, not even a mouse.

No doubt Lucien's snoring had scared all the rodents away.

She sat by the fire. The hour grew late. She should sleep.

The *Markgräf* had invited her to morning prayers to begin the Christmas celebrations in the family chapel. She realised she had not been to church since The Wolf Tower fell. How strange it would be to do that simple thing. Pray. Before God. Give thanks. Listen to a sermon. Sing hymns. Praise the Lord.

She had done that virtually every day since she'd been old enough to do anything. Now the ritual seemed alien. Removed from that world to inhabit one of fear, loathing and vengeance, she had felt no need or desire.

She had two men, one demon, the *sight*, four horses, steel and shot, armour, powder and provisions. Her mother's jewellery. And Flyblown. Whatever he was.

God now seemed... surplus to her requirements.

She watched the flames.

She did not want to go to the Chapel in the morning.

She did not want to go to the *Markgräf's* bed either.

But she was not in a position to choose. Necessity deemed otherwise.

So, she would drop to her knees and give thanks to the God who'd done nothing to help her. Just as she would... do whatever the *Markgräf* might want of his wife.

For a hundred men-at-arms.

Perhaps it was a test? Perhaps if God saw the sacrifices she was prepared to make, he might finally decide to come to her aid. God helped those who helped themselves. So she'd once read...

Her eyes turned to the door.

It would open shortly.

Two soldiers stood outside. But neither of them would enter. It wouldn't be Renard, either. It would be the *Markgräf*.

Something swelled and rolled in her stomach.

No matter. Soon he would come to her chamber every night. To her bed.

Her eyes moved back to the fire.

Something pulled at her. Unease. Anxiety. Familiar and alien.

The dread stone.

Was the *sight* warning her about the *Markgräf?* No, she didn't think so.

This was how she'd felt in the weeks before The Wolf's Tower fell.

If she went to bed, would she dream of fire and blood again?

She rose and hurried to the window. There was little to see even after she'd wiped away the beads of moisture. Just darkness. Pressing against the glass.

Her eyes swept the room. Lingering where the shadows hung thickest; no figure emerged. She'd have to cope without Flyblown's advice.

She didn't know what was happening, but she'd sworn she would never ignore the sight again, whether its warnings came in whispers or howls.

Lucien awoke with a blubbering start to peer at the candle she'd scooped up enroute to the small adjoining room he shared with Renard.

"What-"

"Get up," she ordered, already returning to the main room of their suite. It didn't take him long to follow; he hadn't even taken his boots off, let alone undress, before collapsing onto one of the side room's two cots.

"My lady?" he asked through a stifled yawn, rubbing down his tousled thinning hair.

"Something is happening."

"Happening...?"

"Trust me."

He nodded and went back into his room. He returned, strapping on his weapons belt.

"What do you want me to do?"

It was a good question. Particularly as she didn't know what was happening.

"Be careful, find Ulrich, come back here."

No quip, no grin. Perhaps he saw something in her eyes. Fear, perhaps.

"Wendel?"

"I don't know. *Something*. I..."

"I will see."

"Since my home was destroyed. I listen to my feelings. I felt it coming, felt something coming. The evil. But didn't really believe it until too late."

"And you have that feeling now?"

"Strongly. Two things. Firstly, the *Markgräf* will come through that door very shortly, the other..." her voice dropped "...people are going to die."

He nodded and turned for the door.

"Be careful, Lucien."

He grinned over his shoulder, "Lucien Kazmierczak is infamous for being careful. No man is more prudent!"

After he left, she stood staring at the door. How long before the *Markgräf* came through it. Minutes? Hours? Did she have time to twiddle her thumbs and wait?

No, she decided, she didn't.

"Take me to the *Markgräf's* chambers, she told the two men outside her door.

They glanced at each other. Such an eventuality was clearly not within the remit of their orders.

"Now."

"My lady-"

She moved closer to the soldier, the older of the two. She assumed he was in charge.

"Now," she repeated in her haughtiest voice, "'tis important."

When he hesitated, she added, "Take me, or I'll go and knock on every door until I find it myself."

One of the many first rules of soldiering Lucien prattled about was knowing when you were beaten. The man-at-arms nodded, "This way, my lady."

The *Markgräf's* private chambers were not far. Another two soldiers waited either side of it. Did he always have a guard?

She went in without either knocking or listening to the soldier's protests.

The *Markgräf* was inside, pacing. Perhaps debating the merits of a nocturnal visit to her rooms.

"My Lord-" one of the men trailing in her wake spluttered.

"Leave us, Germaine, please," he said.

"My lord..." the soldier bowed, she curtseyed.

"The hour is late?" the *Markgräf* said once they were alone.

Did she tell him immediately? Warn him? He knew her mother had the *sight*; he suspected she did too. But it wasn't something you told anyone lightly. Such things could cost your life if they reached the wrong ears.

The *sight* told her nothing about whether she could trust this man, Flyblown's mark remained equally quiet. And yet she trusted him enough to marry him.

"You need to turn out your guard," she said, her mouth deciding.

"I'm sorry?"

"There is danger tonight."

"What danger?"

"I'm not sure exactly..."

232

"Then-"

"You asked me earlier if I had the *sight*, like my mother."

The *Markgräf* nodded.

"I do..." her eyes moved to the flames; eager tongues flicked around the logs.

"And your..." he dropped his voice "...*sight* is telling you there is danger?"

"Yes, my lord. My gift is not as strong as my mother's, I believe. But when it whispers, I listen. It whispers now."

"We found no sign of any demon..."

"There's likely a connection."

"Devilish mischief?"

"Perhaps."

A deep sigh escaped the *Markgräf's* lips.

"You were about to come to my rooms, I believe?"

He hesitated, then smiled, "I was considering it."

"You wanted to come to my bed."

He hoisted an eyebrow, "Your *sight* told you this?"

"The *sight* told me you would come through my door. The rest I worked out for myself. A man only comes to a lady's chamber for one reason at this hour."

"Perhaps you have an uncommonly low opinion of men?"

"I'm eighteen years old, my lord; I know little of men. But I am not a fool."

"You are asking a lot of me, Solace. I wish to know your intentions are... as you say they are?"

"I will honour my wedding vows, whoever I make them to. But I will not take you to my bed before you make your vows to me. And give me the means to destroy my enemies."

"I wish-"

"My lord, there is no time! Please, raise your guard. Just as I knew you would come to my chamber, I know a great danger is afoot."

"I turfed my entire household into the cold, searched my home from catacombs to rafters, and found nothing. I have six corpses to bury. And no demon. Perhaps you can understand my reluctance..."

"No. I can't. If I am to be your wife, you must trust me. As I must trust you..." she stared levelly at him "...do you wish me to be your wife?"

"I wish for what I have always wished for from the day I first set eyes on your mother. For Elenore to be my wife."

"I am not my mother. Nor can I ever be. But I am the closest you will ever get to her. On this side of heaven, at least."

Nothing much played across his face. Some men wore their thoughts and feelings for the world to see. The *Markgräf* of Gothen wasn't one of them. He wanted her; she was sure of it, but enough to give her what she wanted in return...?

Within her, the dread stone turned.

Something *was* happening.

There was a time and a place for seduction, but this wasn't it.

She crossed to the nearest window. There was no more to see from it than the last time she'd looked from hers.

"My lady?"

The *Markgräf* remained by the fire's glow.

"You must raise the guard... there's danger... I feel it..."

"Ettestein is well protected; there is nothing to fear."

"You sound like my father! He insisted time and again there was nothing to worry about on the last night of his life..." she took a step back towards the *Markgräf,* "...he didn't listen to me. And he ended up being roasted alive in the fire of our Great Hall!"

Her hands covered her mouth. Something was crawling up her throat. Horror, screams, tears, memories, the dread stone of her *sight* trying to claw its way out of her? She didn't know.

The world wanted to slip away, spin from her grasp and send her into the darkness. She fought it. Not again. She couldn't let it happen again. She didn't want to have to hide from them, run from them, climb into a chimney and listen to the footsteps of her hunters. She didn't want to hear the screams again. She didn't want to put a pistol under her chin and pull the trigger. It couldn't, it couldn't-

"Solace!"

Fingers dug into her arms. Her eyes snapped back into focus.

"Father..." she whispered at the face filling her vision.

Of course, it wasn't her father.

Except, for a moment, it was. And Renard, and Flyblown and Sergeant Lutz, Tutor Magnus, Torben. Lucien too. And, behind them all, Saul the Bloodless' bright, laughing eyes.

Her knees sagged, and she slumped against the *Markgräf.*

"Elenore," the voice in her ear breathed.

Arms enfolded her. Warm, strong, safe.

Just an illusion. Another delusion. For them both.

No safety existed in this world, but oh, how she wished

she could let herself believe otherwise.

She wanted to open her eyes and be a little girl again, one who wanted nothing but her father's love, lived in a world without monsters and believed thick walls and strong arms sufficient to keep evil away.

Breath escaped her in shaky bursts, but the dread receded a little.

She stepped back.

The *Markgräf* allowed her, but his hands moved to her shoulders as if afraid she might bolt away.

He did not really look like Father; it was just the beard. The same colour and trim, shot through with filings of iron-grey. The face beneath was cut quite differently. Still, perhaps she would ask him to shave off the beard as a wedding present if they did wed.

In addition to giving her a hundred men-at-arms.

A giggle tried to squirm out of her, but she strangled it. She was acting strangely enough.

"My lord," she said finally, "please..."

"Are you unwell?" a hand found her hair above her ear, and he stroked it gently. She was unsure if it made her feel comforted or like a dog.

"No, my lord, 'tis the *sight*. Usually, 'tis... weak... just a sigh in the night, but sometimes... it roars. It frightens me, it..."

"Sssshh..." concern momentarily broke the mask of his face, "I remember your mother suffered the same."

"She did? Father never talked of her *sight*. He was afraid the witchfinders might hear of it..."

"We were very-"

"Later!"

She knew little of her mother. Father had rarely spoken about her; most of what she knew came from servants, but a yawning chasm stretched between her and her mother's memory. Perhaps the *Markgräf* could help fill some of that empty space with his memories of Elenore. She would like that. But not now.

The dread stone swelled inside her again.

"Please, my lord, summon your men and go... to the gates... now!"

She didn't know what was happening at the gates; the *sight* seldom filled in every detail and never presented her with maps and letters. But the sense, the feeling, the knowing told her something important was happening, and it was happening at the gates.

And if it wasn't stopped...

"It will happen again..."

Chapter Seven

The footprints disappeared before he reached the bottom of the stairs.

It didn't matter. He knew where to go.

He barrelled through the castle clutching the burning torch, nailed boots clattering on the stone flagstones. Distant lights, distant voices. But no cries of alarm aimed at him or anyone else.

Unlike The Wolf's Tower, no enclosed courtyard filled the centre of Ettestein; the castle was a solid stone block, sprouting towers and buttresses as it soared out of its rocky bluff above the Elbe.

Stables, a smithy, barns, a church, pig styes, chicken coops and clusters of cottages laid between the castle and the outer wall, but the fortress itself existed only as a home for the *Markgräf* of Gothen and as a projection of military force upon the surrounding lands and people.

The upper stories were warm, comfortable and well furnished, the lower levels spartan and designed to be defended should any enemy ever breach the gates.

They would find out how well designed the narrow corridors and thick doors were if he didn't get to the gates soon.

A small barbican housed the gates in the front of the castle; his breath came in a series of panted rattles by the time he hurtled into it and skidded to a halt before the heavy oak doors.

"Guards!"

His voice echoing around the stonework was the only reply.

The silence increased his sense of unease. No lord left his gates unguarded in a time of war.

The main gates, bands of iron reinforcing planks of thick oak, were barred, but a smaller door sat within them. And it wasn't.

Sweeping the torch back and forth, he searched for traces of blood but found nothing.

He set the torch in an empty cradle, drew his father's sword and pushed the door open.

The hinges needed a good oiling, but, otherwise, nothing untoward happened. Still panting clouds of freezing breath, he ducked through the door.

No guards were outside either.

Snow melt had plastered the path from the castle to the outer walls with thick mud. He slithered down it as fast as he dared before reaching level ground. Then he started sprinting again.

A veritable village had grown along the track running from the castle to the two towers marking the gate in the outer wall. Originally stables, smithies and armourers plus some barns; however, the war had swelled the castle's population beyond the fortress's capacity to house them all. There was a tavern, church and cottages all of which looked like they had been here some time, but a shanty town of simple shacks spread beyond them, tents to house refugees from the surrounding villages of Gothen seeking the protection of their lord.

It made for a poor killing field. Once an enemy broke through the outer defences, plenty of cover would shield them from the overlooking castle upon its rocky outcrop.

He sucked in freezing air as he ran towards the Gate Towers; it felt like drawing shards of ice into his lungs.

Braziers burned in the towers and along the battlements, orange islands of light holding back the greater night.

But nobody was in sight.

No men huddled around the fires, warming their hands, sharing jokes, easing the burden of a long frosty night with their fellows. The walls were empty. The towers were empty.

Nothing moved.

What am I doing?

He kept running, boots slapping and sploshing through the muck.

Waking the garrison and sealing the castle would be more useful, but that would mean leaving everybody outside to their fate. Soldiers. Men. Women.

Children.

He ran harder.

Not again.

His foot slipped on a patch of ice, and he nearly went down, windmilling his arms to just about keep upright.

A few soft lights glowed in the windows he shot past, but most were dark and silent. The inhabitants keeping warm in their beds till Christmas dawn broke and light returned to the world.

He hoped they were going to live to see it.

The towers on either side of the outer gates loomed higher

as he approached. There should be guards, but he could see no one.

He slowed. Partly with caution but mainly out of necessity.

A year ago, such a run would have barely left him breathing heavily. Now, with his broken withered body, gorge threatened to fill his mouth while his heart drummed frenetically.

Beneath the gatehouse, something moved.

A figure. Heavy-set and bulky but moving swift and nimble. In a way the real Sergeant Iskra never would.

He drew a pistol and walked forward, hand shaking with the rest of him.

Could he get close enough for a shot before the gates opened?

He didn't think so.

"Wendel!" he screamed.

Iskra's head snapped in his direction. A feral grin flashed in the shadows and a hand rose in a casual wave, then the demon returned his attention to the gates.

An oak beam, as thick as a man's waist, barred them. It would have taken four men to lift it clear. Any lingering doubt that the real Iskra wasn't lying dead somewhere, and the only connection with this one was the blood on his boots, disappeared as the demon lifted the beam with no more effort than he would have picking up a spade.

Every part of him wanted to wheel away and run.

He'd been here before.

And he'd all but sold his soul to the Devil.

He ran towards the demon.

241

What's going to come through that gate?

Was the rest of the Red Company here? This time dressed in Imperial livery rather than blood red cloaks?

Ready to go to work. Ready to slaughter for silver and blood? Ready to round the women and children up once more? To celebrate Christmas with their own dark, satanic feast?

He had only seconds before the gates were free to swing open.

A pistol was a clumsy inaccurate weapon at anything but close range. On the battlefield, armies fired in volleys to maximise the chance of damaging an enemy.

But he had no choice.

He slid to a halt, heels biting into the icy mud to gain purchase.

I must defend the breach.

I must stand.

Whatever the odds.

He levelled his pistol and gulped sharp, freezing air.

Two forms huddled in the corner of the gatehouse. The guards. How many had Wendel killed tonight? It didn't matter. Nothing mattered. If Wendel freed the gates, a wave of slaughter would break upon Ettestein.

He sucked in more air and willed the tremor from his hand.

"The one thing that can't be taken from a man is his honour; he can only give that away..." he whispered at one of the monsters who'd shown him his own cowardice and convinced him, albeit briefly, to give them his.

"Bastard," he added.

242

Then pulled the trigger.

*

"What will happen again?"

He was still holding her arms, still filling her vision. His scent teased her nostrils. Beneath it, the earthier aromas of sweat and tobacco that most men carried with them.

The list of men she'd been this close to for any time was short. Torben, Father, Renard.

Torben could not stand even her to touch him for long. Father was a distant man whose gestures of affection and familiarity were sporadic at best. As for Renard... well, that had been out of necessity... and although the closeness had stirred certain... *curiosities*... well, she'd had far more important things to fill her head with.

And still did!

"What happened at The Wolf's Tower... blood and fire. Slaughter..."

For a man she was warning about the danger to his home, the *Markgräf* didn't seem overly troubled. In fact, he seemed far more concerned with stroking her hair with his thumb.

My lord...?" she pulled away from him.

"That will not happen here."

"You do not believe my *sight*. You think me some... charlatan?"

"No. 'tis just... Ettestein is well defended. And 'tis Christmas. My nephew would never attack, even if he had enough soldiers. Which he doesn't."

"There is a demon here, my lord. Who comes from a company of demons. I do not know where they are; I do not know who will threaten Ettestein's gates tonight. But threatened they are..." she stepped away from his touch completely and retreated to the fire "...perhaps you should invite your nephew to the Christmas feast if you are on such friendly terms with him."

The *Markgräf* followed her after scooping up the glass of claret he'd been drinking before she'd disturbed him.

"Gottlieb wouldn't attend a Protestant celebration. He is a devout Catholic, as are all his side of the family. Which is a continuing source of friction between us..." the *Markgräf* shrugged and drowned his drink, "...that and his avarice for things which are not his."

He filled the glass again.

"How badly does Gottlieb want Ettestein and Gothen?" she asked.

"He'd cut off his right hand for the *Markgräfschaft*. He believes my grandfather usurped his and stole his inheritance. He is quite singularly driven, to the extent he has somehow persuaded the Emperor to give him troops. No doubt a promise to return my lands to Catholicism also played a part in fooling the Emperor..." he shook his head before sipping his claret, "...dark days."

"Would he be prepared to enlist the aid of demons? Would he sell his soul?"

He stared at her over the glass' rim.

"My nephew is a weak man of many faults, but still..."

"I didn't tell you why the Red Company came to The Wolf's Tower, did I?"

"A monster sent them, I believe you said."

"A monster hired them. A man. A rich man. A man used to

244

getting whatever he wants," her eyes dropped to the fire for a second, "a man who wanted me..."

The *Markgräf* moved beside her once more. She thought he wanted to touch her again; instead, he cocked his head, "Tell me."

"We don't have time. The point is, this is what the Red Company does... they hire themselves to greedy, powerful, ruthless men who are using the cover of the war to take whatever they desire. A man hired them to take me for him. Another man sits beyond your walls and badly desires what is inside them. He has an army, but not one large enough to take Ettestein. Yet here he is, in the middle of winter, when most armies do not take to the field. And in these walls is a demon of the Red Company," she pinched a smile, "do you follow my logic, my lord...?"

"You said he was here to kill you?"

Was it a sin to lie to the man you might be marrying? Probably one of the more minor ones.

"He is," she said, "but why not kill two birds with one stone?"

The *Markgräf* glanced at the window. Something akin to uncertainty played across his face for the first time, "Is this Red Company here?"

The dread stone swelled inside her, bleak and ominous, but it did not answer questions. Flyblown's mark tingled oh so faintly. If Saul the Bloodless was near, Flyblown would have warned her, wouldn't he?

"I don't know, my lord..." she reached over and took his hand, "...but I beg you, please... believe me... we are in danger..."

He smiled a rare smile and moved closer to her, "How could I not believe you?"

She knew little of these things. The fact that she knew more about demons than she did about love occasionally dragged her spirits down, but, whether due to her sight or otherwise, she knew the *Markgräf* would kiss her. Or try to. Should she let him? Oh, Lord, it was all so confusing!

As he leaned in closer, still clutching her hand, the opening door rescued her from the dilemma.

She looked around and stepped away from the *Markgräf* in one.

"Father- erm... oh... sorry..." Lebrecht spluttered.

He seemed a man desperately trying not to look aghast.

She supposed being alone in the *Markgräf's* chambers at such an hour might easily be misconstrued. Probably at any hour.

"Ah, just the man!" the *Markgräf* said, not batting an eyelid.

Lebrecht looked at her, then his father. He found a smile, albeit not a very convincing one.

I could be his mother soon...

Another thought best buried for now.

"Lady Solace has brought me fresh concerns about your cousin. I think it prudent we raise the garrison. Get men onto the walls and see what the bugger is up to, eh?"

"'tis Christmas, Father, surely-"

"Now, Lebrecht! If you please."

The young nobleman opened his mouth. He had the air of a man with so many questions he couldn't decide which one to throw out first.

"Yes, Father, of course."

"Wait," she blurted, "I will come with you."

"My dear," the *Markgräf* began, "'tis no place for-"

"My father told me to go to my room when the demons came to The Wolf's Tower. If I'd listened to him..." she shook her head, "...I am not someone you will ever need to protect, my lord."

She didn't wait for an answer. After gathering up her cloak she breezed past Lebrecht.

When the young nobleman stayed in the doorway, she stopped and looked over her shoulder at him.

"Come, don't tarry. We have men to drag from their beds..."

.

Chapter Eight

The wheel turned, the powder fizzed and ignited, the pistol fired.

The demon moved.

Splinters erupted from the gate where Wendel's head had been a moment before.

He swore.

Iskra's grin flashed at him.

"I see I'll be having to have a wee word with you, so I will..." the demon's voice escaped the sergeant's lips as he started lifting the gate's bar once more.

Stuffing the spent weapon back into his belt, he drew his father's sword and ran forward.

"No!" he screamed, "Talk to me now!"

Wendel's shoulders sagged, and he let the bar fall back into place again.

"Now you're getting annoying."

The demon spun on his heels, but the face that turned to him was neither Iskra's nor Wendel's. Instead, his true demonic countenance bared its fangs.

This is where I die...

The thought seared through him as he charged the last few feet, screaming at the monstrosity.

It was going to happen sooner or later. Pursuing the Red Company was not a recipe for a long life. Still, making enough noise might raise the alarm and at least stop whatever dark business Wendel was about.

He slashed the sabre at Wendel's pale, elongated head.

The demon danced out of the way.

"Ah, now, I didn't want to kill you, but if you're gonna be such a noisy bugger I'll have no bloody choice."

Steel sliced air again, nowhere near the demon's head.

"What are you doing, Wendel?"

"Just earning some silver from a fat fool who wants a bigger chair for his fat arse. Saul likes silver, and few things on this Earth are better for making silver than war."

Wendel jerked playfully towards him, laughing at how he flinched away.

"Now, tell me, why are *you here?*"

He tried feinting left and then slashing right.

It didn't fool anyone.

"To kill you."

"Well, you're making a pig's arse o' that, if you don't mind me saying!"

"You can die," he panted.

"Oh, everything dies, so it does. But just because I can, don't mean I will."

Again, the demon effortlessly slipped out of the path of his blade.

"You will die," even he couldn't hear any conviction in those words.

"One last chance, young Ulrich, run along now. Let me do my work, you and your lady will have time to get away."

The demon stared at him with its bottomless eyes. Wendel hadn't even bothered to draw a weapon. He supposed the blood smeared around its slashed mouth and soiling Iskra's tunic showed he didn't really need to.

"Why? Why give me the chance?" he swept the blade towards the demon's midriff for a bit of variety.

"Ah, well, the thing is, Saul still likes you. You made quite the impression on him, in fact. He sees potential. Saul sees the darkness in you..."

He swung harder; Wendel dodged just as easily.

They circled each other in the flickering light of the tar torches and brazier beneath the gates' stone arch. He, hunched forward, knees bent, sabre held outwards, forehead creased by furrows of concentration, the demon, pale and ungodly, but straight-backed and easy.

"There's a red cloak waiting for you, boy... you just have to ask..." the demon showed its blood-flecked fangs, "...take a knee and kiss a hand. Then the world could be yours..."

He found a laugh from somewhere.

"I will never serve you."

"No?"

"Just ask Torben."

Wendel stared at him. Then winked. The grin accompanying it too distorted and gruesome to call knowing, but that was still the word that came to mind.

He screamed, lunged, slashed, spun and slashed again.

Wendel pirouetted away.

Behind him, the corpses of two guards huddled against the door, throats reduced to bloody ruins.

"Silver, women, wine, song, any pleasure that takes your fancy. All yours. Saul wants you. And he can make any dream you have come true..." Wendel leaned in sharply, "...you just have to call him *master*. Again."

This time fury drove him forward. This time Wendel didn't step away.

Instead, icy fingers caught his wrist and yanked him towards the creature's black eyes, where bands of colour eddied around the fathomless pupils.

How many people have seen this and lived...?

"I have no master."

"Should I ruin your other arm too, Ulrich?" the monster's head tilted, inhuman eyes blinked. When he didn't reply, the demon gave his wrist a savage twist, sending his father's sword spinning from his grasp.

Wendel pulled him close enough for the abattoir stink of his breath to soil the air, close enough to see tiny scraps of flesh trapped between the elongated teeth, close enough for the blood on his chin to glisten in the torchlight.

"We can give you paradise, but you'd rather remain in this purgatory, this nothing, this empty lie o' a life..."

He tried to twist away, but both Wendel's arms encircled him, locking him into a devil's embrace.

"I am not you!"

"No, but you could be. And deep down, you know you want to bend your knee and call me master again. Because that's the only road that doesn't take you to oblivion, to nothingness."

"Better that than being you," he hissed.

Wendel laughed, the breath that played over his face colder than any winter's gale.

"You are parched, Ulrich. I can taste it on you. The desire. The need. You thirst for happiness, contentment, to be more than you are. And there is only one way you can sate that thirst and be who you were born to be."

Again, he tried to squirm away; again, Wendel held him tight.

"And you want to know how?" Wendel came close enough for their noses to touch, "By kissing the vein, that's how. Like Torben did. By casting away your weakness and becoming a god..."

He wanted to spit in the demon's face, curse, scream, batter the thing to a pulp with his fists. Instead, Wendel threw him aside like a child's discarded toy to splatter in the freezing mud and horse shit half a dozen paces away.

As he lay, winded, hot fire fizzing up and down his withered arm, the demon scooped up his father's sabre and tossed it into the air. It sailed spinning over his head to land somewhere close to the first dark building back along the path.

"If you can live with that thirst o' yours, go, Ulrich, me boy. If you take a step forward when you stand up," he opened his hands, "be prepared to take a knee or die."

The demon's face became Iskra's again.

Then he turned back to the gate and began lifting the bar without waiting for an answer.

He scrambled up, trying to push Wendel's taunts away. He only thirsted for the demon's head at his feet. He turned and ran to his father's sword.

I do not want that... I do not... I do not...

He had not cut Solace's rope as she escaped The Wolf's Tower when Saul offered him the chance to join the demons. He would not do it now. His life would be spent at his mistress' shoulder as she walked the Night's Road.

Nothing more, nothing less.

The familiar grip of his father's sword provided a brief comfort, but by the time he'd retrieved it and span around to face the demon again... Wendel was gone, and the gates hung open.

And through it Imperial soldiers poured.

*

"You should go to your rooms," Lebrecht didn't look at her.

"You'll find I struggle doing what I'm told. I often drove my father to distraction..."

In fact, the last time I ever saw him, he slapped my face...

Her eyes dropped to her feet.

The memory hurt her far more than Father's hand had atop The Wolf's Tower that dreadful night.

"'tis no place for a woman."

"I am no ordinary woman..." she pulled back her cloak to reveal the long dagger hanging from her belt. It still felt more comfortable at her side than it did in her hand, but Morlaine, Lucien and Renard had all been teaching her how to use it with differing degrees of unenthusiasm. She'd improved, but a hundred men-at-arms were a lot more valuable than a single blade.

Did wearing it make seducing a man harder? Possibly. But pretty dresses and artfully teased hair were useless to a woman travelling the Night's Road.

Lebrecht looked like he would say something but thought better of it.

Their footsteps echoed along the corridor. It was close to

the witching hour, she suspected, and most of Ettestein's inhabitants had been in their beds for hours. They encountered no one enroute to the nearest barrack rooms. There were several in the castle housing the *Markgräf's* men. Who might soon be *her* men too.

"What is this about, my lady?" Lebrecht asked as they turned into another empty, dim corridor.

"Our demon is still here. And is causing mischief."

"We have found no trace of any... demon."

"Your father believes me. That is all you need to concern yourself with."

"Father is not a man to... believe anything lightly."

"All the more reason to do as he says then." When the young nobleman said nothing, she added, "Your brother fears I have cast some spell over the *Markgräf*. Do you harbour similar notions?"

Lebrecht snorted a laugh, "All beautiful women are capable of casting spells, my lady; 'tis not witchcraft!"

She glanced at him out of the corner of her eye.

He thinks me beautiful?

Such words from a handsome young prince would once have caused... *fluttering.* Now...

Before she could acknowledge the fact that, in some deep, locked away part of her, they still might, they arrived at a heavy, iron-studded door.

"We are here," he said, pushing open the door, "perhaps it best you wait outside while I make myself unpopular with my men."

"I don't care about popularity."

"Their language might be... unsuitable. Soldiers are a

254

coarse bunch."

She smiled at that, "I grew up surrounded by soldiers, my lord. I'm sure yours don't know any different curses from mine."

"You are a difficult woman to dissuade..." his smile was soft as he looked back at her, door half open.

"I believe stubborn is the word you are struggling for, my lord."

"Yes, yes..." Lebrecht nodded, "...that does seem the most appropriate one."

Inside, the barrack room was a black vault.

Lebrecht reached out and plucked a lantern from its hook in the wall.

"C'mon, lads, as much as you need your beauty sleep, I want you-"

She nearly ploughed into his back as the young *Markgräf* pulled up short.

He swept the lantern before them, illuminating a dozen narrow beds against each wall.

None of the huddled forms moved.

"What-" she began.

Then she saw the blood.

Lebrecht hurried to the nearest bed. She followed. A man lay there. Throat slashed open; eyes sightlessly fixed upon the shadowy ceiling.

"Dear God... how?" Lebrecht moved from bed to bed. In the lantern's swaying light, they found every man the same.

"Wendel," she said through the hand pressed against her mouth, still standing at the foot of the first bed.

His eyes met hers, face as pale as the dead men

surrounding them.

A table stood at the back of the room with half a dozen chairs around it. A man sat slumped face down on the table; as Lebrecht came closer, the lantern light revealed another sprawled on the floor.

She hurried after the nobleman to remain within the circle of light.

Several pitchers and numerous cups littered the table.

She picked one up and sniffed. It smelt only of wine.

"A sleeping draught?" she raised her eyes to his, "They would not have all slept otherwise while..."

Lebrecht took the cup from her and smelt it too.

"How?"

"Wendel can steal any man's face. He must have gone into the kitchens and laced the wine..." she shook her head "...we should not have allowed people back into the castle..."

"That was our decision, not yours," Lebrecht threw the cup to the floor. He stood, panting, breath steaming around him, before kicking one of the chairs over.

"Why would this demon do such a thing? Some dark amusement, some-"

"So there are less men to fight..." she said. It seemed obvious to her, but she knew the nature of the Red Company.

He stared at her, the lantern light dancing in time to the tremor in his hand.

"This was never about me..." the dread stone inside her roiled, pushing against her senses even more forcefully than the surrounding shadows filled with the dead.

"Then-"

"I fear your cousin's ambition is far greater and darker than your father feared, my lord."

Lebrecht span away for the door, "Come, he could not have killed all of the garrison, we must-"

He stopped in the doorway.

When she joined him, she heard the distant toll of a bell too.

"The alarm..." he said, already running down the corridor "...the castle is under attack!"

.

Chapter Nine

Come, Ulrich! At them!

Poor, brave Vinzenz's doomed last words echoed around the back of his mind as the soldiers rushed towards him. They wore the colours of the Empire rather than the Red Company's, but, for a moment, he was returned to the courtyard of The Wolf's Tower as the demons and their minions poured out of the smoking Darkway upon a wave of slaughter.

Vinzenz had charged the enemy; he'd defended the breach. And he'd been cut down in seconds.

And here he was again.

Facing overwhelming odds as an enemy surged through a breach.

One of the Imperial soldiers spotted him and fired a crossbow.

The bolt whizzed past his ear.

He remained rooted to the spot, the insane urge to charge the attacker coursing through him. It wasn't a breach he could possibly hold. It would be suicide, but his legs nearly took him forward.

Did he want to die?

Of course not.

Saul sees the darkness in you...

Another bolt thudded into the mud next to him.

He turned and ran. Ignoring the thoughts and fears

struggling within. This was not the time for reflection!

His first instinct was to sprint back along the track to Ettestein Castle. If he could make the gates, he could bar them and protect those inside the main castle from the Imperial soldiers.

Never leave a gate unlocked or unguarded.

Old Man Ulrich's familiar voice slurred in his ear.

He knew that well enough, yet he'd done it anyway and chosen to pursue Wendel. If he'd secured the castle and raised the alarm...

This really *isn't the time for reflection!*

But he'd never make the gate. It was too far, and they were too many. They didn't want to use firearms, but they had crossbows. They couldn't all be such poor shots.

Instead, he scrambled up the incline towards the nearby buildings lining the track.

No voices called out, though another bolt slammed into the wood as he ducked between two cottages.

They want to keep quiet. They know the castle is open and unguarded. They can deal with whoever is in the village after securing the fortress.

He hunkered out of the crescent moon's thin light in deep shadow.

No soldiers pursued him.

He'd made a mistake. A bad one. And people were likely going to die because of it. He was a fool as well as a dishonourable coward.

If nobody else discovered the castle was open the Imperials would seize Ettestein. Perhaps they would act honourably and take prisoners where possible. But this war was a brutal one. Atrocities had been committed by both sides and after twelve years, many held the kind of grudges that could only be salved by blood.

He turned and scurried deeper into the castle's village. He couldn't reach the fortress before the Imperials but could still raise the alarm to warn those inside.

Which, he realised with a sick twist of the stomach, included his mistress.

The church stood taller than any other building along the track. Its wooden tower stark against the scattered stars.

He hurried as best he could, stumbling several times in the mud and the strewn clutter disguised by the night's cloak. Snatches of voices broke the silence as he passed by; a few lights burned dimly in the cottages, the commotion waking souls from their slumbers. A door opened.

"What's happening?" a gruff voice demanded from a doorway.

"The castle is under attack! Arm yourselves," he spat back without pausing.

The door slamming shut was the only reply.

He found the church and burst inside; two candles lit the pulpit. He locked the doors behind him and hurried through the aisle of empty pews.

A curtain hung in the doorway beyond the pulpit. He swept it aside after snatching one of the candles.

A single rope hung in the simple room.

Placing the candle on the floor, he sheathed his father's sword, then wrapped the rope around the wrist of his good arm and pulled as hard as he could.

The bell in the wooden tower above began to ring.

He could do no more.

The thoughts he had pushed aside earlier rushed back.

Why?

Saul sees the darkness in you...

More lies.

If Torben thought his future lay with the demons of the Red Company, then perhaps Solace's brother was not the tool Saul thought.

But why had he chased Wendel and left the castle open?

To kill the demon. To save lives.

But how could he have hoped to kill that monster?

He would have saved more lives locking Ettestein's doors against the invaders.

No, that wasn't true. The village was full of women and children. The old and the helpless. He was trying to save them. To atone for leaving the women and children of Tassau to Saul's satanic feast.

Not because he wanted to-

"What the blazes do you think you are doing?!"

Eyes he hadn't realised he'd closed snapped open.

An elderly man with unruly white hair stood in the doorway, wearing a nightshirt and a blanket around his shoulders.

"Who are you?"

"I'm Pastor Wilhelm; who the hell are *you?* And why are you ringing my bell in the middle of the night? Are you drunk, man?" Wilhelm scurried across and tried to seize the rope.

"The castle is under attack!"

"What?"

"The Imperials have come through the gate. We must warn the castle!"

Wilhelm blinked. The Pastor's gnarled hand on the rope did nothing to stop him.

"How?"

"Treachery!"

"But…" Wilhelm spluttered, "…'tis Christmas!"

"The Emperor's men don't appear to have consulted their calendar, and if they did…" he shouted over the wildly clamouring bell, "…the gifts they bear are dark ones!"

Pastor Wilhelm's mostly toothless mouth hung open.

"Here…" he pressed the rope into the old man's hand "…keep ringing it."

"But-"

"Keep fucking ringing it!" he snarled.

The old man jumped but began pulling.

He yanked out his spent pistol and reloaded it, a fumbly business when you only had one hand that did what it should. And even more so when it shook.

Saul sees the darkness in you…

He concentrated on the pistol.

Above the bell's toll, fists pounding on wood started echoing through the church.

"What's that?" Wilhelm might be old, but nothing wrong with his hearing.

"Visitors…" he stuck his head through the curtain. As far as he could see in the gloom, the door held well enough for now.

"You locked the doors?" Wilhelm asked when he looked back.

"Of course I locked the doors."

"But the doors of the house of God are always open!"

"Then why put a lock on the door?"

Wilhelm blinked a couple of times as if trying to focus. He'd eased up on the rope too.

"Ring that bloody bell loud enough to wake the dead..." he grabbed the rope above Wilhelm's liver-spotted hands to show the old man how, "...loud enough so God might notice I've had to lock the door to one of his houses!"

"There's no need for blasphemy, young man."

He glared at the pastor but said nothing. He needed all the help he could get. The man might be old, but at least he had two good hands, and between them, they set the bell ringing frenetically.

Wilhelm's eyes drifted back to the curtained door, "What if they are my flock seeking sanctuary?"

"Unlikely."

"Why?"

"Just call me a pessimist."

Wilhelm's hands slipped from the rope, "I will go and see," he panted, wiping a hand across his already glistening forehead.

"No!" he shoved the rope back at the Pastor, "Keep ringing it; we need to warn the castle. I'll check."

"But how will you know if they are friends or enemies? You're a stranger here?"

"'tis simple, Pastor. The locals will not be trying to kill me... or you."

"Oh..."

"How many ways are there into the church?"

"Just the front doors."

The windows were set high to let in light, too far above the height of a man to offer easy access. Only one point to defend. And no other way out.

"Only stop ringing that bell if you're dead!" he almost screamed in the old man's face. Wilhelm flinched and nodded.

Bullying a defenceless old man was not honourable. Bullying a pastor wasn't wise either; they tended to have friends both in this world and the next, but the bell had to keep ringing.

Would the Imperials be at the castle gates yet? Probably, unless they had run into more resistance, but they had to keep sounding the alarm.

He pushed the curtain aside and headed into the church, lit now by only the single candle on the pulpit.

Ahead, the door rattled and shook. Shouts and curses came from the other side; they didn't sound much like the helpless and innocent seeking sanctuary.

He moved to the door. A single wooden bar locked it. Sturdy, but by no means unbreakable.

"Open the door! In the name of Emperor Ferdinand, open this fucking door!"

It started shaking more forcibly. The crack of breaking wood began competing with the bell.

He dragged a pew over and propped it against the door. Then another.

It didn't sound like there were too many. A small group spared from the main attack to silence the bell. Still, he had only one pistol shot and one good arm.

Above the tower, the bell wasn't ringing as loudly.

And one tiring old man in his nightshirt.

Still, he'd die cleanly in the fight, but the pastor might well end up on the pyre and burnt as a heretic.

He grinned to himself as he dragged another pew over.

Always better to think on the bright side.

The bar bulged inwards, wood splintering.

Ignoring the protests from his bad arm, he dumped the latest pew against the others and stepped back, panting.

They would be inside soon.

The door shook again, accompanied by a crack as the bar snapped.

Very soon.

*

"Where are we going?" she called after Lebrecht.

"I'm going to the gates; you're returning to your rooms."

"No, I'm not."

He skidded to a halt before a stairwell.

"I can't keep you safe down-"

"I don't need you to keep me safe."

She came forward and raised her chin. Challenging him in a way most women wouldn't dream of. But, of course, she wasn't most women anymore.

"My lady…"

She swept back her cloak to show him the blade at her side.

"I can look after myself."

"A battle is no place for a woman. Go to your rooms."

"No."

He blinked.

He *really* wasn't used to this.

"I haven't got time to argue with-"

"Then don't, my lord. Either throw me over your shoulder and take me back to my rooms kicking and screaming, or I come with you," another step forward, another rise of the chin, "which is it to be?"

"Fine. Be it on your own head. The things men do in battle... 'tis not just killing... 'tis..."

She laid a hand on his chest and pushed him gently towards the stairs, "I know what men are capable of, my lord; I know exceedingly well..."

He shook his head and ran down the stairs.

She followed.

"Why?" he asked, not looking over his shoulder, "Why come with me?"

"This is a demon's doing. And I want that demon's head. Preferably after he's told me where I can find the rest of his foul company. Then I can take all their heads too."

Lebrecht laughed.

"What's so funny?"

"Very little, my lady. 'tis just that I hope I never have cause to upset you."

"'tis generally... inadvisable," she agreed.

"I-"

The sound of gunfire and screams cut off his next words.

"Dear God," Lebrecht came to a halt, "They're in the castle!"

"Then best we be rid of them quickly," she said. Her voice was firm and strong, but what hid underneath wasn't. She was running into a battle.

"My lady..." Lebrecht pleaded again, as he drew his sword.

"I've burned men alive. I've blown men to smithereens. I've killed demons. One with a knitting needle through the eye. I know what I am doing."

She slid her blade free and grinned at him. Lucien grinned a lot; something she assumed soldiers did to mask their fear.

He shook his head and hurried on.

"This way," he said when they got to the next floor, "tis quicker to cut down here to the north stairs; they will bring us to the First Hall."

Lebrecht led her down a corridor of unadorned stone walls.

More bells rung out the alarm. These ones inside the castle. Wendel hadn't killed everyone.

They had almost reached the door at the far end of the corridor when three men burst out of it.

All wearing Imperial livery.

Lebrecht threw himself at them without hesitation.

The first he caught by surprise, flashing blade opening the man's throat. Blood arced over the wall as he staggered back into his companions.

"Run!" Lebrecht screamed.

She assumed he was talking to the Imperial soldiers, so raised her blade. It was a duelling dagger, similar to the one she'd lost in Madriel. Light enough for her to wield and wickedly sharp, thanks to Morlaine's whetstone, but she'd have to get close to use it.

As the dying man folded to the floor, the other two stepped

over him, pushing Lebrecht backwards.

The Imperials were swordsmen, and both knew their weapons. They didn't perceive a young woman, even one holding a long dagger, as much of a threat. They were both ignoring her too.

More fool them.

As they continued to push Lebrecht back along the corridor, frantically parrying and dodging blows from his two assailants, she grabbed a tar torch from its black iron cradle.

She rushed in. Ducking under Lebrecht's backswing before thrusting the torch into the nearest soldier's face.

Screaming, he staggered away, swatting the flames from his face. He lost his footing and fell backwards. She threw herself forward. Flattening him. His head cracked against the stone floor. Dazed eyes in a red face tried to focus upon her.

She plunged the dagger into his throat.

Blood gurgled out of his mouth.

I've burned men alive. I've blown men to smithereens.

But she'd never looked into a man's eyes and watched him die.

There was fear, panic, incomprehension. The smell of piss mixed with the stink of blood over her hands. Other things too. Probably.

His eyes grew wider. He was trying to say something. But only blood came.

Should I say sorry...?

Should I offer a prayer...?

Behind her, steel crashed on steel. Someone else would

die very soon. She should make sure it wasn't Lebrecht. But she struggled to rip her eyes from the dying man's.

How easy it is...

The soldier's eyes bulged. Straining as if trying to escape the prison of their sockets. Perhaps it was his soul pushing to be free of the flesh. Bloody bubbles popped around his mouth. Then stilled. The eyes widened no more. The chest she found her knee pressed against stopped moving.

...to slice away a life.

Blood slickened her hand. She wiped it on the man's tunic. There were more pressing matters. But she found the dead man's stare hard to break. How different they looked without life behind them.

This was not a demon...

Unlike the men she'd killed in The Wolf's Tower, he didn't serve a demon either. She hadn't spared them a moment's thought. But this man, with his flat dead eyes. What wrong had he ever done her? Save stand in her way. Perhaps-

A cry dragged her away from the dead soldier's eyes.

Behind her, Lebrecht was on his knees, desperately parrying a series of savage blows from the Imperial soldier.

She rose smoothly, bloody dagger in her hand.

Lebrecht cried out; the soldier above him intent on hammering the young nobleman into the ground.

The soldier was a tall, powerfully built man.

But that wasn't going to stop her.

The Imperials wore stiffened leather jerkins riveted with iron beneath their tunics. No cuirass or chain, but still enough to take most of the force she could put into a dagger thrust.

So, she jumped onto his back and plunged the blade into his neck.

It worked well enough the first time.

The man screamed and staggered forward. Tripping over Lebrecht, all three ended up sprawling over the floor together.

She rolled away and sprang back to her feet. Whirling around, dagger ready to finish the Imperial soldier.

The man gagged, hand clamped to his neck as he tried to crawl away from Lebrecht. He slumped face down to the floor, twitching a few times before growing still. At least she didn't have to look into this one's eyes.

She checked the stairs over her shoulder, lowering the blade to her side when no more soldiers came through it.

Steel twitched against her leg. She gripped the fencing dagger tighter, but when that didn't do anything to stop her hand shaking, she focused her efforts on not vomiting.

Lebrecht pulled himself up onto one knee. Blood trickled down his cheek from a gash on his temple. She couldn't decide if the look on his face was one of awe or horror. Perhaps a little of both.

"Next time, save your breath for the fight, my lord. I do not run any more..." she said, offering a hand to help the young nobleman up, "...I only stand."

Chapter Ten

The door flew open, crashed into the pews he'd piled against them and bounced back.

Gruff curses shot through the gap.

He tried to count the voices.

Know thy enemy, son, always...

Old Man Ulrich had been a great believer in that. It was not knowing his own soul that had always been his father's problem.

He steadied and calmed himself.

Wait.

Be patient.

They'll come to kill you quick enough.

More good advice.

The pews screeched backwards as the men outside put their shoulders to the door.

How many do there need to be before I have no chance?

Four, he decided.

Probably.

Between gloom, obstacles and surprise, he could down three men.

A year ago, he could have killed more.

A year ago, he thought he could take on the world.

But a year ago, he'd been a fool.

Now he was a fool with only one good arm.

He smiled at that.

He was pretty sure there were more than four of them.

The smile faded.

He'd known his death was imminent from the moment they left The Wolf's Tower with Morlaine, but he'd expected to die at Solace's side. Why that might constitute a better death, he didn't know. But he'd stood shoulder to shoulder with his mistress, facing Saul and his demons as they burst into the library. He hadn't wanted to die, but such a fate would have at least reclaimed his honour. Some of it, anyway. Giving your life was the ultimate way of fulfilling your oath, of doing your duty. Like Sergeant Lutz had.

But this?

Cut to pieces alone in a church.

His duty was to be at his lady's side.

His life for hers. Who was he giving his life for here?

An old pastor with one foot in the grave already?

He could put down his weapons and offer surrender. Perhaps they would accept it. Perhaps not.

These were men, not demons. But in war, that distinction was not necessarily a great one.

The pews jerked backwards, and one toppled over.

Would they try squeezing through one at a time as soon as a big enough gap appeared? He could kill more than three of them if they were that stupid.

A gloved hand came around the door.

He stayed himself from stepping forward and taking the man's fingers with his father's sabre.

They didn't know who was in here.

Just an old pastor for all they knew. Put a sword through those fingers, and they'd have a much better idea. Be less rash. Less hasty. More dangerous.

Surprise, Ulrich, my lad! 'tis always the sharpest blade you can carry.

"Yes, Father..."

If he did surrender and they didn't kill him, would they give him to Wendel? Was Saul nearby, waiting for him to bend his knee and kiss his hand?

Perhaps.

Perhaps not.

He licked his lips.

Saul sees the darkness in you...

The bell tolled wearily.

It didn't matter. The Imperials would be at the castle gates by now. He'd done all he could to warn them.

His eyes rose to the windows. Too high for him to climb out of.

The door screamed; pews toppled. Men shouted.

Nobody was asking for surrender.

The Emperor saw this as a place of heresy and insurrection, not worship. Perhaps they wouldn't kill Pastor Wilhelm. Perhaps they would.

He shook his head.

I'm going to die for nothing.

Saul sees the darkness in you...

Well, perhaps not entirely.

The dead could give away their honour no more than they could their souls.

I could lay down my weapons...

The pews finally crashed aside, and the door flew open.

A soldier staggered off-balance through it.

But I'm not going to.

He raised his pistol and shot him.

The door opened to the right. He stood to the left. The Imperial soldier never saw him, swathed in shadow, before the pistol ball took him in the temple.

He dropped the pistol, as the man crumpled to the floor. His father's sabre hung from his weak left hand; stepping forward, he took a two-handed grip and hacked at the second man through the door. The soldier stumbled over the first, so the blow took him on the back of the shoulder rather than his head.

Still, the force was enough to send him to the floor.

Two more men crashed into the church, hurdling their prone comrades and scattered pews.

"Stop!" a voice cried, "this is a house of God!"

Nobody seemed much inclined to listen to Pastor Wilhelm.

Which was a pity.

He backed away from the corner to give himself more room to manoeuvre and swing his sword.

One of the soldiers came at him; he parried his blow and dodged away. His companion hung back a little. Prudence or cowardice?

Two more men followed them inside.

Fuck.

"Gonna put your head on a fucking spike!" one of the men, tall and hook-nosed, shouted.

It appeared surrender wasn't an option.

He barged into the first soldier, pushing him back into the others, then retreated along the aisle.

Two of them followed him; the other two went to each side,

vaulting over pews to get behind him.

None of them carried pistols. Which was something. You should never turn your nose up at a few more seconds of life.

Behind him, Wilhelm wailed, beseeching God to strike down the defilers of his church. He wasn't sure if Wilhelm included him amongst the defilers. Probably.

The hook-nosed soldier and another, who looked like he wasn't old enough to have started shaving, came towards him down the aisle, but neither seemed overly keen to come within striking distance. They were waiting for their friends to get behind him so they could rush him together and cut him to pieces.

His best and only chance was trying to make for the door. If he could get around them and outside...

The other two had passed him and hurtled down between the pews; once both were in the aisle behind him... well, everything would be over. Wilhelm implored them to stop between his calls for God's help.

He wasn't going to hold his breath.

He darted between two pews to his right.

"Fucker!" one of them roared; he didn't look back to see which one.

He ran as hard as he dared in the poor light; there wasn't much room between the pews, the seats on one side and the backs of the next pew on the other both brushed against his legs.

The soldier who had been making his way between the pews was heading back, but he was a barrely load of lard and couldn't squeeze between the pews without turning sideways.

Once he reached the wall, he spun around and heaved the pew with its back to his pursuers over.

The hook-nosed Imperial stumbled, and the lad behind ploughed into the back of him.

It wouldn't buy him much time, but every second was currently worth a fat bag of silver.

He ran along the wall back to the door.

The fourth Imperial sprinted back along the opposite wall. Sadly, he wasn't a barrely load of lard. That bugger was tall and lithe. Quick too.

If God intended to surprise him and intervene, a thunderbolt in that direction would do the most good. Despite Wilhelm's desperate pleas, however, none were forthcoming.

He would make it to the door first, but rather annoyingly, the soldier he'd hacked across the back hadn't had the good grace to die. Instead, he'd pulled himself to his feet, ashen face glistening with sickly sweat. As unsteady as he looked, he blocked the door along with the other debris.

The soldier raised his sword. There was no time to fight. The man's companions would be on him in seconds.

He put his shoulder down, hurdled one of the fallen pews and charged into him full tilt.

The Imperial more waved his sword at him than made a meaningful swing. Still, it hissed alarmingly over his head.

His shoulder slammed into the wounded man's midriff, and they flew into the night together, landing in the mud outside the church. The man, uninterested in continuing their fight, stayed where he was, moaning softly.

He managed to disentangle himself and jump cleanly to his feet, but the other soldiers were erupting out of the church, the tall, nippy fellow first.

A wild slash forced the man to swerve away, and he took the opportunity to run, but his boot slipped in the muck, and he went down hard on one knee.

A blade swept out of the night. He twisted and managed to block the blow, but only just. His whole arm juddered. The soldier was strong as well as fast.

The others poured around him. He didn't even know which shadowy form to lift his blade towards.

I'm dead...

Someone screamed.

He was surprised to find it wasn't him.

One of the soldiers, it was too dark to even tell which, flew through the air to slam into the side of the church.

A flash of silver.

Another scream.

Something wet splattered his face.

A body fell into the mud next to him.

Metal screeched against metal.

"What-" A truncated shout and a thud that sounded like flesh and bone hitting something much harder.

Then silence.

Save for a few groans.

He blinked.

He wasn't dead.

A figure emerged above him, dark against the star-strewn sky.

He lowered his blade.

"Thank you," he panted, "I was starting to think you'd forgotten about us."

Morlaine sheathed her sword, "I've been worried that you might have sold my horse..."

*

"They came up those stairs," she peered into the gloom, "we might run into more of them if we go this way."

"That shouldn't be a problem. You can kill them too."

She stared at him.

"I saved your life. I didn't do it to garner gratitude, but still..."

He flashed her a smile that was neither comfortable nor convincing.

How strange.

If she were a man, Lebrecht would likely have slapped her back and enthused about what a deadly fellow she was. But being a woman... why should that unsettle him so?

Of course, women were not supposed to go around killing men. It certainly wasn't anything she'd ever aspired to, but she found his reaction rather peculiar.

"After you," she said, opening a blood-smeared hand towards the stairs.

Right now, however, she had other matters to put her mind to.

And her blade.

Wendel.

The demon was still here. Whatever politicking, power games and greed between Gothen and the Empire, the *Markgräf* and his nephew drove this violence, the demon remained her primary concern.

Vengeance. Nothing else mattered.

She looked at the blood on her outstretched hand. Then dropped it. No matter. She'd cut the throats of a hundred men if it gave her a chance to take the head of one of the monsters who'd destroyed her life.

Lebrecht headed down the stairs, she followed. The sound of fighting grew louder. Whatever foul deeds Wendel had committed, he clearly hadn't been able to kill the entire garrison in their beds.

It was an old castle, like The Wolf's Tower, built before gunpowder changed how men fought. The staircases and corridors were narrow and designed to be defended against invaders.

It made her think of home.

It made her think of how her home died.

What if it wasn't just Wendel here? What if the whole Red Company were inside? What if they reached the bottom of these stairs and found Saul and the rest feasting?

Footsteps echoing up the steps wrenched her thoughts back.

Lebrecht stopped. Sword ready, knees bent, free hand outstretched to keep her behind him. To protect her.

How quaint.

She readied herself too.

The footsteps came fast. Just one man. And given the laboured breathing that accompanied them, it certainly was just a man.

A figure hurtled around the corner. And pulled up sharp.

"My lady!" Lucien gasped.

She brushed past Lebrecht.

"What's happening down there?"

"A bit of a scrap," Lucien found one of his familiar grins.

Blood splattered his face and coat. None of it seemed to be his.

"What's happening?!" Lebrecht repeated the question.

Lucien sagged against the wall and sucked in a breath, "The Imperials are through the Gate House and into the First Hall, but they're being held there. I don't know how they got in-"

"Wendel," she said.

"Fuck..." Lucien wiped a hand over his flushed face, smearing blood across it.

"How goes the fight?" Lebrecht asked, eyes fixed down the stairs.

"Hard. Would have been harder if someone hadn't started ringing the church bell. A few men got to the gates just as the first Imperials turned up. Couldn't stop them but slowed them enough until more Gothen men arrived. Now..." he shrugged, "...no one is giving quarter."

"Then why are you running away?" Lebrecht demanded.

The mercenary stiffened, "Lucien Kazmierczak never runs away."

"Why-"

"I saw three Imperials make the stairs. I went after them," he glanced at her, "my first duty is to Lady Solace, not Gothen."

"No more made it?" she asked.

"They were forced back."

Her eyes moved to Lebrecht, "Why?"

"Why?"

"Why leave the fight? Why send men deeper without securing the entrance? If they are pushed out of the castle, 'tis over, isn't it?"

Lebrecht nodded.

"Up to mischief," Lucien growled.

"Not any more," she showed him her bloody hand.

The mercenary raised an eyebrow. He looked a lot more impressed than Lebrecht had.

The young nobleman's eyes turned back up the stairs, "The soldiers your demon killed, they were the Household Guard, my father's personal troop..."

"Those three were going after your father?"

"The demon killed the Household Guard?"

She and Lucien asked the questions over each other.

"Why didn't the demon just kill my father? Easier to kill one man than a dozen?"

"Your cousin wants the *Markgräf* alive..."

Lucien nodded, "Your father dies, then you become *Markgräf*. And the fight continues. Your father falls prisoner... he can order your men to lay down their arms. He could be persuaded to name Gottlieb his rightful heir."

"My father would never agree to that!"

Lucien conjured a dark smile, "All men break, my lord, given enough time and pain..."

"And no more men made the stairs?"

"Not that I saw... though I confess I was a bit occupied."

Indecision played across Lebrecht's face.

"Will your father stay in his chambers?" she asked.

"No. He will come to the fight."

"Then best you wait for him there… Gothen needs every sword it has in that fight, my lord…"

"But…"

"We cannot always protect the ones we love…" she whispered, seeing her own father storming away over the roof of The Wolf's Tower's barbican. She resisted the urge to touch the cheek he'd slapped.

It was never going to stop stinging after all.

Lebrecht nodded.

"My brother?

"In the thick of the fighting."

He nodded again, then started down the stairs, "As I should be."

"Renard?" she asked Lucien.

"I haven't seen him. When the church bell rung, I headed for the castle entrance. I was one of the first to arrive…"

She touched his arm and then turned to follow Lebrecht.

"My lady, 'tis a charnel house. You should-"

Lebrecht called back before disappearing around the curve of the stairwell.

"You try stopping her…"

Chapter Eleven

"Dear God in heaven..."

Pastor Wilhelm peered out of the church doorway, shielding a candle against the breeze with a bony hand. His eyes took in the scattered bodies.

"This man..." Morlaine said, nodding at him, "...is one of the most feared swordsmen in the Empire..."

Whatever else you could say about the demon, he had to admit she was very good at keeping a straight face.

"God be with you, my son," Wilhelm said. Then slammed the door shut in their faces.

"This seems an opportune time to leave," she said, moving to his side, "where are your companions?"

"In the castle," he said, nodding towards Ettestein, "the one currently under attack."

"Unfortunate," the vampire sniffed.

One of the Imperial soldiers began to climb onto all fours.

He kicked the man's sword out of reach, "Best you stay where you are for now, friend..."

The soldier turned groggy eyes upwards. Then collapsed back into the mud.

He looked at Morlaine, "Should we finish them?"

"No, keep watch," she said.

The demon crouched over each of the men in turn; it was too dark to see what why, so he concentrated on looking for more Imperial soldiers. None appeared.

"Two are dead," she said, the words flat and slow.

"And the others?"

"Will live…" she span away, "…come, we'll find Solace and Lucien, then return to the road. We've wasted enough time already."

"Wendel is here."

She stopped. Sharply.

"Tell me."

He told her what he knew as they walked to the stables; occasionally, she took his elbow to guide him around some unseen obstacle in the deep shadows. They saw nobody else. The rest of the Imperial force had other priorities, and the servants and refugees living outside the main fortress kept their doors locked.

When they reached the stables, he put his back against the wall as he finished explaining what had happened since they parted.

"Do you think he's still here?"

"It wasn't that long ago he opened the gates for the Imperials. He could have left, his work done. He could still be here. It depends on the terms of his employment," when Morlaine stared at him, he shrugged, "I don't think he is doing this as a favour for Emperor Ferdinand."

"And the rest of them?"

"I've seen only Wendel. He said he was on his own, but…"

"Vampires lie," Morlaine finished for him.

"You saw nothing?"

She shook her head, "No, only the Imperial encampment. If Saul was close, I would know."

"Something, at least…" he ran a hand over his face. He

wanted to curl up and sleep. God, he was a shell of a man. In more ways than one, "What do we do?"

"Find Wendel and kill him."

She made it sound simple.

The castle, stark against the stars atop its rocky crag, pulled his eyes.

"Solace is in there."

"Wendel is more important."

"Not to me."

"If we don't kill Wendel tonight because we try to save Solace instead, then every life he takes will be because of us. I have enough bodies on my conscience already."

"So do I," he levered himself away from the wall; the sounds of fighting drifted through the night. It wasn't coming from the castle, "You must know as well as I what can happen to women when a battle finishes and the slaughter begins."

Morlaine's eyes glistened in the shadows. But she said nothing.

Something flashed and cracked in the darkness. A musket or pistol. Up on the walls. Some of the *Markgräf's* soldiers still resisted outside the castle. He supposed Wendel only killed the ones near the Gate Towers. Others would have been patrolling the rest of the outer walls.

"My purpose here is not to rescue Solace."

"You rescued me."

"I wasn't prepared to let you die. There's a difference."

"I'm sorry I put you to the inconvenience."

He started walking towards the castle.

"Ulrich!"

Morlaine moved in front of him.

When he tried to brush past her, she seized both his shoulders, fingers digging into his flesh hard enough to make him wince.

"What do you think you can achieve in there?"

"Save my lady's life. 'tis worth considerably more than mine."

"One sword will make no difference to a battle."

The evidence of fighting punctuated the night; a shout, a scream, a musket's retort, the hard sound of steel connecting with steel, the softer sound of steel connecting with flesh. But the castle was too far away for such sounds to escape its innards.

They might be getting the Christmas feast going early, for all he knew.

"How can you tell there's fighting in the castle? Someone might have closed the-"

She cocked her head, "I can hear the screams, Ulrich."

He bit his lip, "And Lady Solace?"

"She is alive. So is Lucien."

Of course, they had both shared blood with the demon, one way or another, so their souls were joined, or defiled, or... whatever damn way Morlaine wanted to explain it.

"Then there is still time to-"

"There is an easier way to end a battle and stop the killing than wading into the middle of it."

His forehead crumpled, "There is?"

She dropped her hands and turned in the opposite direction, where the sounds of men dying were loudest.

After a couple of paces, she looked over her shoulder.

"Come with me, and I'll show you..."

*

She thought she had witnessed Hell before.

Perhaps if she'd seen what became of her father and the women and children of Tassau at Saul's hands, she would have no doubt.

But the First Hall of Ettestein Castle was worse than anything she'd seen in The Wolf's Tower with her own eyes.

A narrow corridor led from the Gate House to the First Hall. Anyone entering Ettestein had to come this way. Its secondary purpose was to greet visitors, do business, receive submissions, pleas and appeals from the lord's subjects, resolve disputes, swap information, enjoy refreshment.

Its primary purpose, however, was a place to kill people.

Gunsmoke choked the air, hanging about the rafters and around the burning candles and lanterns.

Blood washed the flagstone floor, worn smooth by centuries of passing feet. Corpses, like broken islands in a bloody sea, littered the length and breadth of the room. Many in a line across the middle of the First Hall, which seemed to mark the high-water line of the Imperial penetration of the fortress. Screams swirled about them. Screams of agony, terror, anger, hatred.

The acrid bite of smoke mixed with the animal stinks of blood, excrement and urine. It only lacked a pinch or two of brimstone.

A weeping man dragged himself across the floor, leaving a dark crimson wake behind him. Along with the entrails spilling from his stomach.

A musket shot chipped splinters from the column next to her head.

She ducked back down.

Better the shooter had aimed at the poor soul smearing his guts over the flagstones than her.

A gallery overlooked the First Hall, providing a platform for defenders to rain missiles down on any invader. Two staircases led off the First Hall, but neither provided a direct route up to the galleries, so they were in no imminent danger of being overrun by the Imperials. Just shot with muskets and crossbows.

Below, both sides had retreated to the mouths of the corridors leading into the north and south ends of the First Hall to regroup, peppering each other with missile fire.

Joachim led the defenders in the hall; Lebrecht kept trying to signal him to send more men up to the gallery to fire on the Imperials. His brother largely ignored him.

"Send too many men up here, and he risks being overrun by the Imperials if they grow enough balls to try and rush him," Lucien explained.

"Send too few and we can't pin them down," Lebrecht added, rolling to put his back against one of the thick stone columns.

Most of the Gothen men bunched in and around the south corridor door, some barricaded behind overturned furniture; a dozen or so musketeers were up in the gallery with them.

"How many men do you have?" she asked, risking a quick peek down through the swirling smoke. At least thirty corpses littered the First Hall.

"Not as many as we should," Lebrecht spat.

One of the Gothen soldiers scurried over to them.

"My lord," the man, young and skittish, handed a bulky wheellock pistol to Lebrecht, followed by bags of shot and powder.

"Go to my brother, tell him we must scour the castle for every able-bodied man we can find. Men-at-arms, cooks, servants, stable boys, everybody. We can hold the invader, but we need to push them out. Understand?"

The young soldier nodded.

"Tell him to spare who he can to gather men. And tell him we need another dozen men in the gallery with muskets and pistols to keep them pinned while we muster our force."

"Yes, my lord."

"And tell him to send men to our father. The Household Guard are dead, and he needs protecting."

The young soldier's eyes widened, but he nodded his understanding and hurried off to deliver Lebrecht's message.

"Keep firing!" Lebrecht yelled at the other men in the gallery as he started to load the wheellock.

A waist-high wall ran between the columns of the gallery. Musketeers loaded their weapons behind the wall and columns before jumping up to fire on the attackers.

"Keep moving, idiot!" Lucien barked at the nearest musketeer when a crossbow bolt whizzed past the soldier's ear before he pulled his weapon's trigger, "If you keep firing from the same position, they will notice and be ready for you!"

"What would you do if you were the Imperial captain?" she asked Lucien.

"Charge," he said, without hesitation, "the longer they stay where they are, the harder it'll be for them. A battle's about momentum. When Joachim pushed them back into the corridor, they lost it. They need to regain it, or they'll bleed to death down there."

"And we need to do the same," Lebrecht added after swinging around the column he sheltered behind to fire his newly acquired pistol.

"Else we're all going to have a long and uncomfortable Christmas…" Lucien said before bobbing up over the wall to fire his.

He cursed under his breath as he came back down.

"Missed."

Another shot took plasterwork off the column. How quickly one became accustomed to people trying to kill you…

A scream ripped through the smoke, terror and torment echoing to the high rafters.

Or perhaps not.

"We must find Wendel…" she said in a lower voice, leaning towards Lucien.

The mercenary raised his eyes from reloading his pistol, "Where should we start looking, my lady?"

She pursed her lips. Wendel was still here. She knew it. Her *sight* whispered the fact silently; Flyblown's mark agreed with warm, smarting tingles.

But where?

Neither *sight* nor mark told her.

She'd insisted she accompanied Lebrecht; now she had, she was far more trapped than she'd been if she'd returned to her rooms.

One of the Gothen musketeers screamed. A crossbow bolt had met his chest as he'd risen to fire.

Lucien glanced up from his pistol.

"Told him to keep moving..."

She scurried over to the musketeer, careful to keep her head below the wall.

The bolt had taken him in the right side of his chest, punching him from his feet. Confused eyes rolled in their sockets.

"Mamma..." blood accompanied the words.

Was there something she could do?

She looked over her shoulder.

Lucien was watching her. He shook his head.

She found the musketeer's hand. He was young, no older than her. The hair covering his chin no more than blonde downy fluff, now darkened by the blood dribbling from his mouth.

Lifting his hand, she enclosed it with both of hers.

He tried to speak, but nothing escaped his lips save blood, gurgles, bubbles and drool.

"Ssshh..."

Morlaine could heal the soldier with a few drops of her blood. But she didn't know where the vampire was, and the young man's soul would soon join all the other dead men of Gothen and the Empire.

She lifted his head onto her lap and stroked his hair while

squeezing his cold hand.

"What is your name? I will pray for you..."

He tried to say something. She leaned in closer but caught nothing understandable. When she straightened up, his eyes stared sightlessly beyond her.

"His name was Polke..." Lebrecht reached past her to close the musketeer's eyes.

"He asked for his mother..."

"He is with her now."

Something thickened in her throat. She looked away. Curls of smoke, or perhaps the souls of the dead, drifted above the wall to gather around oak rafters.

Lebrecht unwrapped her fingers from Polke's.

"You should not be here, my lady."

His hands, she noticed, lingered atop hers.

Her eyes snapped up.

"None of us should be here. But powerful men must play their little games. They must have their heart's desire, whatever the cost..."

She lowered Polke's head to the ground, stroked his hair... then reached over and scooped up his musket.

"My lady?"

"I know how to use one of these too."

Father had taught her. Several lifetimes ago.

She tugged off the bandolier containing Polke's powder and shot, then crawled along the wall. Lucien's advice was sound. Best not to linger in any one place.

Lebrecht scurried after her.

Polke died before firing the musket, so it was still loaded. Long, heavy and cumbersome, it wasn't easy to use, but accurate to around a hundred paces if you knew what you were doing. And it made a satisfying noise. Which might at least drown out the screaming in her head.

Another death to chalk up to the Red Company.

Men might be fighting men here, but they would have stone walls between them if Wendel hadn't intervened. For silver, for power, for a fool's greed.

Killing Saul and his demons would not rid the world of evil... but it would save countless lives.

"My lady!" Lebrecht hissed in alarm as she stood behind a column, musket held before her.

She ignored him. Counted to three, rolled around the column, raising the musket.

It was a snaphance flintlock, an improvement on the wheellock more commonly used in the Empire. Polke had pulled the hammer back. All she needed to do was find someone she wanted to kill and pull the trigger.

A barricade of upended furniture blocked the mouth of the north corridor leading to the Gate House; barrels had appeared too. Through the swirling smoke, men with muskets and crossbows huddled behind them. More figures lurked in the dark corridor behind.

Heart pounding, she found a crossbowman reloading his weapon, crouching, half turned away from her and not fully protected by cover. He was being careless. Was he the man who'd killed Polke?

She hoped so and pulled the trigger.

The hammer sprung forward to hit the steel. White sparks flew, the powder ignited, the gun barked and coughed smoke.

She rolled back behind the column without waiting to see if she hit anyone.

Lebrecht crouched at her feet, scowling as deeply as any disapproving scold.

She flashed a smile.

"See, I do know what I am doing..."

Someone screamed in alarm. She didn't pay it much heed as screams echoed all around the First Hall.

Then the world roared, shook and went white.

.

Chapter Twelve

"Oh, there's one other thing."

"Yes?"

"Lady Solace intends to marry the *Markgräf* of Gothen, so he will give her an army to fight the Red Company..." when Morlaine stared at him without reply or expression, he added, "...don't worry, I'm sure you are invited."

"That would not be my primary concern..."

He flashed her a grin and went back to waiting. He didn't know what he was waiting for any more than what he was grinning at. The demon was being cryptic about what she planned. Probably for the best. If he did know, he wouldn't like it and get upset.

Strangely, the urge to laugh bubbled up inside him.

Perhaps it was something to do with expecting to die only to discover God still had a use for you. He felt rather light-headed. Cheerful, even.

As far as he remembered, the last time he'd felt cheerful was a particularly drunken night shortly before The Wolf's Tower fell.

Then he thought of sitting beside Madleen, sharing a blanket on a freezing night in Madriel's Market Square.

"What are we waiting for?" he asked, the cheerfulness fading as quickly as it had arisen.

"The right moment."

Cryptic. Still.

They crouched in deep shadow between two wooden cottages near the Gate Towers. Mud sucked at his boots and the back of his thighs burnt. The rest of him shivered.

He felt Morlaine's eyes turn on him whenever he fidgeted. He tried not to fidget.

The sounds of fighting had faded. Either the Imperials had mopped up all resistance from the Gothen men, or the *Markgräf's* troops were rallying for a more organised attempt to retake the Gate Towers. Or perhaps all the fighting had moved into the main castle.

"You know, you can let me in on your plan. I won't tell anyone..." when the demon stayed silent, he slashed a finger back and forth across his heart, "...promise."

"Be quiet. I'm listening..."

He could hear nothing. He doubted the village inhabitants had all slept through the attack, but they were staying out of sight. No lights burned, no doors opened. Waiting until morning to find out if they had a new master. And hoping no one kicked in their door to murder, rape and steal before then.

Morlaine reached out and rested a hand on his arm.

Still yourself.

He even held his breath.

The sound of boots slapping through mud came out of the darkness.

Running feet, heading to the castle. He didn't look until after they passed. Morlaine pressed a finger against her lips.

When she rose, he did the same. Though with less grace and more grunting.

"Well…?"

"They have sent more men to the castle; they must be confident they have control here now."

"Why is that good?"

"There will be fewer men guarding their lord."

"Gottlieb?"

"Yes, you said he was the *Markgräf's* nephew?"

He nodded, "*Freiherr* Geiss."

"And Wendel's employer?"

"Wendel said a fat fool was paying him because he wanted a bigger chair for his fat arse. Something like that. I took it that was who he meant."

"Then we shall take him, and he will call off the assault."

He frowned, "How do you know he is in the Gate Towers?"

"The kind of man who hires vampires to do his dirty work will not be leading an army from the front."

He conceded the point with a shrug, "And how will we persuade him to do as we ask?"

"Leave that to me."

He was content to leave everything to her, though that was hardly an honourable thought, even if she wasn't really a woman. She had saved his life. Just as she had Solace's in Madriel. The longer they spent in the demon's company, the greater their debt to her grew. A realisation he found unsettling.

She moved by him, summoning him to follow with a flick of her hand.

The demon's sword stayed sheathed, but he kept hold of his.

They crept along the back of the buildings, past humble

cottages, then a barn, followed by a few more cottages. The ones he had fled between after Wendel opened the gates for the Imperials.

They crouched at the corner of the last one. It was maybe thirty paces from the towers.

The gates remained open; four soldiers stood around a brazier, a couple leaning on pikes, the others cradling muskets. Lights burned inside the right of the two towers flanking the gates. If Morlaine was right, Gottlieb would be there, awaiting news that his men had seized Ettestein. If he still waited, then the castle was yet to fall and the *Markgräf's* men still fought. Which meant they had heard his warning and been able to mount some kind of defence.

"What do we do now?"

"I'll disarm the guards... then we find this Gottlieb."

"Disarm?"

"I only kill if I have to."

"Wendel?"

"Was made vampiric by Saul. He is a monster of my bloodline. Him, I have to kill."

"Is he here?"

Morlaine sighed, "I don't know. I can't sense him, but the link is dilute, and the ability is not absolute. It's not like seeing or hearing."

"I'll leave him to you if he is."

Her dark eyes moved from the tower to him.

"He didn't kill you when you tried to stop him?"

He shook his head.

"Why?"

"I... don't know..."

Morlaine's gaze lingered. Then she stood up, unbuckled her sword belt and handed it to him.

"Why?" he asked, taking the sword.

"Women don't carry swords. I don't want to alarm them."

The belt was too small for his waist, so he fastened the buckle and looped it over his shoulder.

"Wait here."

She pulled her cloak more tightly around her and set off towards the Gate Towers.

He was still wondering how she would disarm four soldiers when she slid the cloak's hood down.

Ah, of course…

Morlaine's stride slowed, shoulders dropped, steps tentative.

As she approached, one of the Imperial soldiers nudged the man next to him. They took a couple of steps forward; the other two remained by the brazier, watching. They didn't seem overly alarmed.

One of the men's eyes swept beyond Morlaine. Ulrich slid further into the deep shadow until the soldier's attention returned to the demon.

Even in the thin moonlight, they could see a fetching young woman. Anyone else they would chase off or kill before they got anywhere near them. But when it came to beautiful women, soldiers could be as blind to their duty and good sense as any other men.

Morlaine called out, her voice hesitant and fearful. She didn't want to cause any trouble, but her little boy had been scared by the commotion and run off. Had they seen him? She knew they were good God-fearing men and would want to help.

He didn't catch the response, but the soldiers beckoned her forward.

Three of them clustered around her. Even at this distance, how they held themselves suggested concern for a missing child was not their prime motivation.

The fourth kept away, not looking at Morlaine but down the lane to the castle. He was the dangerous one. Wary and cautious.

When his hand started creeping towards his pistol, he stopped himself. Too far for a pistol, and even if it wasn't, the sound would likely bring more guards running from the tower.

Morlaine was on her own.

Something he suspected the demon was well used to.

Figures moved atop the tower, but no one was looking down at the gates.

All Morlaine had to do was overpower four armed men.

And then they would have to deal with whoever else was inside that tower...

*

"Solace!"

She frowned; someone slapped her cheek.

Forcing her reluctant eyes open, she found Lucien's face far too close to her own.

"Did you hit me?"

The concern on the mercenary's face ebbed.

"Ah, you don't appear dead after all."

She pushed herself up, causing Lucien to rock backwards

to avoid her forehead connecting with his.

"What happened?"

"Grenades. The bastards used grenades."

Smoke floated around them, thicker than before. Dust too.

Polke's musket lay by her side. Lebrecht sat against the column, face pale, clutching his left arm with his right hand. Blood oozed between his fingers.

More screams rose from below. Shouts and curses too. Metal crashed against metal.

Lucien's gaze followed hers.

"They threw grenades and charged. Bit underhand, really…" he sniffed.

Somewhere, bells rung. In her head, she realised after a few seconds, trying to shake them away.

Beyond Lucien, a musketeer lay dead on the floor. What was left of him. Her eyes bounced away.

Further along the gallery, another musketeer sprang up to fire, eyes wide and white in his sooty face.

A crossbow bolt knocked him from his feet.

Things did not appear to be going well.

She fumbled for the musket and used it to shakily climb to her feet. Lucien rose with her, then half pulled, half dragged her to the back wall.

"We need to be away from here…"

She could barely hear him for the damn bells.

"I do not run anymore…" she spat through gritted teeth.

Lucien touched her face; she jerked her head away as he showed her fingers sticky with blood.

"You're wounded."

"I've hurt myself worse farting…"

Someone had said that to her once. It took a few turns of the wheel before she remembered who. Sergeant Lutz. As they'd hidden in The Wolf's Tower's chapel. Just before he died. Before he sacrificed himself for her.

Before he sacrificed himself for nothing.

"'tis just a scratch."

Lucien's concern did not melt any.

"Check Lebrecht."

"He's fine," Lucien said, not looking around.

More explosions shook the castle. More screams and billowing clouds of smoke. Everything was hazy now.

One of the surviving musketeers ran, fast and crouched, to Lebrecht.

"They've taken both sets of stairs!"

Lebrecht squinted at him as if he didn't quite understand. Perhaps he could hear the bells too.

"The stairs don't lead directly here," Lucien said, "but they will get here eventually."

She knew that already but nodded anyway.

"The only way out is down there... we have no choice but to fight."

"Castles always have a second exit. We just need to find it."

"I don't run," she insisted; besides, she needed the *Markgräf's* men; she needed her army.

Lucien shook his head. For a moment, she thought he would walk away and leave her there. Instead, he crouched next to her and reloaded his pistols, lips pressed into a thin, hard line.

"You do not have to stay. You owe me nothing."

"Lucien Kazmierczak is famed for always following his heart..." his mouth softened into a lop-sided grin, "...'tis a failing he has never learned from despite the many times it has left him neck deep in cow shit."

"And I have your heart, do I?"

"All beautiful women have my heart," he winked, "another failing."

She fumbled shot and a powder charge from Polke's bandolier and began reloading the musket.

"My father taught me," she said, noting Lucien's attention.

"You do not have a good singing voice?"

That made her laugh, despite the screams, "I have an *excellent* singing voice. Because of my brother's... troubles, there was always a likelihood I would inherit Tassau, so, Father thought I should know how to fight if I needed to. Quite prescient of him, really."

Lucien nodded, "My father taught me how to be a baker."

"That... didn't work out?"

"I kept burning the bread. And getting into fights..." it was his turn to shrug, "...in the end, we agreed soldiering was a better fit for me than baking. Well, when I say *agreed*, I mean he threw me out and told me not to come back after one misunderstanding too many."

"Fathers..." she wriggled into the bandolier once she'd loaded the musket.

"Fathers..." Lucien agreed, a pistol in each hand.

They looked at each other, then hurried back to the balcony.

Lebrecht's skin was the colour of dirty snow, but he nodded at her.

303

"All together," she called.

Lebrecht, Lucien and the musketeer all nodded.

"One, two, three... now!"

She rose smoothly, the musket butt hitting her shoulder as she stood.

Smoke made ghosts of men.

Stay calm...

Half protected by a column, she searched for a target.

A flash of light, diffused by the churning smoke, caught her eye.

A soldier held a lighted grenade in his hand, the fuse fizzing as he pulled back his arm to hurl it onto the gallery. He was tall and muscular; you had to be strong to throw those heavy metal balls any distance.

So, he made a big target.

Her shot took him in the shoulder. His scream bled into all the others as he crumpled, the grenade dropping from his hand.

She rolled back behind the column as a roar washed over every other sound.

Afterwards more screams came.

Further along the gallery the three men were safely reloading their weapons.

Ducking down, she scurried over and slid to a halt next to Lebrecht.

His face was an ashen mask as he tried to pour powder into the muzzle of his pistol.

"Let me, my lord," she said, plucking the weapon from his shaking hands, "How bad is your arm?"

He shook his head, "'tis nothing."

Blood darkened the left sleeve of his jacket. Pistol shot or other shrapnel, as well as gunpowder, commonly filled grenades. A piece must have torn through his upper arm.

She rammed the ball home, primed the pan, tugged back the cock and handed him the gun before commencing loading her own musket.

"How long till the Imperials get up here?" she asked.

"Depends how well they know Ettestein."

"How well does your cousin, Gottlieb, know it?"

"Well enough, sadly."

"Do we need to fall back?"

His eyes moved to the nearest doorway, "This is my home..."

"You'll do it no service dying here."

He bit his lip, pulled himself up and fired. He came back down so hard on his arse she feared he'd been hit.

"They have pushed Joachim's men out of the First Hall... bloody grenades. A coward's weapon. I should not be surprised cousin Gottlieb armed his men with them." When she stared at him, he added, "Please excuse the language, my lady."

"Recent events have helped me see the benefit of cursing. At the appropriate moment, of course."

"Of course..." he found a watery smile.

"What should we do?"

"If we fall back... they will have the First Hall. We have to harry them, make it harder for them to get more men into the castle. It will buy time for Joachim to organise and rally. If he still lives..."

"We stand then?"

Lebrecht nodded, "There are many choke points in the castle, and they are not a big force. They expected to sneak in and take us in our beds. If we hurt them enough..."

Besides the four of them, she thought another four or five musketeers remained alive in the gallery. The extra men-at-arms Lebrecht asked for had not yet arrived.

If the Imperials made their way up here before the Gothen men...

Assuming any Gothen men were coming at all.

Chapter Thirteen

"Come on... come on..."

Frosted breath escaped him alongside the hissed words.

Morlaine stood with the three soldiers, still talking. The fourth stayed by the brazier. Did she want him to come closer too? Could she tackle four men together? He knew only too well how fast and strong the demons were, but she had to do it silently or she would alert however many Imperial soldiers were inside the tower with Gottlieb.

Assuming the *Markgräf's* nephew was even there in the first place. If Morlaine was wrong and *Freiherr* Geiss preferred being in the thick of the fighting, they would need another plan.

One of the soldiers took Morlaine by the arm. Rather than snapping it in two, she cowered away from him.

The fourth soldier turned to the others, barking at them.

Arms waved, voices raised.

The soldier holding Morlaine edged her towards the tower where no lights burned in the upper windows.

The men didn't seem very interested in her missing child.

They looked like they wanted to help her with something else entirely.

He strained to pick out words, but nothing carried far enough for him to hear clearly. But the fourth soldier didn't look happy with the others.

Perhaps he thought they should stick to their jobs and

watch for enemies. Maybe he just didn't have a taste for rape. Not all men were beasts.

Which was a shame because if Morlaine lured them inside… well, they were going to get a lot more than their cocks were bargaining for.

One of the three with Morlaine went over to his comrade. Heads close together, they both talked fast; the fourth soldier, who seemed older and stockier than the others, jabbed a finger at the lighted tower several times, then the castle.

The younger man shrugged and threw his arms wide.

He didn't care.

Then he hitched a thumb at Morlaine.

Something he cared a lot more about, by the look of him.

The other two soldiers held Morlaine. When she tried to wriggle free, one of them hit her, and the other clamped a hand over her mouth. He leaned in close to her ear and said something. His friend laughed.

The older soldier shook his head and turned his back on his comrades; when he waved a dismissive hand, the other three manhandled Morlaine to the second tower. The demon made a bit of a show of struggling but eventually allowed them to bundle her inside. One of the soldiers grabbed a tar torch from its fixing, followed the others inside. The door crashed shut after him.

He tensed, shoulder to the corner of the cottage and waited.

The remaining soldier moved to the brazier. He warmed his hands, then took up a musket and leaned against it. The brazier cast an orange glow across his face.

Several times he glanced at the tower door, but his attention bounced away each time. He didn't have the air of a happy man.

Minutes dragged by.

What was happening in there?

He fidgeted and shivered, fingering the worn leather binding wrapped around the hilt of his father's sword.

The remaining soldier's head jerked up towards the door.

He called out and took a couple of hesitant steps. Shaking his head, he hurried over. Pushing open the door, he stuck his head inside.

And something yanked the rest of him in.

Ulrich started running.

Not straight down the track to the gates but further along the wall. The guards atop the tower were likely paying the most attention to the path up to the castle. Only thin light dusted the world, but if a guard looked in the wrong place, they would spot him.

It wasn't a long run, but he expected a cry of alarm every time his boots slapped into the muddy, sodden ground.

None came, and he sagged against the wall when he reached it, comforted by its thick shadow as he caught his breath.

Nobody stood in the pools of light cast by the braziers and tar torches dancing in the icy but fitful breeze.

Unsheathing his father's sabre, he moved along the wall as quickly as he dared.

Beyond the second tower, the Imperial soldiers had stacked a dozen bodies against the wall like damp lumber. Mostly Gothen men, from what he could see. He ignored them and crossed to the tower door.

He hesitated, hearing nothing. Then Morlaine's voice.

"Come in, Ulrich."

The circular windowless room held a table, a couple of simple chairs, and stairs curling up the far wall to the next level. And four men on the floor.

Tied and gagged, all seemed unconscious. One bled heavily from a head wound, another's nose was not where it had been ten minutes earlier, while the third's right arm bent more times than it should.

Morlaine stood over the fourth, the older soldier. She was panting slightly. Blood covered her face.

His eyes bounced to the soldier. Blood darkened his neck too.

"You-"

"Yes," she snapped, "I fed. Go and fetch a cloak from one of the dead."

"But-"

"Quickly!"

He slipped her weapons belt off his shoulder and left it on the floor before hurrying outside. He ripped the cloak from a body atop the pile, holding his breath against the stink of blood, piss and shit.

Back inside, he fixed the torch to the wall.

Morlaine crouched over the man with the broken arm. Blood dripped from her clenched fist in his mouth, which she held open with her other hand.

"What are you doing?"

"Healing him."

"Why?"

310

Dark eyes flicked in his direction, "So he can use his arm again."

"But... they... were going to rape you."

She straightened herself, then crossed to the older man she must have fed from, "They were never going to rape me."

"They didn't know that... they didn't know... what you are."

"What I am?" she seemed amused by that.

"The next woman they try to rape is unlikely to be a demon."

"I am not a demon; I keep telling you this. I am a vampire. There is a difference."

Blood dripped into the older soldier's mouth. He groaned and stirred, his tongue sliding out to lick his lips.

He took a step backwards, fingers scrunching the dead man's cloak.

Morlaine rose to her feet and licked her left palm. She'd opened it with a dagger. By the time her hand fell to her side, blood had stopped dripping from the wound.

She held out her right hand, "The cloak?"

He didn't quite throw it at her.

She wrapped the cloak around the older soldier as gently as any mother with their child.

"What... are you doing?"

"He has lost a lot of blood. He will be more susceptible to the cold until my blood restores him."

"Won't you have them all in your head now?"

"I am used to it." When he continued to stare at her, she asked, "What would you rather I do, Ulrich? Slit their throats?"

"That would ensure they don't rape anybody else."

"They didn't rape me."

"But-"

"It's an interesting philosophical debate, but we don't have the time. My blood will also keep them asleep. By the time they awake, this will all be over, one way or another, so I am not being completely altruistic."

She moved to one of the other men, took off his helm and cloak and handed them to him.

"They'll know I'm not one of them," he said.

"If it causes a second or two's hesitation, that could make the difference between you living or dying. Your choice."

She was right, but he didn't think he would ever accept a thing the demon said without reluctance.

He wrapped the cloak over his own and put on the Imperial helm. It rattled around his ears, but he decided against checking if any of the other men possessed a smaller head.

"Ready?"

He nodded, the helm bouncing with him. His eyes, however, lingered on the men.

"If they ever rape another woman, will we not be responsible?"

"No, Ulrich. I will be responsible, it's not just vampires that have a monster inside them. Everybody does. I can't kill all the monsters in the world. Just the ones I created. Hopefully, they might think twice about attacking a defenceless woman again."

"I think you have a higher regard for humanity than I do."

She snorted at that.

"Come," she moved to the door, "let's end this before too many more people die."

"We might have to kill people to do that."

"So be it. If we have to take five lives to save a hundred, I will pay that price. But I will not take a life lightly. Or unnecessarily."

"Understood."

He followed her outside.

No one waited for them.

As they walked to the second tower on the other side of the gates, light flashed in the castle entrance, illuminating tendrils of smoke curling into the night sky.

"What do you think is happening in there?"

"The World's Pain…"

He slowed his feet, "Is this why Saul is doing this? Causing more slaughter to hasten this… vampire prophecy?"

She shrugged without breaking stride, "Silver, power, greed, lust, desire to bring about the end of the world of men. I don't know. I don't care. All I am interested in is stopping what I started by killing him."

Morlaine paused before the closed door of the second tower, "If Wendel is here, leave him to me. Understand?"

"I'll keep myself busy with the smaller monsters."

"Probably best…"

With that, she drew her sword, pushed open the door and went inside.

*

An experienced musketeer could load and fire his weapon twice every minute.

She wasn't an experienced musketeer.

Smoke stung her eyes, her head throbbed from the wound she'd suffered when the grenade exploded, and her shoulder felt like a mule had kicked her.

She wasn't loading and firing even once a minute, especially as she scurried from place to place to fire so the Imperial musketeers and crossbowmen wouldn't be waiting for her blonde head to pop above the balcony.

Back to one of the columns, she reloaded her musket. The portrait of a stern-faced man looked down at her. Presumably one of Lebrecht's ancestors. The painting hung askew; a musket ball had torn a hole clean between the man's eyes.

Hopefully, that wasn't a portent.

After wiping sweat and blood from her forehead, she primed the musket's pan and cocked the weapon.

The fight, it seemed to her, boiled down to no more than a game of chance. Could she step out of cover, fire the musket and return to safety before anyone shot her. So far, she'd won every time she'd played. But it was time to roll the dice again.

And in this game, you only got to lose once.

Another scream cut the air. A musketeer on the eastern side of the gallery went down clutching his throat.

I am not going to die here.

It seemed absurd that God would let that happen after all she had survived in the last year.

Of course, whether God shared a similar view on

absurdity was likely a matter of some theological debate.

She rose and swept her musket across the First Hall to find someone to try and kill amongst the ever-thickening smoke and strewn corpses.

She fired at what might have been a man. The mule kicked her again. She went down. Something whizzed over her head.

Another few minutes of life won.

She crawled to the next column and started loading the musket again.

A young musketeer crouched behind the balcony wall a little further on. She didn't know his name. In fact, other than Lucien and Lebrecht, she didn't know anybody's name.

"What's your name?" she called.

His head shot up from ramming powder down his musket's muzzle. If it'd been the portrait on the wall that had asked him, she doubted he would have looked more surprised.

"Thimo... ma'am..." his eyes quickly dropped to his weapon.

She'd have thought he was blushing if she didn't know better.

"Call me Solace."

His hands primed the weapon's pan. They moved fast. Thimo probably could fire twice a minute. If she wasn't distracting him.

He muttered something she didn't catch.

Thimo didn't seem much of a conversationalist, but as this wasn't really the time for talking, it didn't matter. She just wanted to know his name. If you were going to die with someone, it was something you really should know.

I am not going to die here!

She concentrated on reloading.

Thimo rose, fired and dropped in one fluid motion. Something slammed into the balcony wall, sending a shower of plaster over the musketeer's head. He was already re-loading.

My turn!

She jumped up with a less grace than Thimo and took longer to fire too. The First Hall was just smoke and shadows now. Still, if it kept someone's head down.

She fell to her knees.

No one had shot her.

I win! Again!

Lucien came down the gallery at a crouching gallop. He skidded to the floor next to her.

"You're going to tell me I shouldn't be here again, aren't you?"

He flashed a black-toothed grin, "Is Lucien Kazmierczak becoming predictable?"

"I'm not going anywhere."

"'tis not our fight…"

"Well… 'tis if I become *Markgräfin* of Gothen."

"A lot of the Imperials are past the First Hall now…" he glanced at the nearest doorway, "…'tis only a matter of time…"

She followed his gaze. Then her eyes moved to the door in the adjacent gallery. Even though there was a wall obscuring it.

"They will come through *that* door."

Lucien's eyebrow twitched.

"I feel it…" she said with certainty.

"Soon?" he asked. He wasn't grinning anymore.

She nodded.

"Then even more reason to leave."

"We can't abandon the First Hall; we're slowing them down. The fewer that get beyond here, the easier it will be for Joachim's men to deal with them."

"We don't know how many Gothen men remain. We don't know how many the grenades killed. We don't know how many Wendel killed," he stared at her, "Do we?"

She shook her head.

Her *sight* told her Imperial soldiers would be coming through that door soon. But on Lucien's questions… it remained silent. The *sight,* when it came, usually painted with a broad brush. It had never been particularly helpful with the specifics.

"Lucien Kazmierczak is famed across the circle of the world for his bravery…" he leaned in closer, "…but perhaps 'tis time to find somewhere safer."

"We must be ready to kill them when they come through that door."

"Has your *sight* ever told you when you will die, Solace?"

"No."

He cocked his head, "I believe I can make a quite shrewd guess. Perhaps I am a seer?"

"Come with me," she summoned Lebrecht and Thimo to follow as they passed. No one else lived on their side of the gallery.

They huddled together beneath the column on the southeast corner.

"Imperial soldiers are going to come through that door shortly…"

Thimo frowned whilst reloading his musket. Lebrecht asked the obvious question.

"How can you know? They could come through any of the doors?"

The east, south and west walls all housed doors. But they were coming through the east one.

"Because I have the *sight*."

Thimo stopped loading his weapon, head jerking up.

"That is not a claim to make lightly, my lady," Lebrecht said.

"Your cousin's men will kill us long before anyone can tie me to a pyre unless we stop them. Now, do you want to save your lives, or denounce me for witchery?"

Thimo appeared confused to the point of appearing like he had a decision to make; Lebrecht let his eyes drift to the east door. Lucien was shaking his head.

Musket fire continued to crackle from the remaining Gothen men on the other side of the gallery.

"What's behind that door?" she asked Lebrecht.

"A corridor, some ten paces or so long, then stairs, only going up to the next floor. But the door is sturdy. It will take time to break down."

"Your cousin knows Ettestein; they will have grenades or gunpowder to blow the door off its hinges," Lucien said, "it won't hold them for long."

"Do you have the *sight* too?"

"Just more years of fighting than all your men here have put together," he cast an eye around the corpse-strewn gallery, "not that that amounts to much at the moment."

Lebrecht bit his lip, "I can't-"

"You know they're coming..." she pointed west, south, then east, "...through *one* of those doors. Even if I don't have the *sight,* there's a one in three chance they will come through *that* door."

Her finger pointed east again.

And so did the dread stone in her stomach.

"How many?" he asked.

"Somewhere between one and a hundred, my lord."

Lebrecht ran a hand through his tousled hair, winced, and put it back on his wounded arm. Blood dripped from the sleeve.

"We should dress that wound," she added.

"If you were leading the Imperials coming towards us," Lebrecht asked Lucien, ignoring both her and the blood, "what would you do?"

Muskets cackled on the far side of the gallery as Lucien pulled a long face, "The most valuable weapon is surprise; that's the first rule of soldiering, as I'm sure you know. So, I'd come through that door as fast and hard as possible. No point pissing about being sneaky."

"And if the Imperial in charge is a more cautious fellow than you?"

Lucien shook his head.

"That door's locked and bolted. Anything else bar blowing it off its hinges warns his enemy where he is. He knows we're armed, and he knows we're occupied with his chums down there," Lucien jerked his head at the First Hall, "he comes through that door fast and hard. No other way. I'd bet your life on it."

"That confident?" Lebrecht found a weak grin.

"Absolutely!"

The east door pulled her eyes once more. She heard nothing above the noise of muskets and men, and even in complete silence she wouldn't be able to hear soldiers rattling towards them.

Except that she could.

"They will be here soon…"

All eyes turned on her.

Lebrecht nodded.

"Then we'd better ensure we're ready to greet them properly. 'tis Christmas, after all…"

Chapter Fourteen

He followed the demon inside.

The room was identical to the other tower, save for the lack of trussed-up Imperial soldiers soiling the floor.

Torches burned, their flames the only movement.

Morlaine pointed to the stairs. Then sheathed her sword and hid it beneath her cloak.

"When we meet someone, tell them you are taking me to this Gottlieb man. That I have information."

"*Freiherr* Geiss," he nodded.

He pulled the Imperial cloak around himself to better conceal his clothes and withered left arm.

"What if he isn't here?"

"Then we ask where he is."

"How ma-"

She shook her head and started to climb the steps curling up the far wall of the circular room.

No more time.

He trailed after her.

The stairs took them to another room no different to the first. Again, empty.

He let out a long breath and looked enquiringly at the demon. She jerked her head upwards. They would carry on till they found someone. Given the height of the rooms, there could only be another two above them in the tower, plus the roof.

What if she was wrong and no one was here?

He held the question. Morlaine didn't have the air of someone harbouring doubt.

A door sat at the top of these stairs. And as they climbed towards it, he began to hear voices. Morlaine raised her hand and extended three fingers without looking back or slowing. After a couple more steps, she added a fourth.

Four men.

At the door, she paused.

Ready?

He nodded.

She pushed open the door.

Inside was another room identical to the first, save it contained furniture and soldiers.

One of the men stood with his back to the door, talking animatedly. His comrades lounged on chairs. None appeared worried about either their arrival or the fact a battle raged nearby.

One of the men, too fat and young to be anything other than a nobleman's son, glanced at them as they entered. His eyes immediately fixed on Morlaine. The others did the same. The talking man babbled on about some "game mare." It wasn't obvious whether he was referring to a horse or a woman.

When he noticed he no longer enjoyed the rapt attention of his comrades, he looked over his shoulder.

And the words ground to a halt.

It must be strange being a beautiful woman.

The thought ricocheted around his head before he

reminded himself Morlaine wasn't a woman. And they would probably have to kill some of these men very shortly.

"This woman has information for *Freiherr* Geiss," he blurted.

Luckily, nobody was looking at him.

"Does she now..." the talking man said, turning to face them. He had been blessed with the face of a dog too enamoured with sniffing its own shit. The rest continued to lounge.

Judging by this bunch, it seemed the Emperor must have hired a lot of fools to fill up his army. Which might explain why his empire was falling apart around his ears.

"I need to see him, sir... 'tis important..." Morlaine curtseyed hurriedly and badly in every direction.

The talking man ambled over to them, fingers hitched in his belt, "Why don't you tell me, and I'll decide how important it is. The *Freiherr's* busy."

The other men found this funny for some reason.

"'tis for his ears only, sir. He'll want to see me."

"I'm sure he'll want to see you. Not sure if it'll be his ears that'll be the most interested part of him, though, lass."

More laughter.

One of the men rose to his feet and joined the talking man. He possessed a sour face and sharp eyes, "Why didn't Klammer bring her up?"

The man directed the question at him rather than Morlaine.

"Busy, sir."

"I don't know you, do I?"

"I'm new..."

"I really need to see the *Freiherr*, 'tis about the *Markgräf*, sir!"

"What's your name?" The sharp eyes narrowed, head jutting forward.

Fuck.

Lost for any words that wouldn't get him killed, he did the only thing he could think of.

He drew his pistol and shot him.

Man and pistol hit the ground simultaneously as he dragged his father's sabre free of its sheath.

Morlaine punched the talking man in the face. He crumpled to the floor even quicker than the man he'd shot.

The other two scrambled to their feet. Morlaine flattened the first while he was still straightening his knees. The second managed to pull a pistol from his belt, but the demon smashed her sword's hilt into his face before he could do anything useful with it. He hit the floor, blood spraying from his ruined nose.

"You didn't need to do that!" Morlaine snapped at him.

The man he'd shot was already dead. He wore a cuirass, but it wasn't thick enough at point-blank range to stop the pistol ball from punching through it.

She glowered at him when he didn't reply. They could discuss the merits of keeping your enemies alive when they had more time. He moved to the next set of stairs, scooping up the pistol of one of the fallen men as he did so.

He expected men to be hurtling down them, but the door at the top stayed shut.

"Is there any rope for these three?"

When he looked around, the demon was slicing her palm

with a dagger again.

"No..." she leant over the first man, opening his mouth to squeeze her blood into it.

"We have time for this?"

"My blood will keep them asleep while they heal, remember?" she said, moving to the second man, pushing himself groggily onto all fours. A small bloody waterfall splashed the stone floor beneath him.

She kicked him in the ribs till he went back down, then smashed his head against the flagstones. The soldier went limp. Morlaine rolled him onto his back and fed him her blood too.

The door above remained closed. He took the opportunity to reload his own pistol.

The demon moved to the final man, the one who'd done most of the talking. He'd managed to sit up, but his eyes were glassy enough to suggest he wouldn't be doing much else for a while.

"Look the other way," Morlaine commanded.

"Why?" he glanced up from his pistol.

"Because I don't want you to see this."

When he continued to stare, her face changed. And the beautiful woman he usually saw no longer looked back at him.

"I need to feed."

"Again?"

"Wendel has fed. He'll have the blood strength. I need it too."

He turned his back on her and concentrated on sprinkling powder into the pistol's pan. He mostly succeeded, despite the shaking hands.

Behind him, a deep, prolonged groan followed by a wet sucking noise.

Master...

He didn't need to see Morlaine to visualise what was happening.

He'd seen it before.

Mistress...

He shook that thought away. Morlaine was not Saul. He had his reservations, but she was a very different kind of monster.

With the pistol loaded, he picked up a second gun from one of the fallen men with his weak hand. Pain sizzled up his withered arm. He winced and forced his fingers not to spring open and drop the weapon.

If I drank her blood...

Mistress.

No.

Better to be half a man than one ensnared by a demon.

Like the three men behind him and the four in the other gate tower.

Wasn't it?

When she appeared at his shoulder, he shuffled away, despite himself.

"I should go first," she said, eyes dark and beguiling in her once more beautiful face, "whoever's up there may be ready when we come through that door.

He nodded, unable to meet her eye. Then stood aside.

She drew her sword.

Specks of blood darkened the pale skin around her

mouth.

Should he tell her?

He decided not to.

Silently, she mounted the stairs. He trailed a few paces behind, the pistol in his right hand levelled, the other at his side. Hopefully, he'd find the strength to raise it if necessary.

Despite himself, he glanced down into the room as he climbed the steps. Three men scattered the floor, for all the world sleeping like babes. The fourth was on his back, sightlessly staring at the ceiling.

Tell me, Ulrich, just who is the monster again?

The voice was his father's, even though it was a question he'd never asked in life.

We are all monsters here, Father.

Above him, Morlaine reached the top of the stairs.

She waited till he was a couple of steps behind her.

Then opened the door...

*

They waited.

They had overturned a table and placed it on the north side of the east door. It wasn't big enough to shelter them all, but it offered some protection.

They had collected and loaded the guns of the fallen. Even she would be able to fire twice in a minute now. They all could. There were sufficient fallen for them all to have more than one musket.

One man, Konrad, had a crossbow bolt in his side. He'd insisted on helping them reload the weapons with bloody, shaking hands. He sat behind them, propped up against the wall.

Another musketeer remained on the west side of the gallery to pepper the Imperials. Few shots came back in return. The men below were either dead or had moved on through the First Hall. She thought the latter more likely.

The men fidgeted. Several kept glancing at her when they thought she wasn't looking. Perhaps they considered her pretty. Or, more likely, a witch who would damn their souls.

Lucien was next to her, on one knee, a pistol in either hand, and two more on the floor, along with his sword. If any Imperials were left after he'd discharged all his guns, it'd be time for the killing to become more personal.

Lebrecht was on the other side of her, then Thimo. The remaining three musketeers, Brandt, Lucas and Hock squatted behind. She'd asked them all their names in turn. Each looked surprised and confused by the question, although Hock still ran his eye up and down her a few times. It took all sorts.

They would stand and fire over their heads in a second row. The privilege of rank.

No one else remained alive on the gallery.

Nine shots between them, another nine in their spare weapons.

Enough?

It depended on how many men came through that door.

I'm going to look very stupid if they come through one of the others.

Still, none of them would live long enough to enjoy

thinking badly of her if that happened.

But it wasn't going to happen.

Her *sight* said otherwise.

Lucien started whistling.

She shot him a scowl. He grinned back at her. Then carried on whistling. Some airy little ditty she didn't know. One probably accompanied by words not suitable for her ears.

Men were peculiar.

She adjusted her musket.

Likely they all thought the same of her.

Lebrecht was staring nowhere. A waxy sheen coated his skin. Was it the poor light or was he starting to turn grey?

"How is your arm, my lord?"

After a few seconds, he blinked and turned his head towards her as if the words had taken longer to make the journey down his ears than usual.

"Good enough."

His sleeve seemed to have stopped dripping blood. That was good. Wasn't it?

"You should let me-"

Something dragged her eyes along the wall to the door. There was nothing to see or hear. But it wasn't any of her five senses telling her to watch.

"Ready yourselves..."

Lucien stopped whistling.

She expected some eye-rolling and headshaking behind her but didn't check. To most men, she was but a woman, which meant her warnings made her either a fool or a witch.

Still, Lebrecht believed her enough to do as she said. More than Father ever had.

And they would find out very soon she was not a fool...

That was when the door exploded.

Even though she was ready for it, the crack, crump and crash, accompanied by a flash and followed by a cloud of smoke, made her jump.

By the time Lucien growled, "Wait for em, lads," three Imperial soldiers had charged through the door, bellowing at the top of their lungs.

They didn't bellow for long.

A volley of shots punched them from their feet and sent them pirouetting to the ground,

"I said wait for em!" Lucien roared.

Another two Imperials came through hot on the heels of the first group and met the same fate. A sixth span towards them but jumped back through the smoking ruins of the door before anyone shot him.

"I told you to fucking wait!" Lucien glowered over his shoulder at the three Gothen men behind him, "We could have got all of the buggers!"

"Got five of them," Hock grumbled, exchanging his musket for the loaded one at his feet.

"But we don't know how many more there are!"

Hock glanced at her. He looked like he wanted to say, "Ask her," but thought better of it.

However many there were, they didn't seem half so keen to come rushing through the door a second time.

"You three," Lebrecht said to the men behind them, "go around the gallery to the other side of the door. They know

330

we're all on this side now."

"Just careful you don't shoot us if more of the buggers come through, "Lucien said, "then you'll piss me off even more than you already have."

Brandt, Lucas and Hock scooped up their spare weapons and trotted off the long way around the gallery.

Lucien glanced at her, "I don't suppose you-"

"No idea."

"Pity," he returned to reloading his spent pistols.

She'd exchanged her musket. Amidst the smoke and confusion, she didn't know if she'd hit anyone with her shot. Killed anyone.

One of the Imperial soldiers was trying to drag himself around the bodies of his comrades back to the door. He wept as he propelled himself forward with his arms. His legs flicked and slid feebly behind him on the blood-soaked floor.

"Leave him," Lucien said, noticing her indecision.

The fact she was even considering killing the wounded man instead of trying to help him distantly appalled her.

Who am I becoming?

She wouldn't become anything other than a corpse if she didn't concentrate.

Once Lucien and Thimo reloaded their weapons, she did the same with hers.

"Do you think they've fled?"

Brandt, Lucas and Hock positioned themselves on the other side of the door. They stretched out on the floor to minimise the chance of being hit by crossfire.

"Only one way to find out..." Lucien said. When she raised

an eyebrow in his direction, the mercenary shrugged, "Someone sticks his head around the door, and we see if anybody shoots it."

"Volunteering?" Lebrecht asked.

Lucien just chuckled.

"So... what *do* we do?"

Lucien stopped chuckling.

"If we just sit here long enough... reinforcements will eventually turn up," Lebrecht nodded behind him, a gesture that made him wince, "probably through one of the other doors."

"So..."

Lucien leaned across her and slapped Thimo on the back, "Think of this as an opportunity, lad."

Thimo looked much more like he wanted to spit.

"Just make your way to the west side, take a peek and see what you can see down there. And try not to get yourself shot; we're getting a bit light on numbers."

Lebrecht nodded his confirmation and grimaced at the same time.

"What would you do if you were in charge of the Imperial soldiers in there?" she asked Lucien after Thimo trotted off.

"Give a medal to whichever of our idiots shot first. If we'd got all the buggers through that door..."

He shook his head when she kept staring, "I really do not know. It depends on how many of them are left. He could wait for more men and rush us, send men to one of the other doors, or keep us bottled up here till they take the rest of the castle."

"They won't take the rest of the castle..." Lebrecht said.

She wished she shared his confidence. And wondered what she should do if they did. This wasn't her fight, after all. All she wanted was Wendel. And a hundred men-at-arms, but the chances of that receded with every fallen Gothen man.

Behind her, Konrad let out a long rolling moan. Head slumped forward, his eyes remained open. He wasn't going to live much longer.

Part of her wanted to go and hold his hand. No one should have to die alone, but the Imperials could storm through the door again any moment. Her cares had to remain with the living.

Across the gallery, Thimo reached a position directly opposite the door. His head popped up, then disappeared equally quickly back down again. No one shot at him from either below or the door.

The final surviving Gothen man-at-arms, she didn't know his name, who had been keeping life awkward for the Imperials, hadn't fired for a while. She doubted it due to him getting bored.

Most of the Imperial force must have pushed beyond the First Hall. Perhaps Lucien's final alternative would prove the correct one. If they no longer presented a nuisance to the Imperial attack, why waste more lives trying to prise them off the gallery?

Thimo came hurrying back, the other Gothen soldier with him.

"How many?" Lebrecht and Lucien asked in unison.

When Thimo replied, "More than us," they both cursed in unison too.

"None left downstairs," the other Gothen man said, wide eyes darting between them.

"Perhaps-"

A grenade clunked and rolled into the galley. They all ducked behind the table before it exploded, sending shrapnel in all directions.

The roar still rang in her ears as Imperial soldiers poured out of the door and into the smoke.

It seemed they still wanted to prise them off the gallery after all.

.

Chapter Fifteen

"Drop your weapon."

"Trust me. It would be better if you dropped yours."

Laughter. High-pitched.

Morlaine blocked the open doorway, so he could see nothing of the room bar the torchlight flickering over the ceiling.

"I expected one of my dashing cousins..." the nasally words almost tripped over themselves, "...this is a surprise. Or is it? Uncle Hendrick sending a *wench* to try and save his bacon. Perhaps not!"

More laughter.

Gottlieb, the *Freiherr* Geiss, he presumed.

"I want you to call your men back from the castle."

Laughter again. Wet and blurted.

"Firstly, they're the Emperor's men, mostly. Secondly, don't be so silly! Thirdly, why not join me for some wine? I'm about to become betrothed, but, well, my beloved to be won't mind. You are rather fetching, after all."

"I will not tell you again. Put down the weapons."

"Are you touched? I think you are. Moonstruck. Or have you knocked your pretty head? Who do you think you are, telling me what to do?"

He fidgeted, unsure what to do.

As Morlaine wasn't budging from the doorway, he

assumed she didn't want him to do anything.

"I *can* tell you what to do because eight of your men couldn't stop me from getting this far."

"I keep telling you, they're not *my* men!"

"Does the Emperor know you're using his men to fulfil your petty ambitions?"

"My ambitions aren't petty. 'tis my birth right! Stolen from me by our grandfather when he embraced Luther's heresy. And the Emperor is always pleased to learn one less heretic prince is fouling his domain."

"When you deal with the Devil, the price is rarely what you think it will be."

"Moonstruck! Pretty or not, best to put you out of your misery. Shoot her!"

Morlaine moved.

He moved too. Just a lot slower.

A musket ball exploded in the door frame, showering him with splinters as he crashed into the room, both pistols levelled. A second shot boomed a moment later but hit the ceiling.

By the time he skidded to a halt and made sense of the room, two Imperial soldiers were bleeding on the floor, and a puffy-faced nobleman had backed into a corner with Morlaine bearing down on him.

A dagger at a girl's throat.

Sophia. The *Markgräf's* daughter.

It seemed Wendel had been even busier than they had imagined.

"What are you?" *Freiherr* Geiss demanded, keeping Sophia between them.

"The price you pay for dealing with the Devil," Morlaine halted before them. Blood darkened her sword. At least one of the soldiers was beyond her help.

The room contained a couple of narrow sagging beds and some functional furniture. More stone stairs led upwards, presumably, to the tower's roof. There had been men up there, but were they the two Morlaine had left crumpled on the floor?

He positioned himself at the foot of the steps, guns raised, just in case. But when nobody came hurtling down them in response to the musket fire, he guessed no one remained up there.

"Please…" Sophia gasped, face flushed, eyes bulging.

"Why is she here?" Morlaine asked.

"None of your fucking business!" Gottlieb sprayed the girl's ear with spittle, making her wince.

The demon's eyes moved to the dead soldier before returning to the nobleman.

"I've had to kill a man. Trust me. That makes it my business."

"Get out of here, or I'll slit her bloody throat! Don't think I won't!" the dagger shook in Gottlieb's hand.

"And then what will you do?" Morlaine asked.

"What?" he frowned.

It clearly hadn't been the response Gottlieb expected.

"After you slit her throat. Then what will you do? Walk out of here alive?" Once more, Morlaine's dark eyes flicked to the two soldiers she'd reduced to bleeding piles of flesh in a couple of heartbeats, "You saw what I did to them. You will be no problem at all."

Gottlieb licked pale, fleshy lips, sweat glistening upon his rose-flushed cheeks. Although still a young man he was already running to fat,

"But... but... I'll kill her!"

Morlaine's shoulders twitched, "She is nothing to me."

She'd said it coldly enough to convince him, and he knew she was bluffing.

Morlaine stepped forward, "No one is coming to save you. Your men downstairs are all dead. I killed them. The rest of your men are fighting in the castle," she conjured a thin smile, "Oh, I'm sorry, do excuse me. The Emperor's men..."

Gottlieb tried to back further away but found himself already wedged hard into the corner, exposed stonework pressing against his shoulders.

"If you kill her. I will kill you. If you let her go. You will live. So long as you do exactly as I say. Do you understand?"

Sophia was panting, Gottlieb was breathing even harder.

"I would do as she says," he offered. If Gottlieb heard him, he didn't respond. His eyes remained fixed on Morlaine.

The demon took another step forward and held out her free hand, "Give me the dagger. Please, I'd rather not kill anyone else tonight."

"You are a witch! No woman could do what you've just done!"

"Call me whatever you wish; just give me the dagger."

"I will see you burn for this!"

That earnt him a smile and a flick of the fingers.

Gottlieb shoved Sophia into Morlaine and dashed for the door.

He managed to half raise one of his pistols by the time the demon caught him and yanked him back by the collar.

"Aaaargh!"

Morlaine cut off Gottlieb's strangled scream by hurling him to the floor. Standing over the prone man, she nodded towards Sophia, climbing shakily to her feet after tumbling into the demon.

"My lady," he put aside a pistol to offer her his hand.

"Thank you," she accepted the help after only the briefest hesitation.

"Are there more men on the roof?"

She shook her head, "No, those two came down when we heard a shot fired downstairs."

Good. That, at least, was something.

"You are Lady Solace's man?" she asked as he retrieved the pistol from the table.

"Yes, my lady."

"And who, may I ask, is she?" Sophia looked at Morlaine, still standing over the panting and shivering Gottlieb at her feet.

"Perhaps that is a question best not asked," when she continued to stare at him, he added, "but she is a friend."

"I owe you my thanks for rescuing me," Sophia brushed herself down and moved to Morlaine's side, "my cousin appears to have gone quite mad."

Gottlieb interrupted his glowering at the demon to glower at Sophia.

"In truth," he confessed, "we did not know you were here."

"Still, you have my gratitude," with that, she bent over and slapped Gottlieb's face hard enough for it to sound like a pistol shot.

"Do you intend to do that again?" Morlaine asked as *Freiherr* Geiss whimpered on the floor.

Sophia thought about it then shook her head, "No, I think once is sufficient for the time being."

"Restraint is an admirable quality..." Morlaine crouched in front of Gottlieb. She took the hem of his cloak and used it to wipe her blade clean of blood, "...though I sometimes struggle with it myself."

Gottlieb tried to scurry away. He walked past them and stood behind the nobleman, "Sometimes she isn't herself at all," he said.

Freiherr Geiss stopped trying to scurry.

"My father is going to string you up for this," Sophia said from Morlaine's shoulder.

"I am just-"

"Shut up!" Morlaine snapped.

Gottlieb settled for scowling. He had the air of a petulant child.

Morlaine turned to Sophia, "Tell me, why are you here?"

"This fool has some silly notion about marrying me."

"It would strengthen his claim on Ettestein," he said, straightening up.

"Lebrecht and Joachim are Father's heirs before me," Sophia said.

"Only if they are alive."

Sophia's eyes dropped to her cousin. She looked like she was seriously reconsidering her promise not to slap him again.

"How did you come to be here, in this tower?" Morlaine

asked.

"A soldier came to my room; he said Father wanted to see me. I thought it strange a soldier bore the message rather than a servant, but... I went with him... then..." Sophia's face crumpled into a frown, "...then I was here... with Gottlieb..." she shook her head as if distracted by a fly.

"You don't recall leaving the castle?"

"No... I... how peculiar... I didn't think it odd before... listening to Gottlieb's ravings... must have... How can I not remember?!"

"The soldier who came to you. Was it Sergeant Iskra?"

"No... I didn't recognise him. Which was odd too; I know most of the men here, if only by sight, though new ones do turn up regularly enough."

He looked at Morlaine.

"Wendel took Iskra's face. I followed Iskra after he left the castle. Sophia wasn't with him."

It seemed unlikely Wendel could have snatched Sophia and brought her here before he killed the guards and opened the gates for Gottlieb's men. Which meant...

Morlaine tightened her lips, "Then it seems your friend was not acting alone..."

Damn...

There was another demon in Ettestein.

*

She fired.

The musket belched fire and smoke, kicking her abused shoulder again.

A soldier went down.

Wounded or dead, she didn't know.

By the time the man hit the ground, she'd dropped her musket and scrambled for the next loaded weapon. When she looked up, she found another Imperial soldier bearing down on her, sword swinging, teeth bared, eyes bulging beneath the dented rim of his gunmetal grey helm.

She froze.

She could throw herself backwards, turn her musket to block the blow, or try and get the muzzle up and shoot him before he took her head off.

Instead, she just watched the wickedly sharpened metal slashing towards her neck.

I will never know vengeance...

The soldier jerked back once, then again, screaming.

Lucien was on his feet, roaring back at the dying man, smoking pistols already tumbling from his hands.

Thimo clubbed an Imperial in the face with his musket's butt as more of them poured out of smoke lit by orange flashes of gunfire.

Something whizzed past her ear. A heartbeat later, another something thudded into the overturned table before her.

Am I going to die here?

The *sight* told her nothing; perhaps it was hiding behind a curtain.

Lucien grabbed her elbow and yanked her to her feet, twisting back to fire a pistol at the men charging them.

For each one that went down, another appeared.

Screams echoed around them.

Lucien snatched his sword, shoved her away and met two

Imperials who'd reached the upturned table.

Thimo was struggling with an Imperial, Lebrecht was on one knee trying to reload a pistol, she couldn't see the other Gothen soldier who'd been with them. Had he run?

She should run. This wasn't her fight. Why was she even here?

An Imperial reared above Lebrecht. She stepped forward and shot him. Another body hit the ground.

Her eyes swept the floor; there were no loaded weapons left.

"Come, my lord!"

The nobleman jumped up, moved away from the table and stumbled over Konrad, whose sightless eyes told her he would suffer no more.

Lebrecht scrambled back to his feet, drawing his sword as he did.

How many Imperials remained?

It was hard to tell; the smoke thickened by the breath. Something must have caught fire.

Steel clashed on steel.

Lucien stepped back and kicked the up-turned table at the Imperials.

"Run!" he shouted at them over his shoulder, making no such move to do the same thing himself.

Another Imperial soldier came out of the smoke at her; she tried to club him with her musket. He easily parried the feeble blow, but it distracted him enough for Lebrecht to dart in and drive his sword into the man's stomach; grunting, he twisted and yanked the blade upwards.

The soldier's guts plopped onto the blood-slicked floor

before the rest of him folded after them.

Lebrecht bundled her away from the fighting.

"Lucien!"

The mercenary was too busy dodging, ducking and parrying to acknowledge her.

Imperial soldiers swarmed around him, but somehow, he danced away from every slash and thrust.

"Move!" Lebrecht bellowed in her face; putting his sword arm across her, he shoved her towards the south balcony.

"We can't leave him!"

Lebrecht didn't reply. Ashen faced, he just kept pushing her away from the fight.

She tried to struggle without knowing why she was struggling. She was no help to anyone in a sword fight. Lucien knew what he was doing.

She hoped.

She sucked at the acrid air and let Lebrecht lead her to the south door.

Once her back pressed against it, he pulled a pistol from his belt and pushed it at her, "Load this!"

He ran back to the fighting without waiting for a reply.

She crouched by the door and loaded the pistol with fumbling hands.

Screams and clashing metal echoed through the smoke. The occasional gunshot, too, though fewer now.

Pistol loaded, she put it by her feet and worked on the musket between coughing fits. Smoke scratched the back of her throat with every laboured breath.

With the musket loaded she settled on one knee, peering for a target. Only phantoms moved. Some of the wooden panelling on the gallery's wall had caught fire, adding to the smoke. Much of the castle was stone, but there was still plenty of wood to burn.

It was impossible to tell friend from foe; shadow and smoke swirled about her.

Fidgeting, she wiped a sleeve across her smarting eyes.

Her only interest in Ettestein was a hundred men-at-arms and the chance to question and then kill one of the Red Company, but whether Ettestein still had a hundred men to offer her or a lord to marry seemed doubtful, and Wendel might well have fled into the night by now, his mischief complete.

So, why was she still here?

She tried to make out Lucien and Lebrecht. Figures danced, steel crashed against steel, screams competed with the spreading flames' crackle. But who was who? The smoke had reduced men to ghostly suggestions and hazy spectres.

She'd known Lucien less than two weeks, Lebrecht for less than two days. Was she going to die for them?

To fight an army, you need an army…

And sometimes, you needed to make sure your army survived to fight another day.

The door behind her was barred.

Leaning the musket against the wall, she pulled it free.

If more Imperial soldiers were coming down the corridor, it was over.

Her *sight* told her nothing.

Which she took to mean they weren't.

Turning back, she found a figure emerging out of the

smoke, but not from the direction Lucien and Lebrecht were fighting. A monstrous apparition, two heads taller than her and almost as broad as the door at her back. Wearing no helm like most of the Imperial soldiers, he smiled when he saw her. Teeth uncommonly white, face splattered with blood, eyes wide and restless. The giant wore Imperial livery beneath the blood.

"Christmas tidings, bitch," he said, reaching for her with the hand that didn't hold a pistol.

She snatched the musket and tried to swing it towards him, but he caught the muzzle and yanked it from her hands.

"Not nice," he grunted, tossing the musket aside.

When she made for the pistol on the floor, the giant grabbed her by the hair and threw her against the door, forcefully enough to rattle both wood and teeth.

Before she could recover her wits, he was hard against her, one hand squeezing her throat. When she tried to struggle, he smashed her head backwards.

"You're pretty," he said, tilting his head back and forth on the other side of the stars flashing in front of her eyes.

"You're ugly," she croaked. Then spat at him.

It was a feeble attempt with his fingers encircling her smoke-dried throat. Most of the spit didn't get further than his gloved hand.

He laughed, pulled her away from the door and threw her to the floor.

Winded and stunned, she fumbled for the blade in her belt, but he slapped her face hard enough to send her reeling before she got anywhere near it. Blood filled her mouth.

She lay on the floor, head spinning as the giant opened the door she'd just unlocked. Then he took an ankle in each hand and dragged her through it.

She screamed despite knowing nobody could help her. If Lucien and Lebrecht still lived, they had their own problems. Her fingers found the edges of the door frame, and she grabbed hold, trying to kick herself out of his grip.

The giant just grunted and yanked her viciously enough to break her grasp. She skidded over the worn flagstones as he tossed her inside.

He turned his back on her as he locked the door behind him.

Less smoke and more shadow filled the corridor. A single torch flickered, and beyond that, a corridor disappeared into darkness. Her first urge was to run, but she doubted the giant would show her his back a second time.

So, she pulled her dagger clear and sprung to her feet.

He was already turning back from the door when she drove the blade towards his neck.

Although a big man, sadly, he was a fast one too.

He ducked, swivelled, caught her wrist and twisted it back in one motion. The dagger clattered to the ground as she cried out.

The giant silenced her with another slap.

She found herself on the floor again; bells accompanied the stars this time.

He stood looking down at her, a grin on his face.

He exchanged the pistol in his hand for a sword; he had another wheellock in his belt alongside several smaller blades. If she could get her hands on one...

"Tell me your name," the giant said, his voice too high and nasally to match the rest of him.

"Celine," she pushed herself up into a sitting position.

When she tried to rise, he put the tip beneath her chin.

"The next time you neglect to call me sir," he said pleasantly enough, "I'm going to cut something off you. Do you understand?"

She nodded.

He raised her chin with the tip of the sword. Blood trickled down the blade.

"Do. You. Understand?"

"Yes... sir..."

"Good, 'tis pleasing you have some manners."

She tried to focus on his eyes rather than the bloody sword. And whose blood might be trickling down it.

No sound troubled the gloomy corridor other than the thunder of her own heart. The giant had closed a door, not only on the battle but on the rest of the world too.

She was on her own. Again.

"Celine..." the soldier teased the word around his mouth, "...why do you dress like a man?"

"Because 'tis much more inconvenient to kill your enemies in a dress... sir..."

He laughed. Given his size, it should have been a hearty roar; instead, it sounded more like someone had unexpectedly trod on a chicken.

"But britches make what I'm going to do to you much more inconvenient," another squawk of laughter, "...what do you say to that, eh?"

What she wanted to tell him was that she'd cut his balls off and stuff them in his mouth. She didn't need the *sight* to know that wasn't the best response to give a man holding a sword to your throat. So, she said nothing.

The giant snorted.

Then he sheathed the sword, grabbed her by the collar and began dragging her down the corridor. She yelped and struggled, but if she inconvenienced him any, it didn't show.

He plucked the torch from the wall as they passed it, then kicked open the first door they came to and pulled her inside.

"Ah, look at this!" the big man squeaked, "all the comforts of home!"

The room was a windowless cell sporting a narrow bed, a stool and the faint stink of damp stone.

The giant threw her onto the bed.

He turned his back to fit the torch into a crude metal ring long enough for her to jump on his back and try to grab a pistol from his belt.

The giant squealed with laughter. He slammed his back into the wall, knocking both breath and sense from her.

The next thing she knew, she was on the bed again.

"Fight if you like," he showed her his rotting teeth, "I quite like that, but you're only gonna make it harder on yourself."

"Haven't you got a battle to fight?"

He tilted his head.

"...sir..."

"The Emperor sent us here to root out heresy," he shrugged and started undoing his britches, "I intend to root it out of your cunt. As good a place as any to look, I reckon."

She backed into the corner, drawing her knees up. The bed squeaked beneath her.

"Be easier if you take those britches off..." he patted the hilt of one of the daggers in his belt, "if I have to cut them off... well, we wouldn't want any accidents, would we?"

"Why should I? You're going to kill me afterwards, aren't you... sir..."

"You're highborn. Fuck a maid and nobody cares, but you could cause me problems, even if you do follow Luther's heresy..." he rolled his massive shoulders and knelt on the bed, "...'tis nothing personal."

She kicked him. The first blow bounced off, the second, he caught, then twisted off her boot, his laughter was as squeaky as the rickety bed's protests.

"Come here..."

He hauled her towards him. She kicked, screamed, punched, clawed, and even bit his hand when it came close to her mouth. All to no avail. An occasional grunt interrupted the laughter as she flailed, but that was the only response she got from him.

I am not going to let this happen!

The thought ricocheted around her mind until he slapped her hard enough to knock the idea clean out of her. When she tried to say something, he hit her again, the blow accompanied by more squeaky laughter.

She felt her britches tugged free, and he was between her legs, forcing them apart.

Making talons of her fingers, she tried to claw at his face,

350

but he just hit her again, connecting with her ear.

Kneeling back, he pulled his own britches down.

She'd never seen an engorged penis, and she whimpered at the sight before he climbed fully on top of her.

"Stop making a fuss; you might even like it," he giggled, "not many of us get to die happy!"

He seized a wrist in each hand and held them down, pinning her completely. Something hard and wet pushed against the exposed flesh of her inner thigh towards her maidenhead.

This is not going to happen!

"Please!" she sobbed, hating the weakness in her voice.

He spat in her face.

Then let go of her left wrist to fumble with his manhood, taking cock in hand to try and guide it into her.

This is not going to happen!

Flyblown's mark suddenly glowed hot, as if in agreement.

She flailed at him with her left hand, but the blows bounced off the giant.

He grunted. The hard warmth was between her legs, trying to find entrance.

"No!" she screamed in his face, "No!"

The soldier laughed his squeaky laugh... then his head twisted to the right, accompanied by a sharp crack.

He slumped forward on top of her, driving the breath from her lungs.

Another face loomed over her.

"Seems you're having a wee bit o' bother, lass, so you are..."

Chapter Sixteen

His bad arm ached like a horse had stamped on him. The rest of his body was little better. Exhaustion dragged all his limbs down.

He was not the man he'd once been. Somehow, he still managed to forget that. Perhaps his strength might return in time, but it was far more likely he'd be dead long before that.

Still, even in his current broken and reduced state, he was more than capable of catching Gottlieb, the *Freiherr* Geiss, when he made another run for it. And then kicking him down the stairs.

"Do try not to kill him," Morlaine said as they stood over the crumpled heap at the bottom. They were in the lower of the tower's rooms, so at least there would be no more steps for him to tumble down.

Morlaine nodded at the door, and he dragged himself to it as she hauled Gottlieb to his feet.

He peered around the door. No one was in sight. Thin tendrils of smoke still curled away from the castle.

"All clear," he said, returning to the others.

Morlaine had brought the four soldiers from the other tower and laid them out on the floor, their weapons piled by the door. None were awake. He'd stayed with Sophia and Gottlieb upstairs, so hadn't seen her do the task, but she'd done it far faster than he or anyone else could have.

The demon grabbed Gottlieb's collar and hauled him to his feet, "Do not do that again."

Gottlieb held her dark eyes for half a second before muttering something and staring at his boots.

Morlaine looked up at Sophia, hovering on the lowest step.

"Do you know how to use a weapon?"

The girl shook her head.

"Would you like to learn? You can practice on your cousin if he tries to escape again."

"Yes, please!"

She wasn't strong enough to handle one of the cumbersome wheellock pistols and was liable to shoot him as anyone else even if she could, so he scooped up a dagger from the collection of weapons taken from the Imperial soldiers.

"We want him alive," he said, reversing the blade and handing it to Sophia, "so best to stick to his arms and legs if he misbehaves."

She took the blade, stared at Gottlieb and then him.

"What about his... *wedding present* for me?"

He shrugged, "If you can find it, feel free to slice it off. Not much around for the birds to eat this time of year..."

Sophia giggled, Gottlieb grew even paler, and Morlaine raised an eyebrow.

"C'mon," he said, leading them to the door.

Once outside, he asked Morlaine, "So, what is our plan?"

She covered her head with the hood of her cloak before answering, "We take our friend to the castle, and he tells his men to leave."

That's what he thought it was, though he'd hoped the demon might have had something slightly more cunning up her sleeve.

"I will say no such thing!" Gottlieb piped up, "Ettestein is my birth- *Oww!!*"

"No one is interested in your opinion, vile pig!" Sophia spat, still pointing the dagger at her cousin.

"She bloody well stabbed me!"

He looked at the arm the nobleman clutched and wrinkled his nose, "I'd call it more of a prick..." he glanced at Sophia, "...maybe a little harder next time, my lady. There's quite a lot of blubber to get through."

Sophia twirled the blade a few times while glaring at her cousin.

"But you can't do this!"

He squared off nose to nose in front of the *Freiherr,* "If you're going to make this much fuss about a little girl poking you with a tiny knife, think what it'll be like if I have cause to hurt you..." he nodded in Morlaine's direction "...and as for her..."

Up close, Gottlieb smelt of bergamot oil and sweat. His Adam's apple bobbed up and down as his eyes bounced to the demon and back again.

"Now, are you going to be a good boy and do as your told, or are we going to have to kill you?"

"And what happens after you kill me?" the young *Freiherr* tried to straighten his back, "my men will just kill you!"

It was the same logic Morlaine used when Gottlieb had a dagger at Sophia's throat.

"Or they'll hoist us onto their shoulders and cheer us to

the rafters."

"What?"

"I know your type. A weasel. Men will follow you because you pay them silver. But they'll despise you because you're sending men to their deaths for your own greed. You're not the kind of man soldiers follow out of loyalty, honour or oath. If we slit your worthless gizzard, they'll leave on the spot. None of them wants to be in there," he jerked his head at the castle, "dying on Christmas morning because you're not as rich and powerful as you think you fucking should be!"

Gottlieb tried to back away but found Morlaine standing behind him.

Old Man Ulrich had worked for plenty of men like Gottlieb. Vainglorious self-entitled pricks who cared more for their hat than the lives in their care.

"Maybe I should take your head now and save everyone a lot of fucking trouble!"

Gottlieb, the *Freiherr* Geiss, was the kind of man used to being spoken to with nothing but deference. Which was probably half the problem.

He didn't even realise he'd drawn his sword till it was at the nobleman's throat. He was vaguely aware of Morlaine's eyes widening. His fury came hot and fast. It had no care for anything but the fool now cowering before him.

"So, what's it going to be?"

Maybe it was the kiss of steel at his throat, the rage in his eyes, or even the novel experience of being weak and helpless, but the bluster drained from the nobleman, and he nodded quickly, "Yes, yes, I'll do what you want. Please don't hurt me!"

When he kept the steel pressed against Gottlieb's neck, Morlaine warned, "Ulrich..."

He blinked. For a few heartbeats, it seemed so much easier to open the snivelling wretch's throat than sheath his father's sabre.

Then the weariness flooded back, and the sabre sank to his side.

Morlaine twisted Gottlieb around and shoved him towards Ettestein.

"I thought you were going to kill him," Sophia said, coming next to him. She sounded impressed.

So did I...

"'tis always best your enemies believe you'll do whatever you're telling them you will do..." he said quietly, fumbling his sword away in exchange for a pistol before hurrying the girl after Morlaine and Gottlieb, "...first rule of soldiering, that."

Sophia nodded.

"You should take shelter in the church or one of the cottages," he said, "this could easily go horribly wrong."

"She will be safer with us," Morlaine said without looking back.

He wasn't sure about that, but he hadn't the strength to argue, particularly as the set of Sophia's face told him she had no intention of doing any such thing. He suspected the girl was as stubborn and headstrong as Solace. Which was some achievement.

He hoped her life wasn't going to develop any more similarities to his mistress'.

356

They hurried under the crescent moon's fey light, their breaths steaming before them. Sophia, who wore no winter cloak, soon began shivering enough for her teeth to chatter.

He stripped off the Imperial cloak covering his own and handed it to her.

"Your father will not be best pleased if I let you freeze to death," he said when she stared curiously at him.

She nodded and wrapped the cloak around her.

As the path started climbing up the slope to Ettestein's gates, Morlaine clamped a hand on Gottlieb's shoulder.

"Stay close…"

Ahead, lights flickered inside the castle's maw, the smell of burning and gun smoke began tainting the crisp air.

This isn't going to work… this isn't ever going to work…

He held his withered arm out, "Stay behind me, but stay close," he told Sophia, "If something goes wrong, just turn and run."

She nodded and moved to his shoulder.

He let his bad arm flop to his side.

The slope was not steep, but to his legs, it felt like climbing the summit of some great mountain.

A couple of figures broke away from the gates and began walking down towards them; there seemed neither hurry nor concern in their manner.

Morlaine tugged on Gottlieb's shoulder and pulled him to a halt.

She glanced back at him, "Best you do the talking."

He could do that. It was raising a pistol or lifting a sword that would be a problem.

No matter. If it came to a fight, they were dead anyway.

He stepped in front of Morlaine and Gottlieb. Sophia moved to the demon's shoulder.

He stopped a couple of paces further on.

"That's far enough!" he shouted at the approaching men.

"Who's this?" a voice called.

"Doesn't matter who I am; we have your lord, the *Freiherr* Geiss. You're to call off your attack and leave Ettestein immediately, or we'll slit the worm's throat. Our comrades also have eight of your men. Frankly, I'd imagine they're of more use, and you can have them back too. If you do as we say."

The two men exchanged glances before one asked, "How do we know you have him?"

He wasn't sure what Morlaine did, but it was enough to make Gottlieb yelp, "'tis true, they took me! Do as they say!"

When the two men just stood there, he said, "If that isn't enough to convince you, I can cut something off and throw it to you. Which bit of Gottlieb, the *Freiherr* Geiss, your commanding officer and representative of Emperor Ferdinand would you like?"

When he half turned back, forcing his bad hand to clasp the hilt of his sword, Gottlieb shouted, "Do as he says, man. Fetch Captain Muntz!"

"Very well, wait there!" the men retreated quickly up the slope.

"At the gates," Morlaine told him quietly.

"No! We'll be in the Gate Towers; you have thirty minutes to march through those them or..."

Behind him, Gottlieb squawked again.

The Imperial soldiers started running up the hill.

"They look convinced…" he said as Morlaine spun Gottlieb around and shoved him back down the slope.

He ushered Sophia before him.

"Have you good eyes, my lady?"

"Yes, I think so."

"Pray keep them peeled; if you see anyone, let me know."

"Are your eyes not good?"

"They are fine, my lady, but we have far more enemies than I have eyes."

She nodded and looked back at the castle.

In truth, his eyes were not the problem. Twisting his neck to look behind him sent spasms of pain down his spine, and he was so exhausted he struggled to maintain the pace Morlaine set for Gottlieb.

Gritting his teeth, he forced his legs on, almost hoping the fat fool would stumble and fall in the mud to allow him a moment's reprieve.

Halfway back to the Gate Towers, Sophia said, "Men are coming from the castle."

"How many?" he panted.

A dozen… more…"

"Are they walking or running?"

"Running."

Morlaine shoved Gottlieb harder without looking around, "Move faster!"

"You'll never-"

The demon grabbed his thinning hair and yanked the nobleman's head back. He didn't hear what she said in his ear, but when she pushed him forward again, Gottlieb's plump little legs broke into a stumbling run.

"Go with... them..." he said to Sophia.

"What about you?"

"I'm protecting... our retreat..." when she kept staring at him, he added, "...please, my lady..."

The concern didn't leave her face, but Sophia hitched up her skirts and quickly caught up with Morlaine and Gottlieb.

Ahead, the Gate Towers loomed above them.

I can do this...

Broken and frozen, he'd made it from The Wolf's Tower to the hunting lodge in the woods. This was but a fraction of the distance, but it suddenly felt so much further.

Pain and exhaustion weighed down his limbs, but surely, it was less than it had been that terrible dawn.

Although, of course, there was one other difference between now and then.

This time, he didn't have Solace to lean upon.

*

Wendel.

She wanted to run away from the demon. She wanted to kill the demon.

The giant's body, which pinned her to the bed, meant she could do neither.

Wendel grinned, pulled over a three-legged stool, and slumped down on to it.

"My, what a night!"

She glowered at him till the grin faded.

"Now would be a good time to say your thank yous, so it would."

"Thank you...?"

Wendel's eyes flicked to the dead man, sprawled over her, "For saving your virtue. Just in the nick o' time, too, by the look o' things. But that's how the hero is supposed to make his entrance... isn't it?"

"You're no one's hero."

"Is it me or is there a distinct lack of gratitude in the air? I didn't have to come here, you know? My work is done. I could be off with me silver to slaughter a nice wee peasant girl or two, so I could. But, no, here I am saving you from this great, ugly lunk."

"Why would you help me?"

"You can't believe I would from purely the kindness o' my own heart?"

"No."

"What have I done to give you such a low opinion?"

"Murder my father, kill everyone I know, abduct my brother, destroy my home."

Wendel waved a hand in her direction, "Oh, that. Well, we're even now."

"No," she hissed, "we're not!"

She tried to push the body off her, it didn't budge. A landslide of flesh and armour trapped her on the bed. She started wriggling to free herself.

Wendel, who now wore his own face, hoisted an eyebrow.

"You need a hand with that?"

"No!"

"For the best, you being not decently dressed..." he licked his lips as his eyes lingered on the exposed flesh of her right leg sticking out from beneath the corpse she wore,

"...and me not being altogether good at resisting temptation..."

She stopped wriggling.

"Ah," he waved his hand again," you've nothing to worry about. I've drunk me fill tonight and... well... Torben would likely be pissed if I fucked you, so..."

Her heart pounded while her breath came in short sharp pants, due to the dead weight across her chest and diaphragm rather than fear.

Wendel smiled at her.

He had a broody, sour face, thick eyebrows and a low forehead that met in a seemingly permanent scowl. Smiling didn't suit him.

She tried wriggling a little less vigorously.

Her right arm was free, but other than her head, she could move nothing else. The giant's left shoulder pressed hard against the side of her face.

"Why did you help me?"

The ill-favoured smile faded.

"Because your brother asked me to."

"Torben?"

"He said you'd likely be having a wee bit o' bother here, in this room, at this moment..."

"You could have just told me before?"

"Aye, but then I'd have to give away I was here to do more than just deliver a message. Which would have put a spoke in me dastardly plan to get Gottlieb's lardy arse into the big man's chair here in Gothen."

"Gottlieb hired you?"

"He hired the Red Company, but Saul reckoned it didn't

362

need our full attention, just someone to open the gates. We have a lot o' demand on our time just at the minute. The war, you see. You wouldn't believe the mischief some of these fine God-fearing noble pricks are getting up to, so you wouldn't!"

She wriggled and stretched her right arm a fraction.

"How did Gottlieb get in touch with you?"

"Oh…" Wendel tapped his temple and laughed, "…think it's best I keep that one under me hat, so I do. Torben's told me you've got some funny ideas. That's why he wants you to take yourself off to Naples or some such place out o' harms way. Before you do anything stupid."

"Why-"

"You're a one for a question, aren't you?" Wendel leaned forward to put a cold hand upon on her cheek, "Let's save time. I'm not going to tell you anything other than I already have. Your brother says, "Go to Naples." 'tis good advice. You'll be happy there. He said it himself. And as we know, wee Torben knows a thing or three about the days to come, don't we now?

Happy?

Torben said she'd be happy.

How could he think such an impossible thing?

With Wendel's eyes filling her vision, she moved her fingers a fraction more.

"I'll only ever be happy when you're all dead…"

"Now that's a disappointing attitude for a young lass to have, so it is. Especially what with me saving your sweet unused cunny from this big fellah and everything!" Wendel gave the dead man's backside a playful slap.

"Well, just you remember, next time some big arse takes a fancy to your sweet arse, I won't be around to save you. Neither will your wee brother..." the demon sat back and wagged a finger at her, "...you'll be on your own..."

"I'll take my chances..."

"So you will, I dare say," Wendel shrugged and rose to his feet, "well, I best be going, nice as it is to chat and hear about all your grand plans to kill me and all."

"Can you at least get this bastard off me?"

She conjured a smile. As much as it hurt, she tried to make it look like she meant it.

"Ah, I've always been a fool for a pretty smile, so I have. Though, the bad language..." he shook his head.

He leaned over her and rolled the giant against the wall with no more effort than pulling aside a blanket.

"Thank you, really," she said, driving the dagger she'd freed from the dead Imperial's belt into Wendel's throat all the way to the hilt...

Blood, dark and cold, spurted over her hand as the demon staggered backwards.

She managed to roll clear of the bed, tugging a pistol from the giant's belt as she did. Wendel lashed out with his free hand, fingers brushed her hair, but she hit the floor and scrambled away before he could grab her.

He tried to say something, but only a wet, gurgling noise escaped.

It wasn't a killing wound for one of these monsters, but they still felt pain and she could rejoice in that.

The room was small; even with her back pressed against the wall, the demon was no more than three paces away.

Black, inhuman eyes looked down at her from Wendel's real face as she cocked the pistol.

Is this how Torben looks now?

Slowly, Wendel pulled the dagger from his throat. Blood and air bubbled as it slid clear. He dropped it to the floor, metal clanged on stone.

Left hand clamped to his neck, the demon stood watching her, no discernible expression on its long, too-thin face.

"You took everything from me..." she whispered.

Elbow resting on her bent knee as she sat against the wall, the pistol remained steady in her hand. That was something. She'd vowed never to show these things her fear again.

"I saved you," Wendel said, the words still thick and wet but understandable. He was already healing.

"The thing you could never understand, demon..." she said, voice as steady as her hand, "... is that after all you and your kind did to me... there is nothing left to save..."

Then she shot him.

Chapter Seventeen

He stumbled, falling to one knee.

Panting, he pushed the point of his father's sword into the mud and gripped either side of the quillon. It seemed an awfully long way back to his feet. Perhaps he should roll onto his back and stare at the stars?

Why go on?

Only death awaited.

Why go through the hardships of the Night's Road? He could reach the same destination so much more quickly by just staying here.

Where is the honour in that, boy?

Old Man Ulrich's raspy voice asked on the back of the breeze cutting the freezing air.

Fuck honour.

He wanted to shout back.

Instead, he forced himself upwards. Pain lanced the length of his withered arm and into his shoulder, a thousand tiny daggers searing his flesh.

Sometimes, the pain is the only thing left to remind you that you're still alive...

"And fuck your worthless fucking drunkard's wisdom, too..." he spat through the gaps in his gritted teeth as he wobbled to his feet.

Once satisfied he wasn't going to fall back down again, he

yanked the blade from the mud and dragged his protesting body forward again.

He didn't look back. No boots slapped the sodden path behind him, but the Imperials couldn't be too far away.

His father's sword dragged his good arm down. He'd move easier if he threw it away; there were plenty of other weapons in the Gate Towers if he needed one, but...

His fingers tightened around the familiar worn leather grip.

All he had in the world was his honour and his father's sword. He'd done his best to cast one aside; he wasn't going to lose the other.

That isn't all you have, though, is it, boy?

"What else do I have, you drunken old fool?"

The Lady Solace. Your mistress. You have her, too. Remember?

He didn't say anything to that, but, he noticed, his feet started moving a little faster.

Raising his head, he squinted towards the Gate Towers; the others were at the door of the right-hand tower. Looking back. Morlaine signalled for him to hurry, then pushed Gottlieb and Sophia inside.

He lowered his head, focused on his squelching boots and tried to make them move faster still.

You say you love her and you hate her...

His boots still felt iron-soled, but he kept them moving and ignored the weight upon his shoulders trying to grind him back into the mud.

...but you do not give your oath for hate, you do not give your honour for hate...

367

Voices sounded behind him. They could shoot him easily enough, but no muskets broke the night's deep silence. They wanted him alive, thinking he was of some worth, something to bargain for Gottlieb's liberty. The fools couldn't see what a worthless, broken thing he was.

...you do not give your life for someone you hate...

The cold cut his lungs while sweat slicked his face. Not much further. Really not much. Then he would be trapped inside a tower with a demon and a girl with only a fat idiot his men likely hated to barter for their lives. And Solace's.

...you only give your life away for love...

One problem at a time. That's how you walked the Night's Road. Until you found the one you could not solve. The one that sent you from this world and shovelled dirt on your lifeless face.

...you only give your life away for Solace.

His stride increased. Ignoring the pounding in his chest, the cold fire in his lungs, the taste of copper in his mouth, he broke into a run. He thought he might have screamed too.

Morlaine stood in the doorway. Face pale and expressionless, hand outstretched.

He feared his knees would buckle before he reached her, but he sucked down a last shuddering lungful of burning air and stumbled into the tower. He suspected his entrance might have involved his face hitting the straw-strewn stone floor if the demon hadn't been there.

"Ulrich...?"

He shook the demon's concern away, "I'm fine... I just lost my footing... a bit winded."

Morlaine only questioned him with her eyes as she slammed the door shut. As it closed, he caught a glimpse of the Imperial soldiers. They were a lot further away than he expected.

He put his back to the wall and waited for his heart to stop hammering.

Once the door's heavy bar was in place, Morlaine grabbed Gottlieb and shoved him towards the stairs.

Sophia came to his side and touched his arm, "Are you...?"

"Just winded, my lady."

She nodded without looking reassured.

Perhaps she found the idea that her safety and liberty rested solely with a broken wretch and a mysterious woman troubling.

Morlaine marched Gottlieb upstairs, "Come, hurry, you need to be at the window so you can negotiate."

Stairs. He'd forgotten about the bloody stairs.

"Do you-" Sophia began when he just glared at the steps on the other side of the circular room.

"No," he said, probably too curtly. He wasn't quite so broken he required a girl's help to climb some stairs.

He pushed himself off the wall and sheathed his father's sword. A pair of muskets sat amongst the pile of weapons they had taken from the soldiers. He slung a bandolier of powder and shot over one shoulder and then a musket in each hand.

Sophia took one from him. He wanted to protest, but the girl had a bold look about her that she was happy to cast in his direction.

"Do you know how to load a musket?" he asked as they started climbing the stairs.

"It looks simple enough..."

"Hopefully, we won't need them, but..."

"'tis prudent to expect the worst."

He snorted a laugh at that.

By the time they reached the next room, Morlaine had plonked Gottlieb in a chair. The three living soldiers on the floor were still as motionless as the dead one.

The room was the only one in the tower with a window facing the castle. A narrow glassless slit built before the days of muskets and gunpowder. Morlaine jerked her head at it.

As he crossed the room he tossed the bandolier at Morlaine, "Show Lady Sophia how to load a musket."

A dozen or so soldiers loitered at the foot of the tower.

"That's close enough!" he shoved the musket through the window for them to see.

"Is your Captain here?"

"He's coming!" one of the men shouted back.

He rested his shoulder against the stonework.

"My men have *Freiherr* Geiss and eight of your comrades. I want to see you withdrawing from the castle, or we'll start tossing them off the roof!"

"But-"

"Do it!"

He pulled back from the window to find three pairs of eyes staring at him.

"What do we do if they realise you're bluffing," Sophia asked him, the musket Morlaine was showing her how to load absurdly long and cumbersome in her delicate hands.

"Who said we're bluffing..."

When Gottlieb shifted uneasily on his stool, he smiled at the nobleman.

"Don't worry, my Lord. If it comes to it, you'll be the last over the edge..."

"Keep watching them," was Morlaine's only comment.

The Imperial soldiers clustered in a knot outside, well within musket range, they made no move to try and break down the tower's door.

Other figures were making their way down from Ettestein, the ranking Imperial, hopefully.

He placed his pistol next to the musket balanced on the window's narrow sill.

How much would they value Gottlieb's life? Enough to abandon the attack on the castle? Perhaps. How well their assault progressed might play a part in the decision too. And whether Gottlieb's podgy fingers were on this company's purse strings. The life of the man who paid you was always particularly precious to any soldier.

The wind bit through the window. He ached to curl up and sleep. He'd forced his broken body to its limit. He was a soldier no longer capable of fighting. What a worthless thing he'd become.

"There's more coming..." he said.

Sophia brought her musket, leant it against the wall, "Will they deal?"

"Your cousin knows the answer to that better than I," he rubbed his good hand over his eyes, "but let us hope..."

"What will happen if they refuse?"

"We will die, you will live," her eyes lingered on him, but he didn't meet her gaze, "you are a *Markgräfin*. You are valuable. Whatever happens inside the castle."

"I would rather die than become that vile pig's wife," she glanced over her shoulder at Gottlieb.

"Death should always be the last choice, my lady."

She threw back her head, "If it comes to it, I will jump from the roof myself."

Now he did turn towards her. Nothing in the set of her face suggested she was anything but serious.

He nodded.

He looked to see how much Morlaine had heard with her sharp ears. The demon stood behind Gottlieb, one hand clamped to his shoulder, her head was tilted towards the ceiling's rafters.

"Morlaine...?"

The demon lowered her gaze.

"Someone is up there."

"The soldiers who-"

One of those was dead, the other bound by Morlaine's blood.

"No, someone else..." the demon shook her head "...we are not alone in here..."

*

The pistol fizzed and fired, black powder sparks burning her hand.

Despite being only a few paces away, Wendel swivelled and twisted his torso. He couldn't avoid the shot, but a dark rose of blood bloomed upon his left arm rather than

372

the heart she'd been aiming for.

"Now you're starting to feckin' annoy me..." Wendel straightened himself, then stepped forward.

Perhaps he expected her to cower, whimper and plead.

No doubt the women and children who'd died after The Wolf's Tower fell had.

Instead, she threw herself at the demon, swinging the spent pistol at his head as she barrelled into him.

Something connected with something, but the demon swatted her away before she could be entirely sure of anything.

Pain fizzed along her spine as she crashed into the wall. She closed her mind to it. Bouncing off the stonework to dive for the bloody dagger Wendel had dropped after pulling it from his throat.

Fingers grabbed her hair as her own curled around the dagger's blood-slickened grip.

"Do you want me to kill you?" Wendel whispered in her ear, yanking her head backwards.

A crushing weight drove her down when she tried to struggle. The demon's knee was in her back, though it felt more like the castle had come down on top of her.

"Is that it, girl?" he hauled her head back, arcing her neck so much she feared it might snap.

The weight shifted, and a frigid breeze she did not immediately realise was the demon's breath froze her ear.

"I can do it, if 'tis what you really want? I understand. Believe me I do. Life... it can be such a burden. I feel it too. All me years weigh heavy, so they do..." he pulled her head further back, tautening tendons till they threatened to pop,

"...just a little more and it'll be over. No more pain, no more loss. Just peace, just silence. Tell me, girl, is that what you want o' me?"

"I want nothing from you!"

Laughter. Then the pressure eased a little.

"There's a thing or three I want from you though, so there is..." Wendel's free hand moved down her back and then squeezed her bare buttocks. She tried to swing back with the blade in her hand, but he released her head and grabbed her wrist before any of the feeble swipes got anywhere near him.

He twisted her wrist till the dagger fell away.

Then he forced her head down against the cold floor while his other hand explored her.

"Ah, don't you worry; I'm just having a little feel, so I am. Your brother wouldn't be happy if I did more than that... but where's the harm in a little feel, eh?"

She tried to buck him off, but the knee in her back kept her down as effectively as if she'd been speared to the floor.

"Stop!" she screamed as his hand pushed between her legs.

"There's no one here to break my neck, so there isn't... hmmm, what have we got here...?"

The fingers wriggling between her clamped thighs found Flyblown's mark, which became so hot her flesh virtually sizzled as the demon touched it.

The pressure on her back vanished and Wendel spun her over. She took the opportunity to try and claw his long, thin bloodless face.

A hand shot out, almost too fast to see, and suddenly she

could no longer breathe.

"Be still..." black, inhuman eyes stared down at her, unblinking. Within the huge dark pupils, filaments of gold seemed to swirl.

As soon as she ceased struggling, the pressure eased enough for her to gulp air.

"Open your legs."

When she tried kicking him instead, Wendel choked off her air again. When she stopped, his fingers loosened their iron grip.

"I'm not going to fuck you, if I wanted to, there wouldn't be a damn thing you could do to stop me..." the eyes drew closer, "...so stop fighting me and open your bloody legs!"

"Fuck you!" she hissed.

"Where does a young lady of quality learn such vulgar language? I think you've been associating with the wrong sort o' people, so I do."

It was hard to discern an expression on the strange demonic face looming over her, but amusement would have been her best guess.

"Now, let's play a little game. 'tis a simple one. I'll choke you till you either open your feckin' legs or you die. No need to look so concerned; it'll be fun!"

Again, the hand around her throat tightened. And this time, it kept on tightening. She tried reaching out behind her for the dagger Wendel had twisted from her grasp, but her fingers found nothing.

Still, the alien face stared down at her. A network of thin blue veins mottled the white skin; she was close enough to see the demon's blood pulsing through them.

Giving up on finding the knife, she tried to claw the thing's oversized eyes, but Wendel arched his back to move his face out of her reach while his fingers squeezed.

Darkness crept into the corners of her eyes, her blows became weaker and even more ineffectual. Fire sizzled her lungs.

"Just open your damn legs, don't be so feckin' stupid!"

Wendel reached down to push her legs apart, but she clamped her thighs together.

I'm going to die if I don't do as he says...

The thought of doing anything one of these monsters wanted sickened her. Even with the black curtain of her own death falling, it impaled her.

I don't want him seeing Flyblown's mark.

She didn't know why but accepted it without question.

"*Jeezus!* But you're a stubborn bitch, so you are!" Wendel rocked back, releasing his grip.

She sucked in desperate gulps of cold air and rolled onto her side. Tears cut down her cheeks as bubbles of snot erupted from her nostrils.

Blinking away tears, she looked across the floor. The dagger lay bloody and discarded just under the bed...

She started to crawl to it.

"There's more than one way to skin a whore..." Wendel grabbed her ankles. She yelped as he pulled her legs apart.

She tried kicking, but he was too strong.

Despite what he'd said earlier, she expected him to force himself on her as the dead giant had intended. Could she reach the dagger under the bed? If she let him do what he wanted, perhaps it would distract him enough. The idea sickened her, but the price of vengeance was not paid in silver.

You paid it in whatever currency it damn well wanted.

But Wendel made no move towards her; his eyes widened at the sight of her right thigh and the five red welts of Flyblown's mark.

"Where did you get this?"

"Get what?"

His hand shot up her leg to cover the mark, icy fingers mirroring the burning slashes, "This..."

"From... childhood," she said, trying to slide further from the demon and closer to the dagger.

Wendel's strange eyes rose as he whispered, "I've seen this before..."

"'tis nothing."

"Do not lie to me, girl! Who did this to you?"

"No one."

The demon shook it's long, thin head, "What have you done...?

She shuffled away from him. When he made no move to stop her, she kept going till her back pressed against the bed.

In a heartbeat, Wendel's human mask returned.

"Have you any idea who you've sold your soul to, girl?" he demanded, heavy brow furrowed, head craning forward.

"I'd sell it to the Devil in a heartbeat for your head," her hand closed around the dagger behind her.

"You price my head too high, so you do..." Wendel headed for the door, "...and your soul too lightly."

"Where are you going?"

"I've wasted enough time, so I have."

Wendel's demonic face might have been largely expressionless, but she saw something flash across his human one she hadn't expected. Not fear, exactly, but certainly unease.

What does he know about Flyblown?

She shoved her curiosity aside; it didn't matter who he was.

The only thing that did was vengeance.

Wendel looked over his shoulder as she struggled to her feet, one hand resting on the latch.

"Keep away from me..." he said.

Saul cannot know about my mark... he will not run away from it...

She didn't know if those words were hers, Flyblown's or her *sight's*. But she didn't question them.

Again, she launched herself at the demon, summoning rage and hatred through her burning throat to scream at him.

Rather than turn to face her, Wendel pulled open the door.

He's running away from me!

Perhaps running was an exaggeration, but he'd turned his back, which was all the encouragement she needed.

She flung herself onto his back, and they twisted out into the corridor together. Left arm around his neck, she tried to reach over and plunge the dagger into his heart, but the leather jacket he wore carried plates of metal stitched into it, and the blade just skidded off.

"Bitch!"

Wendel bent violently forward, throwing her over his shoulder to smash into the corridor wall.

She kept hold of the dagger, but pain exploded in her side before she could even try to regain her feet and do anything with it.

The demon kicked her, hard enough to crack a rib or two. And if the first kick hadn't, the second certainly did.

It must have hurt more after she'd jumped out of a window to escape the Man from Carinthia in Madriel, but as she remembered nothing of that, this felt worse than anything she'd experienced before.

She lay on the cold stone, every breath filling her torso with fire.

"Now stay where you are," Wendel shouted.

"I'm... never... going to... stop..." each word was an agony, each movement even more so, but she forced herself to look up at the demon looming over her.

Wendel looked like he wanted to say something, before shaking his head and turning away.

Clenching her teeth so hard she feared they might shatter; she started crawling after him.

.

Chapter Eighteen

He stared at the ceiling but heard nothing.

Save the voice whispering in his head.

The one that wasn't his father.

Master...

He swallowed, "What do we do?"

"Tie him up," Morlaine said, nodding at Gottlieb and already moving to the rope left over from trussing up the other imperial soldiers, "then we check."

He much preferred the idea of Morlaine going but nodded all the same and kept watching Gottlieb in case the nobleman decided it an opportune moment to try and escape.

"My lady..." he nodded towards the window, "...please keep an eye on our friends but stay out of sight. I want them thinking we have men-at-arms in here."

Sophia hurried to the window. She scooped up one of the muskets and thrust the barrel out into the night air. She grinned when he cocked an eyebrow, "I can be a man-at-arms!"

He smiled, despite himself. Then remembered what waited upstairs.

The smile faded.

"Look," Gottlieb's eyes bounced between them as Morlaine returned with some rope, "let us talk about this. I can make you both very rich if you-"

"Shut up, or I'll gag you as well as bind you," Morlaine yanked the nobleman's arms behind his back.

"Bad luck," he told Gottlieb, "very few people in Christendom are completely uninterested in money. But you've managed to find two of them."

Morlaine seemed to suppress a rare grin while Gottlieb yelped like a small dog as she tightened the rope around his wrist. When the nobleman made to speak again, he tapped the pommel of his father's sword with a finger. Gottlieb let the words die in his mouth.

Morlaine tied his ankles to the chair. It wasn't the sturdiest piece of furniture, but Freiherr Geiss lacked the strength or guile to get himself out of it.

A shout from outside stopped them before they could move to the stairs.

"Their Captain..." Sophia said, peering down from the side of the window, "...I think."

Morlaine hesitated and glanced at the ceiling again.

"I haven't heard anything up there," he said.

"Neither have I," the demon replied, "but something *is* up there..."

He believed her. He didn't want to, but he did. Still, he crossed to the window.

"We have to deal with this first."

"But-"

"Your friend hasn't been inclined to come down and join us yet... let us do this first."

"Who's there?!" he shouted without giving Morlaine the time to disagree with him.

"Captain Muntz," the voice came back.

"Is he in command?" he asked Gottlieb, looking over his shoulder.

When Gottlieb only glowered back at him, Morlaine slipped a finger of steel from her scabbard.

"Yes," the *Freiherr* mumbled.

Despite his noble birth, the man seemed to possess no more backbone than a jellyfish. Which at least made things easier.

He rested his good arm against the stonework. The window was marginally wider than his head; none of the imperials had raised muskets or crossbows, so he didn't think he was in much danger.

"And you are...?" Muntz asked.

"That doesn't matter. We have the *Freiherr* Geiss and the men you left guarding the gates; get your soldiers out of Ettestein if you want them back in one piece."

Muntz moved closer to the tower and put hands on his hips.

"We have prisoners too, my friend."

"Then we can exchange them once you're out of the castle."

"We've shed a lot of blood here, to-"

"Then best not to shed anymore!"

He turned back towards Gottlieb, "Order your men to leave."

The *Freiherr* tried to look defiant...

"And you will release me, unharmed?"

"Yes, my lord."

"On your honour?"

382

He wondered what concept of honour allowed Gottlieb to justify all the death he had caused, trying to kill members of his own family and force his fourteen-year-old cousin into his marriage bed. He'd wager a different kind to the one he'd had drummed into at his drunken father's knee.

"On, my honour. You will be freed. And all your men we hold here."

"Oh, yes, of course, them too…" Gottlieb nodded.

"Tell Muntz to leave."

Gottlieb looked at the window and then down at himself. Perhaps they'd been too hasty tying the bugger up.

Morlaine lifted the chair and carried it to the window with no more effort than if it didn't have a podgy young nobleman trussed up upon it.

Sophia's eyes widened, and she glanced at him.

He moved from the window and let Morlaine place chair and nobleman in front of it.

"There are some things it will be best you forget about this night for our… *convenience*," he told Sophia quietly.

She nodded. Eyes still wide.

"Order them to leave, my lord."

Gottlieb worked his lips together as if he had something to consider before calling down, "Muntz! 'tis *Freiherr* Geiss. Call off the attack and pull the men back to camp!"

"My lord, the castle is nearly ours! We have prisoners to exchange for you."

Morlaine, leaning against the wall next to the window, had pulled her sword free and ran a whetstone along it; dark, fathomless eyes never left the nobleman.

"You have your orders!" Gottlieb shrieked.

He looked over the *Freiherr's* head. Below, Muntz had retreated to the knot of men behind him and appeared deep in animated conversation.

"Will they agree?" Sophia asked.

"It depends how much they value your cousin's life. Given the conversation, there appears to be some debate about its worth."

"They would let us kill him?" Sophia's eyes grew wide again.

"Probably not. But if they guess how few of us there are, they might decide to storm the tower. If their beloved leader dies in the assault..." he smiled at Gottlieb "...well, of course, that would be a tragedy, but they would have the castle. Which the Emperor no doubt prizes much more highly."

Morlaine gave her blade another swipe with the whetstone.

"They will obey my orders!" Gottlieb's assertion might have carried more weight if his words hadn't come out as a high-pitched squeak.

He checked the window again. Muntz was still talking to his lieutenants.

"How would you make us rich?" he asked Gottlieb.

"With silver! With gold, with anything you want, all you have to do-"

"You have coin on you? Or did you expect us to simply take your word?"

"I have coin..."

"Where?"

When the nobleman said nothing, he slapped his face.

"I don't have time for games. Where?"

Morlaine ran the whetstone along her blade again. Even more slowly.

He crouched till he was at eye level with *Freiherr* Geiss. It was all he could do to stop himself from landing on his arse. Hopefully, he'd be able to stand up again.

"My lord, there is only one way you leave this tower alive. Where is your coin?"

"In my pocket," Gottlieb said, eyes refusing to meet his.

He found the purse in the second pocket he checked.

"Where's the rest?"

"That's all I have!"

"Soldiers are little more than thieves rich men give weapons to; you'd never leave your valuables back at camp. Where is the rest? Do I have to strip you in front of your cousin? Show her what she will miss by not marrying you.?"

Sophia giggled; Morlaine scraped her blade a little harder.

"Women can be so *cutting*... don't you think?"

Gottlieb swallowed. His eyes darted about the room before he muttered, "I have a money belt."

"Of course you do..." he patted the nobleman's cheek.

"Come with me, my lady," he said, heading for the stairs.

"Where are you going?" Morlaine asked as Sophia followed him across the room.

"I'm going to talk to Muntz man to man. Get that money belt."

He thought Morlaine would object but didn't wait to find out.

Downstairs, he lifted the bar off the door, "Lock this as

soon as I'm outside. I'll knock twice, take a breath and knock twice more to come back in. Otherwise, don't open it."

"Are you sure this is wise?"

"No," he conceded, "but Muntz and his men will want more than your cousin in return for leaving Ettestein. Trust me, if there is one thing in this world I understand, my lady, 'tis soldiers."

"Won't Gottlieb just demand his coin back?"

"The nobility prize their honour; he'll abide by any agreement rather than risk public disgrace and ridicule."

"But he hasn't agreed to anything!"

"He will..."

"Your friend-"

He raised a finger to his lips.

"Oh, yes," Sophia nodded, "I should forget her."

He smiled, then sucked in air. He felt a thousand years old without looking anywhere near as good as Morlaine did.

"Two knocks, a breath," he opened the door, "and two more, my lady."

"I understand."

He stepped into the sharp night air. Lady Sophia closed the door behind him.

Once he heard the bar fall into place, he walked halfway towards Muntz and his men before asking, "May we talk like honourable men, Captain?"

Muntz took off his helm. He was young for a captain, which meant he was either exceedingly capable or the minor son of a family wealthy enough to buy his position regardless of any talent for soldiering.

"Of course," Muntz nodded at his men and came to meet Ulrich alone.

"Are you minded to accept our terms, Captain?"

"You have a business-like air about you, sir. I do not even know your name?"

"My name is of no importance. Trust me, Captain. I am no one."

Muntz's eyes flicked over him, assessing.

"As I said, we are close to taking the castle."

"Your lord has ordered you to retreat. I have guaranteed his safety if you comply."

"Emperor Ferdinand is my Lord, sir, not *Freiherr* Geiss," Muntz offered a thin smile, "and the Emperor wishes Ettestein cleansed of heretics and returned to the true faith."

"And the Emperor gave explicit instructions, did he?"

Muntz tilted his head, "The Emperor wishes his Empire cleansed of heretics and returned to the true faith. He has been quite explicit about that."

"If you do not withdraw, we *will* kill him."

"And a terrible loss that would be..."

"And your men we captured along with him..."

Muntz's smile faded, "That would be more of a loss," he conceded.

He pulled out Gottlieb's purse and offered it to the Imperial Captain.

Muntz gave him a questioning look.

"Recompense for your inconvenience and loss."

"I have lost a lot of men tonight; despite the assurances I received that I would lose none."

"An advance in good faith, the remainder when you take your men through those gates."

Muntz's eyes moved from the purse to the gates, to the tower and then back to Ulrich.

"Your silver?"

"Your lord's... he prizes his life highly and is willing to pay handsomely for it."

"I doubt he has enough on his person."

"He has a lot of person."

Muntz laughed, and some of the tension eased.

"How many of my men do you have alive in there?"

"Eight... two are dead. I am sorry."

"I persuaded the *Freiherr* to keep his worthless friends with him, hopefully they are the ones you killed..." he sighed and shook his head, "...'tis war."

"It doesn't have to be."

Muntz let out a deep breath to steam in the frigid air.

"Letting blood on Christmas Day, 'tis a bad business. I advised against it... but the *Freiherr* said his men could only do the deed tonight."

"His men?"

"Traitors, I assume. They opened the gates for us. I guess he paid them handsomely or promised to do so... do not ask me their names. I don't know them."

"There was more than one?"

Muntz nodded.

He resisted the urge to look over his shoulder at the tower.

He held out the purse again, "Come, Captain, let's end this now and save some lives. 'tis Christmas; we need to make amends to the Good Lord."

Muntz met his eye with a steady regard and a calm air. He'd met plenty of officers in his life; he had an inkling Muntz was one of the better ones.

"Very well," Muntz took Gottlieb's purse and quickly lost it within the folds of his cloak without opening it, "I have your word my men will be released unharmed?"

"Yes, Captain. And *Freiherr* Geiss too."

Muntz smiled, "Of course."

"And the Emperor will forgive you?"

"Our orders were to dissuade the *Markgräf* from interfering with the Emperor's blockade of Magdeburg. A show of strength, a few days at the gates as a warning, then back to Magdeburg, but *Freiherr* Geiss got other ideas."

"He thinks Ettestein should be his."

"God save us from the greed and ambition of rich men."

"'tis the soldier's curse."

"Indeed!"

Muntz held out his hand; he took it without hesitation.

"I do not know the names of your traitors, but I hope you take their heads," Muntz said, voice dropping, "I did not care for them at all. There was something most off about them."

"What did they look like?"

Muntz pulled a face like he'd found sour beer in his cup, "One short, stocky, dark, the other taller with bright red hair, tangled in spikes. Both as pale as corpses. They spoke German with an accent. English, perhaps... do you know who they are?"

"Yes, thank you, Captain, I do..."

*

One of the monsters who'd murdered her father, stolen her brother and slaughtered everyone else she cared about sauntered off down the corridor with little apparent urgency.

The Bastard thinks he can't be hurt!

"Everybody…. hurts…" she spat blood through her teeth.

That might be so, but she wouldn't catch the demon by pursuing him on her hands and knees.

She didn't know what the effort of trying to stand would do to her ribs. But impotently watching Wendel disappear through the door at the end of the corridor would hurt a damn sight more.

Turned out it hurt a lot.

She swallowed the scream down to a whimper. One fat tear escaped her eye, and she swatted it away with the back of her hand. Despite wanting to charge after Wendel, she had to slump against the wall to prevent herself collapsing back onto the floor.

Sucking in snot and freezing air, she began staggering down the corridor, shoulder bumping the wall with every stride.

Wendel was at the far end of the corridor, almost consumed by the shadows.

Left arm wrapped around her midriff, she tried to move faster.

Why am I so cold?

It took her a moment to remember her legs were bare.

Cold didn't matter, pain didn't matter, being half naked

didn't matter.

Her free hand tightened upon the dagger, its blade darkened by the demon's blood, which had already dried to a black powdery crust.

Only one thing mattered.

"Demon!!!" she screamed as Wendel tugged the door open.

He didn't look back.

"Devil!!! Coward!!! Don't run from me!!!"

Turned out screaming hurt even more than walking.

More tears came.

Wendel slipped through the door and disappeared without looking back.

Like Father had done atop the barbican of The Wolf's Tower the last time she'd seen him, furious with her, thinking she'd killed his men in the Darkway, her face smarting from his palm. Heading off to his death.

Whereas Wendel was simply going to disappear into the night, yet again unpunished for his evil. Free to destroy more lives.

You don't possess foresight, Solace, just ignorance. Your mother was a sick and troubled woman... and clearly so are you...

"Father..."

She ignored the pain. Ignored the tears, ignored the frigid air on her bare legs and concentrated only on the dagger in her hand.

"...I'm sorry..."

Nothing answered. Only the ragged gasps of her breathing disturbed the silence.

Were they still fighting?

She tried to look over her shoulder to the door at the other end of the corridor, which opened onto the gallery but stopped herself. It didn't matter enough to be worth the effort.

The door drew closer; Wendel hadn't shut it after him.

Her knees almost buckled before she reached it.

If I go down, I'm not getting up for a while...

And if I get there, Wendel will be gone anyway.

She pushed her feet on, momentum taking her forward as much as anything else.

Darkness kept creeping into the corners of her eyes. She shook her head to keep it at bay.

Not giving up. Not!

She staggered into the door and managed to get some fingers around the edge to stop it from closing.

The temptation to slide down onto the floor almost overwhelmed her. Instead, she yanked the door open and stumbled through.

Another corridor. Narrower, shorter. Stairs going up to the right, down to the left. No demon.

Her eyes fell to the floor. No blood on the flagstones. The wounds she'd inflicted would have killed any mortal man. But Wendel wasn't mortal. And he wasn't bleeding anymore.

She scrunched up her face as an agonising wave crashed over her, threatening to wash away her senses. She clutched the open door till it passed.

Wendel was leaving the castle; he would be heading down. She took a step to the right.

Wouldn't he?

Something tugged her in the opposite direction.

Slowly she turned around and headed towards the stairs going up.

He went this way.

Yes, of course, he did.

She knew no such thing. Except that she did.

Flyblown's mark tingled and glowed; that spot on her inner thigh the only part of her that wasn't cold. The only part, she suspected, that wouldn't feel like dead flesh if somebody touched her.

It was a thought she didn't care for.

She headed for the stairs.

The pain in her ribs felt like it was easing a little. Or she'd been telling herself it was long enough for her to start believing it. Either way, she moved more freely. By the time she made the stairs, she was able to let her left hand drop away from her side.

The staircase ascended into deep shadow; she could touch either wall without stretching. The stone steps were ice beneath her feet, pulling her body heat - pulling her soul - down into itself.

Another image she didn't like.

Although darkness obscured the top, she didn't think it was a long staircase.

Hot knives drove into her side as she lifted herself to the next step.

At least it better not be.

Wendel... Wendel... Wendel...

She breathed through her teeth in time with each step.

It might have taken ten seconds to reach the top or ten

minutes. However long, it was enough to convince her the pain from her ribs wasn't easing after all.

Another door awaited her. Closed. She'd suffered a lot of discomfort for nothing if the bastard had locked it behind him.

Voices floated from somewhere. Distant. Not shouting or screaming. She paused, hand on the latch, waiting to see if they came closer. They didn't. The silence swallowed them. She remained alone.

The door swung outwards.

Why would Wendel lock it? He didn't think she would follow him through the castle. He didn't think she would follow him to the ends of the Earth and on to Hell itself. He didn't think she would kill him. He didn't know her.

Another corridor, even narrower and more dimly lit than the last.

Only a couple of feeble rush lights held back the darkness. There were no windows.

She dragged herself forward, teeth grinding against each other. Doors lined either side of the corridor. Wendel wasn't looking for somewhere to hide; he intended to slip away into the night. Corpses and soldiers packed the castle's main entrance, so he would leave by another route.

Flyblown's mark pulsed in agreement.

By the time she reached the door at the far end, sweat slickened even her bare legs.

What do you intend to do if you catch him? You can barely walk?

One bridge at a time.

After steadying herself, she pulled open the next door.

394

More stairs, spiral ones this time, twisting up into complete darkness. She thought about going back for one of the rushlights, but she couldn't spare the time or energy.

I'm not afraid of the dark anymore.

Or the monsters that live in it.

She started hauling herself upwards.

The darkness quickly wrapped itself around her. Left shoulder brushing against the stonework, she found the thickest part of each next step with her foot before pulling herself up.

She ignored the nothingness like she ignored the pain by losing herself in a greater nothingness, a greater pain.

The price of vengeance is not paid in silver...

Pounding heart and ragged breath were the only sounds, the cold numbing her bare flesh the only sensation beyond the hurting.

Fingers tightened around the dagger, the leather grip damp with sweat. Blood too. Her own as well as the powdery remains of Wendel's.

Ahead, the darkness softened. A window's grey light allowed her to distinguish the steps. No monster awaited her.

He isn't going to wait for me. If he wanted to kill me, he would have already.

I have nothing to fear but fear itself.

She snorted out a shaky laugh at that. She didn't know why. It wasn't worth the twist of bright torment in her side.

The steps brought her to the window. Just a thin slit in a recess cut into Ettestein's thick skin. She snatched a moment to suck in bitter air. In the distance, she could make out the Elbe, a silver thread in the fey moonlight. Distant voices floated out of the night. No sounds of fighting accompanied them. Perhaps it was over. Perhaps Ettestein had fallen. Was everyone dead? Renard? Lucien? Lebrecht? The *Markgräf?*

She didn't know. She didn't know how their deaths would make her feel, either. Would she feel anything? Did the capacity for grief still live within her, or had Saul and the Red Company burnt it like they had The Wolf Tower itself? Leaving behind just another shattered, broken thing no longer capable of sustaining life?

Turning from the window, she expelled everything from her mind.

Nothing mattered.

She would deal with the dead when Wendel was lifeless at her feet or gone back into the night. Until then...

She turned the blade in her hand.

Other windows came and went, transitory slivers of moonlight. Snatches of voices too, alien and unreal. They came from another world. They meant nothing.

The pain ebbed and flowed with each step. One foot after the other. Every one taking her closer to vengeance. Or a slice of it, at least.

A door appeared around the curve of the staircase.

"Give me strength..."

She didn't know if she was beseeching God, the Devil or Lord Flyblown. She would gladly take whatever help she could. But as no strength washed into her bones, she assumed they were all deaf to her pleas. She was on her own.

For a few seconds, she stood before the door, panting, hurting, twisting the dagger back and forth in her shaking hand.

Then she shoved it open.

The cold slapped her. She ignored it. She knew pain.

A couple of hurt-racked steps took her onto Ettestein's battlements. Moonlight washed the frost-glistened stonework.

"Wendel!"

The demon had climbed up between two crenelations to stand on the very edge of the battlement. An impossible descent for anyone else, but one of these creatures could probably clamber down a sheer wall without too many problems.

It was up to her to make it a problem.

She burst into a run.

Though *burst* and *run* were both optimistic descriptions for the agonised shuffle, she forced her tortured body into.

The demon grinned.

"You don't give up, do you girl?"

Her reply was a guttural, primal scream.

Wendel turned to face her, then waved.

Her legs took her forward… and then they took her down. Knees buckling, she crashed onto the frozen stonework, more jarring pain, mouth filling with copper.

She leveraged herself up on her arms, panting breath steaming into the night.

That's when she saw the body.

A woman. Young. One of the maids by her simple dress.

"She was hiding from the fighting up here," dark smears,

she noticed, blurred the monster's mouth. He shrugged, "Which was handy as I had to eat to heal, thanks to you..." his eyes flashed back to the dead woman, "...not so handy, for her, o' course."

It was Dorothea, the maid who'd laid the table in the cottage a few hours and half a lifetime ago.

"Bastard!" she made to stand but only got as far as one knee. She still held the knife, but the dozen paces to the battlements where the demon stood seemed like a chasm. She could try throwing it at him, but she could try spitting at him too; there wouldn't be much difference.

Wendel leaned against a crenelation, left elbow on the icy stonework, right finger waggling at her, "You know, this one's on you. If I hadn't needed the blood, I'd have left that wee girl be, so I would. This is what happens when you interfere..." the waggling stilled into a pointed finger, "...very bad things!"

With a strangled grunt, she hauled herself back onto her feet.

"You'd have killed her anyway."

Wendel pulled a long face, "Maybe, maybe not, but you'll have to live with that, just like all those who died in The Wolf's Tower."

She took a single step forward. Then stopped.

"They didn't die because of me!"

"We were there for you, so we were. If you'd been born ugly..." he laughed. She felt her face twitch and twist, the words biting deeper than the freezing breeze atop Ettestein.

She wanted to scream at him but didn't have the energy. So she took another step forward.

"Go to Naples, Solace. What's done is done. You can't save your brother, either. He's gone too."

"Torben will never be like that."

"No?" Wendel shook his head, "You know I said I didn't kill that farmer and his family? That weren't no lie. I didn't. Was your big brother, so it was. Said it needed to be done so you d be here in Ettestein when we came to do our bit of work for that fat fuck Gottlieb. Said I'd do that job too, but he wanted it for himself, so he did. Got a taste for the dark work now, so that boy has. Took a few o' our lads and had themselves quite the time while I came here and did some chatting with the fat lad who thinks his arse should be sitting in this here lord's chair."

"Liar!"

"You can't rescue him, Solace. Think that's why he did it, to convince you he can't be saved..."

Fury pushed her forward. A monster's lies would not distract her!

"Would love to chat, so I would, but you've kept me too long already, so you have!"

She tried to make her feet move faster, tried to tell herself no agonies sliced through her with every breath, let alone every shaking step.

"God help me, I will kill you!" the words that escaped upon her steaming breath did not even sound like hers.

Wendel just grinned.

Two pains, different and new, seared through her. The first, a hatred, black, pure and with nowhere to go. Pushing, pulling, stretching and ripping her soul. The second was Flyblown's mark, glowing suddenly so hot it felt like a cattle brand was pressing into her inner thigh.

Wendel waved again, then span around to show her his back as he prepared to clamber away down the side of the castle.

Until his foot slipped away from him on the frosty stonework.

He teetered on the edge, hand shooting out, trying to grab a hold of something.

Then he toppled backwards with a strangled cry.

Now her feet did work; now she could ignore all her pain.

Would a fall kill one of these things?

If he died instantly, then yes.

And falling hundreds of feet onto your head should do that.

She slumped against the battlement, leaning out to peer over, hoping to see Wendel's shattered body motionless below.

Instead, two wild, wide eyes stared up at her in the moonlight.

He'd managed to catch the edge of the pitted battlement with one hand.

She drove her dagger into it. Deep enough for it to vibrate against the stone beneath, then ripped it back, tearing the hand in two.

Wendel screamed and let go but grabbed the edge with his left before he fell.

"Please!"

She stared down at him, seeing nothing but fear in the straining set of his face.

"Did my father say that as you roasted him alive?" she

held the blade above his hand.

Wendel said something, but she couldn't make out what it was.

"I suppose not; he did have an apple stuffed in his mouth at the time, didn't he?"

She shrugged and sliced off one of the demon's fingers.

More screams. Enough to bring a smile to her face. But not enough to make him let go. So she hacked off another one. The little finger this time. She found the crunch of parting bone particularly satisfying. Blood spurted over the ice, and Wendel started slipping away. He was trying to get his ruined right hand up to grip something, but the fingers didn't seem to be working. They healed quickly but not instantly.

"Help me, please!"

She pressed the blade across the remaining fingers, hooked over the very edge of the stonework.

"Help you? Why should I do that?"

"I'll do anything you want... please..."

Would he tell her where the rest of the Red Company were? Would he tell her the truth about Torben instead of black lies? Would he give her a way to kill Saul the Bloodless?

Possibly.

Could she trust him?

No.

"There's one thing," she whispered, "do it, and I'll spare your life."

"Anything!" Wendel's remaining fingers slipped back across the ice-flecked, blood-slickened stone.

She held his eye.

"Can you turn back time and give me my life back?"

Wendel stopped struggling. He didn't answer.

"I thought not."

With the palm of her left hand on the blade, she pushed down and sliced off the demon's last fingers with a grunt and a twist.

And then watched him tumble and spin down to oblivion with a smile on her face.

Chapter Nineteen

Gottlieb was initially reluctant to tell Muntz the silver in the money belt was his. However, after Morlaine crouched down and whispered a few things in his ear and all the remaining colour drained from the nobleman's waxy face, he did as he was told.

"We need to go now," Morlaine's eyes flicked to the ceiling once Muntz sent word to his men to call off the attack and leave the castle.

"Can you watch the window and your cousin?" he asked Sophia.

"Of course."

"If he tries anything, don't kill him, but short of that…"

Sophia nodded vigorously, then turned towards Gottlieb, "You are not going to do anything but sit there, are you, cousin dearest?"

Gottlieb glowered at the girl.

If he could slip the knots, he didn't doubt the *Freiherr* would try to escape. If only to prevent his silver from going to Captain Muntz.

He checked the bindings again. If Gottlieb had been trying to loosen them, he hadn't gotten very far. He nodded at Morlaine and smiled at Sophia.

"I'm in charge," Sophia announced from the window, twisting the dagger in her hand, her eyes moved to Gottlieb, "best you don't test me..." she smiled sweetly before adding, "...vile pig!"

He trailed Morlaine to the stairs; she drew her sword as she mounted the first step.

"You might not need that," he said.

The demon looked over her shoulder and cocked an eyebrow.

"A hunch," he said.

"I can smell what is up there," Morlaine replied, then continued, sword still in hand.

He followed.

The top room was as they had left it earlier, save for the red-haired man sitting cross-legged on the table.

"Christmas tidings!" he beamed and waved. The seasonal bonhomie somewhat undermined by his waving with a severed hand.

"Oh," he said, glancing at the imperial soldier sprawled on the floor, "he won't miss it; he was already dead. I *did* check."

Morlaine took a step forwards. The man blinked and kept smiling.

He stepped ahead of Morlaine and put his arm across the demon.

"Wait..."

"I can smell Saul on him..." she said, eyes not leaving the other demon.

"No one gets to choose their parent. I didn't..."

"Morlaine..." he said, still holding his arm across her, "...this is Henry Cleever."

"We don't require introductions, Ulrich."

Morlaine knew who Cleever was; she'd extensively questioned Solace and him about the demons they encountered in The Wolf's Tower. It was one of the few times she'd looked interested in what he was saying.

Gently she pushed his arm down and started towards Cleever.

The demon smiled, "You're not going to kill me tonight, Morlaine."

"I'm not?"

"This is not the day I die."

"Did Torben tell you that?"

"He has told me many things..."

Morlaine raised her sword. She was too far away to strike him, but that didn't mean much given the speed these monsters could move.

"The future is not set in stone, Henry Cleever; I decide my fate. And yours."

Cleever blinked, but his smile didn't waver.

"A debate on the nature of free will is always fascinating, but I'm not sure we have the time, do you?"

"You certainly don't."

"What do you want, Cleever?" he asked. Morlaine wanted to take Cleever's head from his shoulders; no good reason why he shouldn't want the same came to him. But the way the demon sat patiently and relaxed on the table suggested he had something to say they should listen to.

And of all the Red Company's demons, of all the monsters he'd briefly called master, Henry Cleever scared him the least.

"Want, Ulrich? What makes you think I want anything?"

"Because you've been sitting up here doing nothing while we try to undermine your... client's plans."

"I haven't been doing nothing!" Cleever held up the severed hand again, "Have you seen this fellow's fingers? They're remarkable!"

They didn't appear remarkable to him, even when Cleever started wiggling them and nodding at him as if revealing something terribly clever.

"I doubt Wendel, or Saul for that matter, would consider you collecting body parts the most productive use of your time, all things considered."

"Oh, they know what I'm like," he popped the hand in a satchel at his side, "the human body is just *fascinating*, don't you think?"

"You are produce of Saul," Morlaine said, the quiver in her voice clear even if the blade remained rock steady, "every life you've taken burdens my soul. You'll take no more."

"Morlaine... we haven't met, but I know you. All vampires are mad, but yours is a particular form of torture, I imagine. Denying yourself everything this world has to offer because of something you did out of love."

"You don't know me."

"Perhaps. But I do have some inkling of the things to come, and Torben has revealed much, much more. You will not always be like this. Years hence, a broken man will rescue you from the darkest of places. And in doing so, he will release you from more than one manner of chain. You *will* know love again, Morlaine..."

"That is as unlikely as you leaving this tower with a head upon your shoulders."

"This man, who is not yet born, is called-"

"Shut up!"

Morlaine moved to the edge of the table, sword raised.

Henry Cleever did not move a muscle.

"Morlaine!"

He didn't think she would heed him, but there was something in Cleever's big dark eyes that made him think they should hear him out.

The blade flashed.

And stopped a hair's breadth from Cleever's throat.

The demon did not flinch.

The dark-haired woman panted, nostrils flaring, though he knew well enough that nothing so simple could exert her physically.

"What?" she asked, eyes not leaving Cleever's.

"Let him say his piece."

"It's just a trick, Ulrich. To keep us talking until Wendel gets here. Trust me. Two vampires are much harder to kill than one."

"Wendel won't be joining us. He had to drop in somewhere else."

"Where? she demanded, "Taking more lives to weigh down my soul?

"No," Cleever shook his head, paying no heed to the steel at his throat, "the Lady Solace has ensured he will take no more lives."

"My lady?" he stepped forward, "Is she...?"

"Bruised and hurting," Cleever's eyes moved to him, "But she will live. As much as what lies before her can be called living anyway. She has her first slice of vengeance. But it is a dish that will not sustain, or nourish, or satisfy..." his gaze returned to Morlaine, "...something I think you know well yourself, yes?"

"You lie," Morlaine hissed.

"All vampires lie. We both know that. But in this case, I speak truly. As you will soon discover."

"But you do not know..."

Cleever's shoulders twitched, "No, I do not have Torben's gift. I do not even have Solace's. But... I can tell the truth of things. I always could. I think that is why Saul chose me, made me... *corrupted* me. But..." he shrugged again, deeper this time, "...I suspect I have been a disappointment to him."

"He has a new toy now?" Morlaine's blade lowered a fraction.

"I believe pet might be a more accurate description. Though Saul thinks of him as more of a weapon."

"A weapon?"

"Saul believes he has a purpose. He was not born... or reborn... out of the random chaos of the world. He certainly does not think he was born out of your misplaced but entirely genuine love. He believes in... destiny. A purpose, a meaning. Something more than being a monster that rejoices in the blood of innocents. He believes Torben can show him how to bring forth the World's Pain. He believes he shall become a god."

"All vampires are mad..." Morlaine said.

"Indeed..."

"So... why *are* you here?" he asked when neither demon did more than stare unblinking into the other's eyes.

"The destiny Torben sees is not the one Saul wishes to hear."

"The future is not writ in stone," Morlaine insisted.

"No," Cleever agreed, "it isn't. What Torben actually sees are the possibilities, but his gift is not so much that, we can *all* see possibilities, yes? 'tis that he sees the probabilities too and understands them..." Cleever's eyes moved from Morlaine to him, "...he is not the boy you remember. Kissing the vein brings many changes. The physical ones... well, you've seen those. The changes wrought to the mind are usually more straightforward. Madness, in one form or another, sooner or later. But, in Torben's case, it lifted the fog from his extraordinary mind. And it gave him... *clarity*," Cleever's gaze dropped to lap, "...the poor, blighted soul..."

"And what are these possibilities and probabilities Torben sees that will prevent me from taking your head?" Morlaine twisted the blade one way and then the other.

Cleever was silent for a long while before he answered.

When he finally did, Morlaine lowered her sword.

*

She opened her eyes.

She had no recollection of closing them but was certain whenever she had, she'd been in a different place.

A figure stood at the end of the bed. It took a breath or two to recognise him in the murky light.

"My lady...?" Renard said, arms remaining crossed.

She tried to prop herself up on her elbows. The spikes being driven into her ribs suggested that wasn't a promising idea. She sank back down.

"Ouch..." was all she managed to say.

Renard came around to the side of the bed and sat on a chair.

"How do you feel?"

"Everything hurts."

"My father once told me pain is the price we pay to be reminded we are not dead."

"In which case..." she grimaced, "...I am *exceedingly* alive."

He smiled.

Perhaps it was the discomfort fogging her brain or the flattering light, but for a moment, in the glow of that smile, he looked like the handsome young man he'd been the year before.

She closed her eyes.

An unnecessary thought.

"What happened?"

"You took a fearful beating. Another one. You are beginning to make a habit of it, my lady."

"You sound like my mother."

In truth, she had no idea what her mother sounded like as Elenore von Tassau died giving birth to her, but he had the good grace not to correct her.

She took a couple of shallow breaths. Then a deeper one. The pain seemed marginally less excruciating. A good sign? She felt her side, strapped with tight linen bandages.

Memories swirled. She tried to catch hold of a few. Renard sat in silence while she put them into order.

"The Imperials?"

"Gone, my lady."

"Gone? We beat them off?"

"No. I persuaded them to leave."

She peeled open an eye, "*Persuaded?*"

"*Freiherr* Geiss became very amenable to seeing the error of his ways once he had a blade at his throat. I believe the scales have now completely fallen from his eyes; he has forsaken greed, avarice and ambition in order to devote the remainder of his days to charitable works."

He shrugged when she stared at him, "I am a natural optimist."

"And that was all it took for the Imperials to withdraw?"

"Their captain proved to be a sensible and reasonable man. Rare qualities in an officer. We were fortunate... though a large amount of silver was required to grease the wheels of his reasonableness."

Her eyes widened and she felt her waist once more. Her money belt was gone!

She tried sitting up.

It was still a mistake.

Renard pulled up his shirt a fraction to reveal her money belt, "the *Freiherr* generously donated the silver. Yours is all here. I resisted the urge to save any more orphans."

She settled back down.

Then tried to push herself back up, "Lucien...?"

"Sadly..." Renard dropped his eyes and pursed his lips, "...he survived. And is now claiming he single-handedly held back an entire Imperial army. I fear he has become even more boastful than the conceited boor you knew yesterday."

"You do not care for him much, do you?"

"That is not true. Of all the people I know who still live, he is my second favourite."

"You only know three people alive."

Renard lowered his voice, "I'm not sure we can count Morlaine as being truly alive, my lady."

"We were overrun on the gallery; how did Lucien survive?"

"He'll tell you he proved such a fearsome foe the Imperials fled in terror from his flashing blade and implacable smile. However, I understand the *Markgräf* arrived with more men to save the day before they could cut the oaf to pieces."

Other questions jostled her from all sides, but Renard must have seen her struggling with them, "You should rest, my lady. Your ribs are broken. The *Markgräf's* physician said it was a miracle you did not puncture a lung. Or freeze to death. Running around with broken ribs and bare legs in winter is most ill-advised," Renard found a smile, "his words, not mine."

She decided to ignore both Renard's and the physician's advice, "Wendel, is he-"

"Dead, my lady. You killed him."

She arched her neck and let out a stale hiss of air. None of the pain tormenting her body or soul eased.

"For certain? You found a body? You-"

Renard did something that surprised her enough to stop the words in her throat. He reached over and took her hand.

"Yes. You were raving about him when they found you. I went to the rocks at the foot of the castle at sunrise. There was a body. More like something from an ancient tomb than a fresh corpse. Morlaine said that is what happens to

412

a... vampire's body after it dies."

"Morlaine, did-"

He stilled her with another squeeze of the hand.

Was it appropriate for a retainer to hold the hand of his mistress? Of course not. But she did not pull away. They had shared a bed before now, after all. They had shared intimacies few men and women ever could. Dark ones that went far beyond mere... touching.

Besides, she found the warmth of his hand comforting.

They remained like that for a while. Holding both hands and eyes.

Only when the door creaked open did he let go and sit back.

"Ah, the patient is awake!"

"My lord," Renard shot to his feet as Hendrick, *Markgräf* of Gothen entered the room.

He looked older as he peered down at her through two black eyes. In addition to the other calamities to befall him recently, he'd also suffered a broken nose,

"How are you feeling, my dear?" the *Markgräf* asked. She thought his tone overly familiar until she remembered she'd agreed to marry him.

A queasy roll of the stomach joined her other discomforts.

Agreed? Promised? Offered? Considered?

Some of her memories were still a touch fuzzy.

"A little sore, my lord."

"You were most brave," he said as if talking to a child. She thought he might try to pat her on the head, "If you could give us a moment, please, Ulrich."

Renard's eyes turned to her before he agreed to anything.

She nodded.

"Of course, my lord, my lady. I shall wait outside."

"A good man," the *Markgräf* said once the door clicked shut.

"Yes, he is."

"Should have given Gottlieb to me after getting the Imperials to leave, but..." he flicked out the tails of his jacket and lowered himself onto the chair.

"Lebrecht?"

"Is well, a few new scars aside. As are Joachim and Sophia. My daughter in no small part to your man. I am very grateful."

She found a smile.

"We have much to discuss," he said, arranging and rearranging the hands in his lap.

How many men-at-arms do you have left?

She kept the question from her lips. That probably wasn't what he had in mind.

"I am very tired, my lord," she said, which was the truth.

"Of course, this isn't the moment. And there will be time aplenty later."

"There will?"

"You are in no condition to ride off chasing... your enemies. You must stay in Ettestein until you are fully recovered."

"A day or two," she conceded.

"I broke ribs once, fell from my horse. It was a lot more than a day or two before I got back in the saddle, and you..." he let the words slide into a smile.

Are a woman.

"I'm a fast healer."

"We shall see."

He leant forward and took her hand, much like Renard earlier, without it feeling at all the same.

"You are lucky to be alive, my lady. If you ride off after more of these creatures…"

"It was not a matter of luck."

"You lived only by God's grace."

"As do we all, my lord."

"I lost your mother. I do not wish to lose you too. You coming to my door is a miracle; by their very nature, one does not experience many such things in one's lifetime."

"We had an understanding; nothing has changed on my part. Has it on yours, my lord?"

"I wish…" he ran a thumb across the back of her knuckles; she resisted the urge to yank her hand away, "…only for you to be my wife. As your mother should have been."

"Then we still have an understanding."

How many men-at-arms do you have left?

He smiled, then climbed to his feet.

"I shall let you rest."

He hesitated, then leant over and kissed her forehead. He'd found time to oil his hair but not bathe. Scents of rosewood and macassar competed with sweat, gun smoke and death.

"Thank you, my lord."

He pulled away a little, but not so far his eyes did not fill most of the world. She thought he might try and kiss her lips. It would be improper, but she did not flinch.

He regarded her tenderly, but all she saw in his eyes were Wendel's... falling, falling, falling into the abyss where they belonged.

She blinked and looked away.

The *Markgräf* coughed and straightened quickly.

"I am sorry, my lord... I am so very tired..." she let her head slump to one side.

Was she overdoing it?

"I shall let you rest. If there is anything you require...

Men-at-arms...

"I will not hesitate..."

He smiled, nodded, rearranged himself, eyes lingering for longer than necessary and finally left.

She let out a shaky breath.

How long would it take before she could ride again?

Too long.

She needed Morlaine.

Chapter Twenty

"No."

"No?"

"No."

"Why not!?"

Morlaine stood at the end of the bed, Lucien with his back against the door, he by the window. Outside, the wind howled beneath the moon.

"Not enough time has passed since you last took my blood. Too much, too often, is dangerous for the mind, body and soul. And the power wanes each time you imbibe from one vampire. Your injuries are not life-threatening. Better you heal naturally. You may have a greater need of my blood in future."

"But it will take too long," Solace slapped her hands on the bed, "I cannot stay here!"

Morlaine cast an eye around the room, "It is comfortable; you are in no immediate danger. Why the hurry?"

"You know why!"

The demon raised an eyebrow, which was as expressive as she ever got.

"I want Bulcher's head," Solace said when it became evident glowering wouldn't be enough to make Morlaine lower the eyebrow.

"How did killing Wendel make you feel?" Morlaine asked.

"*Feel?* What does it matter how it made me feel?"

"Vengeance corrodes the soul. It never tastes as sweet as you think it will. That disappointment just makes you want more, makes you think if you can just pour enough blood, it must eventually fill the emptiness within. But no matter how many you kill, Solace, it never will. It will never make you whole again. It can never replace what you have lost. I was hoping what now turns inside you will make you see this."

"We want the same thing. We should be working towards achieving it... not..." she slapped her hands on the bed again, harder this time, "...sitting around doing nothing!"

"Wendel was not the only demon of the Red Company here," he said, ignoring the look he got from Morlaine. They had agreed to say nothing to Solace until she was stronger. But she seemed strong enough to him. And convincing her she didn't immediately need to jump on a horse might at least calm her down.

"What do you mean?" she demanded.

"Henry Cleever was here too."

Solace's eyes darted back to Morlaine, "You killed him?"

"No."

"He escaped?"

She shook her head, "We... I... let him leave."

Solace struggled upright, nostrils flaring, the cords in her neck straining, "You did... *what?!*"

Perhaps this wasn't the best way to calm her down after all.

"He brought a message from your brother," he said.

"Go to Naples? Yes, I've already had that one!" Solace grew

red in the face, anger transforming her into someone he didn't recognise.

The fingers of his right hand moved against each other as he remembered the feel of her hand in his.

He dropped it to his side.

I love her, and I hate her.

But neither mattered.

"Actually, yes," Morlaine said when he remained silent, "but he knows you will not go. He will keep trying to persuade you, but he does not expect success. Partly because he knows you..."

"...and partly because he sees the future. Including yours," he finished.

"What does he... see?" Solace asked, looking back and forth between them.

He exchanged a glance with Morlaine and decided to let the demon do the talking.

"Cleever says... your brother is not always lucid. He rambles. He contradicts himself; he is often confused. He does not know how much of that is an act for Saul's benefit."

"Then he is not a monster! He is trying to help me, I kne-"

"Solace," Morlaine shook her head, "all vampires are mad. Your brother is no different."

"Yes, yes, so you keep saying... but he *is* helping me. He sent Wendel here knowing I would kill him and Cleever..." she frowned, "...is helping him?"

"All vampires are mad," Morlaine repeated, "they are also deceitful and untrustworthy. I fear Cleever is no different."

"Yet you let him live?" Lucien asked, rubbing his stubbled

chin.

"He wants Saul stopped."

"Why?"

"Because Torben fears he will destroy the world if he isn't..."

A long deep silence fell upon the room until Lucien asked, "So... why wasn't he just lying to save his own skin? Many a low fellow will promise the moon and the stars in return for their worthless hides," the mercenary started scratching his scalp. He looked either confused or his lice were being more bothersome than usual.

"He wanted to see us, waited for us. He had the opportunity to run before we found him. He had no interest in fighting," Morlaine said.

Still scratching, Lucien asked, "If he wants Saul stopped, why doesn't he kill him himself?"

"He can't."

"He's squeamish? A pacifist?" Lucien pulled a long face, "I assume he has no problem with the sight of blood?"

"A vampire cannot kill their maker."

Lucien stopped scratching. His eyebrows shot up, "No?"

"It's the shared blood... I don't know why. I have heard of cases where vampires have overcome this to slay their maker. But it is very rare. And it has terrible consequences..."

"So, we must do this Cleever fellow's dirty work then?" Lucien snorted.

"And Lord Torben's," Ulrich pinched his nose, stifling a yawn.

"Saul cannot kill you?" Solace asked Morlaine.

A faraway look flickered in the demon's dark eyes. It was the only answer she gave.

"So..." Lucien broke the following silence, "...I assume Cleever has or will do something to help us stop Saul?"

Again he exchanged a look with Morlaine; this time the demon said nothing.

"Yes. And he told us where we'll be able to find Saul the Bloodless."

"Where?" Solace sat up straighter, eyes bright behind the grimace twisting her face.

"Magdeburg."

The grimace became a frown, "But we were going there anyway. For Bulcher."

"On 20th May 1631."

"But... that's months away! How...?"

"That's the date Saul and his demons will be in the city."

"Why?" Lucien asked.

"Because Lord Torben says that's the day the city's walls will fall to the armies of the Emperor," he said quietly, "and the suffering will be terrible. Biblical. Corpses will carpet the city and the Elbe will run red..."

"Torben has told Saul this, and the vampires will come to feast amongst the carnage because they won't be able to resist..." Morlaine's voice was barely a whisper.

"And *that's* when we must be in Magdeburg to destroy the Red Company?" Solace asked.

"That's the night we have to be there..." Morlaine nodded, meeting no one's eye, "...when the killing begins, when the World's Pain comes to the streets of Magdeburg. Cleever says they won't take the soldiers of the Red Company with them; only the vampires will be present. And the slaughter will distract them, make them careless as they revel and dance in the blood of innocents. That's when we must be in Magdeburg... when the walls fall..."

A Dark Journey Continues…

The Night's Road – Book Four

When the Walls Fall

Follow Solace, Ulrich, Morlaine and Lucien's journey as they pursue *Graf* Bulcher and Saul the Bloodless in *When the Walls Fall* the next instalment of *The Night's Road…*

In the Company of Shadows

If you'd like to read more dark tales from the world of *In the Company of Shadows*, there are currently two free novellas (available as eBooks only) – *The Burning* & *A House of the Dead* – available. Both are set shortly before the events of *Red Company*. To get your free copies just visit andymonkbooks.com.

The Burning

The madness of the 17th Century witch burning frenzy has come to the sleepy village of Reperndorf.

Adolphus Holtz, Inquisitor to the Prince-Bishop of Würzburg, is keen to root out evil wherever he deems it to be. His eye has fallen on young Frieda and he fancies she'll scream so prettily for him when the time comes.

Frieda has already witnessed one burning and knows from the way her friends and neighbours are looking at her that she will be next. She seems doomed to burn on the pyre until a mysterious cloaked stranger appears out of the depths of the forest...

The first novella of *In the Company of Shadows* expands the dark historical world of *In the Absence of Light* and the shadowy relationships between humans and vampires.

A House of the Dead

All vampires are mad...

The weight of memories, loss, the hunger for blood, the voices of your prey whispering in your mind, loneliness, the obsessions you filled the emptiness inside yourself with, the sheer unrelenting bloody boredom of immortality could all chip away at your sanity.

And love, of course, one should never forget what that could do to you...

Mecurio has hidden from the world for twenty years in the secret catacombs beneath the city of Würzburg known as the House of the Dead, a place of refuge for vampires away from the eyes of men.

He tells himself it is so he can complete his Great Work without the distractions of the mortal world. But it isn't true. Time is slowly stealing the woman he adores from him and he has hidden their love away in the shadows of the House of the Dead to await the inevitable.

When a vampire whose bed he fled from a hundred and twenty-seven years before, arrives in search of information, he sees the opportunity to do a deal to save the woman he now loves for a few more bittersweet years. But all vampires are mad, one way or another, and when you strike a deal with one you may not end up with what you bargained for...

Books by Andy Monk

In the Absence of Light
The King of the Winter
A Bad Man's Song
Ghosts in the Blood
The Love of Monsters

In the Company of Shadows
The Burning (Novella)
A House of the Dead (Novella)
Red Company (The Night's Road Book One)
The Kindly Man (Rumville Part One)
Execution Dock (Rumville Part Two)
The Convenient (Rumville Part Three)
Mister Grim (Rumville Part Four)
The Future is Promises (Rumville Part Five)
The World's Pain (The Night's Road Book Two)
Empire of Dirt (The Night's Road Book Three)

For further information about Andy Monk's writing and future releases, please visit the following sites.

www.andymonkbooks.com

www.facebook.com/andymonkbooks

Printed in Great Britain
by Amazon